HEARTSTAR

HeartStar

BOOK THREE:
Walking in Three Worlds

ELVA THOMPSON

HEARTSTAR
BOOK THREE: WALKING IN THREE WORLDS

iUniverse books may be ordered through booksellers or by contacting:

iUniverse
1663 Liberty Drive
Bloomington, IN 47403
www.iuniverse.com
1-800-Authors (1-800-288-4677)

ISBN: 978-1-5320-4115-0 (sc)
ISBN: 978-1-5320-4116-7 (e)

Library of Congress Control Number: 2018902008

Print information available on the last page.

iUniverse rev. date: 03/14/2018

Contents

ACKNOWLEDGMENTS

Thank you to my husband, Harold and my reader, Randy Hutchinson for their support.

THE STORY IN THE MORTAL WORLD SO FAR

On her father's death, Emma Cameron moves into her childhood home and, with the help of her hired hand, Jim Lynch, starts a market stall business. Life is good, until a mysterious faerie being called Trevelyan of Wessex intrudes upon Emma's life and the latter begins to be drawn back into her dark and haunted past.

Emma finds out that she is a being from High Faerie who has taken human form to embark upon a perilous mission to find a powerful sapphire, a star-gate to nine dimensions that was lost in the War of Separation and was located under a hill called Dragonsbury Ring.

Emma and Jim go to Dragonsbury Ring but are beaten to the sapphire by a coven of powerful satanists. The couple are joined in the quest by animal activist Sue Browne, who owns Greenfern Animal Sanctuary, and Omar St Louis, a powerful West Indian mystic. In their pursuit of the sapphire, the friends are plunged into a nightmare world of torture, rape, and murder.

They find out that the sapphire is in the possession of Sir Giles Kingsbury, a wealthy satanic paedophile, and that he planned to activate the star-gate at a sabbat on Beltane Eve. Determined to retrieve the sapphire before it could be used to open the gates to Pandemonia, a portal to the black gulfs of the abyss, Emma and her friends drive to Brising Manor, Kingsbury's country home. They follow the procession of cowled, cloaked figures to a cave in the catacombs underneath the Kingsbury family chapel.

In the cavern, Emma and company see the sapphire upon the altar stone. Equipped with bracelets of invisibility that Trevelyan gave them, they storm the crypt in an effort to recover the stone. But their plans go awry, and in the mayhem that follows, Emma is seized by the arch-demon Zugalfar and taken to the crypt under Dragonsbury Ring to be sacrificed.

CHAPTER I

A QUANTUM LEAP

Emma slowly came to her senses. She was lying on cold, dank earth surrounded by ebony darkness. Her throat was dry and sore, and her body stung as if some hungry beak had been pecking at her skin. As she shifted position, her body cramped, and she grimaced as pain racked her arms and legs.

Memories of being swept up in a rushing nightmare of deathly cold swamped her being. The icy claw of Zugalfar had burned like fire as she was swept screamingly into space. Her mind still echoed with the deep, cracked sound of his malignant laughter as he'd hurtled towards Dragonsbury Ring.

The crypt was cold. Emma shivered. She knew that as soon as the satanists regrouped, they would come to Dragonsbury Ring. She would be raped, tortured, and sacrificed. It was her blood that would bathe the sapphire and open the gates to Pandemonia, her suffering that would free the hordes of hell and loose them upon the earth. Desperately trying to block out images of the horror that was to come, she forced her mind to focus on finding a way out of her predicament.

Emma staggered to her feet, and using her faerie sight, she looked around. She was standing at the centre of an inverted pentacle surrounded by double rings. Peering into the darkness, she saw a sight that shattered her resolve.

In the far corner of the cave, darker than darkness, she could see the huge, hunched, and cowled shape of Zugalfar suspended in the air and surrounded by the foul yellow radiations of the pit. The arch-demon was still and seemed lifeless. He appeared to be sleeping, but she knew he didn't sleep. Under his blood-red hood she could see the blue radiations of the sapphire glowing on his scaly brow.

A glimmer of hope flashed through Emma's mind. If she could summon her faerie nature, she might still be able to escape. After all, she told herself, she had routed Zugalfar once before and she could do it again. Her mind clung to the thought as one clings to a rescuing rope when sinking in a bog.

Her first task was to get out of the circle. Once free, she could hide in the darkness at the bottom of the steps. She still had in her pocket the cosh she had taken to the sabbat, and she might, with the element of surprise, be able to fight her way out. She wondered how many satanists had survived the burning horror of the sabbat. Many were dead, and it would take a little while for the rest of them to regroup and get to Dragonsbury Ring.

Knowing she had a brief respite before the satanists arrived, Emma forced herself to be present. Tiptoeing in a kind of silent panic to the edge of the circle, she tried to step out of the geometric. As she raised her foot, an overpowering force struck her in the solar plexus. She fell backward. For a moment she was too startled to think. She had hit a barrier that prevented her escape. A fury erupted within her. Determined to find out what had prevented her from leaving the pentacle, she crawled forward to the edge of the circle. Putting out her fingers, she touched an invisible smooth glassy surface that burnt her skin like ice. Quickly withdrawing her fingers, she sank back onto the earth floor. She was trapped. Zugalfar had erected a barrier to contain her until the satanists arrived.

The understanding brought a wave of panic. Her breath came in short gasps, and a cold film of perspiration broke out upon her face. Sobs welled up in her throat and tears trickled down her cheeks as she came to terms with the seeming inevitability of what awaited her. She knew that she had the power deep inside her psyche to forge a way out, but the slow vibration of fear was blocking her faerie power, and she couldn't flip the switch to positive. She thought of Omar and heard his deep, sonorous voice in her mind singing about positive vibrations.

Emma made herself sing the song. At first, her voice was weak and shaky and sounded like the squeaking of a mouse, but as she sang, her voice grew louder. She began to move with the message. She felt her mind change from fear to strength, and her resolve began to harden.

Alone in the dark, Emma reflected on her life. It appeared to her that there had been a dark conspiracy against her from birth. She sensed that Zugalfar had prior knowledge of the pledge she had made at the council in High Faerie long ago and had cast sorcerous spells to deliver her human form into a cult of devil-worshippers.

The understanding that she had been groomed for sacrifice since birth tore at Emma's mind. In that instance, she was doubtful of her place in this or any world. Her mother had been a weak woman, a victim of Emma's father. It was with sadness that she recalled her mother's tearful haggard face the day before she blew her brains out with a shotgun.

Only her grandmother Emily had stood between Emma

and the clutching darkness that groped for her in nightmares. After Emily was murdered, the attacks began. That's when Trevelyan arrived. Emma knew that without Trevelyan's vigilance and intervention, she would have already perished.

She thought back to the sabbat and how Zugalfar had used Trevelyan's image to trick her into stepping into the pentacle and giving him the sapphire. It seemed that Zugalfar was always one step ahead of her. His malignancy had tracked her, attacked her, and trapped her in this dark impasse.

Suddenly she heard the sound of a door creaking open above her head, and then came footsteps on the stone stairs leading down to the crypt. Adrenaline coursed through her body. The satanists were coming to start the preparations for her blood sacrifice.

Deciding to play dead so as not to attract their immediate attention, Emma lay down on her stomach, facing the bottom of the steps so she could see what they were doing.

The darkness was suddenly pierced by the beams of two flashlights. Resinous torches were lit and placed in the holders on the walls. Emma could smell the acrid smoke of bitumen. The inside of the cavern became visible. In the trembling light, she saw that the image of Zugalfar had disappeared. Switching to faerie sight, she saw him still limply hanging in the corner of the crypt. For a moment she wondered why the arch-demon could not be seen in the third dimension. Then, in a rush of insight, she realised that Jim had confounded Zugalfar's agenda at the sabbat by killing Giles Kingsbury. The satanic high priest had been the conduit for evil, and his death had broken the energetic link between the arch-demon and the mortal world. If Kingsbury had lived, Zugalfar would have sacrificed Emma and her friends at the sabbat, but fate had played against him. He had been thrown back into the abyss, and that meant, she reasoned, that he could not manifest again in the mortal world until called by blood sacrifice. Even though Zugalfar was conscious of her presence in the crypt, he was powerless to hurt her. He was impotent until called again by blood. The understanding powered her will to get the sapphire and escape.

Through half-closed eyes, she watched as two cowled and robed figures approached her. Her fingers tightened on the cosh. Every muscle was tensed for action. Slowly drawing her hand close to her body, she waited. Her mind was clear of fear, and she wasn't going to give up without a fight.

The satanists entered the circle freely. Emma recognised they were not affected by Zugalfar's holding spell. She realised the barrier was a frequency field specifically designed to contain her physical form and her faerie resonance. Only her High Faerie power would be able to overcome it.

She felt rough hands on her body, turning her over. One of the hooded figures started ripping off her clothes. Opening her eyes, Emma brought up her hand. With all the strength she could muster, she smashed her attacker in the head with the cosh.

The crypt reverberated with shrieks and curses. Scrambling to her feet, Emma lashed out at the other one. There was a crack as the cosh collided with his nose. Blood spurted out on the ground. Emma gave him a kicking as he stumbled from the circle.

A low moaning wind began to blow from within the pentacle, coiling around her knees and pulling her towards the two upright points of the inverted star. At the base of the uprights were two ruby stones pressed into the earth that represented the glowing eyes of Baphomet, the satanic goat.

Emma's breath caught in her throat. There was blood

spattered on the ground around the stones. From the rubies, a red mist was forming. Lurid light leapt into the air and, coalescing above her, began to take on the huge, hunched shape of Zugalfar. In her fight with the satanists, some blood must have been spattered on the rubies. Zugalfar was evidently using it to try to materialise within the pentacle. If he succeeded, she was dead.

In a panic, she bent down and grabbed both of the rubies, pulling them from the earth. Attached to the stones were thin stiletto daggers. As she held them in her hands, waves of malevolence surged through her body, and vomit choked her throat. For a moment she was paralysed with terror. Then, obeying a sudden impulse from deep within her mind, she touched the rubies to the topaz jewel on her necklace.

The air electrified around her. Sparks flew. She felt a jolt of charge throughout her body. A ghoulish wind of ice roared and twisted around her, beating up out of the shadows from spaces behind and underneath the pentacle. Bolts of red and yellow lurid light struck the floor of the cavern. A spectral image of Zugalfar seemed to consume the entire crypt.

Emma kept her eyes lowered. Using faerie sight, she saw the limp form of Zugalfar still hanging in the corner. She understood in a flash of insight that there had not been enough blood to ground him in the mortal world. As a result, he had been thrown back into the abyss by the vibrations of the topaz.

Knowing that in his present state Zugalfar could not harm her in physical reality once again powered Emma's confidence. The pentacle underneath Dragonsbury Ring had for centuries been used for human sacrifice. It was Zugalfar's place of calling, and therefore his point of entry into the mortal world. The rubies were his eyes. Once they'd been removed from the pentacle, he became blind to the third dimension.

Not wanting to leave the daggers in the crypt for the satanists to find, Emma put them in the deep inside pocket of her jacket. Looking around, she saw the two satanists standing against the wall by the steps, mopping blood from their faces with the bottoms of their robes. She had to make her move now, or else all was lost.

Centring her mind, Emma tried to access her High Faerie power. As her consciousness entered the stillness of the quiet mind, the crypt and the peril she was in seemed to recede. She heard words in the language of the HeartStar echo though her head, and she repeated them under her breath. There was a sensation of warmth at her throat. Pulling the topaz from her necklace, she felt the jewel vibrating in her hand. Sending her will into the stone, she saw the stone morph into a long, glowing knife. She was ready to try to break Zugalfar's spell and escape from the circle.

"Eh – hon – na – hessh," she screamed, driving the sound of the last syllable deep into the ground. The words echoed around the cavern. She felt the floor vibrate beneath her feet. An emerald sheen began to pulse around her as the power of her true nature swept through her body. Holding the knife before her, she drove the blade into the barrier. Sparks flew in the air. She heard a crack like splintering ice as the barrier dissolved in a sickly yellow flash.

Emma stepped out of the circle. She had to get the sapphire and escape. Visualising an emerald octahedron around her, she streaked to the back of the cavern where Zugalfar was hanging. Then, jumping up, she snatched the sapphire from his brow and held it to her heart.

For an instant, she felt a shortening of her breath as if

something was trying to stifle her, but it was soon followed by a feeling of expansion. She could hear the music of the spheres in the great vastness of infinity.

Dimly in the recesses of her mind, she heard shouts, and footsteps coming down the stairs.

"There's the bitch!" a high-pitched voice shrilled. "Get her. Let's strip her and stake her down before the others arrive."

For a moment, Emma was struck with fright. The coven had arrived.

She did not move or try to run. Gripping the sapphire in her hand, she sent her intent inwards and opened her mind to the power of High Faerie. The pulsing emerald shield around her began to strengthen, and then it blazed with light. Seeming to be looking at herself from outside, she watched as the monsters in human form staggered back, shielding their eyes against the faerie glare.

The sapphire was enveloping her emerald octahedron in glittering shades of blue. Feeling a prompt from deep within her psyche, Emma willed herself into the sapphire star-gate. Then, using her intent, she propelled herself through the low vibration of the crypt, and down the hillside to the hedge by the road. In a burst of dazzling blue light, she found herself standing on the grass beside the hedge with the sapphire in her hand.

THE STORY SO FAR IN THE FOURTH DIMENSION OF FAERIE

Long ago in the mists of time, the realms of Humanity, Faerie, and High Faerie were all one world, with the sentient creatures of all three realms living in harmony with each other. But evil entered the world of humankind. The Cathac, the great horned serpent from the stars, insinuated his thoughts of conquest into the dreams of chieftains, filling them with pride, a lust for war, and murderous intent. When the stars aligned and formed a glittering pentagon in the sky, the Cathac had attacked the triad world of Faerie. Long and bloody was the battle. The Cathac had druid sorcerers in his ranks. With dark spells, he had ripped the world of Humanity away from Faerie and made its inhabitants mortal.

Ke-enaan the Danaan wizard had fought alongside the High Faerie hosts in the War of Separation. After the splitting of the worlds, he had been doomed to stay in the fourth dimension of Faerie for an age until the stars formed a pentagon once more. With his friend Trevelyan, he had pledged to protect the Faerie Worlds and the HeartStar of the High House of Air, the emerald light of High Faerie that was the living essence of all green growing things.

The time had come. The stars of prophecy were blazing in the sky, the containment spells that bound the Cathac in Faerie would soon dissolve, and the will of the enemy of life would come alive in Lower Faerie. The sapphire star-gate that had been lost in the War of Separation had appeared upon the airwaves. War was at hand.

Ke-enaan had revealed to Kilfannan and Kilcannan of the House of Air, that Niamh and Caiomhin, their creators from the fifth dimension, had been imprisoned in the Outer Darkness and could be consumed by demons at any time.

To try to free their creators, Kilfannan and Kilcannan, along with Aine, daughter of Manannan Mac Lir, and other elementals, set out on a perilous mission to find the stolen key made of air. On their journey, the Company of the Key was attacked by Crom Dubh, the headless coachman, and the souls of Kilfannan and Kilcannan were taken to Crom Dubh's haunted world in Under-Earth.

Knowing that Crom Dubh would return for the bodies of the sylphs, Ke-enaan ordered Thorn-Haw, the dryad of the sacred hawthorn tree, to take Kilfannan and Kilcannan's bodies to Trevelyan's house in England.

Using his cunning mirror to check on Trevelyan, Ke-enaan had seen his friend of ages become locked in deadly battle with Crom Dubh and then collapse upon the floor.

Chapter 2

DARK ALLIANCE

Consumed with anxiety for Trevelyan and the House of Air, Ke-enaan bent his will upon the glass, but the pearly surface did not clear. He tried again, but to no avail. A feeling of unease stole over him. He felt a cold, nervous pricking down his spine as he realised the mirror was being attacked to prevent him from viewing Trevelyan and the company.

The skin on the back of his neck began to prickle, and he suddenly had the impression of being watched. He looked searchingly around his hall; there was mischief afoot, but he could not define it. To look for answers to his doubt, he decided to consult the oracles of sea and sky.

Ke-enaan left his hall. Stepping out onto the short, damp turf that bordered the road, he looked across the grey stone wall at the western marches of the sea. The ocean was troubled, steely, and foam wracked. He sensed, beneath the frothing surface, a living malice alive within the water. To trace the source of the evil influence, he sent his mind to Under-Sea.

His senses led him to a ghostly, cyclopean pillared underwater city of stained marble arches and dank weed-wracked temples. Chill currents swept around his thought, shooting his attentiveness with icy darts of hostility and warning.

Through the gloomy waters, he saw the grotesque hull of a huge galleon lying at anchor in a slimy festering dock. Nearby was a domed temple. As his mindfulness moved closer, he saw light flickering through the open door. A giant of a man dressed in oilskins and a flat black hat was standing with his hands raised before a mighty altar fire wreathed with coiling, flaming serpents. His rasping voice, thick with the ugly tones of Under-Sea, boomed waves of sorcerous incantations, which vibrated through the water.

A thrill of fear ran through Ke-enaan's being as he recognised the oilskin-clad figure. It was as he feared. Manannan Mac Lir, the Son of the Sea, had awakened. The sight of Manannan filled Ke-enaan with dread. He called back his thought before it was noticed and danger came upon it. He had been present when Luillin, grandson of the Danaan king Nada, had stabbed Manannan through the heart, and had born witness to his ruin on the red bog of Magh Cuilenn. With the help of the Cathac's sorcery, Manannan's dark spirit had left the bog and was reunited with his hideous frame.

The water had spoken and revealed Manannan. Now it was time to consult the oracle of air. Taking a deep breath to steady himself, Ke-enaan turned his eyes southward to the sky above the Giant's Cliffs.

A thunderhead hung over the cliffs, a grim red beacon betokening evil to come. Banks of low heaving clouds were rushing north across a threatening leaden sky, accompanied by squalls of twisting rain. Ke-enaan stared at the writhing, serpentine cloud banks, and sensed for a moment, he saw within the swirling vapours a menacing symbolism, a directiveness of movement. It was as if his being had caught a horror before his eyes had seen it. His intuition warned him not to look away. He gazed piercingly at the clouds as they scudded overhead. And whether by chance or fate, a slight clearing of the air revealed a darker shape riding within the cloud.

The air became infused with charnel stench. He heard the throb of a thunderous incantation resounding above him and on all sides. The air shook with malice. The clouds thinned, and for a moment he caught a glimpse of the death coach. The hunched shape of Crom Dubh was in the driver's seat and, with raised whip, was driving his horses forward. A swamping wave of sickness and repulsion swept through Ke-enaan, and his faculties faltered for a moment as the fume closed in again. The Cóiste Bodhar, the death coach, was racing north towards Crann Sidhe.

Swiftly returning to his hall, Ke-enaan sat down before the mirror and tried to bring it to his will. The pearly sheen upon the glass did not clear. He noticed that the wall around it was tinged with the tainted yellow light of Lower Faerie. Sending his mind into the stone, he looked for the blocking spell.

Woven in a web around the perimeters of the mirror was a filmy grey mass flickering with flame. Ke-enaan swallowed hard. Fronds of fiery flecks were snaking up the walls and across the ceiling. The enchantment was spreading like a net across his hall, closing his thought and energy from broadcast. In desperation, he sent a plea for help to Thorn-Haw on the airwaves, but his plea came ricocheting back in mocking echoes.

In dismay he realised that a dark fire spell of sabotage had been cast against Black Head. He would need dragon fire to breach it. Without the mirror or access to the airwaves, he could neither warn nor aid Trevelyan and the House of Air.

Ke-enaan poured himself a goblet of elixir and gulped it down. The weight of ages bowed down upon his shoulders. He felt drained and impotent.

A sudden rush of heat fanned his back. Turning round, he saw Trax fly through the eyehole window in the western wall. In a blur of golden flame, the dragon expanded in size and settled on the floor before him. "Fell tidings," Trax crackled in the language of the flame.

The dragon's eyes glowed like molten gold as he went on to tell Ke-enaan of Crom Dubh's taking of the souls of Kilfannan and Kilcannan at the gates of Crann Sidhe.

"Fly from Crann Sidhe to Trevelyan," Trax flared. "Tell him evil tidings; tell him to make ready. Protect sylphs from Crom Dubh."

"I need thine help," Ke-enaan said urgently. "The mirror and the airwaves hath been blocked by a foul fire spell from Lower Faerie, and dragon fire is needed to dispel it."

The air crackled around the dragon. The blue-flame firelight dimmed in the hearth as Trax summoned every last degree of fire power to himself. As the dragon's belching flame consumed the glass, Ke-enaan advanced on the mirror and, uttering incantations, placed his palms on the surface of the glass. Wave after wave of power and fire the two sent coursing through the mirror. As the blocking frequencies dissolved and the flickering flames faded from the hall, they heard a squeal of frustrated and malevolent anger.

Sensing that the evil presence in his hall had yielded before their spell, Ke-enaan said, "With the might of thy flame and the power of my heart, the spell hath been dissolved."

Trax stretched his neck. Fire issued from his nostrils. "Leave now. Gorias unprotected."

Ke-enaan bowed before the dragon. "May the fire of Axar sustain thee on thy journey to Gorias, and protect thee from the fey fire of our enemies."

With a snort of farewell flame, Trax shrunk in size. Rising into the air, he flew out of the window and into the gloom.

Gathering his resolve, and knowing an assault on the House of Air was imminent, Ke-enaan resonated on Trevelyan's frequency and sent a sonic boom of impending threat across the airwaves. Sitting back down before the mirror, he bent his will upon Trevelyan.

The glass was slow to clear. It showed him nothing but swirling charnel dust and darkness. He saw the veil of death suddenly rent asunder by the light of many fiery suns. In that instant, images poured into his mind. Stifling back a gasp, he saw the hideous bulk of Crom Dubh consumed by flame. Panic seized him as he saw Trevelyan stagger forward and fall down. Star specks of light were escaping from Trevelyan's body into the room and out through the walls into the night. His atoms were spinning off into space. Ke-enaan knew his form would soon disintegrate altogether. Braxach was lying on the floor by the cold hearth, and Ke-enaan saw with dismay that fire was leaking from a wound in his side. He watched with bated breath as the dragon rose, grasped Trevelyan's body in his talons, and flew out of the study window. In his own mind, Ke-enaan heard the dragon's fiery thought. *Bring Trevelyan: Black Head.*

Ke-enaan got up from the mirror. The fall of Trevelyan weighed heavily on his mind as he waited anxiously for Braxach to arrive. He needed to think. Pouring himself a goblet of elixir to steady his thoughts, he sat down by the dragon fire and gazed into the flames.

It was clear to him that the Cathac, having conquered the world of humankind, had turned his lust for subjugation to the fourth and fifth dimensions. It seemed that a new War of Separation was about to begin. Staring into the fire, Ke-enaan sensed in the sinuous movement of the dancing flames a veiled threat, a harbinger of danger, and saw a horrible familiarity in the dark events that were now occurring.

Warmth in the air field caught his attention. Braxach flew through the eyehole in the wall, gently laid Trevelyan's body on the rush floor by the hearth, and then sank down in exhaustion.

"Greetings, Ke-enaan," the dragon flared weakly. "On way to Axar; seek spell to undo fey fire. See evil in cloud; battle against death coach. Trevelyan rout Crom Dubh; fall in effort."

Ke-enaan looked in anguish upon the pale face of Trevelyan. His body was a transparent two-dimensional cut-out of his former self, and there was a pellucidity about him that intensified with every passing moment. A sense of urgency surged through Ke-enaan's mind as he frantically searched for a way to stop further dispersion of Trevelyan's energy.

"Braxach!" he said. "Even though thou art injured, 'twouldst be possible to set a yellow fire in thy breath for me to weave the geometry of restraint around Trevelyan's body? I fear he will soon be beyond our aid."

A feeble yellow flame issued from Braxach's nostrils. Catching the fire between his hands, Ke-enaan cupped it like a ball. The flaming sphere began to pulse and expand, until he could no longer contain it. As he opened his hands, the flame darkened into fir light and formed itself into a cube of dragonite, the densest vibration found in Faerie. The dark green cube slowly revolved in the air before him. Uttering words of power, Ke-enaan lowered it over Trevelyan's body. Then, taking a small blue sapphire from his robe, he placed it on the top of the cube.

"If thou still hast the power of flame, send a jet into the jewel," he said to Braxach. "Then I will send it into space to draw Trevelyan's scattered particles to the living fire within the stone."

With an effort, Braxach drew back his head and sent a thin flame into the jewel. The stone glowed and, gathering brightness, pulsed from blue through indigo to violet. The colours mingled together and began to glow as one, and formed into a circle.

Ke-enaan heard the air crackle with charge. A vivid magenta light began to grow, bathing the cube of dragonite in a dazzling burst of outer spectrum colours, the hues that vibrated beyond the visible light of the third dimension. Stepping back, he made passes with his hands and created a small nebulous disc of spinning light that formed into a spider's web. Setting the sapphire at the centre of the web, he placed the disc into the mirror and sent the hoop spiralling into space.

Turning to Braxach, he said, "'Twill take some time for Trevelyan's atoms to be collected, for they hath travelled beyond the stars. Pray, let me staunch the wound in thy side, for thou art weakened by every flame that escapeth from thy heart fire."

Ke-enaan took down a bottle of powdered root from a shelf next to the hearth. Taking a handful, he blew it gently into the dragon's gaping wound. Then, calling on Pa'gnac, the turquoise gas, he summoned the knitter of flesh to him. "'Tis the stauncher of escaping flame," he said, as a shimmering light coalesced into a serpentine shape before him, "and 'twill close the rift from which thy fire escapeth."

The gas coalesced into a shining ball and, settling on the wound, disappeared inside. Turquoise light blazed forth, travelling in rivulets along the open gash. Slowly the leaking flames faded; the flesh knitted together and scales appeared.

"I thank thee," Braxach roared as blue flame gushed through his nostrils.

The hall blazed with turquoise light, lingered for a moment, and slowly vanished.

"Trax hath but lately left my halls," Ke-enaan said, sitting down. "He flies to Gorias and will stand guard over the sky above the city." He paused for a moment and then resumed. "Whilst we wait for Trevelyan's atoms to complete their return, tellest me of the battle in Gorias, for methinks 'twas a dragon's claw that inflicted the wound upon thee."

The crest upon the dragon's head gleamed in the firelight. A small jet of flame issued from his nostrils, and in the fire was an answer. "Zugalfar's legions attack Gorias. Ngpa-tawa, Lord of Fire Descending, betray HeartStar, join Cathac's legions."

Ke-enaan's eyes widened in shock. He rocked back in his chair. "This is grave news," he muttered. Ngpa-tawa, he recalled, had been present at the council in High Faerie, long ago. The Lord of Fire Descending had taken his seat at the table and was privy to all their plans. It was clear now that it was Ngpa-tawa who had revealed to Zugalfar the identities of the four faerie warriors and conspired with the water moon to steal their memories at birth. Ke-enaan swallowed hard.

Ngpa-tawa's allegiance to the HeartStar was only a mask he had worn while spying for the Cathac.

"Dragon Nag-ta cast fire spell around city," the dragon flared again. "Cannot breach spell; battle in sky. Many enemies fall in ruination. Nag-ta dragon wound Braxach; fire dragon dead. Becuille, master sphere of Ophire, set ruby cube to guard Gorias. Evil fire spirits hidden in fey fire attack citadel. Lord of Fire fled south. Hide in halls."

Ke-enaan realised that the Cathac had empowered Ngpa-tawa with the secret of dark fey fire, and the fire lord had used the withering heat to surround Gorias. How long the emerald city would endure the hungry molten heat, he did not know. Doubt took him. For energetic support, he merged his mind with Braxach's. In the swirling field of fire rising into air, he was transported to a place where words have no meaning. In the silent communion that knows no separation, the two of them shared the understanding of the betrayal of the HeartStar. Those who had made a dark alliance with the Cathac against the living Green were revealed and their plans laid bare.

Their awareness fluttered together. The fire in the hearth blazed with outer spectrum colours. As it grew dim, and the blue flame waxed again, the communion of minds was over.

"If our ancient serpent foe is to succeed in his mission, he will attack on all three fronts at once," Ke-enaan said. "Niamh and Caiomhin have been tricked and trapped in the outer darkness, and Gorias is in peril."

At this Braxach snorted. His lids slid across his eyes, and a fire devil shot around the hall. "First I am," he flared. "Found by Nuadan; he of the star brow. Fight on till flame die."

The dragon's crackle returned Ke-enaan to the past. During the War of Separation, he and his brother Creidne had been with Nuadan on the beach at Fanore searching for signs of the Cathac. In the sand dunes they found a gold-flecked turquoise dragon's egg, which they took to the fire city of Finias, the flaming tower of the south. In the great hall of Blaze, they had borne witness to the hatching of Braxach the Green. The Lord of Fire Rising had seven other dragon eggs in his possession. All of the great winged worms were hatched that day to fight Zugalfar and his legions.

In the War of Separation, the Cathac and his dark company of druids had conjured a dark-fire spell deep within the labyrinths of Lower Faerie. Human blood they had fed the flame, until it consumed everything in its path. This was fey fire. The Cathac had used the dark enchantment to devour five dragons in the War of Separation. Only Braxach, Trax, and the traitorous Nag-ta had survived.

Ke-enaan recalled the counter-spells that he and Creidne had cast against the ravenous flame, but all their efforts to turn the fey fire on itself had failed.

"All these long years, we have feared the day when the cycle of time and prophecy are complete in their revolutions," Ke-enaan said, breaking the silence. "That day hath come, and events are moving with the speed of a snake." He sighed. "Tonight is Bealltainn in the mortal world. It is the last chance for Emma and her friends to take possession of the sapphire and return it to my halls. All will be lost if she fails ..." His voice trailed off as if the sound of the words hurt him.

After a long pause, he resumed. "If Emma fails, the Faerie Worlds will be assailed by every realm of horror and by every hideous dimension that evil hath the power to mould." He glanced at Trevelyan's body resting under the cube of dragonite.

"Without Trevelyan, Emma hath no spiritual protection.

She is our last surviving warrior of the heart in mortal form. If she cannot access her faerie nature, she will be defenceless against Zugalfar and his coven of devil-worshippers. The rites will be spoken in unhallowed places, blood will be shed, and night will walk forth. We must pray that Trevelyan returns in time to be of aid to Emma and her friends."

Braxach stirred. The firelight glinted on the golden-pointed emerald armour running along his spine. Lifting his head, he flared, "Bealltainn fire burn on cliffs; guard this night. Then travel to eternal fire cavern; find sire Braxa. Undo fey-fire spell."

"'Tis said that the counter-spell to turn dark fey fire into the cold blue flame of dragons was lost in the mists of time," Ke-enaan responded. "And no living being but the Cathac and the treacherous Lord of Fire Descending hath the knowledge to invoke it. Mighty in power was my brother, but our wizardry came to naught, and those of the fire breath perished in the evil flame." Ke-enaan's mouth hardened and his eyes glittered midnight in the firelight. "While Ngpa-tawa lives, he is a danger to us all. He may come forth with the Cathac and Manannan and use the fey fire against us."

Ke-enaan felt a rush of hot dragon breath upon his face. "Braxa hath knowledge; reverse flame of fey fire. Destroy Ngpa-tawa. Save Gorias."

Ke-enaan shivered as a chill crawled across the back of his neck. He passed two fingers over the space between his eyes to block the darts of fear that had been fired at him from some infernal pit of darkness. To find his sire, Braxach would journey through the perilous illimitable vastness of the void beyond the stars to Axar, the fire world of the nine suns, the home world of dragons. To get there, he would first have to battle the hungry shape-shifting blasphemies that hunted for food in the endless onyx labyrinths of space. Space. The sound echoed through his being and brought him to the present.

Pouring himself another glass of elixir to fortify his spirits, he said to Braxach, "Let us pay heed to Trevelyan and see what the mirror may hold. Time is short, for night is falling in the mortal world and the blood rite is at hand. Without Trevelyan's help and guidance, the HeartStar, Emma, and her friends are in great peril."

Together they looked into the mirror and saw teeming starlight caught within the web of the star-catcher. Ke-enaan smiled. "'Tis complete," he said. "Drawn by the fire in the jewel, Trevelyan's atoms are as one. He will awake soon. Pray! Send a flame to release his body from the dragonite that contains it."

A bolt of green flame issued from the dragon's nostrils, and the cube of dragonite collapsed into nothingness. Taking the star-catcher from the mirror, Ke-enaan let it hover above Trevelyan's body. He watched as the outer spectrum colours engulfed his friend's limp form. To ground Trevelyan's atoms into Faerie, he began to sing softly the tones of the fourth dimension, vibrating the sound until the hall shook with the music of the heart. As the echoes died away, Ke-enaan joined Braxach at the hearth.

"If all goes ill for Emma, Zugalfar will bathe the sapphire in her blood," Ke-enaan said. "Then he will come hither to the cliffs, and the gates to Pandemonia will open. There will be a second Separation, and the Faerie Worlds will be sucked into the abyss. If he does not succeed and Emma triumphs, Manannan will use his dark magic to free the Cathac, and together they will ride once more upon the sea of desire and destruction. We are to be damned on either hand. This night and the dawning of the morrow will be fraught with malice, sorcery, and nightmare dread."

A voice whispered in Ke-enaan's mind that it was pointless to go on—they had already lost. He saw a vision of his brother dead upon the field. A lump formed in his throat and tears came to his eyes. Evil visions were trying to repeat, impinging on his mind and eclipsing his connection to the HeartStar. One thing that succoured him in that moment was the company of Braxach. Mighty in power was the dragon, and wisdom flowed like flame from his fiery exhalation. Warmth surrounded Ke-enaan in his doubt. He felt dragon breath upon him, giving fire to his heart and will.

Braxach rose and flexed his wings. "Go now. Keep watch on Giant's Cliffs. Kill enemy."

"Fare ye well, Braxach, son of Braxa. May the eternal fire beat within thine heart."

With a farewell gush of flame, Braxach took to the air and flew out through the eyehole into the gathering dark.

A weight lifted from Ke-enaan's mind as Braxach departed for the Giant's Cliffs. Whether good or evil prevailed in the mortal world, and whatever the fate of the sapphire, he knew that Braxach would be there to defend the Green as he had since his beginning.

Ke-enaan turned his attention to Trevelyan, who was sleeping peacefully by the fireside. Taking his hand, he found the flesh was warm and firm. He knew that Trevelyan would soon awake.

CHAPTER 3

THE RETURN

From the depths of starlit consciousness, Trevelyan felt his atoms streaming slowly back from the prodigious wonders of the void to the halls of waking. A shiver ran through him as his bones, muscles, and nerves knitted back together and realigned into the fourth dimension. Opening his eyes, he felt life coursing through his being. Raising himself on one arm, he looked about himself in confusion. His eyes roved over the green rush floor, the vaulted ceiling, a table stacked with manuscripts and ancient texts, shelves stacked with glass jars of herbs and unction, and a blue flame fire burning brightly in the hearth.

The hall seemed familiar, as did the noble and concerned face that peered expectantly into his. He gazed at the blue-cloaked figure but could find no meaning to his image, no anchor to steady the chaos of his own disorganised sensations. He realised that he did not know who he was or where he came from.

"Friend of Ages, thou hast returned," he heard the man say. He felt himself being raised and taken to a chair by the fireside. "Sit thee by the fire whilst I bringeth thee a glass of elixir."

Trevelyan's eyes were drawn into the mystical flickering firelight. His consciousness clung to it as a rock in an endless ocean of forgetting. The energy of the fire was friendly and supportive. Bathed in its radiance, his memory began gradually to return. He knew who he was, but at the same time he was beset with images of some hideous memory that couldn't quite be realised by his conscious mind.

Immersed in the firelight, he felt the breath of dragons upon his face. Wisps of golden nebulae surrounded him, and far off he heard the melody of the stars. He felt himself slowly taking root, swelling with substance, and imbuing the space around him with his memory. His fingers began to tingle with energy, and he felt warmth rise into his head, invigorating his mind and will.

Ke-enaan returned with the drink. With a trembling hand, Trevelyan took the glass and sipped upon the elixir. He looked at the tall figure beside him. The lazulite ring on the man's finger was sparkling, reflecting the firelight in hues of blue radiance. The sparkle turned into flame. As the blues merged together in the hearth, Trevelyan's memories flooded through his being.

"Ke-enaan!" he cried in recognition, gazing into the wizard's sea-grey eyes that mirrored change in wind and water. "How did I get to Black Head? I have no recollection." He tried to rise but felt a restraining hand upon his shoulder.

"After Crom Dubh was vanquished, thou didst fall, and the stars called to thee," the wizard answered. "Thy form was dissolving. 'Twas only in the nick of time that Braxach brought thee to my hall."

Trevelyan looked at Ke-enaan in consternation. "The House of Air. Are they safe?"

Ke-enaan gave a grim laugh. "Kilfannan and Kilcannan

are safe—safe as anything is safe in this fell time. They are in pursuit of the thief who stole the key made of air, travelling north with the House of An Carn and the rest of the company. Thorn-Haw and his trees keep watch on them. He is my ears and eyes upon the road."

Trevelyan heaved a sigh of relief, and then suddenly his countenance fell and his back stiffened. He saw Emma's face in his mind and visions of the sapphire. The satanists had the space gate. On the night of the Beltane fire, they were going to use it to open the gates to Pandemonia. Overcome with fear and panic, he said with a choke in his throat, "What day is it in the mortal world?"

"'Tis Saturday, the thirtieth of April."

Trevelyan struggled away from Ke-enaan's grasp. Sending his mind to Emma's kitchen, he looked at the wall clock. It was half past eleven. "The sabbat in the mortal world will be in a few hours," he said anxiously. "Let us consult the looking glass and see where Emma and her friends are."

Ke-enaan brought a second chair. The two sat down before the mirror. Resonating on Emma's frequency, they looked intently into the pearly sheen. When the glass cleared, they were looking down on Brising Manor estate. The manor was dark apart from a single red light that burned like a watching eye from the pillared portico at the entrance.

Trevelyan's eyes were drawn to a torchlight procession of robed figures who had stopped at the entrance to an old, grey chapel glimmering evilly in the fitful spectral moonlight. Demons were flying overhead. He shivered at the sound of their hideous croaking voices. A little ways behind the procession, he saw four figures threading their way through a crumbling cemetery. It was Emma and her friends.

He noticed that he could not see the purple glow of the

asafoetida bracelets he had given them to wear at the sabbat. The bands of grass held the high energy of bending-light and would protect them from the sight of demons in the third dimension and Lower Faerie. In consternation, he looked closer at their energy, and saw, with dismay, the dull red glow of waste in their bodies. He shot up straight in his chair.

"We have been undone!" he cried out, looking at Ke-enaan with shock in his eyes. "Emma and her friends have eaten food when I told them not to, and the devil's bane bracelets I had woven for their protection are not upon their person." After pausing for a moment in thought, he said, "'Tis obvious that Zugalfar has found a way to influence Emma. He has accessed her mind and cast a spell upon her and her friends. He has clouded their judgement and drowned my words from their ears. I have failed in my duty to protect Emma, betrayed her by my lack of vigilance. I have proven false." Choking back a cry of despair, he got up from his chair and made a move towards the door.

"Stay!" Ke-enaan thundered. "Thou canst not blame thyself. 'Tis Emma in her unawakened state that hath betrayed herself, her friends, and us! Part of her essence is connected to High Faerie, and the other dwells in the flesh. … The flesh is fearful, and therein lies her weakness." He put his hand supportively on Trevelyan's shoulder. "'Tis not by chance that Crom Dubh struck the House of Air at this portentous time, for the will of the Cathac is upon him. The enemy knows that even though thou art skilled in wisdom, thou art singular in form. The Cathac sought to send Crom Dubh against thee in the hope of a double blow. His will was to destroy thee and the House of Air, and leave Emma without hope."

"There is no time to lose. I must go!" Trevelyan said, struggling away from Ke-enaan's grip.

Trevelyan's hand was upon the door when Ke-enaan stopped him.

"'Tis not prudent to take the road, for the coming of Trax and Braxach to my halls will not hath gone unnoticed. In truth, the fate of the Green hangs on a knife edge, and any misbegotten step will lead to its destruction. Thou must take my secret way," he said, ushering his friend away from the door to an arch at the back of the hall.

Trevelyan followed the wizard down a flight of stone steps and onto a flat grey rock. They were in a cavern, standing next to a pool fed by a cascading waterfall.

"There is a tunnel yonder," Ke-enaan said, pointing to a dark space behind the curtain of falling water. "The passage will take thee to the surface, to an entrance to the outer world. When the path ends and thou canst go no further, stand before the rock face and utter the words of opening, 'Tash-Ka. Tash-Ka.'" He repeated it again. "The rock will shift and give thee passage, and then close behind thee." He sighed heavily. "Long hath this door and passage remained a secret for dark days such as these, friend of all pasts. Be cautious in thy travel to the mortal world, for the Cathac hath cast dark dream spells upon the desolate, grey limestone pavements of the Burren, and the portal doors to the mortal world are watched. Stand still now while I bend light around thee."

Trevelyan saw a faint band of wavering outer spectrum colours form around his body.

"Thy invisibility will only last until you step through the portal door to England," Ke-enaan warned. "When thou emerge from the gate, be ready to defend thyself, for thou will be visible to friend and foe alike. I will give thee what aid I may. Fare ye well."

They stood for a moment in silent communion. And then with a nod of farewell, Trevelyan took his leave.

The passage led slowly upward and then widened into a flat space, ending in a damp rock wall. Standing in the gloom before the stone, Trevelyan uttered the words of opening: "Tash-Ka. Tash-Ka."

The sound gathered power, ricocheting off the passage walls in chorus. As the echo died away, he felt the stone quivering beneath his feet. The rock in front of him dissolved. He found himself looking out through a small cave mouth at the night-cloud-ridden sky. Stepping out of the passageway into the windless air, he walked quickly down the boulder-strewn hillside to the walled fields beyond.

As he approached the fields, the clouds became lower and the night darker, and on the air he could taste mischief and malevolence. He remembered Ke-enaan's warning of dark spells on the Burren. Even though he was invisible to demon sight, he proceeded with caution. Time was pressing, and he knew it. A delay here could cost Emma and her friends their lives. But, he told himself, there is oft a spill between the cup and the lip and he could not take any chances.

Up ahead, he heard a hawking sound. The air became thick with goblin taint. Goblins were guarding the portal. Trevelyan was sure they had known of his presence at Black Head and that they were now guarding the portal gate he commonly used to cross from Ireland to England. To find another portal would take time—time he and Emma did not have. He would have to get by the goblins and into the passage tomb the best way he could.

In his haste to get nearer to the portal, he stepped on a pile of dry twigs hidden by the darkness. As they cracked and broke beneath his feet, he heard the shouts of goblins.

He had walked into the goblins' early warning system and given his presence away. The piles of dry twigs were set in a semicircle round the portal gate. Springing over them, he stood back in the shadow of a wall and waited for a chance to get to the portal.

"A spy! A filthy spy!" the cry went up.

Out of the gloom, half a dozen goblin guards came towards him, jabbing and slicing at the darkness with their knives and daggers. In an effort to distract them, he took a deep breath and threw his voice over the far side wall onto the hillside.

"Over here, numbskulls!"

The goblins stopped in their tracks and looked about in confusion. Trevelyan shouted again, this time even louder.

"I've outwitted you once more, you good-for-nothing numbskulls!"

"After him! There's gold on his head and we gets to eat his body. The boss promised," he heard a goblin growl. With jeers and yells, the goblin guards ran in the direction of the sound.

A knocker flitted past Trevelyan and took up guard at the entrance to the portal. He stared at the vile creature. It was Sageuz, the brother of the knocker whom Aine had killed at the battle in Kinvara. Deciding his best chance was to lure Sageuz away from the portal, Trevelyan sent his voice to the top of the hill he had just come down and shouted. "Knocker scum. Can't even see a sylph off! And what of Aeguz?" he taunted. "Dead is what he is!"

The knocker bared its needle teeth and hissed but did not move. "Get him," Sageuz screamed after the goblins. "Find the spy and bring him back alive! Alive, I sayest!" he yelled after them. "Thou canst have thy fun with him after I am done."

Hearing Sageuz call for pursuit, a knocker who had been

waiting just inside the portal ran out between the uprights. "What is going on?" he hissed.

"Our supper's got away," Sageuz snarled. "But my magg of goblins is a hundred strong and they are scouring the Burren, so he won't get far. Let us stay and wait." His eyes gleamed viciously into the darkness. "If the cur doubles back, he may make his way here ... and we shall be ready." He drew a dagger from under his shapeless grey cloak and stood in the opening, blocking access to the portal.

Trevelyan was at a loss. The clock of Emma's life was ticking. His ruse to draw Sageuz away from the portal had failed, and now he had another knocker to contend with. Behind him, he heard shouts and curses. The goblin guards were returning empty-handed.

There was a loud bang over the far wall. The field lit up like it was day, and the ground beneath his feet shuddered for an instant. The knockers hissed and, drawing their cloaks across their eyes, stepped back into the portal.

Trevelyan's heart fell, an air of helplessness descending on him. His fear for Emma and her friends was mounting, and he was plagued with doubt that he would arrive in time to help them. He was going to have to rush the knockers at the portal. After all, he told himself, he had the element of surprise. He was about to make his move when the air was suddenly split with curses from the adjacent field and shrill goblin voices rose in outrage.

"The maggot-ridden scum has murdered the chief. Curse him!"

The howlings and oaths increased. Hearing the growing commotion, the knockers glided away from the portal and over the stone wall into the next field.

Trevelyan seized his chance. He realised that Ke-enaan had

created a diversion and that it was now or never. As he rushed forward into the portal, his motion was suddenly arrested. It seemed he'd run into an invisible stone wall. Falling back in surprise, he saw the uprights at the entrance to the portal begin to flicker with veins of lurid fire. The veins expanded into arteries of flame. His ears roared with the droning chant of sacrifice. In between the pillars, a ghastly vision was playing. He saw a projection of himself at the sabbat, standing in the pentacle with Zugalfar and urging Emma to join him in the circle.

In horror, he realised the fear that had haunted him since the battle under Emma's house had been realised. Heaven and earth seemed to rush together with the sound of thunder, and he was thrust into a black void without beginning or end. Trevelyan did not scream, but all the stars above screamed his agony for him. He was faced with a terror that nothing in his experience could parallel. Doom had struck. The understanding that Zugalfar had replicated his image to trap Emma filled his soul with withering regret. For a moment, he was transfixed with grief, and then he felt Ke-enaan on the airwaves encouraging him, telling him that all was not lost. Trevelyan tried to pull his resolve together. Instead of sinking into the bottomless pit of despair, he stirred with new courage. Stepping into the portal, he willed himself to the giant oak tree that was the faerie gate at Hillside.

There still may be time to save Emma, he thought as he walked out of the tree into the sunlight. Whatever it took, he would do his best to save her. If he had to go into the crypt at Dragonsbury Ring, he would need a mortal with him. Resonating on Jim's frequency, he saw him sitting on the sofa at Emma's, swigging brandy from a bottle.

Jim Lynch lurched to his senses. He felt groggy; his head was throbbing and the overpowering stench of wild garlic made him feel sick to his stomach. Looking round, he saw he was in a patch of dense woodland. Then his memory flooded back like a slap of icy wind on a warm day. Splinters of horror and loss wounded him like shards of glass. Emma had walked into the pentacle and given herself up to evil after all they had been through. It didn't make sense. Nothing made fucking sense. The shock of his situation instantly sobered him up.

The last thing he remembered was a succubus calling to him. In his haste to be with her, he had ripped off the ring Trevelyan had given him for protection and, in the process, lost control of the car and plunged down an embankment into a patch of woodland. The succubus had been beckoning to him from deeper in the trees. Consumed with desire, he had set off at a run towards her, but before he could reach her, she had disappeared.

Jim shivered with the implications of his plight. If he had reached the succubus, she would have murdered him. He looked around the gloomy wood with sudden fright. He had to get out of the trees and back to the car before she reappeared. He looked down at his injured knuckle and wondered what had become of his ring. Without the peridot, he had no defence against her.

The overpowering odour of wild garlic swelled around him as he staggered through a patch of star-white lily flowers. Stumbling up a bank, he saw his car at the bottom of the incline. As he drew nearer, he noticed the driver's door was hanging open. Getting into the driver's seat, he closed the door and turned the key in the ignition. The engine fired to life. He drove up the bank and onto the road.

A few minutes later, he pulled into Emma's driveway and,

turning off the engine, brooded on his loss. In that moment, he thought about killing himself, ridding himself of all the ugly truths about reality he wished he hadn't realised. Life wasn't worth a shit anyway without Emma.

In frustration, he beat his fists on the dashboard a couple of times. Then, putting his head in his hands, he leant over the steering wheel and cried bitter tears. Suddenly remembering the bottle of brandy in the cabinet at Emma's, he got out of the car and walked along the path to the house. Taking the key from under the mat, he opened the back door. All he wanted to do was drown out the terrible scenes playing over and over in his mind.

The liquor cabinet was in the sitting room. Walking into the room, Jim caught a glimpse of his reflection in the wall mirror. He started back in shock and then peered at the almost unrecognisable face that stared back at him. His tawny eyes were dull and bloodshot. His mouth was lacerated and swollen where his teeth had punctured his lip in his fight with the mamba at the sabbat. His braid had come undone, and strands of filthy yellow hair tumbled around his face. There was dried blood on the sleeve of his jacket and on the bottoms of his trousers. He looked like a wild man. He thought for an instant about taking a shower and cleaning himself up, but then he decided he'd rather drink instead.

Taking out the brandy, Jim removed the cap. Sitting down on the sofa, he started swigging from the bottle. In the midst of his morbid self-destructive thoughts, he was suddenly aware that there was someone in the room with him. He looked around and saw a small silver-haired man dressed in a Georgian-style black riding coat, white cravat, breeches, and boots standing by the door.

Jim stared at Trevelyan with a mixture of fear and rage.

"Where the fuck was you when we needed 'elp?" Jim stormed. "You deceived us. Emma's lost. Everythin's gone to shit, and it's all your fault."

"Jim Lynch, I am not your enemy," Trevelyan replied calmly, producing a peridot ring from a pocket in his waistcoat and handing it to Jim. "This, sir, belongs to you," he said. "You are fortunate indeed to be alive! The dispelling frequency of wild garlic sent the succubus back to her wood in Faerie, and while the scent lingered on your clothing and your shoes, she could not approach. The Green saved you from being drained of life."

So intense was the scrutiny, the power, that Trevelyan exerted over him in that moment that Jim's cheeks grew hot with shame. He fidgeted in his seat. He was embarrassed. Trevelyan had given him a ring for protection against the succubus, but in the heat of lust, he had ripped it from his finger and thrown it away.

"Come!" Trevelyan commanded. "There is no time to lose. A chance still remains to save Emma. We must take the faerie gate at Hillside to the tumuli by Dragonsbury Ring."

A chance to save Emma! Jim thought. His spirits rose as he got up and followed Trevelyan through the kitchen door into the sunshine.

A cloud covered the face of the sun, shedding a forbidding light on the land, as they walked round the back of the house and took the footpath to Hillside. Jim looked east towards Dragonsbury Ring. The thought of going there frightened the life out of him and he wanted to be sick. He was desperately afraid, but if there was a chance he could save Emma, he would walk into hell and back. He suddenly baulked at the idea of what his life had become: demons and devils and

35

death. For a moment, he wondered if he was mad and he'd wake up institutionalised.

"This is the portal gate that will take us to the tumulus near Dragonsbury Ring," Trevelyan said, stopping in front of an ancient oak tree. Taking Jim's hand, he pulled him into the tree trunk.

Even though Trevelyan had taken him into Faerie, Jim had never been through a portal gate before. Emma had told him there was an electromagnetic grid laid across the earth and that where the lines of force crossed there was a space that connected to every other cross space on the grid. By using intent, you could travel at will. The tree, he thought, had to be growing on an energetic crossing.

In the next instant, he found himself next to Trevelyan a few yards from the lay-by beneath Dragonsbury Ring. The air was damp and there was a stink of rot in the air. Even the bright new hawthorn leaves unfolding in the hedge failed to cheer him. He was sick to his stomach with fear for Emma and himself. He didn't know how to deal with demons. For a moment, he was paralysed with fear.

Jim felt Trevelyan's reassuring hand upon his arm and realised that the faerie understood his feelings. "There's Sue and Omar," he heard Trevelyan say.

Looking back along the road, Jim saw Omar's lanky frame and Sue's short, stocky body hurrying towards them. Omar's dreads were flying behind him. Sue was wearing a black balaclava and carrying a shotgun in her hand.

"Follow me," Trevelyan said as they came alongside.

The light was gloomy under low grey clouds as they walked along the verge towards the stile leading to the footpath. They were a few yards away from the track when Jim heard the purr of an engine coming along the road. His hackles rose as adrenaline pumped into his blood. He wondered if it was satanists going to Dragonsbury Ring. He knew the bastards weren't going to give up. They were regrouping. Hell-bent on sacrificing Emma, they were using her blood to open the gates to Pandemonia. He fingered the flick knife in his jacket pocket and hoped he wouldn't have to use it.

Trevelyan and Omar disappeared over the stile.

"Quick!" Jim hissed, helping Sue over the step. "There's a vehicle comin'. Any moment it's goin' to come round the bend, and then the driver will see us."

Trevelyan bent light around them as Jim stepped onto the footpath. A few seconds later, a Range Rover sped by and disappeared around a corner. They heard the roar of its engine as the vehicle drove off the road and up the track leading to the summit of Dragonsbury Ring.

The footpath was muddy and slick. Jim kept his eyes on the ground and concentrated on his footing. The close press of damp trees was depressing and claustrophobic. He was glad when he stepped out into open air.

Jim, Sue, and Omar stood for a moment in the shadow of the hedge, awaiting Trevelyan's instructions.

Jim couldn't bear to look at the hill. Zugalfar had Emma. It took all his willpower to keep him from running back along the path and screaming out his fear. He glanced at Trevelyan. "What we goin' to do now?" he whispered.

"Nothing," said Trevelyan. "We are going to wait."

Jim noticed Trevelyan was staring at the summit of the hill with a strange gleam in his eye. *Wait for what?* he silently fumed. *Emma is in the crypt, and God knows what is happening to her.*

"What do you mean, do nothin'?" Jim retorted angrily. "Stop playin' fast and loose with Emma's life. Why aren't we

goin' up the 'ill? We know where the entrance to the crypt is."
He wondered why Trevelyan was stalling. Doubt crept into
his mind again. He heard the sound of cars on the road. The
remnants of Kingsbury's coven were going to the summit.
Soon it would be too late to save Emma. He felt a flush to his
face. His hands were trembling.

"There are vehicles comin'. Soon it's goin' to be too late to
save 'er. We must go to the crypt at once," Jim cried out. "We
are wastin' precious, precious time!"

He heard Sue mutter in agreement.

Trevelyan's face was impassive. Turning to Sue, he said,
"Go and get the car, m'dear."

"I thought we came here to save Emma's life," she said
sharply, gesturing to the shotgun she was carrying.

"Emma is about to save herself," Trevelyan said, offering
no further explanation. "Do as I say. Omar, go with Sue. Take
care: there are murderers from the sabbat about, and we can't
take any chances you'll be recognised. I can only bend light
around you when we are together, but I must stay here. Go
quickly now!"

For a moment, Sue hesitated. She looked at Omar in
bewilderment.

"Let's do as he says, mon," Omar whispered. "Come on!"

Jim, staring helplessly at Trevelyan, noticed a look of grim
satisfaction on his face. A cold wind blew up and rain began to
fall. Jim shivered. The suspense of waiting made the seconds
pass with nightmarish slowness. The horror of the past few
hours was suddenly too much for him. Putting his hands in
front of his face, he began to cry with loud, heaving sobs
that came from deep within his soul. He loved Emma. She
was lost, and he was desperately sad and broken. If he were

a real man, he'd put away his fear, go to the crypt, and save her himself—or perish in the trying. But he was too afraid.

He felt an arm tighten around his shoulder. "Jim," Trevelyan said softly, "there are evil days ahead of us. Let us work together, not as two, but as one. Will you not trust me?"

Jim looked up. He felt his lips trembling. "I don't understand," he said miserably. "Why we are standin' 'ere and Emma's in the crypt with them ..." He broke off suddenly, and gulped back tears.

"Jim!" Trevelyan said, looking him straight in the eye. "Know that Emma has triumphed. She has accessed her faerie nature."

Jim was speechless. He didn't know what to think. His emotions were see-sawing, and he could barely hold himself together. He felt Trevelyan take his hand in a firm grip. "Come with me," he commanded.

The two walked along the inside of the hedgerow. They had not gone far when Jim saw a sudden flash of brilliant blue light touch the ground a few yards in front of them. He gasped in disbelief. Emma was standing just a few feet from him. Her red hair hung greasily around her heart-shaped face, and the sprays of freckles on her cheeks stood out like inkblots against her pale skin. The dark circles underneath her eyes told him of the terror she had endured. He could smell the rottenness of hell upon her ripped and filthy clothes. In a haze of unreality, he saw her give Trevelyan the sapphire. They stood together for a moment, and then Trevelyan disappeared. Emma turned towards Jim. With a sob welling in his throat, he took her in his arms and hugged her. Able to feel her body shivering, he hugged her tighter. "I thought you were lost," he sobbed into her neck.

"Me too," Emma said faintly. She pulled away and looked

him in the eye. "I don't feel very well, Jim. I'm giddy and nauseous."

There was the sound of a car on the road on the other side of the hedge beeping its horn.

"That's Sue and Omar," Jim said to Emma, putting his arm around her shoulder. "Come on! Let's take you 'ome."

A few yards away there was a gate in the hedge. Jim helped Emma over. Then, stepping out into the road, they saw Sue's car. The back passenger door was open. After sliding Emma into the seat, Jim got in beside her.

"Praise to Jah, you are safe, mon," Omar said to Emma. He leant over into the back seat and touched her hand. "You okay, mon?"

"I'm just a bit out of it," Emma answered, managing a smile. She could see the concern in Omar's eyes. He seemed to have aged in just a few days. His dreads were greyer, and his dark skin was ashen, lined, and careworn.

Omar patted her hand. "I and I can imagine, mon," he said, lapsing into Jamaican patois.

"Yeah! You gave us a few bad moments. It's good to see you, mate!" Sue said, driving off along the narrow road. "Do you mind if I roll the window down? There's a bit of a pong in here. No disrespect to you, Emma. I'll soon get you cleaned up when we get back to Greenfern."

"Where'd Trevelyan go?" Jim asked, looking round the car.

"He has taken the sapphire beyond the five dimensions for safekeeping," Emma answered. "Then he's coming to Greenfern. Hopefully he'll be waiting when we get there."

Sue put her foot down on the accelerator. "We've got to get the hell out of here. I think we are in for trouble."

"Trouble?!" Jim queried.

"Yes. When we stepped through the hedge into the lay-by, a Range Rover from Kingsbury's estate went slowly by. Feodora St Clair was driving. We tried to take cover, but it was too late. She saw us and got on her phone immediately." Sue sniffed. "I'm sure the witch won't forgive me for trying to throttle her or you, Jim, for killing Kingsbury," Sue said. "They'll know by now that Emma took the sapphire from Zugalfar and then escaped the crypt. Feodora saw me and Omar in the lay-by. Her lackeys will have run my licence plate by now. They know we picked up Emma, and they also know where I live." She heaved a sigh of resignation. "We had better get ready to protect ourselves from black magic and, as soon as we get back to Greenfern, build an astral fortress in the sanctuary room."

Looking in the rear-view mirror, Sue saw a Range Rover speeding up behind them. "Kingsbury's lackeys are behind us," she shouted, "the same fuckheads who tried to kidnap me. Hang on! One of them has a gun."

"They think Emma has the sapphire, mon," Omar said. "Dem wicked sons of Babylon are goin' to try to kill us. I will send my loa to slow them down."

A bullet whizzed past the driver's window. Sue swerved across the road. Then, putting her foot down on the accelerator, she gunned the car forward, and didn't slow down until she turned onto the Eastbourne road. "Did we lose them?" she asked breathlessly.

Omar looked back. "They're finished, mon. My loa have returned." He sniggered. "Dem sons of wickedness were so intent on gettin' us that they missed a corner and crashed into the bank." He gave a deep, rich laugh and then began to sing about positive vibrations.

The words of the song echoed in Emma's mind. She

found herself singing along. And just as in the crypt under Dragonsbury Ring, she felt her energy returning.

Sue reached into the console and brought out a flask. "I need a drink. I don't know about you," she said to the others. "It's hot lemon." Sue took a drink and then handed the flask to Emma.

It was near eleven when they got back to Greenfern. Emma was very glad to be back in Sue's cheerful kitchen with its warm Aga and the bright copper-bottomed pans hanging from the wall.

"You've got blood on your clothes from the sabbat, mate," Sue said to Jim, looking at the sleeve of his jacket. "Why don't you go and clean up? You can put your dirties in the washing machine. There's clean sweats and T-shirts in the airing cupboard. I'm off to run a bath for Emma."

Quickly following Sue upstairs, Emma went into the bathroom. She took off her ripped jacket. Then, after removing the rest of her torn and soiled clothes, she stuffed them into a plastic bag. The ruby-encrusted daggers she had taken from Dragonsbury Ring were in the inside pocket of her jacket. She had to decide what to do with them.

"Okay, mate," Sue said, helping Emma into the bath. "There's shampoo and conditioner on the rack, and I've put a little lavender oil in the water to cleanse and calm you. When you are done, there's a clean sweatshirt, clean tracksuit bottoms, and a pair of running shoes on the bed in the spare room. I've got to tend to the animals and get a fire lit in the sitting room. I'll see you later."

Emma relaxed into the warm, lavender-scented water. The events of the past twelve hours had rendered her numb and unable to piece her thoughts together. Yet she felt something had shifted in her inner space, an unknown power source that she had tapped that had now become the known—but she couldn't quite grasp its source.

How long Emma languished in the bath, she couldn't recall, but after a while, she got out of the water and towelled herself dry. Going into the spare room, she got dressed. Picking up the bag of clothes, she went downstairs to the sitting room, where she collapsed onto the settee and gazed out through the window.

While Emma was in the bath, Jim showered and changed his clothes. He stared into the mirror. His eyes were still bloodshot, his swollen lip was painful, and his head began to ache. Brushing his hair firmly back, he fastened it into a ponytail and then went into the kitchen to make a pot of tea. Looking through the kitchen window, he saw Sue and Omar in the yard tending to the animals. When the tea was brewed, he took the tray into the sitting room and put it on the table.

"Are you feelin' better, Em?" Jim asked pouring the tea and handing her a cup.

Emma nodded. "I was just wondering where Trevelyan's got to," she said. "He told me he would be back in the twinkling of an eye. It's been much longer than that. You know, Jim." She paused for a moment. "Trevelyan said something odd to me after I had given him the sapphire."

"What was that, Em?"

"He told me I was now a three-world walker, but he was gone before I could ask him to explain."

"A three-world walker, eh?" Jim repeated, gazing at her. "I've no idea what that is."

With Emma framed in the light of the window, Jim noticed how different she was from the Em who had gone with them to the sabbat. He had never seen her look so beautiful.

Her dark red hair had turned to burnished copper, and her emerald eyes were now turquoise and gleamed with timeless, wisdomed age. He sensed a mystical energy around her that he knew was only an echo, a shadow of High Faerie, a realm far beyond his know-how to enter or describe.

A few minutes later, Sue came into the sitting room, followed by Omar. She looked at the clock and then switched on the television. The breaking news showed police cars, ambulances, and fire engines in the car park at Brising Manor. A commentator at the scene reported that a sinkhole had swallowed the family chapel during a special service. The number of casualties was as yet unknown.

"A sinkhole!" Sue exclaimed, raising her eyebrows. "Fucking unbelievable! But Joe Public will swallow it, just like he always does. If it's on the TV news, it has to be true."

Omar laughed and shook his head. "People believe anythin', mon. The truth has been carefully hidden, the narrative manufactured, and these wicked sons of Babylon continue to do what they've done for thousands of years. They think they are invincible."

"Well, they are, sort of," Jim remarked. "They own the media and the judiciary. I mean, they got us all sewn up. No doubt, the police will be under orders to sweep all the damnin' evidence of satanism and child sacrifices under the carpet." Glancing at Emma, he said, "What do you make of the sinkhole business, Em?"

Emma grinned. "I think a sinkhole is quite plausible. After all, they are happening all over the world and they are constantly in the news. And if the public were told the truth, they wouldn't believe it anyway. Seriously, how many people would believe that the chapel was destroyed by a child-eating demon and by a satanic ritual that backfired?" She gave a grim laugh. "Literally backfired!"

Jim topped up his tea. He felt like shit. His hangover had gotten to the throbbing headache stage, and his jaw was sore and bruised. "Do you 'ave an aspirin, Sue?" he asked.

"There's a bottle in the medicine cabinet, mate. You know where it is. Help yourself."

Jim went into bathroom to get an aspirin. When he came back, he asked Sue, "Is there any word from Tony?"

Sue shook her head. "I expect he's still recovering from the trauma of the sabbat, the poor man."

An uneasy silence descended on the sitting room. Sue rolled a cigarette.

"You want one?" she said to Jim.

He nodded. "My nerves are frayed and a smoke will 'elp to settle me down." He lit a cigarette and inhaled deeply. "I wanted to go 'ome to Emma's and get back to our business, but after what's 'appened, I think we'll 'ave to stay 'ere for a while and see 'ow things iron out."

"There's safety in numbers, mon. Dem sons of wickedness will be comin' for all of us," Omar said, nervously fiddling with his dreads. "They'll want vengeance and our blood for what happened at the sabbat. I killed a high-rankin' member of their wicked order, the voodoo mamba that sacrificed my Lucy."

Emma turned and looked out of the window at the depressing grey sky. Going inside herself, she resonated on Trevelyan's vibration but could find no sympathetic match upon the airwaves. All she could see and hear was shimmering blue space. She tried to concentrate on the colours and see what lay beyond, but she found the light absorbing her, sucking her into it.

For a moment, the blue light confused her, and then the understanding dawned that the sapphire star-gate was open. Trevelyan had left the Faerie Worlds and had travelled beyond her frequency to interpret.

She took a deep breath and leant back into the cushions. She had accomplished what Trevelyan had asked of her and, at the moment, was still alive to tell the tale. Against impossible odds, the sapphire had been wrenched from the jaws of evil, but she knew that Feodora and Zugalfar would hunt her and her compeers with a vengeance. The thought of Zugalfar sent a chilling shiver down her spine. She wished Trevelyan were there to support her.

Suddenly remembering the daggers she had in her jacket pocket, Emma fished them out of the bag and stared at them. The stones were set at the top of a pair of small stiletto daggers with thin, cold blades. The daggers conjured up visions of robed and cowled figures, the stink of bitter incense, and the spattered blood of sacrifice.

"I took these daggers from the pentacle under Dragonsbury Ring," Emma said, showing them to Sue, who physically recoiled at the sight of them. Seeing Sue's reaction, she added, "I wasn't going to leave the rubies in the crypt. Taking Zugalfar's eyes in this dimension is a major blow against him."

"There's centuries of suffering held within those stones, and they'll be vibrating with the frequency of hell," Sue said, standing up and reaching for the smudge pot on the shelf. "We are dealing with satanic power objects, mate. I have to think about the welfare of my animals. Once Zugalfar is called by blood, he'll be able to sense your whereabouts even though he can't see you. Having the rubies here is like a magnet to the Devil." She nervously ran her hands through her ash-blonde hair. "I'm sorry, but they can't stay in the house. Or on the property," she said adamantly, putting the smoking smudge pot on the table. "There's a churchyard about four miles from here. You can bury them there. Right now, that's the only hallowed ground I can think of."

"I agree with Sue," Jim said, peering at the daggers. "I think we should get them off the grounds as soon as we can. I mean, if Zugalfar can use them to materialise, they need to be as far away from 'ere as possible." He looked at Omar. "What do you think?"

"Jah has dealt a blow to evil, mon," Omar responded. "But in the circumstances, we need to get rid of the daggers before they can betray us. Once called through ritual and blood, Zugalfar will sense their whereabouts, and dem sons of wickedness will find us." He paused for a moment in thought. "Sue! Do you have any agrimony in the house? The herb is potent against wickedness and will temporarily block any demon sight until we can find a place to bury the daggers."

Sue nodded. "I do. I'll go and get a bowl." She hurried off into the kitchen.

"I know where the churchyard is in Appleton," Jim said. "What do you say, Em? We'll take the daggers there and bury 'em."

The scent of the flat-cedar smudge filled the room. Emma took a deep breath of the purifying smoke and wafted it over her head and around her body. Realising that Sue was frightened for her animals, she didn't blame her friend for wanting the daggers gone from Greenfern. The rubies were fraught with malice. Zugalfar's mortal minions were psychopaths, the kind that liked to torture living things. The helpless animals in Sue's care would be the first thing to be slaughtered.

Emma gave a sigh of resignation. She had brought this evil

on Sue, Omar, and Jim. If anyone had to distance themselves from Greenfern, it had to be her. This was her fight; it was not fair to involve the others in her hell world. Tony had suffered. His daughters were dead, and God knows who was next.

Emma suddenly made up her mind. She would leave the sanctuary and take the daggers with her. She thought about Trevelyan and how much she needed his advice. He had said he would be back shortly, but he hadn't yet arrived. She knew something had prevented his return. Fear tried to get a foothold in her mind, but she was ready for it.

Sending her attention onto the airwaves, she tried to find Trevelyan's vibration, but again she found no trace of his resonance to key into. She wished he was with her. He would know what to do with the evil power objects. But the bottom line was that she had to leave and take the daggers with her.

"Jim!" she said after a while. "I think it's best I leave. The daggers will only draw Zugalfar and his servants to the sanctuary, and being the low-life lackeys that they are, the animals will be at risk. I can't take that chance." She looked into his face. "You can stay here if you want to, until … whatever happens. It's me Zugalfar wants, and me he will come after."

"I'm not leavin' you, Em. If you're goin', so am I. We're in this shit together, right?" He nervously rubbed his neck. "Trevelyan will be back soon. 'E'll 'elp us."

"I hope so, Jim."

"But we got to get rid of them daggers, Em. They're givin' me the 'eebie-jeebies."

Emma could feel Jim's anxiety as keenly as her own. The dark power objects were a liability, a magnet for evil. To hold the negative power of the rubies in check, she passed the daggers through the cedar smoke.

"Ouch!" She started back, almost dropping the daggers. The blades felt like fire and ice and burned her hands. Not wanting to put the daggers on the table because of their negativity, she jostled them from hand to hand.

"What's up, Em?" Jim asked in alarm.

"The daggers burnt me," she said nervously. "I hope Sue hurries up with the herbs."

At that moment, Sue came back into the room with an aluminium box full of dried agrimony and put it on the table. "This is the best container I can find." She stared at Emma. "Are you all right, mate?"

Emma nodded. "I put the daggers through the smudge and they burnt me," she said, checking her fingers. "They are so cold, they've made my hands numb."

Moving the top layer of leaves and flower heads to one side, Emma swiftly placed the daggers in the centre, and then covered them over with the herbs. She turned to Sue and Omar. "I think it's best if Jim and I leave the sanctuary and take the ruby daggers with us. The last thing we want to do is put you two and all the animals at risk. If we are not here, maybe Zugalfar and the satanists will leave you alone."

Sue looked startled. "Leave! That's not going to solve anything. Feodora's lackeys know you left Dragonsbury Ring in my car," she said quickly. "They are going to come after you and me ... all of us." She shook her head. "Even if you do leave, they'll still come here. It's the only clue to your whereabouts they have, apart from the daggers in the box. Just get rid of the power objects and come back here. That will put Zugalfar off our scent for a while. The old adage rings true: there's safety in numbers."

"They's tryin' to divide and conquer, mon. That's the way of wickedness. We need to stay together." Omar held up his hand with fingers splayed. "One at a time, our fingers can be broken." He brought them together in a fist. "But together we are strong. We are in this struggle together, mon."

Sue looked at the clock. "It'll be midday soon and the sun will be overhead. That's the best time to bury any negative power object. Take the daggers to the churchyard and bury them, box and all."

"Sue, do you have a pendulum I can borrow?" Emma asked. "I didn't think to bring mine, and I'm going to have to douse for the place to bury the daggers. Oh! And a jacket. Mine's ruined."

Sue nodded. She disappeared through the door and came back with a pendulum and an anorak, which she gave to Emma.

"While you are gone," Sue said to Emma, "I'll burn your ruined clothes. We don't want any grime on the premises that is connected to the crypt under Dragonsbury Ring that the coven could use against us in a psychic attack."

"Thanks, Sue," Emma said, putting the pendulum in her pocket. She picked up the box of agrimony containing the daggers. "Let's get on with it."

"Okay," Jim said, putting on his coat. "We'll 'ave to take your car, Sue. Ours is back at Emma's."

"Okay, but you'd better keep your eyes peeled, mate. Kingsbury's mob might be looking for the car," Sue said.

"See you in a little while," Emma said, following Jim through the door.

CHAPTER 4

BATTLE MAGIC

The wind was brisk and cold and the sky heavy with the threat of rain as Emma and Jim walked along the path to the car park.

"Don't look like the sun's goin' to show up today, Em," Jim commented, opening the tool shed door and taking out a shovel. "That's a pity, considerin' what's in the box."

"The sun's still shining behind the clouds," Emma answered. "Its virtue isn't lessened by the fact that we can't see it."

Jim sniffed. "I know, but at least I'd feel better if the sun was shinin'."

"The cemetery at Appleton's not far," Jim said as they left Greenfern and drove along the high-banked twisty road towards the village. On the way, he told Emma about his drinking and the succubus attack. He glanced sheepishly at her. "I 'ope you don't mind, but I polished off 'alf your brandy. And then Trevelyan arrived."

The thought of Jim's drinking made Emma nervous. She glanced at his finger to make sure he was wearing the peridot ring.

"You're quiet, Em. I'll give you a penny for your thoughts."

"I was thinking about why the daggers burnt me when I passed them through the smudge," Emma replied.

"The ruby daggers are evil, Em. They are the eyes of Baphomet in the pentacle under Dragonsbury Ring. That's why they reacted to the purifyin' frequency of the smudge."

Emma was unconvinced. "I think there's more to it than that." She paused and then said, "They didn't burn when I had them in my pocket, or when I took them out and showed them to Sue. Something's changed."

She sensed that there was a connection between Feodora and the change in the energy of the daggers. She wondered if the satanist had carried out a blood sacrifice. If so, Zugalfar would have taken root in the pentacle and taken possession of her mind. Feodora would then be a conduit for the arch-demon, and may have awakened his connection to the daggers.

Emma realised she had underestimated Zugalfar. Having thought that he was blind in the mortal world without the ruby daggers, she had not reckoned on him possessing Feodora, body, mind, and soul. Her eyes were now his eyes. Emma knew that as long as she had the daggers in her possession, she and Jim were in the gravest danger.

"I think Feodora has carried out a blood sacrifice," she said anxiously. "And, as a result, Zugalfar is aware of us."

"That quick!" Jim exclaimed.

Emma nodded. "That's the only explanation I can think of for the energetic change in the daggers."

"Perhaps it was one of 'er own coven she murdered." Jim sniffed. "That's what's called expediency!"

"I think Feodora's lost too many of her coven to sacrifice any more. With her contacts, she can pick up her phone and order a child of any age or either sex for immediate delivery. There's no problem if you are part of the satanic club and in the know. Millions of children go missing every year and are never found. And that's surprising what with all the surveillance cameras around."

"Nobody's really lookin', Em," Jim said. "The 'igher-ups in the police are too busy protectin' their rich paedophile buddies. It's just the same as the 'unt." He gave a sigh of exasperation. "I don't think the 'ellfire club ever went away. If you can pay, you can play. 'Ave you ever noticed 'ow the media never fingers the 'igh-rankin' paedophile priests and politicians until they kick the bucket?" He glanced at Emma. "All I know is that this is a sick fuckin' world run by even sicker people."

Emma nodded. "They are not people, Jim. That's the point. Shakespeare had it right when he wrote, 'Hell is empty and all the devils are here.'"

"Ain't that a fact," Jim said in agreement. "I've always thought this place was 'ell."

They passed the speed restriction signs and drove along the high street. The village had the atmosphere of the old coaching days with its wide street, inns, and picturesque bow-fronted shops. Jim drove through an alley behind one of the inns into a broad car park. The old stone church with its square tower was on the opposite side of the square and fenced in with tall, dark trees.

Jim parked outside the dark weather-worn arched gate leading to the entrance of the church.

"I'll take the box," he said, opening Emma's door. "Don't want you to drop it."

Emma smiled. "Thanks. It's awkward trying to get in and out of the car without using my hands."

Jim looked uneasily at Emma as he handed her the box. "The box feels really cold, Em."

"It seems heavier too, and the metal is bloody freezing," she said with a shiver as they walked through the gate and followed a pathway that ran around the church to the graveyard at the back.

The cemetery was old, green, and still. Emma, looking thoughtfully around, noticed a yew tree growing amongst the cypress and firs. "Come on, Jim," she said, leading the way along a grass-grown path bordered by stained and tottering grave stones. "There's a yew tree at the back of the graveyard. That would be the best place to bury the daggers. Yew is a magical tree, and its ability to contain dark power objects is strong."

At the end of the path was an old and scarred oak seat shadowed by a huge yew tree. The branches had grown into the ground and formed into separate but linked trunks. Emma handed the box containing the daggers to Jim and then took the pendulum from her pocket. Holding the pointer over her palm, she visualised the daggers and asked the spirit of the yew tree if the dark objects could be buried there. The pendulum swung to the left, answering no. Emma tried again but got the same response.

Suddenly the air around her seemed to flock with hidden listeners. A green mist was rising from the yew tree and then began to spiral towards her. She was instantly surrounded by a cloud of tiny emerald octahedral forms, and heard the plaintive whisperings of the Faeries of Place in her ears. "The power of the yew cannot contain the dark magic of the daggers," they said in hushed tones. "You must leave and take them with you."

Emma felt a tinge of despair, followed by panic. She had felt sure that the yew tree would accept the burial of the daggers. Now they had to find another place. Her anxiety began to deepen as she took the box back from Jim. It was even colder, and felt like a lead weight in her hands.

"Let's go, Jim. We have to find another place—and quick."

"I saw the Faeries of Place surround you, but I couldn't 'ear what they was sayin'," Jim said as they began to retrace their steps.

"They said that the yew tree did not have the power to contain the evil in the daggers," Emma responded. She took an anxious breath. "That confirms what we suspected. Feodora has called Zugalfar, and he has sent his will into the daggers. If we don't bury them soon, I fear he will lead Feodora and her yobbos to them, and may even be able to materialise himself."

"You mean materialise out of the box, like a genie from a bottle? I don't like the sound of that."

"That's exactly what I mean, and I don't like the sound of it either. We have to find a place to bury these suckers—and fast."

They walked quickly back along the path through the churchyard to the car. Jim took the box as Emma got into the seat.

"Gosh, Em," he said in alarm, "the box is freezin', and there's fissures formin' along the sides and on the top." He stared at his fingers. "My 'ands are turnin' red. They feel numb from the cold." He looked at her anxiously. "I think you'd better put somethin' between the box and your knees."

Emma looked around the car and saw a blanket on the back seat. Reaching over, she grabbed it and put it over her knees.

The metal groaned as Jim put the box on top of the blanket. The chill was still there. He was right: the metal was breaking down. Even though the daggers were covered by the agrimony and metal, Emma could feel malevolence flowing from them. Feeling anxious, she took a deep breath to steady herself. What if they couldn't find a place to dispose of the box before Feodora caught up with them? She shut off the thought. Thoughts were charges of energy, and with the evil enhancement in the box, any negative scenario she harboured in her mind could manifest.

"Where's the nearest church?" she asked.

Jim thought a moment. "Denhampstead. It's about four miles along the Eastbourne road."

Emma gulped. She could hear tiny cracking sounds coming from the box.

"Gun it, Jim," she said. "I don't know how much longer the box is going to last."

Jim drove along a hedged narrow road towards Denhampstead. The road seemed to wind on forever; four miles was beginning to feel like ten.

"How much further?" Emma asked, fidgeting in her seat.

"About a mile."

They drove past the speed restriction signs and into the village.

"How much further is the church?" Emma said again as they drove along the broad shop-lined street.

"Just up 'ere, Em."

Hearing Jim take a quick intake of breath, Emma looked into the rear-view mirror. A Range Rover was behind them. One of the headlights was missing, and the bumper was smashed in. She recognised the sallow evil face of the driver and his sidekick from Dragonsbury Ring. There was another Range Rover behind them. For a moment Emma caught a glimpse of the haughty face of Feodora St Clair. Both vehicles were surrounded by the evil light of the abyss.

"Fuck! 'Ang on, Em!" Jim cried out.

Emma gulped. Zugalfar and Feodora had not wasted a second. They had found her and the daggers.

Knowing they were being pursued by psychopaths from Brising Manor, Jim swerved into a side road without indicating.

"Em! Watch the mirror. I got to concentrate on drivin' if we are goin' to make it out of 'ere. If they catch us, they will kill us. I 'ope they didn't see us turn." His hopes were soon dashed. Checking the rear-view mirror, he saw both Range Rovers closing in behind.

The road looped round the village green and out the other side back to the main road. Putting his foot down on the accelerator, Jim raced to the junction. There was a gap in a long line of cars he could squeeze into. With his heart hammering in his chest, he sailed out into the traffic. Adrenaline was pumping through his veins as he accelerated around the car in front of him and sped along the high street. Looking in the mirror, he saw that his pursuers were edging out into the road, trying to force an opening in the traffic.

The area around Denhampstead was familiar to him from his anti-hunting days. He soon turned off the high street into a hedge-banked narrow lane.

"I think we better give up the idea of the church in Denhampstead," he said breathlessly. "I don't fancy a run-in with Feodora and 'er thugs. If they catch up with us and you still 'ave the box, we'll be in deep shit, Em."

"I know," Emma said despondently. "I was sure we could have buried the box on any hallowed ground. We can't." She took a shallow breath. "What the fuck are we going to do, Jim? The ruby daggers are so negatively charged that only a few elemental strongholds will be able to contain them. We found that out with the Faeries of Place in Appleton churchyard. We need to find a place of power where ley lines cross—and we don't have much time. It's not going to be long before the box will fall apart and the rubies be exposed. Then God knows what will happen." She shifted awkwardly in the seat. "The damn box is so heavy that it feels like lead weight on my legs. Even with the blanket in between, it's chilling my body."

She felt her shoulders and back tense up. It was becoming difficult to breathe. "We have to get rid of the box, Jim," she said in a panic. "Is there a tumulus, a stone circle, or an ancient hill fort anywhere nearby?"

Jim thought for a moment. He remembered a Neolithic site from his hunt-sabbing days. The place had stuck in his mind. A hare had been cornered by the hounds and, making a dash between two yew trees, had suddenly disappeared.

"There is a place we could try," he said thoughtfully. "It's an old site from the Neolithic period. You know, them round barrows and the like. Bit of a stone circle there, too."

Emma felt the tingle of portent. Neolithic sites were normally built on a power point, a focus of ley line energy harnessed by a circle of crystalline sarsen stones. If any place could subdue and neutralise the evil in the daggers, it would be there. Hell was resting on her knees. She felt that the darkness had for an instant been breached by diamond light. "Take me there, Jim!" she cried out. "As fast as you can!"

"Em," Jim said as he sped around the bends, "there's only a narrow bridleway into the site and the same way out. If we get caught up there, them soulless fuckers are goin' to 'ave us at their mercy. And they 'aven't got any mercy."

"We'll just have to take the chance. We have no other choice."

"Yeah!" Jim said in agreement. "We'll 'ave to jump the fences as we come to them."

Jim began to slow down. His palms felt sweaty on the steering wheel. Biting his teeth into his lip, he scanned the road ahead for the turning to the barrow downs.

"There are no vehicles behind us," Emma said, checking the rear-view mirror. She suddenly felt nauseous as an ugly vibration coursed through the box and into her legs. "Hurry, Jim!" she yelled.

Jim turned off the tarmac road onto a green lane. The track was narrow and tree-lined, ending on a slight rise. He parked the car on the overlook and quickly opened Emma's door. He helped her out of the car and then got the shovel from the back of the vehicle.

Emma stood on the top of the slope and looked around. Below her, about half a mile away, she saw a meadow of low mounds overgrown with grass. The mole-like mounds were barrows, burial places from the Neolithic period. Some of the barrows were long, and others were shaped like inverted bowls. Here and there were the stumps of sarsen stones that had once formed a circle.

Using her faerie sight, she saw the energetic outlines of the standing stones that had once graced the circle, and for an instant, she revisited a time where satanic priests had heated up the stones in an effort to destroy them.

But the monsters had failed to destroy the fourth dimension of the heart—the connection to the living Green of leaf and bud and tree. The geometric grids and power sigils created through the ages had endured, and in them Emma viewed a time before the Separation. Using her expanded awareness, she gazed at the circle. In the centre were two yew trees covered in glistening red berries. Their upper limbs were bent over to form a heart shape, and the stone stumps reminded her of guardians standing like sentinels against the grey forbidding sky. Her heart told her that in between the trees was the place to bury the ruby daggers.

"Em," Jim said, "that's the yew trees I told you about, where the 'are disappeared."

Before Emma could answer, she felt the box groan. Then the rivets started popping. She choked back a cry. The hint of a red fume was escaping through the fissures on the top.

"Zugalfar's trying to form," she shrieked. "Somehow we have to stop him." Her mind raced frantically, seeking a solution. Around her she saw the golden heads of dandelions blooming in the grass. Trevelyan's words came flooding back to her: "Dandelions, m'dear—the garblus, as it is known—is the protector of High Faerie." She wondered if the power in the flowers might be able to slow the evil that was trying to take shape.

"Jim! Pick some dandelion flowers and put them on top of the box. Quick!"

Jim bent down, swiftly picked some dandelions, stood up, and laid them across the fissures. The red fume was suddenly shut off.

"Let's make for the yew trees while we can," Emma said, setting off down the hill towards the barrow downs.

They had barely made it halfway down when they heard the sound of car engines behind them and a screech of tyres. Doors were slamming, and the sound of angry voices split the air. Glancing over her shoulder, Emma saw four threatening figures standing on the rise above, staring down at them. Feodora was moving her hands in cabbalistic gestures and screaming out a wild incantation.

"Run to the yew trees!" Emma shouted desperately to Jim.

The box began to vibrate and pull her hands towards the ground. A low, moaning wind blew up around her. The box was so heavy, she had to almost bend double to carry it. It was only her will that kept her on her feet and moving forward.

Craning her neck back, she saw the huge, hunched, astral shape of Zugalfar towering over Feodora's mortal form. He had taken possession of her body and was empowering her to cast a barrier spell to stop Emma and Jim in their tracks.

Emma, calling on her inner resources, sent an octahedron spinning into Feodora's witchcraft to break the pattern of her spell. She heard a crackle and a loud pop as the enchantments clashed against each other, and then she saw Feodora throw up her arms and stagger backwards.

Taking advantage of the respite, Emma stumbled forward through the stones to the yews. The box was suddenly comparatively weightless to what it had been before and was growing warmer. Emma looked around for Jim and saw he wasn't with her.

Jim reproached himself as he followed Emma to the bottom of the hill. He had driven into a dead end; there was no way they could get back to Sue's car. They were stuck in open country, and the only thing they could do was bury the box at the yew trees and then run across the barrow downs to the copse beyond. He was sure the thugs had guns and wouldn't hesitate to use them. He and Emma would be sitting ducks.

A few yards before he got to the ring of stones, Jim was struck by a chill that instantly drained his strength and stopped him in his tracks. He felt weak in every limb. The bones in his body were aching, and each step forward was an effort. The weight of the shovel was almost unbearable and for a moment, he thought of dropping and leaving it behind. But reason spoke to him and Jim realised that he needed a shovel to dig the hole and bury the daggers.

Seeing that Emma had made it to the yew trees, he tried desperately to fight off the malaise that was spreading through his muscles. He heard a loud popping noise, and suddenly the restraining pressure on his body eased. With an effort of will, he moved forward through the ring of stones to the yew trees.

"I only just made it, Em," he said breathlessly as he joined her. "Somethin' was tryin' to stop me from movin'."

"Feodora cast a restraining spell against us," Emma responded. "Thankfully it didn't work as well as she would have liked and we made it through."

"What's 'appenin' to the box?"

"All the leaden weight has gone from it, and that means that Zugalfar's energy has left the daggers. While you bury the box, I'm going to try to harness the energy of this sacred site to keep Feodora's sorcery at bay."

"What's the point of buryin' the box, Em?" Jim muttered, leaning on the shovel. "They are only goin' to dig it up again."

Emma could hear defeat and resignation in his voice. In spite of the predicament they were in, her intuition told her to block out the negative reality and concentrate on burying the box.

"Focus, Jim," she said sharply. "Let's get the daggers buried. I sense this is the place."

Emma looked back at Feodora. The priestess was shrouded in the lurid light of Zugalfar once again, and a wave of shimmering vapour was streaming from her hands and surging down the hill towards the yews. Emma sensed its vibration. It was flesh-vaporising magic, and if it reached them, their bodies would be burnt to cinder. Putting her hand on her necklace, she sent her will into the jewel. As the topaz changed into her faerie knife, she saw a set of symbols appear within her mind, sigils that she recognised as battle magic, but she could not place their meaning. One of the sigils started to pulse. Obeying a command from within, she used her knife to trace the magic symbol in the air, and then sent it crashing against Feodora's fire spell.

A stench-filled hot wind stung her in the face, making her eyes tear up. Through the blur, she saw the burning wave of fire slow down and then begin to stall.

The awful infra-bass tones of Under-Earth echoed down the hill and across the meadow to the yew trees. The grey clouds turned red, and the wall of scalding vapour began to move forward and push against the standing stones.

"Jim!" Emma cried out. "I can't hold back the fire spell any longer. And there is a red fume rising from the box. I can hardly hold it together."

"Quick, Em! The 'oles ready," Jim said, stepping back.

Emma bent forward. As she put the box into the space, all the rivets popped out, the top fell off, and the metal plates separated, exposing the agrimony. The green of the leaves had faded into a dirty brown. As she stepped away from the hole so Jim could shovel the earth back in, she once again saw the sigils in her mind. One of them was glowing. Taking it as an image to dissolve Feodora's spell, Emma traced the sigil in the air with her knife and sent it spiralling against the shimmering wave of fire that was trying to consume the standing stones.

There was a crack and an intense flash of light. The light was so bright that it temporarily blinded her. When her sight returned, Emma saw that the hungering fire had stopped and was returning up the hillside to Feodora. She also noticed that Zugalfar's spectral image had vanished.

In a flash of intuition and memory, Emma realised that by tracing the sigil with her topaz knife, she had activated the High Faerie power stored in the ring of stones. Old timeless magic woven before the time of Separation had thwarted both Zugalfar and Feodora's sorcery.

A piercing scream of rage blasted the silence. With the screech still ringing in her ears, Emma instinctively grabbed Jim's hand and pulled him into one of the yew trees.

There was a giddy space filled with a kaleidoscope of images. She saw lofty pinnacles of porphyry stone that glittered with rose-red sparks and beheld glints of tiny flames rising from a golden meadow with gentle hills behind it. Around the towering citadel was a ring of sarsen stones, and above these was a canopy of long, curved, interlacing streaks of turquoise and magenta light that formed a protective arc above the citadel. Her eyes were drawn to the topmost pinnacle. A blue radiance shined through the windows. Emma understood that she was looking at the energetic radiations of the sapphire star-gate before the time of Separation.

Seven tall men dressed in outer spectrum colours appeared to her in inner space. There was no aura of earth about them, and yet they were familiar. She felt their kindly glowing eyes reach deep into her psyche. Forgotten memories surfaced in her mind, and she saw herself at the council in High Faerie long ago. She recognised the seven figures as the lords of the elemental realms who had pledged to save the Green. They had seen ahead in time what would befall her, and had worked beyond mortal space and time to give her what aid they could in her time of need. Her faerie nature had resonated on their frequency and brought the old magic in the stone circle to life.

No dark spell could approach the sanctity of the yews or the sacred earth that had engulfed the daggers.

The vision changed and she saw the breaking of the worlds. The meadow around the citadel was stained with blood and full of hungry shrieking. Druids on dark horses dragging bodies in their wakes charged through the sarsen stones. The air was full of flying hooded forms hauling nets of human skulls that they had harvested. Hither and thither they rode through the clouds, with flaming swords slashing at the glowing arc of turquoise and magenta light above the citadel.

The earth groaned; mighty winds began to blow. The groaning became a cataclysmic roar. The ground heaved and split apart. The pinnacles of the citadel crumbled and fell, and Emma saw an intense flash of sapphire light.

In the tumult that followed, she saw seven bodies fall, and she realised that there were seven grass mounds within the stone circle. At the time of Separation, the lords of the elements had vacated their bodies in the mortal world and had translated their being, and their reality, into the fifth dimension. But the sapphire was lost and left behind.

Just as she had pulled Jim into the yew tree, Emma had quickly looked back. There were no yew trees, no freshly filled in hole, just grass and winds and barrow downs. Emma realised the trees could only be seen by those with faerie sight.

In the next instant, she found herself holding Jim's hand and standing outside of the giant oak at Hillside. She breathed a sigh of relief. "That was too bloody close for comfort," she said to Jim. She noticed he looked pale and drawn.

"I'm still wonderin' 'ow we got 'ere." He pulled on his earlobe. "I'm not cut out for this, Em," he said miserably. "I think I need a change of underwear."

"I found something out," she said to Jim as they walked

slowly down the hill. "The yew trees can only be seen with faerie sight." She laughed. "All Feodora could see were two people digging a hole on the barrow downs."

"Really!" He looked at her with interest.

"And, I daresay, the hare was a thought form that was sent to lead you to the stone circle. I think you were shown the yew trees so that at a future time you could take me to the right place to bury the daggers."

"You mean I was spiritually set up!" he exclaimed. His haggard face broke out in a smile.

They turned onto the footpath that led to Emma's house.

"All I know, Em, is that I'm starvin' 'ungry."

"I'm hungry too, Jim, but we can't eat until all this is over. Feodora and Zugalfar will be coming for us tonight. They still think I have the sapphire. We'd better get back to Greenfern as soon as we can and help Sue and Omar with the preparations."

They reached the step. Emma opened the door. "Come on! At least we are safe for now. Let's go and clean ourselves up. I don't know about you, but I want to wash all the shit of the last few hours away."

Once inside, they took a shower and changed their clothes. While Emma made a flask of hot lemon tea to take with them on the ride back to Greenfern, Jim went next door to tell Maggie, their friend they were okay, and to ask her to feed the cats and keep an eye on the place for a while longer.

On the journey to Greenfern, Emma had a chance to think about what had transpired on the barrow downs. So much had happened, and so fast, that it was difficult to gain clarity or an understanding on what had energetically taken place. She closed her eyes and saw again in her inner vision the scenes that had flashed before her eyes when she'd stood between the yew trees.

The thought that the Neolithic site had been the home of the sapphire filled her with awe. She saw again an image of the glittering citadel and its pinnacle of sapphire light in the days before the Separation.

"You're quiet, Em," Jim commented as they drove through Appleton. "I'll give you two pennies for your thoughts!"

Emma smiled. "I'm a bit distracted, still trying to make sense of the visions I saw at the yew trees. Did you see anything?"

"No! I was too scared," Jim admitted. "To be 'onest, Em, I thought we'd 'ad it."

"One thing I found strange," she said, "was I saw seven figures and recognised them as the elemental lords from High Faerie. But there were eight in attendance at the council. I wonder what happened to the other one."

"Beats me, Em," Jim replied. "That's a question for Trevelyan. I 'ope 'e's all right," he added.

The events of the last few hours had driven Emma's anxieties about Trevelyan to the back of her mind. He had been gone for too long. She sent her mind onto the airwaves to try to find his resonance, but all she saw was shimmering blue light.

CHAPTER 5

INTO DARKNESS

After Jim and Emma had left Greenfern, Omar and Sue went to the sanctuary room to get the space ready for the ceremony. They moved all of the furniture out of the room and put it in one of the barns, and then spent the next hour washing the walls and ceiling, paying special attention to the floor. The room had to be spotless. Any trace of dust or dirt could be used by negative entities to manifest and attack them.

When all was clean, they took the mops, brooms, and buckets back to the kitchen.

"What's next, mon?" Omar asked, helping himself to a glass of spring water.

"We have to construct the pentacle, mate," Sue answered, rummaging through a drawer in the sideboard. "I'll get the chalk, a ruler, and a ball of string. You'll find a gallon jug of spring water in the fridge, and five little silver cups in the china cabinet."

"Okay," Omar replied. "Do you have any cornmeal, mon?"

"I think I do. What do you need cornmeal for?"

"Veves, mon, have to be drawn with cornmeal."

Sue looked at him in surprise. "You mean to draw voodoo symbols in our astral fortress?"

"Yes, mon. Veves are drawn to allow my loa to have a focus in the circle. That way they can keep wicked loa out." His dark eyes flashed as he looked at her. "Zugalfar will have a host of bad loa in his wicked legion. Voodoo is like any other kind of magic. It can be used to hurt or to heal."

Sue nodded and said no more.

When they had collected everything they needed to build the protective geometric, Sue picked up the smoking smudge pot and they headed to the sanctuary room. With the smudge pot in one hand and a ball of string in the other, she stood at the centre of the room while Omar took the other end of the string. Then, using Sue as a pivot, Omar measured twelve feet and drew a chalk circle on the floor. Once the first ring was drawn, he measured out eleven feet and drew a second circle, this one inside the other one. When the circles were completed, he said, "We have to draw a five-pointed star, mon. Do you want to do it?"

"No." Sue shook her head. "The points have to touch the outer circle, and it has to be exact. If the geometric is off by a fraction, the circle will be useless as protection and we will all be in danger. I'm not very good at geometry, so I know you could do a much better job than me, mate." She laughed. "A safer job, I mean. Anyway, I'll leave you to it. I'm going to load my cats and dogs up in the van and take them to my friend in the village. I'll only worry about them if they are in the house. I don't want anything to happen to them."

Omar nodded. "Good thinkin', mon."

With the help of his loa, string, and measure, Omar drew the microcosmic star. When he was satisfied the proportions were correct, he drew veves and cabbalistic sigils in the points of the pentacle. Dipping his finger into the spring water, he traced a water circle just within the first line of chalk, and then he joined all the symbols he had drawn together. Next, he placed a green candle in the points of the star and put the silver cups into the valleys.

He had just finished constructing their spiritual refuge when Sue came back in through the door.

"Good job, mate!" she said, looking appraisingly at his psychic fortress.

"We's done here, mon," Omar said, stepping through a narrow space in the outer rings he had left open. "I'll light the candles and put water in the cups when we's ready to enter the circle."

Leaving the smoking smudge pot in the room, they returned to the kitchen and sat down at the table. The grandfather clock in the hallway chimed five o'clock.

"I wonder what's keepin' Emma and Jim, mon," Omar said worriedly. "They should have been back a while ago."

"That's just what I was thinking. I hope nothing's happened to them. The ruby daggers were bad news. Let's hope they've got shot of them."

"The daggers may be bad news," Omar answered, "but Emma did the right thing by takin' them out of the pentacle at Dragonsbury Ring. It's a case of damned if you do and damned if you don't, mon." He ran his hand over his dreads. "What's next to do?"

"We have to feed the horses, goats, and chickens and put them away in the barn for the night."

Sue and Omar were tending to the animals when Jim and Emma came driving down the track and parked in front of the house.

"Hello, mates!" Sue called as they got out. "We were

wondering where you'd got to. Is everything all right?" She came over. Staring at Jim, she said, "Where's my car?"

"Er … while we were buryin' the daggers, Feodora and 'er louts caught up with us," Jim replied. "We 'ad to leave the car and run for it. Otherwise they would 'ave caught us. The car is on the 'ill above the barrow downs near Denhampstead. We can go and get it if you like."

"We can't risk going for it now, mate. It'll be dark soon and we still have things to do. We'll wait until the morning."

"If you are finished with the animals," Emma said, "we should go into the house. There is a lot to tell and talk about."

"I've still got a couple of jobs to do," Sue replied. "Go on in. Omar's making some hot lemon to warm us up. It's a bit nippy out here."

Emma and Jim went into the kitchen. Omar was putting the teapot and cups on a tray. "Good to see you, mon," he said. "Where you been all afternoon?"

"It's a story and a 'alf," Jim said, shaking his head. "I can't really believe I'm 'ere."

Just then, Sue came into the kitchen. "Everything is taken care of," she said, pulling off her boots. "Ah! The tea's ready. Let's go into the sitting room. I built the fire up. It should be warm in there." She smiled at Jim and Emma. "I'm interested to hear what happened with the daggers. You were gone so long, me and Omar thought something bad had happened to you."

"It nearly did!" Jim murmured.

They took their tea into the sitting room and sat down in front of a roaring log fire. When they were settled, Emma told Sue and Omar about their struggle with the daggers.

"Good grief," Sue remarked gravely, when Emma had finished telling them what had happened. She topped up all the cups and got a pack of tobacco from the kitchen. "Anyone like a smoke?"

Emma nodded quickly. "I'll take one."

"Roll one for me," Jim said. "It might 'elp to level me out a bit. I feel like a basket case."

Sue sat down on the settee next to Omar. "I think we should have had a tarot card reading before Emma and Jim left with the daggers," she said. "Then at least they would have known the full extent of the evil they were going up against. The cards would have also shown what I suspected, that the daggers were still energetically connected to the abyss and could come alive. That's why I wanted to get them out of the sanctuary."

"Yes, mon. The cards would have told us that hallowed ground was no defence against the wickedness in the daggers." Omar's eyes flashed. "But we had no time."

"You're damn right about that," Jim responded. "If we 'ad stayed 'ere any longer, we'd 'ave 'ad a lot of problems. There would 'ave been no place to bury the daggers and no tree to escape through. We got out of 'ere just in time."

Omar pushed back his dreads. "I and I will read the cards before we go into our astral fortress, mon. They will tell us what our best defence is against the wickedness that will come callin'."

The talk about the daggers made Emma tense. She also felt guilty. She had endangered her friends and risked the well-being of the animal sanctuary just by taking the daggers there. If she and Jim had not gone to Greenfern, Sue, Omar, Lily, and Tony would have been spared the horror that had become their lives, and Tony's daughters would be still alive. The events of the last few hours suddenly became too much for her. Sobs erupted from her throat, and her body shook with the pain of her release.

"It's okay, Em," Jim said, putting his arm around her. "You got nothin' to cry about. You saved me today, and the Green."

Sue brought a tissue. "Come on, mate! You've given me a real purpose in my life. If we don't stop Feodora's plan for a demonic takeover of the world, life won't be worth living. We are Mother Earth's last stand, and you, Emma, are her champion." At that, Sue started crying as well.

"Em's gettin' good at faerie magic," Jim declared, trying to lighten the conversation. "She pulled me in through a yew tree on the barrow downs and out of an oak tree at 'Illside just behind 'er 'ouse. Now that takes some doin'." He thought for a moment. "Sue! You were with me that day when the 'are disappeared on the barrow downs. Do you remember the yew trees?"

"No. I was too busy trying to fend the police off. But I remember that none of the sabs could get over the hare's disappearance." She laughed. "The beaglers were at a total loss. It was great! When we go back for my car, I'm going to look for the trees."

The four of them sat smoking and spent a few pleasant minutes planning a trip to the stone circle. "We'll take offerings and say thank you," Emma said.

Omar laughed. "Well, as long as you don't expect me to cut off a finger, mon."

"Hardly!" Emma countered, smiling. "That would be a blood sacrifice!"

Their relaxed conversation didn't last long, their thoughts soon turning to darker matters.

"Well, at least we got rid of the daggers for good," Emma

said, stubbing out her cigarette in an ashtray. "That is a big setback for Feodora. The daggers must have been in Kingsbury's family for generations, and claimed the lives of thousands of innocents. They were supremely powerful dark objects." She smoothed back her hair. "I can hardly believe that we succeeded in getting them buried."

Jim stirred in his chair. "Em, 'ow do you think losin' the daggers will affect Feodora's sorcery? Will she be less powerful?"

"I don't think so," Emma answered. "Zugalfar will take possession of Feodora through a blood ritual, and can still appear in the astral like he did on the barrow downs. What it will stop, at least for a while, is Zugalfar materialising under his own will. He needs a connection with this dimension, which we have temporarily put a stop to."

"That maybe," Sue said, lighting another cigarette. "But Feodora saw Emma in my car. The satanists will think she has the sapphire. I'm pretty sure that Feodora and her followers will mount a psychic attack on us, and a physical one as well." She took a long pull on her cigarette. "Woody and Gillian are gone. I can't think of anyone who would come and stay here at such short notice, and under the circumstances …" Her voice trailed off. "Now Tony's gone, I can hardly call the police," she added. "The chief constable was part of Kingsbury's coven. God knows how many satanist coppers there are at the station."

Jim nervously rubbed the back of his neck and looked at Emma with concern. "It's not only the sapphire Zugalfar's after. 'E knows Emma is the last of the faerie warriors sent to stop 'im, and for that reason alone 'e wants 'er dead."

Emma swallowed hard. "Or worse."

"Over my dead body, Em," Jim muttered, nervously puffing on his cigarette.

The striking of the clock brought them back to their immediate reality. Sue put her cigarette out and got up. "It's six o'clock. We'd better get a move on. I'll go and get my tarot cards. After the reading, we'll have to shower, wash our hair, and change our clothes."

Emma found a duster and cleaned off the table while Jim went looking for the smudge pot. "Anyone know where the incense burner is?" he asked.

"Yes, mon. It's in the sanctuary room," Omar replied. "Look in my rucksack. There's some frankincense resin in a little packet. We'll use the abalone shell on the sideboard as a burner."

Jim put the frankincense resin in the shell and set light to it. By the time it was smoking, Sue returned with the tarot cards. After passing them through the smudge, she put them on the table.

After smudging themselves, the four of them sat down. Omar shuffled the pack and then laid the cards face down upon the table.

"I want us to all touch the pack with our middle fingers—the positive finger, mon." He smiled. "All we are goin' to do is ask for guidance."

Bowing his head, Omar sat silently for a moment, and then he laid five cards face up upon the table in the shape of a cross.

In the centre was the nine of swords, with the moon and the high priestess on either side. Above the centre card was the nine of wands, and below it was the ten of wands.

Omar gazed at the cards, interpreting their meaning. His eyes rested on the card at the centre of the cross. "This is the crux of the readin', mon," he said. "The nine of swords shows us the now situation. We are the target of sorcery. Wicked spells are bein' cast against us to make us afraid. We have to become fearless spiritual warriors in order to beat back dem sons and daughters of the Devil."

"I don't think I'm cut out to be a spiritual warrior," Jim said drily. "I was so frightened on the barrow downs, I almost lost my reason." He took a quick glance at Emma and blushed.

Emma smiled knowingly. "That's what our personal battles are all about, overcoming fear."

Omar looked up from the cards. Pushing back his dreads, he said, "Positive vibrations, mon. That's all we got that's ours." He paused for a moment and then carried on with the reading. "On the left of the centre card we have the moon. The card tells us not to let our fear cloud our judgement. On the right is the high priestess. She is tellin' us to go inwards for our salvation, to use our intuition and receive inner guidance." He looked up and smiled at them. "We have to trust our intuition."

"Even when our intellect is telling us something different," Emma added.

"The last card is the ten of wands, and its message is to use our will and intent to overcome whatever dem sons of Babylon throw at us. That means positive vibrations, mon." Omar got up quickly from the table and began to sing his favourite Bob Marley song. His upbeat voice was so infectious that they all started singing along.

"Got to focus on positivity and Jah love," he said at the end of the song.

"Thank you, Omar. I needed that little boost," Emma said appreciatively. "I think it's a very positive spread. It tells us exactly what to do: move into a spiritual space, connect with our inner strength, and trust our intuition." She took a deep breath. "But as we all know, it's easier said than done."

Sue looked out of the window. "It will be dark in forty minutes. We have to be in the circle by then. There are two bathrooms in the house. We have to shower and wash our hair. I've got some clean clothes in the airing cupboard. I'll go and get them."

In a couple of minutes, Sue was back. "I found four pairs of warm sweatpants and tops. I've even got a large long one for you, Omar." She started laughing. "And lots of thick socks."

"Are we goin' to the Arctic?" Jim said with a grin.

Sue smiled. "Once the shit starts, it's going to be bloody cold, mate."

After they had all showered and changed their clothes, they met up in the sitting room. "Let's go!" Sue said. She took a bottle of spring water from the fridge. Grabbing a flashlight and matches from a shelf, she followed the others to the sanctuary room.

Emma, Jim, and Sue took their blankets into the circle. Omar lit the candles at the five points of the star. Then, entering the pentacle, he closed the opening in the double circles with a piece of chalk. Once the circle was closed, he filled the silver cups half full with spring water.

"Just a thought, before we get comfortable," Emma said. "Feodora will conjure Zugalfar, and all the legions of hell will come against us. No matter what horrors appear, they cannot harm us as long as we stay in the pentacle. If one of us tries to break out of the circle, it's up to the rest of us to stop that person from leaving it."

"There's another thing we should pay attention to," Omar said. "We may find ourselves under attack from within our minds. Bad loa can influence us to take unconscious action that can endanger all of us. So let's be vigilant of our thoughts, mon."

They sat back-to-back in the centre of the star. Emma faced east and Omar west. Jim was on Emma's right facing south, and Sue on her left in the north. The room was dark, the only light coming from the candles that were burning steadily in the five points of the star. Time passed slowly. The waiting weighed heavily on their nerves.

As night deepened in its long, slow march to dawn, they heard the sound of footsteps outside. There was a loud knock at the sanctuary door.

Sue stiffened. *Who could be calling at this late hour?* she thought. It had to be urgent.

"Sue!" a voice called out. "Are you in there? It's me, Woody."

Sue did not answer. *That can't be Woody,* she said to herself. *He went to Farnham with Gillian to visit her grandmother in hospital. They are not coming back until tomorrow.*

The knocking became louder. "Sue! Are you all right in there?" Woody's voice came urgently again. "Let me in." The locked door handle to the room worked vigorously. "I've got a badly injured dog for you to look at."

Sue suddenly felt conflicted. She could hear the whimpering of a suffering animal just yards away. But knowing the desperate spiritual conflict they were soon to be engaged in, and the deceptions of the black art, she doubted it was Woody at the door. "I thought you told me you were going to stay the night in Farnham," she said loudly so he could hear her through the door.

"We were going to stay the night, but on our way back from the hospital we found an injured dog in the road and brought it straight here. Sue, please help this poor little chap!" Woody pleaded.

Sue's mind was torn in two. Her life was dedicated to saving animals, but she couldn't leave the circle. She began to worry what would happen to Woody and Gillian if they were at the sanctuary when the demonic attack began.

"Woody! You must leave now, mate!" she shouted. "Take the dog to a vet and get the hell out of here. Just trust me. I'll explain later. Go!"

"We can't go anywhere, Sue. The engine died as we drove into the car park, and now the car won't start!"

Evil was already at work at the sanctuary, Sue thought. It had drained the power from Woody's car so he and Gillian could not escape. She suddenly felt responsible for their safety.

"What are we going to do?" Sue asked the others. "We can't leave Woody and Gillian out there to be murdered."

"We have to, mon," Omar responded.

"No," Sue argued, getting to her feet. "I have to let them in. The only place they will be safe is in the pentacle with us." She took a couple of steps across the pentacle in the direction of the door.

Before she could reach the edge of the outer circle, Omar tackled her and, throwing his arm around her neck, jerked her back to the centre of the pentacle, her chin held fast in the crook of his elbow. Sue's body suddenly went limp. He wondered if she had fainted. He looked down at her face. "Sue!" He patted her gently on the cheek. "Wake up!"

"What happened to me?" she said, opening her eyes and staring at him.

"You tried to break the circle, mon. I had to stop you. I hope I didn't hurt you," Omar answered, his dark eyes full of concern. "You were thinkin' it was Woody and Gillian outside, but my loa told me that it was devils masqueradin' as your friends."

There was a loud, heavy thud on the door, followed by silence.

Sue felt fear snake through her. Omar had warned them when they entered the circle that evil spirits could influence their minds and get them to take action that would put all their lives in danger. She had fallen into the trap. It was the perfect imitation of Woody's voice that had fooled her. Whoever sent the spell had tried to trick her into breaking the circle. If Omar hadn't stopped her, it would have been the end of all of them.

The atmosphere grew tense and strained as they sat back down again.

Sensing a subtle change of energy in the room, Emma shivered. An icy chill crawled down the back of her neck. It felt like an oppressing pain that slowly spread into her shoulders, forcing them down and sapping at her power of action. Using her faerie sight to view Lower Faerie, she penetrated the cloying darkness. A black shadow was moving slowly around the outer circle. It seemed to pulse, elongating and contracting like a spring that is suddenly pulled tight and then let go. She nudged Omar with her elbow. "There's an evil presence in the room," she whispered.

"I can sense it too, mon," he murmured. "My loa have retreated. Wickedness is movin' stealthily around the circle, lookin' for any weakness in the design of our astral fortress."

The malevolent silence grew heavier. Beyond the outer ring, Emma saw a dull red glow appear. There was a terrific crash against the door, followed by another. The walls of the room shook, the floor vibrated, and the temperature was dropping fast.

A cold film of perspiration broke out on Emma's face as the red glow began to spread around the outside of the circle. She felt fear trying to take control of her mind. Taking a deep breath, she steeled her will against it. The attack on their astral defence was beginning. She needed to stay centred.

"Let's all stand up and face it, mon," Omar said. Stench flooded the space around them.

Jim helped Emma up. The four of them formed a ring at the centre of the pentacle, their hands clasped together and their bodies back-to-back.

Piercing the darkness, Emma saw an indistinct shadow suspended in the air outside the outer ring. It darted forward and passed swiftly around the circle, looking for a way in, but drew back as if stung when it tried to breach the circle. Round and round the shadow moved, and then it disappeared back into the darkness in the corner of the room. It seemed to retreat, but Emma sensed its malign determination to break into the circle and destroy them. She let go of Jim's hand and, putting her fingers on her necklace, sent her will into the stone. The topaz morphed into her faerie dagger. Holding it before her, she waited.

The temperature in the room grew even colder.

Jim was restless. The sabbat and the struggle with the satanists on the barrow downs had frightened him badly. He felt drained and unsettled. The last few days were a horrific blur of fear, and now he was sitting in a circle waiting to be attacked by demons once again. He could feel his body shaking, could hear his stomach rumbling, and could feel his throat, which was parched and sore. He wanted to scream, to shout out, anything that would relieve the suspense, break the awful silence. He wished that whatever was going to attack them would hurry up and get it over with.

Standing in the darkness, he started thinking about how he had gotten into this mess. It had started when he applied for a gardening job with Emma. He'd been out of work for some time, and it seemed that working for Emma was an answer to his prayer. They had hit it off and even started a market business together. In the beginning everything was good. Then Trevelyan had shown up and their lives had gone to pot and the nightmare had begun. The upshot of it was that he had fallen in love with Emma. He thought back to the evening he had made dinner for her, bought her roses and champagne, and even put on her favourite music. He had wanted to deepen their relationship. There was no way she could have misunderstood his intentions. He didn't want to be just her friend or employee; he wanted to be her lover. He had to face it: Emma wasn't romantically interested in him.

The understanding that Emma didn't fancy him began to make Jim feel resentful. The truth was that she didn't think he was good enough for her, he told himself. He couldn't blame her. When the succubus had possessed him, he had tried to rape her. The thought of the succubus frightened him. He instinctively felt for the peridot ring upon his finger. It was missing. He remembered that he had taken it off when he showered and had forgotten to put it on again. Fear thrilled down his spine as he stared resignedly into the darkness. He thought that for an instant he could see an indistinct shape standing outside the outer circle. The shape took on meaning, and Jim saw the slim body of a well-endowed naked man. A face appeared in the darkness with amber catlike eyes. Small oak leaves and acorns were blooming in the figure's skin. Jim, sensing it was demon, tried to look away, but the hypnotic eyes exerted a strange fascination for and influence over him. He tried to raise his hand to his eyes to block out the apparition, but his muscles would not obey his mind. Fear engulfed him as he realised he could not cry out or tell the others what he was experiencing.

The vison faded. Jim could move once more. He was about to whisper to Emma what he had seen, when he took a quick intake of breath. He noticed that her clothes were becoming diaphanous and he could see the outline of her body. His eyes rested on her breasts, and he suddenly realised he could see bare skin through her clothes. The sight of her naked body aroused him. He began to ogle her. Finding himself strangely energised, he felt another will impinging on his thoughts.

"You want to fuck her, but she thinks she's too good for you," a voice whispered in his mind. "She's a tease. She's a bitch."

Yes, she is a tease, Jim agreed. He began to fantasise about ripping off her tracksuit bottom and dogging her in the pentacle. He'd make Emma his bitch and no one else's. He heard a soft voice murmuring in his mind, egging him on and telling him that once Emma experienced his sexual power, she would be eternally his and no one else's.

For a moment he was overcome by the horror of his thoughts. What was happening to him? Again he tried to alert the others to what was going on, but he couldn't voice his thought. He struggled to fight off the impulse, but the sexual tension was becoming unbearable. The logic of the voice in his head was irrefutable; he was no longer in control. As all decency was blotted from his mind, he became an instrument of lust. Dropping Omar's hand, he threw himself at Emma. Knocking her to the ground, he tried to pull off her tracksuit bottom and force her legs open with his knee. Emma fought back. In the struggle, Jim kicked over one of the water cups in the valleys of the star.

A savage cry of triumph split the air. A stench-filled wind blew up, swirling round and round the outer circle with ever-increasing violence and strength, and the darkness lit up with the dreadful yellow light of the abyss.

Omar whipped round. Grabbing Jim by the back of his sweatshirt, he pulled him off of Emma.

"Let me go," Jim raged, kicking to get free.

Omar saw that Jim's good-natured face was twisted and ugly, his teeth were bared, and his eyes were glowing with the hot light of lust. Knowing Jim had been possessed by bad loa, there was nothing Omar could do but punch him into oblivion for all their sakes. Drawing back his fist, he slugged Jim in the face. As Jim fell, Omar pushed his limp body back into the centre of the circle.

As Emma got up from the floor, she saw grey, wispy shadows massing in one corner of the room. Jim's attack on her had left her shaky. Taking a deep breath, she swallowed hard and pushed away her fear. Tightening her grip upon her knife, she stared into the darkness. The shadows in the corner seemed to knit together and form a hunched and cowled shape which expanded outwards and upward into the astral form of Zugalfar. Without warning, the arch-demon rushed forward, gathering form and solidity as he swept over the outer circle and towered above the pentacle.

The candles in the points of the star flickered wildly and then went out. Sue had the terrifying idea that the sanctuary room was no longer part of her house, that it had been transported into a no-man's-land of horror. Picking up the matchbox, she struck a match and tried to relight the candles, but a gust of icy air blew it out. She struck another match, but it spluttered out before the wood had caught. The darkness seemed to close in around her, siphoning the positivity from her mind. Seeing visions of her animals being butchered, she had the overwhelming feeling that all was lost. Their astral fortress was not powerful enough to combat the combined force of Feodora's coven and Zugalfar with his legion. Sliding to the floor, she put her head down, placed her arms around her knees, and started repeating over and over again the opening lines of Psalm 18. "The Lord is my rock, my fortress and deliverer."

Emma realised that fear had allowed Jim's and Sue's minds to become possessed by a demonic thought form. They could no longer help her to defend the circle. She felt Omar move beside her.

"Spiritual warriors, mon," he said, patting her on the arm. "Positive vibrations. Let's send this wickedness back to hell."

Over the tumult, Emma heard Omar calling on his loa to return, and saw a flash of purple as he brought out the amethyst stone he carried for protection.

Zugalfar was gyrating above the circle. His blind eyes were swivelling in their sockets, and his long pointed ears were cocked forward. Emma knew he could not see her and that he was listening for her breath. His claw was groping blindly around the interior of the circle, and his dreadful talons were just inches from her face. Throwing caution to the wind, she took a shallow breath of the stinking air and drove the blade of her dagger into Zugalfar's groping claw.

There was a shriek of rage; sparks crackled in the air, and the stench of sulphur became almost overpowering. She saw Zugalfar's image shrink back and then begin to wax again.

In the dim recesses of her mind, Emma thought she heard more heavy blows on the door and the wood begin to splinter.

The hideous grating baritone of Under-Earth and the foul speech of the abyss blasted through the room. Zugalfar was calling on his legion for the final assault upon their astral fortress. Emma heard Omar's voice in her mind: "Let's finish the devil off together."

Sigils of the battle magic that she had seen on the barrow downs flashed before her eyes. One of them was blazing with the outer spectrum colours of High Faerie. Tracing the outline with her knife in the air above her, she used her mind to set it rotating around the circle. "Eh – hon – na – hessh," she shouted.

The sigil blazed forth in the murky light. Emma saw the veves that Omar had drawn between the circles lift off the ground and, spiralling into the centre of the circle, join the sigil she had made.

"For Lucy!" she heard Omar yell. The amethyst in his hand lit up, blocking the light from the abyss. Lightning flashed, and a thunderous crack vibrated through the room.

"Eh – hon – na – hessh." Emma commanded the phonetics to rise above the tumult. Power throbbed above her, and she saw the image of Zugalfar hurled backwards by some mighty invisible force. Plaster cracked and popped and fell from the walls. Part of the ceiling caved in, barely missing their bodies as it fell inside the circle.

Suddenly the wind died away and there was silence, broken only by the pounding of their hearts, and the patter of bits of plaster falling on the floor. Emma found the matches and lit the gutted candles. She saw Jim rubbing his jaw, and Sue sitting up beside him.

Sue struggled to her feet. "What a nightmare." She suddenly burst into tears and clung on to Emma's arm.

The faint light of dawn was coming through the hole in the roof as they left the circle. Sue was hyperventilating as she stepped through the broken door into the conservatory.

She noticed there was blood on the floor, but it didn't really register in her mind. She had to make sure her animals were all right. A cockerel was crowing in the barn when she went through the side door and out into the yard. Opening the door to the barn, she gave a sigh of relief. Her animals were fine. Leaning up against the wall, she tried to calm her breathing. It had been a hellish night.

Sue was suddenly aware of a green Range Rover parked next to the tool shed. It looked like one of the vehicles from Kingsbury's estate. She stiffened and looked wildly around but saw no one. She was just about to check out the Range Rover when she saw Omar and Emma appear around the side of the house. They were hurrying towards the tool shed.

"What is one of Kingsbury's Range Rovers doing here?" Sue asked, walking over to them.

"I don't know, but there's a trail of blood from the conservatory to the tool shed, mon," Omar answered. He opened the shed door and looked in.

"There's nothin' but blood in here," he said, shutting the door. "Let's take a look in the Range Rover."

Emma's face was white and strained. "There are two dead bodies inside the vehicle."

Sue stared at Emma in bewilderment.

"Two dead bodies!" Sue exclaimed, peering at the bodies through the window. "Those are the fuckers who tried to kidnap me when we went to Dragonsbury Ring. It appears they've been shot." Sue glanced nervously at Emma and then at Omar. "Who the fuck did this?" She paused. "I mean, whoever it is has done the world a favour, but what are we going to do with two dead men and one of Brising Manor's estate vehicles on the property?"

"I don't know," Emma replied. "In view of the

circumstances, we can't call the police, and we can't leave the vehicle here either. Let's go and find Jim." Taking Sue's arm, she propelled her towards the house.

When they got inside, Emma saw Jim and Tony sitting across from one another in the kitchen. Tony had a rifle slung across his shoulder. A pistol was lying on the table, with a half-drank cup of tea beside it.

CHAPTER 6

THE AVENGER

Chief Inspector Tony Farran was on his way out of his office. It was lunchtime; he was going home to get a bite to eat. Walking to the exit, he was suddenly confronted by Giles Kingsbury.

"Hello, Sergeant," Kingsbury said, demoting him at a stroke. "I've come to see the chief constable."

Tony tried to keep his cool. He wanted to punch the supercilious fucker in the face. "He's still on leave and won't be back until Monday morning," he said. "Can I be of assistance?"

Kingsbury glared at him. "Assistance! Is that what you call poking your nose into my business?"

"I'm just doing my job, Mr Kingsbury. I have reason to believe you have committed an offence, and I am investigating it."

Kingsbury snorted and ran his fingers across his receding hairline. "If you think you can get the better of me, you're welcome to try," he hissed. He looked down his nose at Tony. "I'll eat you for breakfast and spit you out."

Tony was finding it very hard to keep his head. He was quivering with anger. "You're a right little charmer, aren't you?" he answered. "I won't rest until you and your pack of yahoos are in the slammer."

"You'd better watch out, Farran, or you will end up like your little trollop of an informant," Kingsbury said in a low voice so that the duty officer at the counter couldn't hear him.

"Are you threatening me, Mr Kingsbury?"

"Yes." He leered evilly at Tony. "You know there's nothing you can do about it. The chief constable is not going to take any notice of your unsubstantiated ramblings. What he will take notice of is my complaint about your ongoing harassment of me and interference in my business."

Tony shrugged his shoulders. "Whatever you say, Mr Kingsbury."

"You'll pay for your insolence, Farran. You'll pay dearly." Kingsbury gave him a withering look. Turning on his heel, he stormed out of the station.

Tony went back to his office to give Kingsbury time to get clear. He needed to think. Tina's gruesome murder had unnerved him. Kingsbury's threat that he would end up like Tina was, in his eyes, an admission that Kingsbury knew a lot more about Tina's murder than he was telling. If Sue was right about a satanic ritual killing, then the chinless aristocrat would have probably performed it himself. He thought about Tina's injuries and shuddered.

There was a spare flash drive in his drawer. Taking it out and plugging it in to his computer, he copied Kingsbury's file and then emailed a copy to Sue. If push came to shove, and his intuition told him that it would, the chief constable would have the file destroyed. It would be accidently deleted; he knew how the game was played. It was better to be safe than sorry, he thought, as he put the flash drive in his pocket.

The fracas with Kingsbury had put Tony off lunch, so he

decided to wade through the ton of work on his desk before the chief constable returned. It was late in the afternoon when he finished getting everything in order. As he got up to leave, the duty officer came through the door.

"Guv," he said. "Your missus is on the phone. She sounds upset, sir. Almost hysterical, I'd say."

Tony sniffed. He was estranged from his wife. She had taken their two daughters and moved in with her mother. He wondered what she wanted. Sick of her infidelity, he was not going to take her back.

"Yes," he said abruptly, picking up the phone. His wife was so distraught that he could hardly make out what she was saying.

Tony froze. Dropping the phone, he felt his body stiffen. A sickening, numbing shock ran through him. His two little girls had been snatched from the front garden of the house while they were playing.

For several minutes his mind was in turmoil, and then a soul-destroying realisation surfaced: Kingsbury had made good on his threat against him. He had punished him by abducting his little girls.

Horrific scenarios formed within his mind. With an effort of will, he pushed them away. He forced himself to think like a policeman and not a father.

He filed a missing person's report and contacted all the officers on duty to mount a search for his daughters. Kingsbury had the chief constable in his pocket, as well as many magistrates and judges. Tony realised that if Kingsbury had taken his children, there would only be a token investigation. Whatever damaging evidence was uncovered by his colleagues would soon be covered up. He understood that if Kingsbury was involved, the only real investigation that would be undertaken to find his daughters would be whatever one he conducted himself.

Looking at the clock, he saw it was five minutes to five. He'd be off duty soon. He'd go home, get changed, take one of his own vehicles to Brising Manor, and find out for himself if Kingsbury was involved in the disappearance of his children.

It was half past six when Tony got to Brising Manor. He drove through the dark, forbidding gates, past the gatehouse, and along the tree-lined avenue to the house.

He parked outside the main entrance. Getting out of the car, he looked around. There were a dozen classy cars parked in the car park. Kingsbury had company.

Standing at the bottom of the balustrade that led to the grotesque pillared porchway, Tony felt every fibre in his body tingling with warning. *This is madness,* he told himself. He'd told no one where he was going; plus, he could be walking into a trap. Before he could bolt back to his car and get the hell out of there, the manor's front door opened and a cadaverous butler in black evening dress emerged. "Ah! Mr Farran," he said in a hollow voice. "Mr Kingsbury is expecting you."

Tony felt apprehensive. He hadn't even touched the doorbell.

The butler showed Tony into the drawing room. Kingsbury and Feodora St Clair were sitting in their bathrobes on the sofa, drinking wine.

Tony shivered inside as he looked at the couple. He had forgotten how ugly Kingsbury was. The satanist's lack of chin, staring glassy eyes, and receding hairline reminded him of the head of a fringed lizard. Kingsbury had a repulsive air about him.

Feodora St Clair was lounging on the sofa like a Grecian

goddess. Tony noticed a glint in her ice-blue eyes as she looked him up and down.

"Ah! Mr Farran. You've arrived. I see you are in civvies," Kingsbury said. He got up and looked out of the window into the car park. "And, you came in your own car, I see. So I assume this is not an official visit."

Tony shook his head. "No, this is a personal visit." He paused for a moment to try to frame his words. Alone in enemy territory, he had to be careful what he said. He was in enough trouble at work already.

"My daughters have been kidnapped," he started. "And in view of the threats you made against me this afternoon, I wondered if you had any information regarding their disappearance."

"Tut-tut, Mr Farran." Kingsley looked down his nose. "My property is invaded by vandals, and instead of trying to find the guilty parties, you come here in a non-official capacity and accuse me of kidnapping."

"I'm not accusing you, Mr Kingsbury. I am asking if you have any information about their disappearance."

"Feodora! What do you make of Mr Farran's answer?" Kingsbury asked in a falsetto.

"I don't care," Feodora said haughtily. "I just want to fuck him."

Tony's eyes widened in disgust. Feodora's bathrobe was lying on the floor. Naked, she started masturbating in front of him.

"What's the matter, officer? Don't tell me you haven't seen a woman masturbate before." Kingsbury giggled. "Don't tell me your sensitivities are offended. I'm sure you've had a hag or two in your time—little fucks in the back of the police car in exchange for dropping a speeding ticket."

Tony shuddered. It was obvious to him now that Kingsbury and St Clair were insane. Both of them were monsters with no decency or morals. He cursed at himself for coming to Brising Manor. He felt like a fly caught in a spider's sticky web.

"I'm going to leave," Tony said, starting towards the door. "I'm sorry to have taken up your time."

As he reached the door, the butler barred his way. Tony tried to push past, but the man seemed to swell and fill up all the space.

"Not so fast, Mr Farran," Kingsbury said. "Don't you want to know where your sweet little women are? After all, that's why you came here, isn't it?"

Turning round, Tony saw Kingsbury giggling and licking his lips. "Oh, Sergeant!" he simpered. "How the girlies whimpered when I stripped them naked and played with their soft little bodies."

It took a moment for the full impact of Kingsbury's words to sink in. Tony felt hatred and outrage consume his being. Blood pounded in his head. He was going to kill the bastard. Lunging forward, he swung his fist at Kingsbury's sneering face, but before his blow could land, he was suddenly grabbed from behind by two pairs of strong arms and pulled backwards. Struggling to get away, he felt his hands wrenched behind his back and the cold steel of handcuffs lock around his wrists.

"The girlies are in a spider-infested dungeon underneath the house, and tonight they will be offered as gifts to the Prince of Devils." Kingsbury gave a hideous grin and obscenely waggled his middle finger under Tony's nose. "I broke them in, so to speak. They were so soft and pliable."

"And Daddy will get to watch them die," Feodora crooned. Her cold eyes were bright and excited as she put her hand between Tony's legs, pushing her body into him. "He feels like a big boy, darling," she said to Kingsbury. "Can I eat him now?"

"Oh yes," he cackled. "You know how I like to watch. I might get tempted to … do a back-door jobby as well."

Realising he was caught like a rat in a trap, Tony tried one last desperate effort to free himself. Taking a slow deep breath, he kicked out at one of the men holding his arms. The man let go of him and staggered backwards, falling down. Tony felt a blow in the small of his back and the pricking of a needle in his leg. The next thing he knew, he was being dragged down a flight of steps into a torchlit dungeon and thrown onto the floor.

The ground was soft, damp, and stinking. A sharp kick in the ribs made him gasp for air. He felt hands upon him, stripping off his clothes. He tried to struggle but found he couldn't move. Whatever they had shot him up with had paralysed him. The handcuffs were removed and he was turned over onto his back.

He was aware that Feodora was kneeling down beside him. He could smell her foul breath as she tried to force her tongue into his mouth. Then she straddled him and started rubbing her body on his member.

Tony desperately tried to blot out any carnal feeling from his mind. Even though he couldn't move his limbs, his sexual organ was responding. He heard Feodora yell in triumph as his manhood took root inside her. He didn't know how long her assault upon him lasted, but finally it was over. He felt her sliding off his body. Still unable to move, he lay there wondering what was coming next. Suddenly in the flickering torchlight, he saw Feodora standing beside him. "Put him in

the pleasure position," she hissed to her lackeys, "so Giles can have a go."

Tony found himself being manhandled and forced to his knees. "He's all yours, boss," one of the men jeered.

"Let Giles have his fun," Feodora said to her lackeys. "Come! Let's go and entertain ourselves in the cell next door."

"So, it's just you and me, Farran," Kingsbury said, dropping his robe. Grabbing Tony around the waist, the satanist started to brutalise him. Tony wanted to cry out but found he could make no sound. From the next cell, he heard terrified screams and shrieking. The sound rang around in his head. It didn't seem to end. He knew it was his daughters. His mind writhed in torment at the thought of what might be happening to them.

Somewhere in his mind, he heard Kingsbury shout, "When you fuck with the bull, Farran, you get the horn."

Tony's surroundings became a blur. When he came to full sense, he found he was spreadeagled on a damp stone slab in a cavern lit by flaming torches. He found he could move, but he was strapped down. From the corner of his eye, he could see a young girl staked out next to him. In a nightmare of unreality, he saw a gap appear in the ranks of cowled and robed figures, and the butler from Brising Manor dragging his two screaming daughters onto the slab and raping them. The girls were just a few feet away from him, but he was helpless and unable to protect them.

Tony closed his eyes. The mental and spiritual pain was too much for him. He must have passed out, because the next thing he remembered was Sue, his lover, taking off his cassock and leading him naked, into the emergency room at the hospital in Denhampstead.

Sue had disappeared. He was taken to a cubicle for examination, and then it seemed all hell broke loose. He could hear the whine of sirens. Ambulances were pulling up outside. Tony knew he had to get out of the hospital as quick as possible. Kingsbury would know by now that he had been rescued, and he'd be looking for him. He realised why Sue had stripped both him and the young girl of their cassocks. Kingsbury's arm was long; he was sure to have informants at the hospital. Anyone who had witnessed the horror at Brising Manor and could testify against Kingsbury would immediately be eliminated. Dead men tell no tales.

Pulling back the curtain, Tony peeked out. People were being brought in to the hospital on stretchers. All the staff were busy with the sudden influx of patients needing care.

Taking advantage of the moment, Tony moved quickly along the corridor. He saw a door marked Private: Doctors Only. Opening the door, he peered in. The room was empty. Along one side of a wall there was a rack of scrub suits, surgical gloves, hats, and bootees. He put on a set of scrubs and a surgical hat and found a pair of shoes that almost fit. Stuffing a pair of surgical gloves into the back pocket of his scrubs, he left the room and started walking along the corridor towards the exit.

Tony walked unnoticed out of the hospital into the cold, damp air. A light rain was falling, so he stood under the shelter by the entrance. He thought about hiring a cab, but he had no cash. Plus, the cabbie might remember him. It was best not to leave a trail in case Kingsbury's henchmen started looking for him. He was wondering what to do when he saw a car pull up outside the entrance. A very pregnant woman got out, holding her stomach. She appeared to be in labour. Her husband was helping her into the hospital. Tony noticed that the husband had left the car running.

Taking the rubber gloves from his pocket, he put them on.

Without looking back, he walked over to the car, got in the driver's seat, and drove out of the car park.

Tony lived outside of Market Thorpe. All he could think about on the drive was getting home as fast as possible. He needed to think and plan his next move. He decided to dump the car in a lane next to a copse about two miles from his house. He would walk from there.

Abandoning the car, he took a footpath through the woods to the lane that ran past his back gate. With luck he'd get inside his house without attracting attention. Peering out through the trees, he saw the lane was empty. It was only a hundred yards or so to his gate, so he set off at a dogtrot.

Retrieving the spare door key that was hidden behind a loose brick in the kitchen wall, he let himself in. Bolting the door behind him, he went into the sitting room and sat down in his chair. Pictures of his wife and daughters smiled down at him from the walls and mantelpiece, but they seemed to him to have existed in another space and time. He felt numb and empty. Safety and a normal life were things of the past. His girls, the light of his life, were gone. Now he had nothing to live for. Putting his hands up to his face, he began to sob.

How long he was in misery, he did not recall, but towards the late afternoon, he began to calm down and get his mind into some semblance of order. Knowing that without a purpose he would seek his own destruction and go mad, he forced his mind into a single thought: revenge. He would slaughter Giles Kingsbury and his bitch. They would know terror. He would do it for his girls, Tina, and all the other victims, and he would do it for himself.

He made himself a cup of coffee and put a frozen chicken curry in the oven.

Sitting down at the table, Tony thought about how he was

going to wreak his revenge upon the satanists. He tried to put himself in Kingsbury's mind. The satanist would know that Sue and her friends had escaped from the sabbat and taken him and the girl with them. In all probability, the sanctuary at Greenfern would be one of the first places Kingsbury's mob would go with orders to kill Sue and her friends or else abduct them for sacrifice. If his assumption was correct, and if he lay in wait for the satanists at the sanctuary, it might give him a chance to eliminate some of them. He made up his mind that as soon as it was dark, he would go to Greenfern and keep watch.

Plugging his flash drive into his computer, he brought up Kingsbury's file and printed out the section that gave the number plates of the vehicles registered to Kingsbury's estate. He needed them to identify any suspicious vehicles near the sanctuary.

Tony took a shower, changed his clothes, and ate his food. After dinner, he made a flask of coffee, and wondered what weapons he would take. He went into his study and, unlocking a cupboard, took out a rifle and a handgun, which he spent the next hour cleaning and loading.

It was getting dark when Tony backed his MG out of the garage and drove towards Greenfern. He had his guns and ammunition, a ski mask, a knife, his cell phone, a tiny flashlight, and his flask.

The narrow high-banked road leading to Sue's place was empty. About a quarter of a mile from the gate to the sanctuary, he backed into a track, switching off the engine and the lights. He put on his mask. After gathering his weapons, he shut and locked the car. Putting the keys in his pocket, he started walking along the road to the gates of the sanctuary.

He climbed over the gate. Following the hedge that bordered the road, he found a hiding place amongst the bushes.

Waiting in the darkness, Tony wondered how he could convince Sue and her friends to help him. He couldn't see why they wouldn't join him. The satanists were rapists and child killers, the dregs of humanity.

Time ticked by slowly as he crouched in the shrubbery. After a while, he saw the glare of lights on the road. Jerking to attention, he watched as a Range Rover pulled up at the front gate of the sanctuary, the driver inside turning off its lights and engine. He heard the doors close and saw two men crawling over the gate. They were talking in muffled tones, but he could not hear what they were saying.

Adrenaline was pumping through Tony's body as he followed the two men like a panther down the hillside. The house was in darkness. He assumed Sue and her friends were in the ceremony room. He saw the beam of a flashlight shining on the path that led to the kitchen door. Keeping in the shadows, Tony tiptoed forward. He heard the sound of breaking glass. The men had smashed the kitchen window, and the door was now open. There were no lights on in the house. Peering through the broken window, he could see the flashlight flickering in the sitting room.

The door to the ceremony room was through the conservatory, but there was a side door round the back that was rarely used. Walking quickly around the side of the house to the door, Tony waited at the entrance. A few moments later, he heard a crash and then the pounding of heavy objects. Removing his gun from his jacket pocket, he attached the silencer and took the safety off. He quietly opened the side door and stepped into the conservatory. Moonlight was filtering through the glass panels. In the dim light, he saw the backs of two men beating down the sanctuary door with sledgehammers.

Hate was in Tony's blood. Raising the gun, he took aim. He shot first one man and then the other. After making sure they were dead, he grabbed them by the feet, one by one, and dragged them to the tool shed.

Once inside, he went through their pockets. They had nothing on them but cigarettes and a Zippo lighter. *No car keys,* he thought. The yobs must have left them in the Range Rover.

Leaving the bodies in the shed, Tony walked quickly up the track and opened the gate. Getting into the Range Rover, he saw the keys were in the ignition. Switching on the engine, he turned around and drove down the track, parking beside the tool shed. Dragging the bodies out of the shed, he put them in the back of the Range Rover. The next job he had to do was dispose of the bodies and the vehicle.

Knowing he had foiled the attack, Tony thought that Sue and her friends were probably all right. Whatever was going on in the sanctuary room, he wouldn't bother them. Feeling cold, he decided to go into the kitchen, make a cup of tea, and plan his next move.

Tony sat down at the table, trying to come to terms with the catastrophic changes in his life. From a good copper trying to protect and serve the community, he had become a thief and a murderer overnight. *But enough of the past,* he told himself. It was the now that was important. He had to get the men's bodies and Range Rover off of Sue's property as fast as he could. The best way to dispose of the problem would be to fake an accident and push the vehicle over the side of a cliff. He thought about a suitable place with a big enough drop-off. He decided to send the vehicle over the cliff into a quarry locally known as the Devils Bowl because of the accidents that had happened there in the past.

Jim was the last to leave the sanctuary room. He felt dazed, his jaw ached, his head felt thick like it was stuffed with cotton wool, and he had a sour feeling in his stomach. He noticed that the thick oak door was splintered and a hinge had broken off. Two sledgehammers were lying on the flagstone floor and there was blood splattered everywhere. Not remembering having heard any noise, he wondered what had happened. In fact, he realised, he didn't remember much about anything that had gone on after he had entered the circle.

Walking through the sitting room door into the kitchen, he pulled up short. Tony was sitting at the table. Jim stared at him in surprise. He had a rifle slung over his shoulder. A handgun and a ski mask were lying on the table.

"What the fuck!" Jim said, startled. "Aren't you supposed to be in the 'ospital? And what you doin' with guns and a ski mask?"

Tony looked at him with dead eyes. "I left the hospital because I was afraid to stay there," he said in a monotone. "Kingsbury's arm is long, and as we are all witnesses to his devilry and murder, he'll stop at nothing to destroy us."

"Kingsbury's dead," Jim said in a flat voice. "I beat 'is 'ead in with a cosh.

Tony stared at him. "Dead, you say? Tell me everything that happened."

Jim pulled nervously on his earlobe, and then went on to tell Tony what had happened at the sabbat. "Kingsbury was about to cut Lily's throat. I 'ad to stop 'im, so I beat 'im to death with a cosh."

"Lily?" Tony questioned. "Is that the name of the girl that was staked out next to me on the altar?"

"Yes," Jim replied. "Lily is Tina's little sister. Kingsbury's yobs must 'ave kidnapped 'er from Tina's flat after Sue and Omar left." Jim glanced uneasily at Tony. "I've never killed anyone before and it's done my 'ead in."

"Don't beat yourself up," Tony remarked. "Getting rid of a child-murdering satanist is no different than killing a poisonous snake that's trying to bite you. This world is a better place without him."

Jim nodded. "Kingsbury is dead, but 'is bitch is still alive." He saw Tony's eyes widen. "After we dropped you and Lily at the 'ospital, we went back to Dragonsbury Ring to rescue Emma." Jim left out the bit about his drinking and the succubus attack. "Sue went to get the car, and as she and Omar were comin' through the 'edge, a Range Rover drove by. Feodora St Clair was drivin'. She saw 'em," he added. "So what's the story on the guns?" He looked inquiringly at Tony.

"Two of Kingsbury's lackeys showed up about half past three this morning. I suspected there would be an attack on the sanctuary, so I was waiting. They broke in through here." He pointed to the kitchen door. "Then they tried to batter down the door of the sanctuary room ..."

"Yeah! I saw the damage," Jim said, interrupting, getting up to retrieve the dustpan from a closet and sweep the glass off the floor.

"The men were going to murder you, so I shot them before they could get in. I dumped their corpses in the Range Rover they drove up in. It's parked outside."

Sitting down at the table, Jim stared at Tony in disbelief. For a moment, he was at a loss for words. When he found his voice again, he said shakily, "You mean there are two dead bodies in a Range Rover outside?"

"Yes, that is exactly what I'm saying." Tony leant across the table. Jim saw a crazy glint in his eye. "Tonight, I need you to help me dispose of the evidence."

Jim shifted nervously in his chair. What Tony was asking him to do was preposterous. "I don't know about that. ... I mean ..."

Before he could finish the sentence, Tony butted in. "You've already murdered Kingsbury, and that means you are in the shit up to your neck."

I'm fucked, Jim thought miserably. *I'm damned if I don't go with him and damned if I do.*

"The bottom line is," Tony said, picking up his gun and stroking the barrel, "if we don't eliminate the satanists who saw us at the sabbat, both of us are likely to face a murder rap."

Jim felt an ugly thrill of fear snake through him. He was compromised and had to go along with Tony's plan. "As you say, I don't 'ave a choice," he said. "What do you want me to do?"

"I'll drive the Rover to the Devils Bowl. I'll start a fire inside, set the cruise control, and send the vehicle over the edge. With luck it should explode when it hits the bottom of the quarry. I need you to follow me in another vehicle and bring me back here."

Jim could hardly believe what he was hearing. "You mean you're goin' to drive the Range Rover to the edge of the cliff and jump out just before it goes over the edge?" He sniffed. "That's an 'ell of a risk. You could be killed."

Tony gave a grim smile. "I'm dead already" is all he said. Emma and Sue came into the kitchen with Omar behind them. When they saw Tony, they looked at one another in shocked surprise.

Sue stared worriedly at the guns. "What you doing here, mate?" she asked, breaking the stunned silence. "Did you shoot those men in the Range Rover?"

"Yes," Tony answered. "I kept watch on the sanctuary all night. Kingsbury's thugs showed up about three o'clock. I'm glad they came." He beamed at all of them. "It gave me the chance to eliminate them."

Emma gazed at Tony. He had a black eye and one of his front teeth was missing. He seemed to have aged twenty years since she had seen him last. His animal magnetism and attractiveness had been sucked out of him. His skin was dry, and there was a cold fire in his sunken eyes. She realised that his agony and loss were so unbearable that he had switched off his emotions and that, in his present state, he was nothing more than an instrument of revenge.

She glanced quickly at Jim. He'd attacked her again, and she noticed the peridot ring was missing from his finger. An ugly chill tingled down her spine. He only took the ring off when he was drunk and easily influenced by the succubus. She wondered what had happened. Deciding to cut to the quick, she said, "Where's your peridot ring, Jim? Why the fuck did you take it off! You know what happens when it's not on your finger."

"What!" He stared in bewilderment at his hand. "Oh!" he exclaimed, hitting his brow with the palm of his hand. "Stupid me! I forgot all about the ring. It's in the bathroom. I'll go and get it." Jim hurried off and soon returned.

Emma sighed with relief as Jim put the ring on his finger. Affairs seemed to be going from bad to worse, with every moment becoming a struggle in an endless war of dark against light. She could hardly cope with all the madness that was happening around her. Zugalfar's attack on the circle, Jim assaulting her, the dead bodies in the Range Rover, and a madman on a mission sitting fully armed at Sue's kitchen table was almost too much for her to endure and still remain functional. She felt it only needed another negative straw to break the camel's back and send her to the hospital to be institutionalised. Taking a deep breath to try to calm herself, she thought about Jim. He was becoming a liability, a danger to her safety; it would be best if she kept her distance.

She tried to reach out energetically to Trevelyan. She needed his guidance, but all she could sense on the airwaves was the shimmering vibrations of the sapphire.

"Tony, thank you for protecting us, and the sanctuary," Sue said gratefully. "I have no doubt that if you hadn't looked out for us, none of us would have been here to tell the tale." She tried to hug him, but he shied away.

What the fuck? Sue thought. They were lovers and confidants, and he had just rejected her.

Sue felt her face flush. Taking a deep breath, she said, "The men will have been missed by now, and Feodora will be looking for them. What happens if the police show up here and find the bodies? We will be arrested, and that means I'm done, and so are all the abused animals that have a home here." Her voice got higher and more strident. "I'm not prepared to take the risk. Hide the fucking vehicle, and be quick about it."

"Calm down," Tony responded. "It's only been a few hours since I neutralised the threat, and it takes an hour to drive from here to Brising Manor. Anything could have happened to them. St Clair probably doesn't know yet that the men are missing, and it will take her a while before she sets the wheels in motion to find them. We'll hide the Range Rover out of sight until it gets dark, and then Jim's going to help me dispose of the evidence. Aren't you, Jim?"

Before Jim could answer, Sue cut in. "Are the keys in the Range Rover?"

Tony nodded.

"Well, if you are just going to sit here while the Range Rover is parked outside in broad daylight, I'll drive the bloody thing into the barn myself, mate."

"That won't be necessary," Jim said. "I'll do it." He looked at Emma. "I need somethin' to eat. Is there any chance of breakfast?"

Emma frowned at him for a moment and then looked away. There was a stolen Range Rover parked in the yard with two dead bodies in it, and all Jim could think about was food.

Sue was getting exasperated. "We'll eat here in a few minutes, Jim. Just go and hide the bloody vehicle before someone shows up and we are dragged out of here."

"Sue! Just calm down," Tony said again. "St Clair is not going to call attention to herself until she knows what has happened to her co-conspirators. That will take her a few hours. Don't worry. I know what I'm doing."

Sue swallowed hard. She was unnerved at Tony's composure. He was talking about murder as if it were an everyday event. She had never seen him act like this before.

"I'll go 'ide the Range Rover," Jim said, going through the door and into the yard.

Sue shot a glance at Tony. He was resting his head on the back of the chair and his eyes were closed. "You can go and lie down if you want to," she said, but he didn't answer.

"All right then, mates," she said to Omar and Emma. "While you two are getting the food ready, I'll order some glass to be cut for the kitchen door. The glass cutters have the measurements from the last time. Then when I'm done, I'll light the fire in the sitting room."

"Okay, mon."

Getting into the Range Rover, Jim drove the vehicle into the barn. Then, closing the door behind him, he walked into the yard. He was glad to get away from the house. There was a strange atmosphere there that wasn't all together to do with Tony. Emma was distant, and it was obvious he'd done something to upset her. She was mad with him for taking off the ring, but he hadn't left it in the bathroom deliberately. Had he tried to rape her again? His memory of the attack on the pentacle was a blur. All he could recall was being frightened. The last time he had tried to sexually assault Emma, Sue had hit him over the head with a flowerpot and knocked him out. He lightly touched his jaw. It ached like hell. *Had I been slugged?* he wondered, walking back to the kitchen.

Soon plates of fried potatoes, eggs, and toast were on the table. They all sat down to eat. "After breakfast," Sue said, munching on a piece of toast, "we need to go and get my car from the barrow downs. The longer we leave it, the better chance it has of being vandalised." Noticing that Tony was not eating, she said, "You all right, mate?"

Tony nodded. "Thanks, but I'm not hungry."

"Sling it over 'ere," Jim said, pointing to Tony's plate. "I can always eat a second breakfast."

"Sue, I'm going to walk up to the road and get my car," Tony said, getting up from the table. "When you've finished eating, I'll drive you to the barrow downs and you can bring your car back."

Jim poured himself a cup of lukewarm tea and gulped it down. "I don't want to be a wallflower," he said to Sue. "Could

I ride along? I need some air, and I like the barrow downs."
He caught Emma's eye. "Maybe the yew trees are still there."

Emma ignored him and looked away.

"Tony's car's not big enough for three," Sue said. "We will
take the van. Jim, you can drive."

After breakfast the three of them left, leaving Emma and
Omar alone.

"Let's go to the sitting room and relax, mon," Omar
suggested. "It'll give us time to assimilate all the shit that's
been happenin'."

Tony didn't say much on the drive to the barrow downs.
Sue was subdued, and Jim felt tension in the air. He turned
off the high street in Denhampstead and drove up the narrow
track that led to the barrow downs. As they neared the top,
they saw Sue's car. Every panel, including the roof, had been
smashed in; the tyres were shredded; and all the glass was
shattered.

The three of them got out of the van and stood looking at
the wreck.

"Fuck!" Sue exclaimed angrily. "The bastards vandalised
my car."

"I'm sorry about this," Jim said apologetically. "But we
'ad to leave your car and leg it. Otherwise they would 'ave
killed us."

Sue was quiet for a moment, and then with a resigned
shrug of her shoulders, she said, "No point in crying over spilt
milk. What's done is done. A car you can replace, but a life
you can't. It's okay, mate. I've got the van."

"I'll call a friend of mine," Tony said, getting out his cell
phone. "He'll come and tow your car away."

Sue looked in the back to see if her toolbox was still there. Jim looked over her shoulder. "Well, at least your tools are still intact," he said, leaning through the broken hatch. Picking up the toolbox, he carried it over to the van and put it inside.

"The tow lorry is on its way," Tony informed them, switching off his phone. "There's no need to wait. He'll call us. Come on, let's go back to Greenfern!"

"Sue," Jim said, as they drove towards the sanctuary, "I blanked out while we were in the circle." He gingerly touched his jaw. "Did someone 'it me?"

"Yes. Omar had to knock you out." She paused and then said, "You were possessed and tried to rape Emma."

Jim felt wretched and sick inside. It was the third time he had tried to rape Emma and could not remember doing it. Now he realised why she was distant. Instead of being an asset to her cause, he had become a liability, and a danger to her life.

"Do you remember anything that happened prior to the attack?" Sue asked.

"Not really. I know that I was terrified the whole time, and freezin' cold." Jim paused for a moment and knitted his brows together in concentration. "There was somethin'," he said slowly. "I saw a glowin' face in the darkness with amber eyes like a cat." He sniffed. "I don't remember nothin' after that."

Gripping the wheel, Jim focused all of his attention on the road. He took a quick glance at Tony beside him in the passenger seat. Tony was sitting bolt upright. His face was like a mask.

Tony was thinking about the car he'd left at Brising Manor. Knowing that many of the satanists had died when the chapel caved in, he couldn't see anything to prevent him from going back to collect the vehicle.

"With all the mayhem going on at Brising Manor," Tony said as they drove along, "I should take the opportunity to get my Renault back. I don't want anyone other than us to know I was there." He turned his head and looked at Sue, who was sitting in the back seat. "You can drive it until you get another car."

"It's madness going back to Brising Manor," Sue said with horrified surprise. "Forget your car. I can use the van until I can scrape up enough for another vehicle."

"Nobody's going to be looking for us," Tony countered. "It's the last thing they would expect."

"Tony! What's got into you?" Sue cried out, bringing her hands to her face. "Have you lost your bloody mind? What you are suggesting is insane."

Tony flipped her off with his finger.

"Sue is right!" Jim exclaimed in astonishment. "You can't be serious! We only got out of the sabbat by the skin of our teeth. And you want to go back? Forget it! It's not worth the bloody risk."

"So nobody's willing to drop me off at Brising Manor then? Is that it?" Tony said angrily. His eyes were bright and excited. "Well, fuck you! I'll get to Brising Manor if I have to hitch." He turned on Jim. "You told me Kingsbury was dead, and there are lots of people missing after the chapel collapsed. Whoever's left at Brising Manor isn't going to be thinking about us, are they?"

Sue tried to reason with Tony as Jim pulled up outside the house. But he wasn't listening. "My mind is made up," he declared as she got out. "I'm going to Brising Manor straightaway."

"You are not taking the van," Sue said in alarm. "It's the only vehicle I have, and it's not going anywhere."

"No sweat! We'll go in my car," Tony snapped.

The last thing Jim wanted was to go anywhere near Brising Manor. If Tony wanted to go on a suicide mission, he could do it alone.

"Tony, I don't want to go to Brisin' Manor, full bloody stop," he said flatly.

"You have to help me," Tony argued. "We are all in this together. If my car is at Brising Manor, I could be fitted up for Giles Kingsbury's murder and all of you will be implicated. All I ask is that you drop me off."

Jim felt bound over a barrel and it irritated him.

"Okay! I'll take you to Brisin' Manor," he said resignedly. "But I want you to know, once you go through the gates, you're on your own."

Tony smiled. "Good! That's settled. Let's get on our way."

"I'd feel better if we went in Emma's car," Jim said. "Your MG is too conspicuous. I'll drive."

Tony was quiet on the journey. Jim wondered what he was planning. As they drove through Hockham's Bridge, Tony began fidgeting in his seat and drumming his fingers on the dashboard. He began to mutter to himself. Jim heard him say, "I wish you had left Kingsbury to me. He's taken everything from me, my children, my dignity, and even my car. I wanted to be the one to stick him."

Jim said nothing, but his unease grew as Tony continued mumbling about the murder of his children and how all those involved deserved to die.

Jim parked the car in a lay-by not far from the crossroads. He was full of misgivings. Tony was not in his right mind if he thought he could waltz into Brising Manor through the main gate.

"Tony," he said, looking him square in the eye, "when Omar and I came 'ere a couple of days ago, 'e told me that Kingsbury had conjured evil spirits to keep watch on the estate and tell 'im if anyone tried to get in."

"Yeah, yeah," Tony said, interrupting. "Kingsbury's dead, and so are his spirits." He gave a grim laugh. "It's a pity you stole my thunder and killed him yourself."

"That's not what I was tryin' to say." Jim tried again. "Omar warned me about the watchers. 'E warned me to control my thinkin', and I didn't listen. I got pissed off because of somethin' I saw on the estate, and Kingsbury's devils were instantly aware of us. We 'ad to run for our lives. Kingsbury shot at us." He took a deep, anxious breath. "I don't want it to 'appen to you."

"Well, if you are so concerned about my welfare, you should come with me into the estate. You know where the side entrance is and I don't. You can show me where it is and then run back to the car. Is that such a problem?"

"Of course it's a bloody problem. I'm scared shitless."

Without a word, Tony got out of the car and started off towards the woodland. Jim, noticing he was going the wrong way, reluctantly got out of the car. "Tony," he called as loudly as he dare. "You are goin' in the wrong direction."

"Well! Show me where the side entrance is, and then you can leave."

"All right! Come on," Jim said, leading the way through the trees and bramble thickets to the track that ran around the estate.

They followed the track to a high stone wall covered in

moss and lichen. About a hundred yards further on, they came to an arched door set into the stonework.

"This is it," Jim said. The iron-studded oak door was ajar. Jim pushed it open and peered through. "This gate is normally locked," he said in a low voice. "Looks like whoever came through 'ere was in a 'urry and didn't lock the gate behind them."

Tony peered into the estate. "Which way now?" he muttered.

Against all his better instincts, Jim decided that if Tony had a hope in hell of pulling off his plan, he would have to take him as far as the laurel bushes before the house, but not one step further. Tony was on his own from there.

Jim took a deep breath. In an effort to keep fear from his mind, he visualised a glowing emerald diamond shape and walked into it. It made him feel better. He knew that if he could keep his mind in neutral, he would not register on the radar of any bad spirits that might be on the watch.

"Tony!" he said earnestly. "If you want to survive and get your revenge, you'd better not be 'arbourin' any violent thoughts."

Tony brushed him off. Patting the gun in his pocket, he answered, "I've got something better."

Jim stared at Tony. He wondered if the copper's obsession with his car was an excuse to go to Brising Manor and murder as many satanists as he could.

In that instant, Jim wanted to run back to the car and get the hell out of there. He could understand that Tony wanted revenge after what had happened to him and his daughters, but he also knew that Tony's negatively charged thinking would put them both in danger.

"Which way?" Tony asked impatiently.

"I'll take you to the bushes in front of the 'ouse, and that's it," Jim answered.

The woodland was quiet. Jim wondered where the rooks had gone. They were not noisy like the last time he was there. Perhaps Tony was right about Kingsbury's demon watchers dying with him. He hoped it was true.

Making sure the coast was clear, they followed a path into the trees and into a clearing full of sheds and pens. Jim kept his eyes on the ground and his mind in neutral. He heard Tony take a sharp intake of breath as they passed the fence filled with bird and animal bodies. The path went on through another small copse and ended at a sward of grass in front of a tall privet hedge.

"Come on!" Jim hissed. He pointed to an arched wrought-iron gate "Through 'ere. This will take us to the 'ouse."

The gate was open. They cautiously set off along a flagstone walkway bordered on one side by tennis courts and on the other by a stand of laurel bushes.

Sticking closely to the shrubbery, they turned a corner. Tony raised his binoculars and, peering through the laurels, looked towards the house. The sight of the forbidding mansion brought painful memories to the surface of his mind. He forced himself to think like a policeman. He would get his revenge on the coven, but right now he was concentrating on his car. It could be used to implicate him. He had to get it back. And if he had to shoot a satanist to get it, he wouldn't hesitate.

Scanning the car park for his yellow Renault, he saw it parked at the side of the mansion along with other vehicles. He gauged the distance from where he stood to the car. It was about two hundred yards—quite a stretch. He wondered if there was any way of getting closer.

Cars were coming and going in a slow but steady stream. He noticed that vehicles coming in to Brising Manor had two occupants and left with one. Realising that the relatives of the missing people were picking up their cars, he saw a golden opportunity to get in and out. They would go back and get the car. Then Jim could drive into the estate and drop him off. To the casual eye there would be nothing unusual. If anyone was watching, he would blend in with the other people who were coming and going.

Noticing a sudden flurry of activity at the house, Tony looked over to the entrance. The front door to Brising Manor was open. He could see a gaunt black-suited man standing on the porch directing events and conversing with a group of people. The figure was familiar. In a sudden flash of memory, Tony gasped with sickening recognition. The man on the porch was the monster who had dragged his daughters into the pentacle at the sabbat, had defiled them, and had then consumed them. A sweat broke out on his face, and his heartbeat quickened. Taking out his gun, he flicked off the safety. He'd kill the bastard if it was the last thing he ever did. Setting out at a run towards the entrance to the manor, he suddenly tripped. As he hit the ground, he heard the gun discharge.

"What the fuck you doin'?" Jim hissed, hauling him back into the bushes. "Fuck your car. I'm gettin' out of 'ere, and you are comin' with me."

They ran as fast as they could to the side door of the estate and back to the road. Tony stopped at the tree line.

"What's up?" Jim questioned. "Why 'ave you stopped?"

Tony said nothing, just stared back along the road towards Brising Manor.

"The car's just down the road," Jim said. "Quick! You've

just sounded the fuckin' alarm bell. What were you thinkin' runnin' off toward the 'ouse like that with a gun? Do you think you're Superman or somethin'?"

"No sweat, man," Tony said. "Whoever heard the shot will think it's just the gamekeeper killing critters for his fence."

Jim heard the sound of a car coming. He pulled Tony into the hedge. A Bentley drove by.

"There are still a lot of cars that need to be picked up in the car park," Tony said as they carried on towards the car. "Everyone came late to miss the press. I've got a plan."

Jim didn't want to listen to any plan. He wanted to get out of the area as quick as possible. He wondered how Tony had talked him into this madness, and what misguided loyalty had made him agree to come back to this horrific place. If push came to shove and he was arrested for killing Kingsbury, he'd rather spend his life in prison than be sacrificed to the Devil. He began to jog back to the car.

"My Renault is parked at the side of the house," Tony said, keeping up with him. "Instead of trying to sneak around and get it, why don't we drive in through the main entrance? You can drop me off, and I can get my vehicle and follow you out of the estate. There is so much traffic coming and going that we'll just blend in."

"I think you goin' back is a bad idea," Jim said when they reached the car. He opened the door.

"I'm going to get my car with you or without you," Tony said aggressively. His mouth was set in a straight line. Jim saw a dangerous glitter in his eye. *He's gone mad*, he thought to himself. He couldn't leave Tony alone on the road; he had to help him, however crazy it was. At least he was prepared to ram his way out of Brising Manor if he had to. He prayed it wouldn't come to that.

"Okay, get in. I'll drive you into the estate," Jim said reluctantly, desperately trying to ward off the many negative scenarios that crammed into his mind.

Jim took off along the Turley road towards the main gates of the estate. He had not gone far when a black Mercedes sped by him, almost forcing him into the ditch, and swerved through the entrance to the manor.

"There's someone in a hurry," Tony said. "Speed up! Let's follow him."

Accelerating, Jim turned in through the gates and followed the Mercedes into the car park. Looking around the forecourt, he saw there were still a dozen or so vehicles outside of Brising Manor, and people were still being dropped off to collect their respective cars.

"Where's your car?" Jim asked, pulling into the car park.

"Over there at the side of the house." Jim drove a little further.

"Drop me here! It's just a stone's throw to my car. Wait until you see me back out." Tony gave a grim smile. "Just in case the car won't start and you have to pick me up."

Jim's heart was beating wildly as he watched Tony move swiftly across the gravel forecourt to the side wing of the house and get in his car. Jim looked nervously around and saw with relief that no one seemed to be taking any notice of either of them.

So far, so good, Jim thought as Tony backed out. Turning round, Jim started driving across the forecourt towards the driveway. The Mercedes that had almost run him off the road was parked outside the entrance to the manor. Two men were inside, and the back passenger door was open. A tall, dark figure was getting in the back seat. Jim froze for a moment.

It was Kingsbury's shape-shifting butler who had sacrificed Tony's girls at the sabbat.

The Mercedes started speeding towards Jim as he accelerated across the forecourt. Realising he and Tony had been sussed and the satanists were trying to block their escape along the drive, Jim pressed the accelerator pedal to the floor. Barely missing a tree, he skidded onto the driveway.

The Mercedes was right alongside and was moving over, trying to push him off to the side and into the trees. Wrenching the steering wheel to the left, Jim cut in front of the Mercedes and gunned the car forward. He felt an impact on the side pane. For a moment he lost control of the wheel, and the car veered madly across the road.

Gaining control of the steering wheel, he drove at full speed to the gates. Checking the rear-view mirror, he saw that the Mercedes had parked across the road blocking the drive and that Tony's Renault had come to a stop behind it. For a moment, he thought about turning round and trying to rescue Tony, but he saw to his horror an estate vehicle driving up and blocking the Renault in.

Jim shifted his gaze to the road ahead and saw two estate workers running towards the gates. He knew they were going to try to prevent his escape and shut him into the estate, and then he'd be caught like Tony.

As the estate workers reached the gates, Jim's mind switched off and terror took hold. Gripping the steering wheel, he drove straight at the men as they were closing the gates. He didn't care if he ran them down. They were all child-sacrificing lowlifes anyway.

The men jumped out of the way as he sped through. Keeping the pedal pressed to the floor, he drove like a madman away from Brising Manor. Passing the speed restriction signs at Hockham's Bridge, he felt the tension in his chest begin to ease. The understanding that he had courted disaster and somehow survived had left him drained and shaken. The coven had captured Tony, and there was nothing he could do about it.

On the drive back to Greenfern, Jim tried to think of what to do next. He was afraid to go to the police and raise the alarm in case the copper in charge was a satanist. The power wielded by the likes of Giles Kingsbury was absolute and showed what a sham the justice system was. The entire establishment from the top to the bottom was bought and paid for by the Devil. The thought made him feel sick. There was no one apart from Emma, Omar, and Sue that he could trust.

It was late afternoon when Jim pulled into Greenfern, got out of the car, and ran to the house. Sue was making bread when he burst into the kitchen.

"What's up, mate? You're as white as a sheet." She looked out of the window. "Where's Tony?"

Jim sunk down in a chair. "Tony didn't make it," he said, his voice shaking with emotion.

"What?! No!" Sue started to cry. Grabbing the tobacco, she quickly tried to roll a cigarette. Her hands were shaking so bad that she couldn't fold the paper. "What happened?" she cried out.

Jim was in such a state that he didn't know where to start. "I knew 'e was 'ell-bent on goin' to Brisin' Manor and I couldn't stop 'im, so I went into the estate with 'im. We was 'idden in the shrubbery. Tony 'ad 'is binoculars and was lookin' for 'is car. Suddenly 'e got 'is gun out and started runnin' towards the 'ouse. He tripped and the gun went off. I dragged 'im back to the bushes."

"Was he hurt?" Sue was becoming hysterical.

"No." Jim hesitated for a moment before he carried on. There was no easy way for him to tell her what had happened. "We legged it out of there back towards the car through the side gate. I was 'eadin' for the road when suddenly Tony stops. I wanted to get away from the estate there and then, but 'e wouldn't come with me. 'E said 'e 'ad an idea that would work, and that I should drive into the car park at Brisin' Manor and drop 'im off." Tears trickled down his cheeks. "It would 'ave worked," he muttered. There was a pause, and then he burst into a spate of words. "It was 'is anger that trapped 'im. I tried to tell 'im about the wicked spirits. I told 'im not to think any bad thoughts, but 'e wouldn't listen," Jim said. "And they got 'im," he added.

Sue staggered back from the counter. With a strangled sob, she fainted.

Jim wiped away his tears with the back of his hand. *Is this fucking nightmare ever going to end?* he thought. He picked Sue up, carried her into the sitting room, and laid her on the settee. He remembered there was a bottle of smelling salts in the cupboard.

"Em! Omar!" Jim called out. "Where are you? I need 'elp." There was no reply. "Em!" he called again.

Sue began to come round as he held the open bottle under her nose. After a few moments, Jim left her on the settee and went in search of Emma and Omar. He went outside and called their names, but no one answered. After a fruitless search of the property, he went back to the sitting room. On the table, he saw a large purple envelope edged in gold. Inside was a note. "We are with Trevelyan" is all it said.

"Fuck!" Jim shouted out. Emma and Omar had gone with Trevelyan, Sue was in a bad way, and Tony would soon be dead. It seemed to him that he had been abandoned—dumped off and left to deal with all the horror that was happening on his own. He started to get resentful. He was a pawn in Trevelyan and Emma's game, and when he needed moral and spiritual support, they had abandoned him.

Seeing a pouch of tobacco on the table, he rolled himself a cigarette and sat down on the sofa. "Fuck!" he shouted to the empty space. "They just left me to deal with all the shit. Well, fuck them. I've 'ad enough!"

CHAPTER 7

TWO IS COMPANY

After Jim and Sue had left for the barrow downs with Tony, Emma went into the sitting room and sat down in an armchair next to the log fire. The room was warm and comforting. It felt like an age ago that she had been able to relax without the immediate threat of danger. She laid her head back on the seat and took some long, slow breaths.

The events of the last few days had numbed her mind by their rapidity and morbidity. She welcomed the respite from the horror that had pursued her, however long it lasted. She sensed that the psychic evil that had shadowed her had been withdrawn; she could no longer feel its presence. How she wished to wake up and find it all a dream and be able to return to the normality of the garden, the market, and her beloved cats.

Emma gazed at Omar as he eased his long body into the chair opposite her. His dreads were even greyer than when they had met, and his long, haggard face was lined and careworn. She'd known him for less than a week, and yet it seemed like a lifetime.

She remembered their first meeting. Jim had found a matchbook cover from a strip joint next to the dig on

Dragonsbury Ring. Trying to find out if the address on the matchbook was connected to the satanists, they had decided to investigate. When they got there, the bar was closed. They'd had a little time to spare before the club opened for the evening. Seeing a brightly painted door across the road with a sign advertising crystals, herbs, and tarot card readings, she had felt an extraordinary magnetic pull to have her tarot cards read. She had felt the same magnetic attraction when she had gone with her grandmother to sacred stones and left food and cream for the faeries in the ring and cup marks. The experience had taught her to follow her intuition.

They entered the premises, and Omar St Louis, the mystic, had shown them into his studio and cast the cards for her. His reaction to the spread was totally unexpected and unnerving for Emma. Without explanation, Omar had given Jim his money back, and then had forcefully rushed them out of the shop, locking the door behind them. That had upset her. The next day, Jim had phoned Omar for an explanation. An appointment had been made for the day after. Trevelyan had accompanied them to Omar's studio for a reading. At the meeting, Omar had agreed to help them find the sapphire. She wondered what it was he had seen in her cards that had affected him so deeply. Now that they were alone, she thought she would broach the subject.

"Omar," she said, "do you remember when we met?"

"Yes, mon. I do."

"You never did tell me why you rushed us out of your studio." Emma grinned. "Not that it's important, especially after what we have been through together, but I'm interested to know what the problem was."

Omar's smile vanished. He was silent for a while, and then he said, "You reminded me of someone I loved very much.

Her name was Lucy, and she had your fine green eyes." He paused. A spasm of pain crossed his face.

"If the memory is too painful, you don't have to relive it," Emma said.

"No! No, mon. I and I wants to talk it out. The tarot spread that I cast for you in my studio was the same cards I had cast for Lucy a week before she was abducted by the mamba. She was raped and sacrificed to the sons of wickedness. You brought the darkness back, and I didn't want to relive the horror." He got up and patted her on the arm. "I and I is sorry to have frightened you, mon. But I was frightened too." He held his hands up in the air as if in supplication to a higher power. "Jah knows the misery I've been through."

Standing up, Emma hugged his long, thin frame. They looked at each other. Tears trickled down both of their faces. "After you and Jim had gone," Omar began, "I cast the cards again, and I realised that the same wickedness that had consumed my Lucy was comin' after you. The cards showed me that I too had a part to play in defeatin' the wicked ones. When you came back to my studio the second time, you had the powerful loa Trevelyan with you. Before the readin', he told me about the council in High Faerie long ago and how you had volunteered to take on human form at the time of prophecy. He told me my Lucy was the warrior of water, and you are the warrior of air."

Sitting back down Emma glanced at him in surprise. "Your Lucy was the faerie warrior of water?"

Omar nodded. "I did not know that at the time. Otherwise I would have forced her to leave Jamaica with me."

"When did Trevelyan tell you about my faerie heritage?" Emma asked. She had been with Trevelyan all the time they had been at Omar's studio and had not heard any conversation about her mission. "Was I there?"

"Yes, mon. You were there. He was tellin' me about you just before the readin'." Omar flicked back his dreads and smiled at her.

Emma thought back to their second visit to Omar's studio. She recalled a tingle in the air after Trevelyan had requested that Omar cast the cards for him. She had turned her attention to the feeling and had joined a silent conversation going on between them.

"I remember." Emma smiled back. "I didn't hear anything that concerned me, but then I was late to the conversation."

"The loa Trevelyan has transferred Lucy's mission onto I and I, mon," Omar said solemnly. "You are east and I am west, and when we combine our polarities, a wave of spiritual power is generated. That's what threw Zugalfar back into the pit, mon. We set up a power wave he could not combat."

Needing to assimilate what Omar had told her, Emma got up. "I'll make a fresh pot of tea," she said, taking the empty cups into the kitchen.

Lucy had been the faerie warrior of water. Emma wanted to know more about her. She was interested to know if Lucy had experienced the same psychic attacks as she had, and if there were any similarities.

"How did you meet Lucy?" Emma asked, putting a tea tray on the table.

"We grew up together in the shanty towns of Kingston," Omar answered. "Lucy was my childhood sweetheart. We was goin' to get married on May Eve. Lucy started havin' nightmares at the beginnin' of April. She started walkin' in her sleep to a churchyard where dem sons of Obeah held their ceremonies."

"Sons of Obeah?" Emma questioned.

"Voodoo priests of the Left-Hand Path."

"So in other words, they are satanists just like Feodora St Clair?"

"Yes, mon," Omar replied, and then continued on. "Lucy told me she was drawn to a sunken grave with a broken headstone. She told me it was a dream, but I was not so sure. I had noticed she seemed to be distant and preoccupied, and kept lookin' over her shoulder as if somethin' was trackin' her. I didn't like it one bit, mon." He paused, his eyes misting over. Passing his hand across his brow, he pushed back his dreads. "I went lookin' for the grave in the daylight, and as I walked through the gravestones, I saw the shapes of evil loa followin' me." His dark eyes flashed and he leant forward. "I could hear them titterin'. I ran out of the cemetery and went straightaway to see Lucy. Knowin' that she was in great danger, I begged her to leave Jamaica and go to another island, but she would not go. She told me flat out she wasn't goin' to leave. I suspected then that she had been spelled by the Obeah men. I was so worried about her that I stayed beside her night and day, and made sure that when we left the house we were always in open spaces." He got up. "Do you want a glass of water?"

Emma nodded. "Yes, please."

Omar went into the kitchen and returned with two glasses of water.

"Cheers!" Emma said as he handed her a glass.

"One evenin' as the sun was goin' down," Omar continued, sitting down, "we were walkin' on the beach talkin' about our weddin', when from out of nowhere a group of Obeah men appeared on the beach behind us. Their faces were painted white. I heard the rattle of their gourds as they advanced toward us." There was a period of silence before he spoke again. "I took Lucy's hand and tried to pull her away, but she fought me. The Obeah men were shakin' their rattles even harder. I knew they were spellin' her, so I picked her up and threw her over my shoulder. She started yellin' and beatin' on my back with her fists, screamin' for me to let go of her. As I started climbin' the path to the top of the cliffs, I was confronted by a huge negress in flowin' scarlet robes and a turban. It was the same mamba whom Jim had killed at the sabbat." He paused again, his face twisted in a grimace.

"Evil loa were clustered around her huge grotesque body. I will never forget her leerin' face and gleamin' white eyeballs as she ogled Lucy. The Obeah men came up behind us. One of them grabbed me, pullin' me backwards, while another blew a powder in my face. I felt giddy and sick, and my eyesight began to get blurry. Lucy got free." He choked up with emotion and then took a long drink of water. "The Obeah men picked her up, and holdin' her aloft like a trophy, they followed the mamba away from the cliffs. I sank to the ground and passed out.

"When the consciousness came back into me, I was filled with emptiness and rage. I had lost my love, and I couldn't bear the terror and angst of what would happen to her. It was soul-crushin', mon. To ease my pain, I started drinkin' rum. For weeks I lost myself. I came to my senses in a back alley. Rats were chewin' on my boots tryin' to get at my toes, and I suddenly realised I had become a victim of wicked loa. They were tryin' to kill me, mon."

Emma got up and refilled their glasses with water. Listening to what Omar was saying about drinking alcohol and engaging in self-destructive behaviour, she saw he had a similarity with Jim. She recalled that after Zugalfar had snatched her from the sabbat, Jim had started drinking, and would have become a victim of the succubus, or evil loa, as Omar called them.

"Go on," she said, sitting down.

"I went to see my daddy," Omar continued. "He lived on the other side of the island. When I was growin' up, he taught me how to read tarot cards and practise healin' and good magic. When I told him what had happened to Lucy, sayin' that I wanted to learn how to counter the magic of the mamba and her Obeah men, he said he would help me. Over the next few months, he taught me songs in the sacred language of our tribe—ancient phonetics used for communication with elemental forces of the earth."

Omar sipped his water. "My daddy painted my body half yellow and half orange and painted hailstones upon my face to give me mastery of the storm. Then he took me to the top of a hill and left me there naked and alone with no food or water." He sighed deeply. Looking at Emma, he said, "I prayed to Jah for understandin' and direction. On the third day, the clouds drew together and lightnin' struck all around me. Hail battered my body, and with it came a message. Jah said to align myself with life and to be positive in my thoughts. At the first hour on the fifth day, my daddy came. Takin' me to his car, he drove me to a waterfall, and sang songs while I purified myself." His lined face lit up with a smile. "That is how I have the loa of lightnin', fire, and drivin' water, mon."

Realising that Lucy's nightmares and the sleepwalking was a carbon copy of what she had experienced, Emma said, "I had nightmares at the beginning of April, the same month as Lucy's, and I started walking in my sleep to a ruined church. I was lucky. I came to my senses just in time, and ran away. Jim saved my life that night."

"It seems that Jah has brought us all together—in the nick of time, mon." He looked searchingly at Emma. "What's the score on Jim, mon? I saw his aura change into an orange glow when he was in the pentacle. His face contorted with lust, and then he tried to rape you."

"This isn't the first time that has happened," Emma said gravely. "Jim is possessed by succubi and incubi, and it's my fault. What's happening to him is because of me."

Omar passed his hands nervously over his dreads and then took another swig of water. He saw the similarity between him and Jim. Wicked loa had tried to kill both of them.

Emma composed herself and started to talk about her past.

"Underneath my house is a temple dedicated to Agdistis. My father used to hold black mass down there when I was a small child. He used me for sexual purposes, and many times an incubus would possess me. I thought I'd got over the memories, but sometimes in my sleep I would see the incubus's catlike eyes and the acorns blooming in his face. My father left me the house in his will. I moved in nine months ago. I needed someone to help me fix up the place and do the garden, so I hired Jim to help me."

Emma got up. "I need a cigarette." She soon returned with the tobacco. As Omar rolled himself a joint, she rolled and lit a cigarette.

"Before I tell you about Jim, I think we need a top-up. Water is just not doing it. I need a cup of tea." The pot was still hot. Refreshing their cups with tea, Emma sat back down.

"It began when I moved back to my childhood home and met Trevelyan," she started. "His house in the fourth dimension of Faerie is identical to mine, and the two are superimposed on one another. In his house he has a secret room. I became obsessed with finding the secret room in mine. Little did I know that the hidden room was a gateway to hell." She shifted nervously in the chair. "I was drawn to a wall in the hallway, and as I was tapping on the plaster to see if there was anything behind it, an incubus pushed its body through the wall and embraced me." She hesitated and shot a glance at Omar. He had his eyes closed and was smoking. "I did not admit it to myself"— her voice was trembling— "but there was an instant when I wanted to go with him through the wall and down into the temple of Agdistis." She puffed nervously on her cigarette. "Trevelyan found the room in my house. To cut a long story short, there was a terrible battle between one of Zugalfar's demon lords and Trevelyan for control of the temple, and for control of me." She grew quiet. After a little while, she said, "I realised when Trevelyan took me into the hidden room that I had been there many times before and been used in satanic rituals. I'd erased the horror from my memory, but after Trevelyan had banished the evil that had taken hold there, my memories came flooding back …" Her voice trailed off.

The air grew dense and oppressive. Omar got up and opened a window. Emma waited until he had sat down before she continued on again.

"Trevelyan asked Jim and me to go to Dragonsbury Ring and get the sapphire. As you know, Kingsbury beat us to it. Once we realised Kingsbury had gotten there before us, there was nothing we could do. We were starting back when a fog came rolling in like a white blanket. It was so thick that we could hardly see each other. Jim remembered he had left a shovel at the dig site and went back to get it. I started down the hill on my own. I felt like a boat floating through an ocean of fog. I couldn't see a bloody thing. On the way down, I felt something was close by me, and I realise now it was the same incubus that haunted the temple underneath my house. I was rescued by the Faeries of Place, but Jim wasn't so lucky. He was lost in the fog, and then raped by a succubus. She has an energetic link to him and can possess him anytime she wants. Trevelyan told me that Kingsbury had held a sabbat under the hill a few hours before we got there and that the satanic ritual abuse of the sacrifice had attracted sexual demons, who were still lingering on the mount when we showed up."

Omar raised his eyebrows in surprise. "Trevelyan is a powerful loa, mon," he said. "Surely he can give Jim a charm to protect him from attack."

"He did," Emma answered. "He gave Jim a peridot ring to wear as protection against the succubus. The problem is that Jim can't keep away from alcohol. When he's drunk, the succubus takes advantage and gets him to take off the ring." She gave a deep sigh. "The truth is, Omar, that Jim wants to be with me. His sexual frustration attaches us to one another on some low level of vibration. That means we both share the same sexual demons, and both of them are exploiting his sexual desire for me. Poor Jim," Emma said. "He doesn't deserve any of the nightmares he's involved in. But he's in it up to his neck, and we can't desert him."

Omar cleared his throat. "Jim saved my life at the sabbat. We were leavin' the cavern when the mamba that had sacrificed Lucy came out of the shadows and attacked me. The mamba was throttlin' the life out of me when Jim stabbed her." He shook his head sadly. "You know, mon, while we were fightin' demons in the circle, Jim was easy prey. He was frightened and couldn't stay in neutral. Fear made him negative, and a wicked sexual loa attached to him."

"That's true, but it's still my fault. I should have made

sure that the ring was on his finger before he joined us in the circle." Emma nervously ran her hands through her hair. "At least Jim's wearing it now; otherwise Sue would be at risk."

Omar leant towards her. "Havin' Tony along is bad news for Jim, mon. Tony's anger will attract evil loas to him, and after what the satanists must have subjected him to, I'll bet there are sexual demons hoverin' around him."

"No doubt about that," Emma answered. "But as long as Jim keeps the ring on, he'll be safe from the succubus, even if there are sexual predators hanging around Tony." She took a shallow breath. "We've all taken a battering."

"We might have taken a batterin', mon, but so have they. We got the sapphire and averted a catastrophe." He grinned. "One thing's for sure, dem wicked sons of Babylon lost many of their high adepts at the sabbat. They were the select, mon, the highest in wickedness from all across the world, and most of them have gone to join their master."

Emma nodded, remembering the cosmopolitan assembly she had seen in the library at Brising Manor. "*Infernus ejus,*" she said. "Hell has its price."

Omar smiled and nodded his head. "Praise to Jah," he said.

Emma rolled herself another cigarette.

"It's goin' to take a little while for the covens to regroup, mon," Omar said. "They've suffered a major setback. They've lost the sapphire; many are dead, includin' Kingsbury and the mamba; and their attack on the sanctuary failed. Two more of their wicked crew are dead, and that's goin' to give us a little time to figure out what we have to do next."

What we have to do next. Omar's words rang in Emma's ears. There were so many imponderables that she didn't know what to do next.

Electricity rippled through the sitting room, Sue's house faded, and they found themselves in Trevelyan's sitting room in Faerie. Dappled sunshine was filtering through the open windows, and the perfume of the flowers from the garden was drifting through the room. Emma looked around for Trevelyan.

"I wonder where Trevelyan is," she said to Omar. "We're in my sitting room at his house. Remember, I told you it was superimposed on mine. It's good to be home." She grinned. "I mean, in one of my houses."

She heard the excited barking of a dog. Trevelyan walked through the door with Chloe at his heels.

"'Tis good to see you," he said to them. "Pray, sit down. Sit down! I will bring us brandy, and then I will tell you the reason for my delay."

Trevelyan brought the drinks. The three of them sat together at the round table in the centre of the room. "Forgive me, m'dear," he said earnestly to Emma, "for not returning to you sooner." He looked at both of them searchingly and, reading their memories, saw the events that had transpired since their last meeting.

"What happened to you?" Emma asked. "I tried to call you across the airwaves but could find no trace of you."

Trevelyan sipped on his drink. "I will explain, m'dear. After you had given me the sapphire, I had planned to take it to Crann Sidhe, but first I wanted to consult with Ke-enaan. Entering the tumulus opposite Dragonsbury Ring, I willed myself to the portal on the Burren. Knowing that the radiance of the sapphire could be seen by friend and foe alike, I hastened as fast as I could to the wizard's halls.

"When I entered the hall, I saw that Ke-enaan was seated at the mirror. He stood up and stared when he saw me. I noticed his face was gaunt and solemn, and his shoulders were hunched forward in an attitude of despair."

"'The Company of the Key have followed the thief to the island of Inishark!' he cried out when he saw me. 'A storm spell hath been cast against them. Come! Look into the mirror.' Joining him, I looked into the glass. All I could see was mountainous seas, and I heard the howling of a gale in my ears. 'See!' Ke-enaan said, jabbing his finger on the glass. I looked closer and saw a small boat being tossed like a matchstick in the turmoil of the ocean. A great wave came, the boat disappeared, and I could see nothing but the tempest of the storm. 'We must make search for the House of Air,' Ke-enaan said in a panic. 'Follow me!'

"Leaving the mirror, we rushed down the steps to the cave beneath his halls. Ke-enaan bent down and, touching the water, sang a note that reverberated through the underground river system. A few moments later a seal man broke the surface.

"'Liam!' Ke-enaan cried out in the language of water. 'The House of Air hast been lost in the storm. Their boat is sinking. Gather thy relatives and search for survivors, and bring them to my halls.' With a twitch of his whiskers, the merrow disappeared.

"Turning to me, Ke-enaan said, 'The sapphire cannot stay here. I hath nothing to shield the radiance, and it canst be seen from far and wide. My power is waning and my defences art too weak to stand the Cathac's attack. Thou must take the sapphire to Crann Sidhe. If thou canst stay free of dark thought, thou might be able to enter a timeline more benevolent than that of the Company of the Key. If thou couldst get the lords of the Ghrian Sidhe to accept the burden of the sapphire, it would be taken beyond the nine dimensions, where neither the Cathac could possess it nor mortal men find it. Thou must go now!'

"Using the sapphire as a gate, I willed myself to the summit of Crann Sidhe," Trevelyan continued. "Pressing the sapphire against the stone pillar, I petitioned the Ghrian Sidhe for an audience. Alfaan instantly appeared in a haze of shifting light. 'Your errand is known to me,' he said coldly. 'By thy presence, thou hast brought great evil to the hill of our long memory. The Cathac is awake. He will divine the emanations of the sapphire on the ether and send forth his hate against the memories in our sacred hill. He will choose a time of great evil and, resonating with it, will bring chaos to our timelines by altering the past.' Alfaan's eyes blazed dangerously. 'For aeons we travailed to free ourselves from the enemy of life. Great battles we have fought … and thou, star-walker,' he uttered with disdain, 'hast brought the evil chance of calamity to our doors. Leave!' he commanded, his dark liquid eyes aflame with fire. 'The sapphire will not rest here.'

"Thinking that the lords of the Ghrian Sidhe would aid me in so desperate a mission, I had not expected a rebuttal. For a few moments I was at a loss," Trevelyan carried on. "While the sapphire remained with me in Faerie, the Cathac, Zugalfar, and the denizens of Under-Earth could see its radiance. I knew the enemy would move hell and earth to claim it.

"Thinking that xonite, the metal of invisibility, might be able to contain the radiations of the sapphire, I took the star-gate to the eighteen-sided xonite tower of BelPa-zach in the sixth density, known as Din-Nemor. There resides Pa-za, keeper of the xonite. He is a powerful and mystical force coexisting within all time, contiguous with all space. I asked him to guard the sapphire until I could take it beyond the stars. He refused, saying, 'The affairs of faraway worlds are of little interest to the xonite. Thou art from Vana the Vale beyond the stars. Canst thou not take the sapphire to safety there?' I did not tell him that I had no time to journey beyond the stars, because I'd read his mind and knew it could not be changed.

"Not knowing what else to do, I took my leave and returned to Black Head with the sapphire." He looked at them solemnly. "The Cathac will have seen the emanations of the sapphire on the airwaves. He has summoned Zugalfar and his legions to the Giant's Cliffs. Ke-enaan and I saw his foul stain upon the airwaves. We are preparing for battle against the demons, and we will need your help to defend Black Head."

Emma's heart sank. She wanted time to rest and recuperate after her ordeal with Zugalfar and the satanists, but it was not to be. She felt her shoulders drop in resignation.

"Do you want us to go with you to Black Head now?" she asked. "What about Jim and Sue?"

Trevelyan shook his head. "I have preparations to make, but I will return for you later today. As for Jim and Sue, they could well be a liability. They have too much fear. We cannot take the risk that they will compromise us in the heat of our defence, so they will have to remain behind."

Emma thought back to the attack on the sanctuary. Trevelyan was right. Even though Jim and Sue had faerie sight, they did not have the spiritual strength or the power of High Faerie to counter their human fear.

"I'll await your return," she said to Trevelyan. She glanced at Omar.

"Irie, mon," he responded. "The warriors of air and water are at your service."

Trevelyan smiled. "To the Green," he said, raising his glass. His face grew serious again. "We must pray the Company of the Key is safe," he said. "Without Kilfannan and Kilcannan, the HeartStar will be lost and our efforts to save the Green will be in vain." He got up. "Now I must return to Black Head and take council with Ke-enaan." He bowed. "I will return within a few hours. Be ready!"

Having to fight her own battle against evil, Emma had no time to think about Kilfannan and Kilcannan, her counterparts in the fourth dimension of Faerie. A chill struck her heart. She had triumphed, but if the House of Kilfenoran were lost, then the Green would fall, and all their efforts to gain the sapphire would have been in vain.

The air crackled, Trevelyan's house faded, and Emma and Omar were back in Sue's sitting room.

CHAPTER 8

THE PRICE OF FEAR

Sue was sitting beside Jim on the sofa when Emma and Omar reappeared. Emma immediately noticed an atmosphere of fear and sadness around them. Jim was pale, and his eyes were red. Sue's face was drawn and streaked with tears.

"Where's Tony?" Emma asked, noticing he was missing.

Jim sniffed, rubbing his eyes. "The satanists got 'im," he said miserably. "There was nothin' I could do. I was lucky to get away from Brisin' Manor myself."

"You and Tony went to Brising Manor?" Emma said incredulously. "Why?"

"Tony was so set on gettin' 'is car ... said it could implicate 'im in murder—and us too, Em. 'E would know; 'e's a copper after all. I did what I thought was best." Jim's hands shook as he told them of the events that had happened at Brising Manor.

When he finished, he got up and, pouring himself a large brandy, knocked it back in one. "I'm sorry about the damage to your car, Em. I'll pay for it to be repaired," he said, pouring himself another one. "All this business with Tony 'as scrambled my 'ead, and I can't think straight."

The pressure of the last few days suddenly became

unbearable. Jim broke down. "I can't do this anymore," he cried out in short, fast gasps. "Tony's gone, and I can't go back to that 'ell'ole and rescue 'im. I don't want to be sacrificed. When is this ever goin' to end? I feel like I'm goin' mad." Grabbing the brandy, he started swigging from the bottle.

Emma felt awful. Her association with Jim had brought terror into his life and had reduced him from a strong and positive man to a shivering, terrified wreck. She knew he wanted to get drunk and blot out all the horror, but that would make him reckless and easy prey for succubus possession. She had to take the brandy away from him.

"Jim," she said gently, putting her hand on his shoulder, "I know our lives have become a nightmare, but I don't think you should drink any more booze. We've got to pull together here. We've got too much shit on our plate without adding to it."

"I know, Em. I'm tryin'," he said, looking into her face. "I'm tryin' to 'ang on to myself. You was gone when I got back. I saw the card in the sittin' room. Why didn't you wait for me? I could 'ave gone with you into Faerie. Did you see my little dog, Chloe?"

"Yes, I did see Chloe," Emma answered, smiling. Taking away the brandy bottle, she squeezed Jim's hand. How could she tell him he had become a liability? She sensed he already knew why Trevelyan had left him behind, but he was so broken that she wasn't going to reinforce his low self-esteem or add insult to injury.

"We can't just abandon Tony," Sue said, drumming her fingers on the table. "What are we goin' to do?"

Catching Omar's eye, Emma sent him a telepathic message. *We can't risk our lives by going back to Brising Manor to rescue Tony. He returned to the estate of his own free will and almost destroyed Jim in the doing. Our mission is to prevent the sapphire from falling into the Cathac's clutches.*

Omar nodded. *I agree, mon.*

"Sue," Emma said gently, "Omar and I can't help you rescue Tony. Trevelyan will be back soon to take us into Faerie. We have to go with him."

Sue stared at both of them in bewilderment for a moment, and then her face flushed with anger. "Do you mean that you are just going to leave me to clear up all this shit and deal with everything on my own? I can't believe I'm hearing this from you." She put her hands over her face and started sobbing.

"Irie, mon," Omar said, sitting on the arm of the sofa and putting his hand supportively on Sue's shoulder.

Gloom descended on the room, and a long and ominous silence followed. Suddenly the quiet was shattered by the chiming of the clock in the hallway. The sound was loud and seemed to reverberate around the room as a reminder of flying time.

"I'm going to do something to help Tony," Sue said, pulling away from Omar. "I don't know what yet, but I'm not just going to abandon him. He saved our lives. Those yobbos from Brising Manor would have murdered us if he hadn't intervened."

"That's true, Sue," Jim answered. "But don't get any silly ideas about tryin' to rescue 'im yourself, because it's 'opeless. Brisin' Manor is like a fortress—and full of fuckin' demons. I don't want to go back in there for love or money. I'm scared shitless of that place. What we need to concentrate on is gettin' rid of the Range Rover and the bodies before the police come lookin'. There's still a trail of blood from the 'ouse to the tool shed that needs to be cleaned up. Once we get it all squared away, you could alert the police that Tony's missin', and then they can deal with it." He glanced at her. "You could make somethin' up about 'im comin' to adopt a dog, sayin' you 'aven't been able to contact 'im."

"That's not going to work, Jim," Sue answered. "Don't forget that the police have my registration, and definitely photographs of me from the hunts. Feodora will have fingered me for sure. I'll be arrested on the spot. Anyway," she said, getting up from the settee, "I need to phone the hardware store and see if the glass is ready for the kitchen window. If the police do come here and they see the smashed window, it will draw attention to us."

"I'll get the hose and start washin' away the blood," Omar added. "We don't know what dem sons of wickedness are up to. The satanists will be gunnin' for us, and I don't want to be arrested for accessory to murder, mon." He got up and stretched, and then followed Sue through the door.

"Em," Jim said hesitantly, once they were alone. "I'm sorry about what 'appened in the pentacle. You know in my right mind, I'd never 'urt you."

"I know, Jim. I understand what happened to you. You have to stay away from the booze and keep the ring on your finger."

Jim flushed. Changing the subject, he said, "Let's go to the sanctuary room and clean the pentacle off the floor. We wouldn't want any nosy parker copper seein' that. If 'e was a Satanist, it would be a dead giveaway that we were at the sabbat."

Emma went into the kitchen to get a broom and a mop.

Seeing the brandy bottle on the floor where Emma had left it, Jim took off the cap and took a long pull. He knew he shouldn't, but one more wouldn't do him any harm. The brandy fortified his courage. He took another long pull, wincing as the fiery liquid coursed down his throat.

It was getting dark when Emma and Jim returned to the kitchen. There was a pot of tea on the table, along with some sandwiches.

"I made us a bite to eat," Sue said, filling the teacups.

After they had eaten, Jim got up, excused himself, and went into the toilet. He needed to think. The knowledge that Trevelyan had excluded him from going with Emma and Omar into Faerie had undermined his already fragile self-esteem. He felt he'd been left to do the dirty work, and he feared he wasn't up to it. He still hadn't recovered from the shock of losing Tony, and the thought of driving the Range Rover over the cliff scared him shitless. The way things were going, he thought to himself, he'd probably die in the attempt. He remembered the booze was still in the sitting room and decided to have another drink to bolster his courage. Leaving the toilet, he listened for a moment. He could hear the others talking in the kitchen. Nipping into the sitting room, he took another long swig of brandy. There were a couple of shots left in the bottom of the bottle. He knocked those back as well.

Emma noticed uneasily that Jim's face was flushed and he was full of confidence when he rejoined them at the table.

"I think we'll follow Tony's plan," he announced loudly. "'E told me what 'e intended to do with the Range Rover this mornin'." He glanced at Sue. "Do you know where Devils Bowl is?"

"It's about twelve miles from here, mate. What about it?"

"Tony's plan was to drive the Rover to the Devils Bowl and start a fire inside. Then set the cruise control and jump out of the vehicle before it went over the edge of the drop-off. 'E said it should explode on impact at the bottom of the quarry. Everyone will think it was an accident, and there will be nothin' to connect us to it."

"It might work," Sue said thoughtfully. "In the last few years, a couple of people have driven their cars over the edge of the quarry, so it wouldn't be the first time people have died there."

"Sounds dangerous, Jim," Omar said, shaking his head. "What if you don't jump out in time?"

Jim raised his eyebrows and sniffed. "You got a better idea?" he said truculently.

"No, mon, I don't," Omar replied quietly.

Emma glanced at Omar. His look confirmed what she suspected: Jim was drunk. With everything that was going on, she had inadvertently left the brandy bottle on the floor in the sitting room. She got up and went to have a look. Jim had been sneaking drinks. The brandy bottle was empty.

"Can I take your car, Em?" Jim slurred as she got back to the table. "We're gettin' a bit short on vehicles."

"No! You're drunk! You'll kill yourself." She found herself getting angry. "What the fuck is wrong with you? You know what happens when you drink."

Jim waggled his ring finger at her. "Don't worry, Em," he slurred. "I won't take the ring off."

Sue got up. "That's enough, Jim!" she said angrily. "I thought you were going to help me dump the Range Rover. It's obvious I can't count on you in a bloody crisis. Don't bother to come with me. You are worse than fucking useless. I'll drive the Range Rover to Devils Bowl myself. I'll walk back."

Sue stormed out of the room, slamming the door behind her.

Jim staggered after her.

"Where are you going?" Emma cried out.

"To 'ave a piss, if that's all right with you," he shouted back.

"Omar! Follow him, and make sure he's all right."

"I'm on it, mon."

Omar came back a few moments later. "Jim seems to have disappeared, mon. You search the house. I'll look for him outside."

Emma ran upstairs. The bedrooms were empty. She suddenly thought about her car and wondered where the keys were. Sprinting down the stairs, she joined Omar in the yard.

"Any sign of Jim?" she said, moving swiftly to her car.

"Nothin', mon."

The keys were still in the ignition. Emma breathed a sigh of relief. Taking the keys out, she put them in her pocket. "The car took quite a bang," she said, looking at the damage. "Jim!" she called. "Where are you?"

"He seems to have vanished," Omar said. "Let's go back inside, mon. We don't want to miss Trevelyan, and it's futile lookin' for someone who don't want to be found."

They went back to the sitting room and sat down by the fire. Emma leant back in her chair and ran her fingers through her hair. "Things are going from bad to worse," she said despondently. "It seems everything is falling apart. Jim's drunk, Tony's been captured by the satanists, and Sue's gone off on a hare-brained scheme to dump the Range Rover."

Omar's eyes glinted in the firelight. "Dem sons of wickedness are attackin' on all fronts. We have to stay in Jah love, mon."

The air tingled with electricity. Trevelyan appeared in the centre of the room. "Come!" he said breathlessly. "There is no time to lose."

Sue's mind was in turmoil as she drove the Range Rover out of the sanctuary and along the road towards Denhampstead.

Her life was crashing into darkness. She had been thrust into a nightmare of unimaginable proportions.

She had tried to talk Tony out of going to Brising Manor to get his car, but he wouldn't listen, and now he had been recaptured. Ever since they had rescued Tony from the sabbat, he had been aloof and strange, in no mood for talking, and had rejected her when she tried to hug him. She wondered if a compulsion spell had been laid against him to draw him back to Brising Manor. Sue brushed away her tears with her hand and tried to concentrate on the road. Tony had said nothing about how he had been taken prisoner by the satanists and marked for sacrifice. There was so much she didn't know, but the fact that his car was even in the car park at Brising Manor seemed to indicate that he had gone there voluntarily.

Now that Kingsbury was dead, she knew that Feodora would need to stay in control of the coven and restore her credibility as high priestess after the butchery and burning of her disciples at the sabbat. The recapture of Tony would cement her position, show that she had taken control back from those who opposed her. Feodora would also need to rebuild her demonic power. Sue knew that she would sacrifice Tony at her earliest opportunity.

Images of torture and horror forced themselves upon Sue as she drove on. All she could see in her mind was Tony's face distorted with agony and horror. Tears trickled down her cheeks. She loved Tony. He was a kindred soul. His compassion was unconditional; honesty was engraved upon his soul; and his sensitive, human vulnerability had stolen her heart. For the first time in many years, she had known love. It was worth fighting for, she told herself. If there was even a tiny chance that she could save him, she would have to try. He had become her world.

She had hoped that after sending the Range Rover over the cliff into the quarry, she could have talked Jim into going with her to Brising Manor in a last-ditch effort to save Tony. Jim had put the kybosh on that plan by getting drunk. She understood that Emma and Omar could not help her rescue Tony; they were needed in Faerie. If he was to be saved, it was up to her.

Driving through the town, Sue thought about her options. She wanted to rescue Tony, but she wasn't going to be reckless. If she followed Tony's plan, she'd be stuck in the middle of nowhere without a vehicle. It would take her hours to walk back to the sanctuary, and in that time Tony would probably be dead. An alternative would be to take the Range Rover to Brising Manor and dump it there. Then it would no longer be her problem. It would also give her an opportunity to spy out the land and see if there was any activity going on at the manor.

She reasoned that there would probably be a camera at the gatehouse, and the gates would be programmed to open automatically for one of their estate vehicles. She could dump the Range Rover in the car park, and then hide in the laurel bushes and keep watch on the house. All she had to do, she told herself, to stay safe was to keep her mind in neutral.

Sue turned off at the crossroads and drove towards Hockham's Bridge. Pulling off the road and getting out, she opened the back door of the vehicle. Feeling with her hands, she found a torch. Switching it on, she started looking for something with which to arm herself. She found a hunting knife lying amongst some snares and traps in the back, and some old sacks. Slipping the knife into her pocket and picking up the sacks, she opened the side door. There was an estate jacket and cap on the floor. Sue quickly put on the jacket.

Tucking her hair up, she put the cap on, and then threw the sacks over the bodies.

She took a couple of deep breaths to steady herself. Then, getting back into the vehicle, she drove on to Hockham's Bridge. On the way, she tried to recall what Jim and Omar had told her about the layout of the estate. Jim had also said that the side door to the estate was open when he and Tony had gone to get the car. That was only a few hours ago. The gate might still be open.

Sue slowed down as she entered the village. Hockham's Bridge was the closest village to Brising Manor, and the Gables pub on the corner of the high street and the Turley road was frequented by workers from the Kingsbury estate. Driving past the pub, she checked the cars on the forecourt to see if any estate vehicles were present. There were none. She turned left at the pub, drove to the crossroads, and travelled along the lane that led past the main gates of Brising Manor.

Not far along the road, Sue saw the dark wall of the estate looming up from a patch of woodland. The jagged glass cemented on the top of the wall glittered coldly in the headlights. She felt a chill down her spine as memories of the sabbat tried to tumble into her awareness. Keeping a picture of Tony's face in her mind, she gritted her teeth and drove on towards the gatehouse.

The wrought-iron gates to Brising Manor suddenly reared up like dark shadows at the side of the road. For a moment the headlights caught the baleful red eyes of the bronze griffins perched on the gateposts. The eyes were glaring down at her. Evil was palpable. For a moment, she wanted to put her foot down and get the hell away from there. Realising that the red glowing eyes were cameras, she pulled her cap down low over her eyes. There was a Brising Manor decal on the windscreen.

She hoped it would be enough to get her through the gates without interrogation.

She saw the gates were closed and the gatehouse was in darkness. There was a moment of indecision. Her intuition was screaming at her to dump the vehicle at the gates and get away from the estate as fast as possible.

Sue hardened her resolve. Turning in, she parked in front of the gates and waited.

A cold sweat broke out on her face and she nervously bit her lip as she waited in the darkness for the gates to open. The baleful red light looking down on her from the cameras on the top of the gateposts did not flash or waver. She wondered if there was something else she had to do to gain entry—a button to be pushed or a password to be entered on an inboard computer. She looked around the dashboard for apps or gadgets but could see nothing. The idea occurred to her that maybe the signal to open the gates was transmitted by a cell phone. She realised that she didn't have a clue, but she knew she couldn't run the risk of anyone coming to the gates to see who was there. The gatekeeper would be familiar with the workers on the estate and would immediately ask questions. She had to get out of there and check the side entrance to the estate that Jim and Omar had told her about.

A dying moon sailed out behind ragged clouds. Something in the moonlight spoke of evil. For an instant, all Sue wanted to do was to turn around and flee from the accursed place.

She was about to back up and turn around when she saw the gates begin to open. There was another moment of indecision. She did not want to drive forward. Taking a few deep breaths to steady her nerve, she visualised Tony's face, and then drove along the tree-lined driveway. The road was oppressive and hemmed in with dark oaks.

The grotesque bronze sculptures set at intervals along the driveway were no longer illuminated as they had been when Sue and her compeers had entered the estate on the night of the sabbat.

When she got to the end of the driveway, she looked around. The car park was empty, the estate seeming to be in total darkness. She could see the tennis courts glimmering in the moonlight and the beginnings of a road that ran past them. That would be her escape route.

Sue looked towards the house. The mansion rose before her like a monstrous silhouette of madness, a psychic shock of evil that chilled her soul. In the pillared porchway hung a red light that cast bloody shadows on the steps leading to the entrance. The big black doors to Brising Manor were closed, and the windows below the frowning gables were dark, reflecting the cold glare of the moon.

Sue suddenly felt panicked. If there was no one at Brising Manor, it might mean that Feodora had taken Tony somewhere else. The only other place she knew the satanists used for sacrifice was the crypt under Dragonsbury Ring. Feeling the horror of the sabbat trying to impinge upon her consciousness, she struggled to stay centred. Getting out of the car, she moved swiftly across the forecourt, concealing herself behind the laurels.

Her determination began to weaken as she stood hidden in the bushes. She suddenly realised how alone and vulnerable she was. Jim had been right. The mansion was a fortress, and even if she did get in, she didn't have a clue where to start looking. Fear snaked through her and she began to shiver. Her heart had ruled her head and brought her to an impasse. The understanding of her situation for a moment froze her action. She worried that she too had been drawn back to Brising

Manor by a spell. *I have to get out of the estate and call the police.* She thought about making a run for the Range Rover and driving out of there. If the gates were automatic, there was a good chance they would open. She didn't dare to think what she would do if the gates stayed closed. Tony had been blocked in the driveway, she recalled. The thought of him brought tears to her eyes. She experienced an instant of confusion. Her mind was getting harder to control. She had tried so hard to stay in neutral, but her emotions kept taking over. She was suddenly afraid that her fear would alert the evil spirits guarding the estate, and they would inform the satanists of her presence. Try as she may, she couldn't stop the morbid scenarios that were crowding her mind. Knowing what would happen to her if she were to be caught, she desperately tried to push away the thoughts of sacrifice.

Pulling herself together, she decided to take a chance with the Range Rover. If the gates were closed, she would have to ram her way through. She was about to make a move across the forecourt, when the doors to Brising Manor were flung wide open. Sue gasped and swallowed hard. Standing on the top of the steps illuminated by the light from the hallway was the gaunt figure of the butler. He was the shape-shifting demon that had cast a spell against them in the anteroom at Brising Manor on the night of the sabbat, the same demon that had sacrificed Tony's daughters. Try as she may, Sue could not quell the thoughts of hate that were raging through her mind. Fear choked in her throat as she looked at the butler. What had brought him out of the manor? Had her negative emotions given her away?

She heard the hiss of tyres on gravel. A dark car shot into view and parked outside the entrance. Two figures got out and raced towards the Range Rover. They were soon joined by the butler. Looking inside, one of them said, "There are two dead members of our coven in the back seat."

There was muttering that Sue couldn't quite make out. She shrank back as the butler turned his scrawny head towards the bushes and flicked out his tongue, sensing the vibrations in the air. Her eyes were drawn once again to the front door. Sue shuddered with fright as a dark shape appeared within the doorway. Feodora St Clair limped out onto the porch and, leaning on a cane, swept her gaze over the laurels. As the light fell on Feodora's face, Sue saw she had been disfigured by a stroke. The left side of her face was drooping like heated wax, while the other side twitched and grimaced.

The butler left the other two men. Gliding up the stairs, he started whispering to Feodora. An estate vehicle pulled up beside the other car, and the butler helped Feodora down the steps and into the passenger seat. Then he got into the vehicle himself. Driving across the forecourt, he turned into the driveway and drove towards the gates. Serving boys were closing the entrance, and the light was cut off, leaving only a crimson tide of shadows on the porch steps.

Sue felt a sense of relief. The satanists were leaving, which would make her escape from the estate easier. She noted that Tony wasn't with them, and wondered if the satanists had taken him somewhere else.

Looking around the car park before she left the laurels, she saw the two men removing the bodies from the Range Rover. While their backs were turned, she stepped onto the flagged pathway that ran alongside the tennis courts. Hurrying forward in the moonlight, she saw the shadow of a hedge looming up in front of her. As she got closer, she saw an open gateway and, walking through it, took cover in the woodland beyond. Jim had told her there was a trail through the woods. Looking round, she searched the grounds. A few yards away, she saw a faint trail leading off into a copse.

Sue followed the path through the keeper's enclosure and into the woodland beyond. *The side door to the estate should be on the other side of the woodland,* she thought. Hastening her step, she saw the wall of the estate suddenly loom up in front of her. Cautiously approaching the lichen-blasted stone, she noticed the side door was ajar. A sense of relief flooded her. She had made it to the gate without being detected. The first thing she would do when she got back onto the road was to go to Hockham's Bridge and call the police.

Pulling the door open, Sue stepped through it onto a muddy track.

Her thoughts of escape were shattered in an instant when she saw a Range Rover parked by the side of the wall. Feodora was standing in front of the vehicle leaning on her cane, with one of the hideous bat-winged demons from the sabbat perched upon her shoulder.

Sue shrank back. She tried to turn and run back in to the estate, but the way was blocked by a serving boy with a revolver in his hand.

The knowledge that she was trapped sent Sue's mind spinning uncontrollably into the blackness of despair.

She felt a cold hand grab her wrist, and she was violently swung around. In a paroxysm of horror, she saw the butler's triumphant glowing eyes just inches from her face. Feodora limped up to her.

"We meet again, bitch," she muttered through the side of her mouth. "Did you think you could try to kill me at the sabbat and get away with it? Your riff-raff friends have been quite costly, and you will pay in torment and in blood." Drool ran out of the side of her mouth. "I will have my revenge, on you and the interfering policeman. There will be a double sacrifice, and your blood will be used to power a new set of ruby eyes for our master Zugalfar."

Visions of the arch-demon burst into Sue's mind. She whimpered as the full impact of what was in store for her flooded her awareness.

Another Range Rover pulled up, and two men got out.

"We've got a bitch to whet your appetites," Feodora mumbled, jerking the right side of her body like she was fucking. "But Alfredo, our much esteemed high priest, is first." She paused. "When you have finished using her, take the bitch to the dungeons." Thrusting her distorted face into Sue's, Feodora wiped her drool on Sue's lips. "Drink up," she mouthed.

"Hold her," the butler hissed to the two men, "while I help our lady Lilith into the vehicle."

Sue shrieked and squirmed as the men sandwiched her in between them. Her chest started to constrict and she began to hyperventilate. She felt their hands feeling her body, and their hot mouths sucking on her face. In a paroxysm of fear, she saw the butler advancing towards her. In his hand was the wooden phallus he had used to rape Tony's daughters.

Her body went into a shaking spasm as the butler began ripping off her clothes. The men were laughing and making comments, but she couldn't understand them. Reality was receding. Her mind numbed as the butler pushed her to the ground and, forcing her legs apart, began brutally raping her with the wooden phallus.

CHAPTER 9

UNREQUITED LOVE

Jim knew Emma and Sue were upset with him for drinking the brandy, but he'd had enough of what was going on and had just wanted to blot out the ongoing horror that had become his life. Maybe the others could cope with the terrifying events of the last few days, but he could not. His nerves were buckling under the strain; he couldn't take anymore. He knew he was drunk, but so what?

Knowing that Emma and Omar were in the house waiting for Trevelyan, he walked unsteadily around the side of the barn, and made his way to the stone wall at the end of the property. Clambering over the wall, he sat down, leant his head against the stones, and started mulling over his feelings.

He thought back to the time he had first met Emma. Maggie had been the one who introduced him to her. Maggie knew he was out of work and looking for a job, so she had recommended him to Emma, who had just moved in next door and was trying to get her house and greenhouses repaired.

He realised that he had fallen in love with Emma at first sight. He also realised that she didn't share his feelings. They got on well and had started a market business together, but in spite of the flowers he bought her and the dinners he had made, she always treated him like a brother. He had hoped that their friendship would develop into a love affair, but his plan had gone awry when Trevelyan arrived. The faerie had embroiled Emma in the understandings of her faerie heritage and her mission as a warrior of air from the fifth dimension, thereby putting the kybosh on Jim's romantic aspirations.

As a result of Trevelyan's interference in their lives, Jim had been parasitised by sexual demons, and had tried to rape Emma on several occasions. The dreams he had that they could be a couple had been shattered, and his association with her had turned his life into a nightmare.

The understanding that Trevelyan was taking Emma and Omar into Faerie and leaving him behind began to bother Jim. He felt resentful. They had just left him to fend for himself, and he felt rejected and alone. It was true that he wasn't a powerful seer like Omar, but he had saved Emma from Zugalfar when she had sleepwalked to the ruined church. He'd also done his best to protect her, at the expense of his own well-being.

He knew in the back of his mind that Trevelyan didn't trust him because of his sexual attacks upon Emma. He reasoned that he was the weak link in the chain that bound them all together, and that his lack of control over his mind was the reason they were not going to take him with them into Faerie. The knowledge that he had become a liability to Emma and a threat to the Green made him feel even more useless and depressed.

His memory of the last few hours was foggy, but he remembered Emma telling him he couldn't take her car to help Sue because he was drunk, and then Sue slamming out of the room saying she was going to dump the Range Rover on her own. He might have been drunk, but she was reckless, he told himself. But still, he had a pang of guilt. He had told Sue he would go with her to the quarry, but he had let her down when she needed him the most. Everything had turned to shit. He wished he was safely out of the chaos and misery that had erupted into reality. He wanted his life back and wished he had never gotten involved with Emma in the first place. Anyway, he told himself, he wasn't good enough for her, and his vision of them being together from the start had been an unrealistic dream.

The effects of the brandy were telling on him; he began to feel dizzy and sick. He felt himself leaning over. And then, tumbling to the ground, he blacked out.

When Jim woke up, the sun was high in the sky. He passed his hand gropingly across his face and rubbed his eyes. Memory came flooding back, and he realised he'd been out cold for hours. Anxiously looking at his hand, he saw with relief that the peridot ring was still upon his finger. In his drunken state he could have easily taken it off and fallen prey to the sexual demons that were tracking him. Getting up, he stretched and looked around. The hills glowed green, the meadows were in flower, and he could hear the babbling of a brook, but the natural beauty of the land was lost on him and did little to improve his spirits. Climbing over the wall, he went back to the house to see if Sue was all right.

"Sue! Em!" he called when he got into the kitchen. There was no response. The house was quiet. Realising that Emma and Omar had already left with Trevelyan and gone into Faerie, he wondered where Sue was. He noticed uneasily that the Aga was out. Looking out the window, he saw that the animals, including the geese and chickens, were still shut up in the barn. He began to feel anxious. Sue would not have left them locked up for so long if she were around. He ran upstairs to see if she was sleeping, but the bedroom was empty.

Knowing Sue would never leave the animals unattended, Jim realised that something had prevented her return. Devils Bowl was only fourteen miles away, and Sue had been missing for over fifteen hours. He started to worry about what had happened to her. If she had been in a serious accident on the way to the quarry, he felt sure someone would have contacted the sanctuary by now. Suddenly realising there would have been no one in the house to answer any calls, he swiftly checked the answering machine. The only message was from Woody, telling Sue that he and Gillian were back. Jim saw Sue's cell phone on the sideboard. He realised that in her irrational state of mind, she had forgotten to take it with her when she left. As a result, she wouldn't have been able to contact him if she needed help.

Sitting down at the kitchen table, he tried to clear his mind. There were two other possibilities, he thought. One was that Sue had not gotten out of the Range Rover in time and had gone over the edge into the quarry, and the other was that she could have broken a leg or an ankle when she jumped out of the vehicle. He would go and look for her, but first he had to find someone to watch the sanctuary and look after things. He remembered Sue talking about her friends Woody and Gillian, and he wondered if their telephone number was in Sue's address book. If he could find it, he would ask them to tend to the animals while he went in search of her.

Going back to the sitting room, he found the address book next to the telephone. Quickly flicking through the pages, he found Woody's cell number. His hands were shaking as he dialled the number. The phone rang and rang. Jim prayed

Woody would pick up. He sighed with relief when he heard Woody's voice on the other end of the line.

"Woody, my name's Jim," he said, introducing himself. "I'm a friend of Sue's. I 'eard 'er mention you, so I thought I'd better tell you that Sue left Greenfern last night and 'asn't returned. Do you think you could come over to the sanctuary and look after the animals while I look for 'er?"

Jim put the phone down. Woody and his girlfriend were coming straight over.

He went into the kitchen and made himself a cup of tea while he waited for Sue's friends to arrive. He sat down at the table and started blaming himself for Sue's disappearance. If he had gone with her, he could have prevented her from doing anything hasty or reckless, and if she had been injured, he could have called an ambulance. *Too late for that now,* he thought. His mission was to find her if he could.

A while later, he heard the sound of a car pull up outside. Opening the kitchen door, he saw a young ginger-haired man and a pretty blonde woman hurrying towards him.

"Hello, I'm Woody," the man said. "This is my girlfriend Gillian."

They came inside and sat down at the table.

"You said Sue was missing," Woody said anxiously. "Where did she go? She hasn't been arrested, has she?"

"I don't know," Jim answered. He couldn't tell them that she'd gone to dump a Range Rover with two bodies inside, and he didn't want to stress them unnecessarily with Sue's disappearance when there was a chance she might come back.

"If you could stay 'ere and look after the animals, I'll go and look for 'er."

Woody looked at him curiously. "How do you know Sue?"

"I went 'unt sabbin with 'er for years," Jim responded.

"Then after blood sports was banned, I moved to Basingstoke and we lost touch. I was in the area a couple of days ago, so I stopped in for a visit."

Woody's face brightened. "It's a pity you moved. We could have done with your help around here. Blood sports might be illegal on the books, but the fuckers are still out there with their hounds killing what they can."

"Instead of prosecuting them for breaking the law, the police protect them," Gillian added.

Jim thought about the chief constable and other high-ranking police officers protecting Giles Kingsbury and his coven. In this world, money, not compassion or decency, did the talking.

"Perhaps she had a call to go and help an animal in distress," Woody said. "She does a lot of rescue work, but she's been gone too long. She would have brought any injured animal straight back here."

"You know Sue," Jim said. "She might have broken into an animal research station somewhere and gotten caught."

Woody look worried. "Did she say anything to you before she left the house?"

"Actually, I was 'ittin' the brandy pretty 'ard. I was drunk when she left," Jim admitted. He felt a flush come to his face and felt guilty once again that he'd let Sue go to the quarry on her own. "If she doesn't show up tonight, could you stay 'ere and look after the animals?"

Woody glanced at Gillian, who nodded. "I think we ought to stay here until Sue gets back," she agreed. "We're both on the dole and live at home. We'll just have to let our mums know we are staying here to look after the animals while Sue's away. We can stay as long as necessary. We've helped Sue a lot with the animals; we know what to do."

Jim felt a sense of relief. At least the animals at the sanctuary would be taken care of.

"If you 'ear anythin' about Sue, call me," Jim said. Taking a scrap of paper from his pocket, he wrote down his own cell number and the phone number at Emma's house.

"If you don't know where Sue went, where are you going to start looking?" Gillian asked.

"First I thought I might enquire at the police station," Jim answered, "to see if she was arrested." Jim felt he had to distract Woody and Gillian with a plausible explanation of Sue's disappearance so that he wouldn't worry them further.

Woody nodded. "That's a good idea. Anyway, we're here, and we'll stay until Sue returns. Let us know if you hear anything."

Jim left the house with mixed feelings. He hadn't wanted to lie to them, but what else could he do? He didn't know them well enough to trust them with the truth. All he needed was to have them looking after the sanctuary so he could get on with trying to find Sue.

For their safety, the less they knew, the better. Jim hoped that for Woody and Gillian's sake the sanctuary would not be attacked by satanists again. In his sad reality, hope was all he had to hang on to.

Emma's car was in the car park. Remembering that he had left the keys in the ignition when he had come back from Brising Manor, he went over to her car. Looking through the window, he saw the keys were gone. Opening the door, he quickly searched the console and glove compartment. The keys were not there. Emma must have taken them with her to prevent him from driving the car while he was drunk. He suddenly remembered the spare key he had taped on the inside of the back bumper. Emma was always misplacing her keys, and he had put one there in case she lost them altogether. Going to the back of the car, he took out the key. Then, getting into the driver's seat, he started the engine.

His anxiety mounted as he drove through Denhampstead and took the road to Devils Bowl. There was only one road that ran past the quarry. He knew he was on the route that Sue had taken. If she had succeeded in safely dumping the Range Rover, she would have had to walk back to the sanctuary. Thinking she may have been injured and fallen down, he checked the ditches on both sides of the road for any sign of her. He felt anxious and tense as he got to the muddy track that led up to the top of the quarry.

He noticed immediately that there were no fresh tyre prints on the track. Sue hadn't been there. Alarmed, he drove to the top of the hill and, leaving the car running, got out and peered into the quarry. There was no vehicle at the bottom, and no traces of a fire.

For a moment he was utterly confused. Then he began to panic. *Where could she have gone?* he asked himself.

He got back into the car and drove slowly down the steep hill to the road. He didn't have a clue what to do next or where to start looking for her. Driving back to Denhampstead, he had a niggling thought that Sue might have gone to Brising Manor on a reckless mission to rescue Tony, but he talked himself out of the idea. As crazy as Sue was, Brising Manor was the last place she would go.

His mind was in turmoil as he drove along the high street. He wished he had Emma and Omar to talk to. He had never felt so alone in all his life. He needed time to think and try to get his scrambled brain together.

Passing the Red Lion pub, he thought he would go in for a drink. He knew he shouldn't, but he had a hangover; a quick pint would help him clear his mind and bolster up his courage. It was early in the evening, so he'd be able to find a quiet spot to sit and think things through.

He pulled onto the forecourt and had a quick look up and down the street in case there were any of Brising Manor's estate vehicles nearby. Then he thought better of parking in such an exposed place. Emma's car could easily be spotted from the high street.

The Red Lion was an old coaching inn. Driving along the alleyway, Jim parked in the courtyard at the rear, out of view of the main road. Going through the back door, he went into the saloon bar. The room was warm and softly lit, with ancient black beams stretched across a low smoke-stained plaster ceiling.

The bar was empty. Going to a small counter, Jim ordered a pint of bitter. He was glad there was no one in the bar. Glancing round, he saw a small table by the window that overlooked the street. From there he could keep watch on the road outside for any sign of Brising Manor's vehicles. If Sue had abandoned the Range Rover in the vicinity and it had been found, workers from the estate might be driving the vehicle back to the estate.

Sitting down at the table by the window, Jim took a big slurp of beer and wondered where to start searching for Sue. He thought the best way to begin was to enquire at the hospital and then go to the police station.

His hangover was wearing off and he was feeling a little better. The pint had done its job. Now he was ready for another one. He got himself another drink. As he was crossing the room to go back to his seat, the door to the saloon bar opened. Two men dressed in barber jackets and corduroy trousers came in and sat down on stools on either side of the counter.

One of them was burly and red-faced, and the other was tall, thin, and chinless. They started talking to the landlord about a country sports fair that had been arranged for the following Saturday. Jim began to get annoyed. Their voices were loud; he wished they'd shut the fuck up and let him think. He would drink his pint and go. He was about halfway through his beer when he heard the red-faced man say to the landlord, "Did you hear the news about the sinkhole swallowing the family chapel at Brising Manor? The owner, Giles Kingsbury, and lots of his guests were killed."

Jim, pricking up his ears, put his head down so the men wouldn't know he was eavesdropping on their conversation.

"I heard about the sinkhole on the news, but I didn't know Mr Kingsbury was amongst the dead," the landlord replied, shaking his head.

"I was in the Gables pub at Hockham's Bridge at lunchtime," the man went on. "Art, the gamekeeper from Brising Manor, was in the bar. I overheard him talking. He said that Giles was having one of his get-togethers on Saturday night, and there were as many as fifty people that got swallowed up by the sinkhole."

"Fifty people? That's a lot," the landlord responded with surprise. "Sinkholes seem to be happening all across the world. I think it's all the fracking that's to blame. Something bad has to happen when they keep drilling holes into the ground." He paused and then said, "There's been a spate of little earthquakes too. Crazy is what I call it."

"Well, let's hope a sinkhole doesn't open up and swallow the pub. I don't want to lose my watering hole," the shorter of the two said, laughing.

"Well," the taller of the two retorted, "we're all using gas and petrol, and in this day and age it pays to be self-sufficient.

We don't want to rely on foreign nations for gas and oil. What happens if they cut us off and put the price up? You'd be complaining about that, I'm sure."

"All I'm saying," the landlord countered, "is, what's the bloody use of gas if we're all dead and buried in an earthquake?"

There was an awkward silence for a moment.

The red-faced man put his glass on the counter and leant towards the landlord. "And that's not all," he said. Jim saw him glance across at him to see if he was listening. Quickly turning his head away, Jim looked out of the window. Straining his ears, he heard the man say, "Two bodies were found this morning in one of the estate Range Rovers. They'd been shot."

"Shot!" the landlord repeated in surprise. "What's this world coming to?"

The man nodded. "Art said they were two workers from the estate. The Range Rover had been stolen, and then it suddenly showed up in the car park. The bodies were in the back seat covered up with sacks."

Jim stiffened and swallowed hard. The bodies had been found. He felt a sensation of bristling fear and dread as he realised that Sue had dumped the vehicle at Brising Manor and had been caught. Swallowing the rest of his beer, he went out to the car. If Sue had been captured, he certainly wasn't going to go to Brising Manor to rescue her.

He sat in the car for a moment trying to deal with the grief that was welling up inside him. He had to report to the police that Tony and Sue were missing. Someone had to listen. After all, Tony was a chief inspector and would probably have been missed by now. In the circumstances, it was the only choice Jim had. He prayed he'd find an officer who was not connected to the satanists at Brising Manor.

He drove along the high street. As he got close to the police station, he saw a black Mercedes pulling into the car park. Jim slowed down to get a better look. He noticed there was a dent on the wing, and he recognised the car as the one that had tried to ram him and had also blocked Tony's escape from Brising Manor. A thin man with sandy-coloured hair got out and went through a side door into the police station.

Jim took a deep breath. The copper was a satanist. He had to get out of there, and fast. It occurred to him that his number plate might already have been circulated. If the car were to be seen, he would run the risk of being stopped by the police and questioned. He knew he would be set up and would probably be arrested as a suspect in the murder of the men from the estate. The more he thought about it, the more he was sure that to get rid of their problem, the satanists would try to pin a murder rap on him, Emma, and Omar. *If they ever come back*, he thought despondently of Emma and Omar.

It took Jim an hour to get back to Basingstoke. On the way, he thought about what he would do with Emma's car. The dent in the side had to be fixed quickly, and a new wing mirror needed to be put on. He had a friend who had a garage and body shop nearby Emma's house. He would take it there. Taking out his cell phone, he dialled the number.

"Dennis," he said when the call was answered. "Someone ran into my car while it was parked and dented the side panel. Do you think you could repair the damage?" Hearing an affirmative, Jim said, "Thanks! I'll drop the car off in a few minutes."

Dennis was waiting for him on the forecourt when he pulled up.

"Your car's taken quite a bang," he commented, inspecting the damage. He smiled at Jim. "I'm not busy at the moment, so you're in luck. It's going to cost a bit though."

"That's all right," Jim responded. "I'm flush right now. Perhaps you could respray the car a brighter colour so it will be easier to see. Maybe red or yellow, but as it is, dull green is obviously askin' for another accident."

"I don't know why they paint cars green," Dennis answered, shaking his head.

Jim felt a modicum of relief. At least Emma's car was out of sight for a few days and wouldn't be so easily recognised by the thugs from Brising Manor once it was repaired and repainted a different colour. He had told Dennis it was his car that was damaged. For Dennis's safety the less he knew the better. Jim doubted there would be a police investigation of any substance. The cover-up at Brising Manor was already underway. Feodora St Clair and the chief constable would not want to draw public attention to Tony and his daughters' disappearance. Jim's fear was that the satanists would try and murder him and Emma.

"I'm back," Dennis said, rejoining Jim. "Do you want a lift home?"

"That would be great."

A bit later, Dennis pulled into Emma's driveway. "Call me in a couple of days," he said. With a wave of his hand, he drove away.

Jim went inside. Going to the bathroom, he looked into the mirror. The face that stared back at him was almost unrecognisable. His skin was lined, there was stubble on his chin, and his braided hair hung greasily down his back. He quickly turned away. He seemed to have aged twenty years in just a few days.

He took a shower, washed his hair, and then shaved and put on fresh clothes. The shower did little to calm his mind. He felt depressed and alone, and wondered when Emma would return from Black Head. The idea occurred to him again that she might never return. Tony and Sue were gone. It appeared that none of them were safe. The more he thought about the last few days, the more depressed he became. He wandered aimlessly around the house. Needing to prop himself up with a drink and knowing Emma's liquor cabinet was empty, he decided to go next door and cadge a bottle of spirits from Maggie. She always had liquor in the house.

Jim had known Maggie and Dave for years. Maggie had known his mother. After his father had left the night before his twelfth birthday and run off with another woman, she had been a great psychological support to both of them. As a teenager, Jim had started drinking and taking drugs to help cope with the trauma of abandonment. Maggie had always been there for him, and stood by him in his darkest hours. She had bailed him out of jail several times and had never talked down to him like the alcohol counsellors the court had assigned to treat him. Maggie understood him.

Maggie was weeding the garden when Jim walked through the gate. She looked up as he walked towards her.

"Hello, Jim," she said, staring at him. "Are you all right?"

Jim hesitated and tried to smile. He didn't answer straightaway. He could see the concern in her face. Even the shower and the shave couldn't hide the ravages of the horror that had engulfed him. He swallowed hard. Passing his hand over his hair with a nervous gesture, he said hoarsely, "I'm just tired." He sniffed. "It's been a long day."

Maggie couldn't believe that in a week Jim had changed from a strapping bloke full of life and energy to a drained and haggard man with bloodshot sunken eyes. It was obvious that something awful had happened to him. He looked like he'd been hitting the bottle hard. She wondered if his falling off the wagon had anything to do with Emma.

"How's Emma?" she said, trying to draw him out.

Jim was at a loss for words. He didn't know how Emma was. She could be dead for all he knew.

"She's stayin' on in Brighton for a few days." Quickly changing the subject, he asked, "'Ow's the market business goin'?"

"We've sold out every time, and not only your vegetables but also our eggs, honey, and preserves." She paused. "Have you seen your garden? It's amazing."

Jim shook his head. He found it hard to switch realities. With the horror of Sue's and Tony's captures still fresh in his mind, he was in no mood to engage in small talk about the garden. He wanted to drink and forget about everything.

"You don't 'appen to 'ave any brandy in your 'ouse? I could 'ave. I'm exhausted. A drink will 'elp me sleep. I'll buy you a replacement bottle tomorrow."

Maggie knew there was something dreadfully wrong in Jim's life. He seemed to have a haunted look about him. She wasn't going to push him to tell her what was troubling him, but it was obvious he was trying to drink away a problem.

Maggie nodded. "Sure. Come on in."

Jim didn't want to go into the house. He felt he couldn't hold himself together and would break down under her questions. Maggie was kind and open-hearted, and even though he needed someone to talk to for advice, he knew that for her own safety, he had to keep silent about what had happened to him and Emma.

Emma's cats suddenly appeared from the bushes in front of Maggie's house and started rubbing round his legs. Relieved by the diversion, he bent down and stroked them while Maggie disappeared inside. The sound of the cats purring calmed him and provided a smidgen of something safe and familiar, which he desperately needed after all he had been through.

Maggie returned with a bottle of gin. "This is all I have," she said, handing him the bottle. She looked at him searchingly. "Why don't you come in for a minute?"

"Thanks, Maggie, but no," Jim responded. "I just want to rest."

"Well, if there's anything Dave and I can do for you, don't hesitate to call."

"I won't," he said, managing a smile.

Turning on his heel, Jim started back to Emma's house. He unscrewed the cap from the bottle of gin. As he walked through the back gate and into the garden, he started swigging from the bottle. He would think about what he was going to do later. Right now the only way to block out his fear was to get drunk and make hell go away.

Jim went into the house. It felt lonely and cold. Going into the sitting room, he sat down on the sofa. He was exhausted. The psychic horror and terrible events of the last few days were taking a heavy toll on him. He realised that he had to get away from Emma to save his sanity. She had once been the centre of his dreams, but now she was the source of his misery and despair.

His only alternative, he thought, was to leave her employment and look for another job. He decided he would stay at the house until she returned from Faerie and until her car had been fixed. Then he would tell her he was quitting the garden and market business, and that if she wanted to carry on, Maggie and Dave would help her. Anyway, he told himself, it wouldn't be his problem anymore. Leaning his head against one of the high scrolled arms of the sofa, he thought about his situation. It wouldn't be easy for him to find work in his present condition. He could barely hold himself together.

Jim took a long swig of gin. It burnt as it went down his throat, but he didn't care. The liquor was a means to an end and would soon put him to sleep. His reliance on booze to get through the day had cost him many jobs, whereas working for Emma had brought stability to his life—that is until Trevelyan had come upon the scene. He could hardly believe that in the space of a week, he had murdered two people and was the accessory to two more killings. He had almost been caught and killed himself.

He thought about Emma and the sexual fantasies he had woven around her. Images of her naked body and what it would be like to make love to her had consumed him for days before the sabbat. Ever since his run-in with the succubus on Dragonsbury Ring, he had found himself masturbating daily. The thought crossed his mind that he might have been possessed by the incubus that had tried to take Emma through the wall into the temple of Cybele underneath her house. Jim took a short breath. An incubus attachment would account for his uncontrollable sexual urges towards Emma.

Jim shivered. The thought of sex with Emma chilled him. She was no longer the human Em he loved and lusted after. She had become aloof and cold. He hoped his lack of desire for her would deter the sexual demons that plagued him, leading them to go off in search of other prey. Perhaps a normal life would be possible again.

He took another long pull of gin and wrinkled up his nose. Gin wasn't one of his favourite spirits, but it would get him blotto, and that was all he cared about.

The drunker Jim got, the more resentful he became. He blamed Trevelyan for taking Emma away from him, ruining his life, and crashing all his dreams. The knowledge that Sue and Tony would still be with them if he hadn't introduced Sue to Emma only inflamed him further. Draining the bottle, he felt himself falling off the sofa. With a bump, he hit the floor.

CHAPTER 10

THE MIND OF THE SEA

Aine, daughter of Manannan Mac Lir, was returning from Crann Conagh to Erin's Point in a bid to join the House of Air. The Company of the Key had hired a boat at the port and were on their way to the island of Inishark to search for the thief who had stolen the key made of air. On the way to Erin's Point, Aine had been attacked by goblins. After killing the goblin chief Grad, she reached her destination.

After exchanging talismans with her brother Nala, she had gained the ability to shape-shift at will without the need to feed on mortals. She and Nala were free of their father's curse, and their combined water element connected them both to the mind of the sea and to everything living in the ocean, streams, lakes, and rivers. Standing on the quayside, Aine had shape-shifted into reptile form, and then dived into the water. As she swam towards the boat, she had seen her father's galleon cutting through the waves. She realised that Manannan had been empowered by the Cathac and, leaving his underwater city, had tried to intercept and destroy the House of Air. Her father had seen her in the water and attacked her with his love vipers in an effort to take her soul and possess her for eternity. High Faerie warriors from the fifth dimension had come to her aid, and together with the faerie host and Nala's strength, they had driven Manannan back to his slime-ridden city in Under-Sea.

Not knowing the whereabouts of the boat carrying the company, Aine dived down into the depths looking for survivors. As she swam towards the island, she became acutely aware of the consciousness of the sea. The voices of seaweed, crabs, lobsters, octopi, and fish were all equally hers. Desperate to find the House of Air, Aine imaged the faces of Kilfannan and Kilcannan and sent a resonance of finding into the sea. All the sea creatures would know her mind; their eyes would become her eyes, and they would lead her to the missing members of the company.

Snaking towards the island, she saw images of the wreck through the eyes of a dolphin that had been in the water where the boat capsized. She saw the company swept from the deck and into the raging sea. Suddenly she heard Nala's warning voice speaking in her mind. The Cathac had freed himself from the Giant's Cliffs and was upon the sea. Aine broke the surface and saw the luminous heaving coils of the Cathac on the horizon. Fear had seized her. Even her triumph over her father did little to stay her terror of the Cathac. Diving down into the depths, she propelled herself towards the island. Through the eyes of seals, she saw the ocean rising in tumult, and blasts of fire and hissing steam blanketing the sea and sky. From the whispering of crabs, she learnt that bodies from the wreck had been washed up on the island. Not knowing if the bodies were alive or dead, she swam as fast as she could to the beach, hoping to find Kilfannan and the Company of the Key.

The sun was rising as she left the water. Morphing into faerie form, she stood on the beach and looked out to sea. The ocean was calm, but she sensed the odour of burnt flesh upon the wind. There was no sign of the Cathac. She wondered if the blasts of fire and steam she had seen through the seal's eyes had driven him back to the Giant's Cliffs.

Aine heaved a sigh of relief that the Cathac had disappeared, but she could still feel the tingling vibrations of the terror and despair that had overcome her senses when she had seen the monster silhouetted against the dark horizon.

Turning her thoughts to finding the company, she checked her belt. Her weapons were still there. Drawing her sword, she moved along the beach searching for any sign of Kilfannan, Kilcannan, and the rest of her friends.

She had only taken a few strides when she heard the sound of a gruff voice cursing up ahead behind an outcrop in the cliff face. She stopped for a moment and listened. The voice was low and raspy but did not have the ugly vibration of goblin talk. Cautiously rounding the outcrop, she saw Duirmuid sitting on the sand nursing his wounds.

"Duirmuid!" she cried out. "Thank the stars, thou art alive." She ran to him and helped him up.

"Aine!" he said, hugging her. "Meself is lucky to be alive. I can't swim and managed to cling on to a piece of wood that broke off from the boat. I was waiting for the light to come before I went along the beach to see if meself could find any more of the company alive." He hesitated. "Or dead," he added.

"What hath happened to the House of Air?" she asked anxiously.

"Meself knows not," he answered, shaking his head. "The sea swept us away from one another."

"Take heart," Aine said, looking at the brightening sky.

"Let us search for our friends on the beach beyond the headland."

They walked swiftly along the sand and round the headland. Bits and pieces of wreckage from the boat had been washed up on the shore, but there was no sign of life apart from some plate-like jellyfish thrown up by the storm.

As they rounded the cliff face, they saw further along the beach two bodies bound in tentacles of seaweed. The forms were flopped like rag dolls at the water's edge on a pile of tangled fishing net.

Aine broke into a run, with Duirmuid close behind. Reaching the nets, they ripped the seaweed from the bodies.

"'Tis Kilcannan and Cor-cannan," Aine said, wiping away the phosphorescent slime that covered their pale faces. "'Tis the work of water serpents," she said in dismay. "They bind their prey like a spider binds a fly."

Crouching down, she touched their hands. Their skin felt cold and clammy. As she looked into their faces, she sensed a shimmering aura of hungry hate surrounding them. Aine passed her hand across their eyes so she could see what had possessed them. In the space around them, she could see the slit eyes of a ghosted water serpent glaring at her.

Using her High Faerie sight, she looked into Under-Sea. In the murky water she saw two huge crested serpents coiled together. They were watching her. Hate blazed from their eyes. Their fanged mouths were open, ready to strike her if she entered the sea. She knew the sea serpents were not going to give up the sylphs without a fight. They would protect their prey at all costs, and would kill her if she tried to stop them. While the sylphs were at the waterline, they were in peril. She had to get Kilcannan and Cor-cannan away from the water's edge and high up on the sand.

Desperately looking round the beach for a place they could be bathed and be safe from the serpents, she saw a pool at the base of the cliff that had been filled with water during the tempest of the tide.

"Duirmuid," she said urgently, "the moment I go into the water, grab Kilcannan and Cor-cannan and take them to the rock pool yonder." She pointed to the bottom of the cliff. "Wash away the foul slime from their bodies, and then lay them on the sand and guard them until I return. Be swift, for every instant they are at the water's edge, they are in peril."

Aine knew what she had to do. "'Tis plain that the serpents are not going to give up their prey without a fight," she said. "I must enter the sea and kill them."

Duirmuid looked at her in concern. "Be careful, Mistress Aine," he said. "The company are scattered. We cannot afford to lose ye."

Putting her hand on the hare talisman, Aine touched Nala's mind and asked him to transfer his spiritual force to strengthen her. The serpents were the seed of Nephelum, the father of all sea serpents. Nephelum had been created by her father's sorcery. She knew that the instant she went into the water, they would be aware of her intent. She had to be fast. The serpents were cunning and their bite was deadly.

She felt her brother's presence. As his spiritual energy flowed through her, she stepped into the water. Steadying her mind, she shape-shifted into a tiny electric eel and darted into the sea.

As she approached the sea serpents, they released clouds of acid-yellow venom to obscure her view, but the sea was her mind and she knew their position from their hateful vibrations. If they thought they could hide and attack her by surprise, they were mistaken. She was too small and fast for them to see.

Diving down underneath their tails, she imaged herself into a sawfish. Wheeling around, she charged at their coiling bodies. With a swing of her head, she swept the saw through their writhing forms and cut them in two. Whirling round, she charged again and hacked at their quivering bodies. Angry hissing erupted through the water. She was suddenly blinded by an acrid cloud of fluid that poured out from the wounds she had inflicted.

Diving into clearer water, she saw the serpents gathering their dismembered limbs and recombining back into their vile forms. Before she could attack again, the serpents separated and, lashing their tails, charged at her from two directions. Their fangs were striking the water around her. Knowing that if she were to be bitten, she would be paralysed, bound, and destroyed, Aine called again on Nala's awareness to support her courage.

Shape-shifting into an octopus, she caught one of the serpents in her tentacles as it tried to bite her. Breaking the surface of the water, she threw the wriggling, snapping serpent high onto the beach. Out of the sea it would be weakened. And she hoped that Duirmuid would see it and kill it. She heard Nala's voice in her mind telling her that the only way to kill the serpents was to cut off their heads.

She suddenly felt a vibration in the water as the other snake mounted an attack. Fronds of seaweed came twisting like green snakes through the sea, coiling around her tentacles, trying to pin them to her side. Hiding in a cloud of ink, Aine morphed back into a swordfish and met the serpent head-on. The fanged mouth was open, just inches from her face. Raising the sword on her head, she chopped at the striking serpent and decapitated it.

Clouds of acid flooded into the water, burning her eyes until she could barely see. Swimming to the surface, she morphed into faerie form. If the seed of Nephelum had captured Kilcannan and Cor-cannan, she wondered if they also had Kilfannan. She sent her mind into the water for clues as to the whereabouts of Kilfannan and Fercle.

Aine heard the whispering of bladderwrack and kelp telling her that Kilfannan had been captured by the meresna. The siren mermaids had taken him to the grotto of Nephelum in the Giant's Cliffs.

Aine swallowed hard. The grotto was the cave where her father had created Nephelum by blood sorcery. Nephelum had been destroyed in the War of Separation, and the meresna had taken his dark, dripping cavern as their abode. The meresna clan was under the control of the Cathac. Aine knew the sirens would offer Kilfannan to the Cathac as a sacrifice. Her breath caught in her throat. If Kilfannan could not be rescued, then the HeartStar would fall and the Green would be no more.

Swimming to the shore, she heard the sea stars murmur of a fire geometric that had been found in the sand at the bottom of the sea by a seal man. *Fercle,* she thought. The water had extinguished his fiery breath, and only the cold fire of a dragon could restore him.

Gaining the beach, she saw Duirmuid sitting on the sand next to the still forms of Kilcannan and Cor-cannan. The severed head and limp body of a sea serpent was lying near him on the strand.

"The serpent will be seagull food," Duirmuid said as she joined them.

"Nay," Aine answered. "Gulls will not feed on the poisonous flesh of the seed of Nephelum. 'Twill only be the sun that can destroy their remains."

Gazing at the lifeless forms of Kilcannan and Cor-cannan lying on the sand, Aine saw that even though the sea serpents had been destroyed, their enchantment was still upon the sylphs. Knowing she would have to reverse the dark magic with a counter-water spell, she knelt down by their side and began to sing a calling song in the language of the water.

Duirmuid saw the outer spectrum colours of High Faerie surround Aine in a nimbus of glowing light. In her song he heard the sound of water falling, the babble of rushing streams, and the oceans battering against rock in the tumult of a storm. He thought he caught the sound of popping—the sound of water bubbles bursting—and then there was silence.

"Kilcannan and Cor-cannan, come out of the shadows," Aine commanded.

Kilcannan was the first to open his eyes. He sat up and, looking around in confusion, cried out, "Where am I? Where is Kilfannan? Where is my brother?" A wind blew up around him. His peridot eyes flashed with fire.

"He was lost at sea," Duirmuid said miserably.

"Nay! Kilfannan lives, for my breathing is not laboured," Kilcannan responded heatedly, getting to his feet. "We must find him! Come, Nephew," he said to Cor-cannan, taking his hand and helping him up. "We must find Kilfannan."

"Wait!" Aine cried out. "There is many an ill step taken in haste." She turned to Duirmuid, who was standing by. "Stay here with Kilcannan and Cor-cannan while I check the rest of the beach. Evil things may be abroad looking for any survivors of the shipwreck. This is the only stretch where anything can land. The rest of the island is sheer rock."

Aine said naught about what she had been told by the mind of the sea. If Kilcannan knew the danger his brother and the Green were in, he would summon the whirling downdraught and his mind would be in chaos. She could not afford to let that happen. They needed a steady mind if they were going to get off the island and get back safely to the mainland.

Kilcannan shivered in the cold dawn. A shadow was upon him. *Where is Kilfannan?* he called to the wind. He tried to remember the last time he saw his brother on the deck, but the shock of Manannan's return upon the sea and the boat capsizing had numbed his mind and he couldn't recall what had happened. He looked down at his belt. All his arms were missing. The diamond ring of resolution, fashioned by Sharn, dwarf lord of the Wicklow Mountains that Ke-enaan had gifted him had also disappeared. In a panic he checked his inside pocket for the Brax. To his relief, his fingers closed upon the little horseshoe.

"My weapons are gone," he said to Cor-cannan. "But thank the stars, I have the Brax."

"Mine too have been taken," Cor-cannan bemoaned.

"Arms can be replaced. Souls cannot," Duirmuid said. "Be thankful yees are still alive."

"How are we going to get off the island and back to land?" Cor-cannan asked Kilcannan. "Perhaps Kilfannan and the rest of the company have been swept inland by the flow tide and washed up on the mainland shore."

Kilcannan thought for a moment. "If we can find a hawthorn tree growing on the island, we can call Thorn-Haw for aid. He will be able to take us off the island. Come, let us search. Maybe there is one growing in the shelter of the rocks."

"Wait for Mistress Aine to return," Duirmuid said gruffly.

"There is safety in numbers. We do not know if enemies are abroad."

Aine checked the beach. Finding no trace of enemies, she ran up a steep path to the top of the cliffs and looked around. The island appeared to be empty. All she could hear was the noisy chatter of nesting birds and the sighing of the breeze amongst the rocks. There was no sign of a boat or of the archaeologists who had taken the thief to the island. She swiftly returned to the rest of the company.

"'Tis all clear," she reported.

"Aine! Let us search the island for a hawthorn tree," Kilcannan said. "If we can find one, we can call Thorn-Haw, and he will be able to take us to Ke-enaan's halls. The wizard will know how to find my brother."

Aine looked at the sky for any sign of spying birds that could reveal them to their enemies. Seeing nothing, she nodded in agreement.

They climbed up a steep path to the top of the cliffs into a bleak world of patchwork of grey stone and green turf.

"There are no trees on the island," Cor-cannan said, disconsolately looking round.

"Let us fan out across the island," Kilcannan urged. "'Twill be quicker. The sooner we are gone from this desolate place, the better."

Splitting up, they combed every nook and cranny in the rock-strewn grass. Kilcannan sniffed the wind searching for the perfume of hawthorn flowers floating on the airwaves. Following his nose, he set off across a grey limestone pavement. After a few minutes of searching, he found a tiny hawthorn sapling growing in a crevice. It had one little stem of budding flowers and a few small leaves.

"Over here!" Kilcannan shouted to the others. "I have found a hawthorn growing in a windbreak."

When they were all together, Kilcannan closed his eyes and, concentrating on Thorn-Haw, sent a plea for help onto the airwaves.

They heard a rustling sound. Thorn-Haw appeared. He looked from one to the other. "Greetings," he rustled. "Where art Kilfannan and Fercle?"

"They were lost when the boat capsized," Aine replied.

"My brother is also missing," Cor-cannan said anxiously.

"Fret not," Thorn-Haw rustled. "Cor-garran is safely at Black Head. Come! There is no time to lose. Hold hands."

When they were linked together, the faun took Aine's hand and pulled them through the sapling and out of another hawthorn tree growing on the Burren a few steps away from Ke-enaan's hidden door. The rock slid back as they stood upon the grass. Ke-enaan appeared. "Quick!" he said, beckoning to them. "There art many enemies upon the Burren to mark thy passage. Make haste!"

Aine was the last to enter. Standing in the shadow of the door, she took a quick glance around the hillside and down to the walled fields beyond. There was nothing moving save a hare. Taking the hare as a sign from her brother that all was well, she stepped inside the passage. As the door silently closed, she followed after the others.

"Brother!" Cor-cannan cried out in joy, seeing Cor-garran sitting by the fire with Doonvannan of the House of Doon. Swiftly joining him at the fireside, he embraced his brother. "'Tis good to see thee safe and sound. How did thee get to Black Head?"

"Liam the seal man found meself adrift in the sea," Cor-garran answered, a smile in his eyes. "He took me to his house made of shells on the seabed. He doctored my wounds and gave me liquor to set a fire in my heart. When I was rested, he brought me hither to the wizard's halls. What happened to thee, brother?"

"Kilcannan and meself were captured by vile serpents. And if Aine had not rescued us"—he paused—"we would hath been lost forever."

"Mistress Aine! 'Tis good to see thee safe," Doonvannan declared as she joined them at the fireplace. "For all roads of earth and water art perilous in the dark days that hath come upon us."

Cor-garran took Aine's delicate hand and kissed it. "My lady," he said. "The House of Air is in thy debt."

Aine's eyes sparkled. Forget-me-nots flowered in her face.

Cor-garran looked around the hall. "Where are Kilfannan and Fercle?" he asked anxiously.

"Liam the seal man heard rumours echoing through the sea that Kilfannan of the House of Air hast been captured by the meresna," Ke-enaan said to the company.

"'Tis not a rumour but a truth," Aine said, sitting down beside them. "The mind of the sea showed me that Kilfannan was taken by the meresna to the grotto of Nephelum."

A fey mood took Kilcannan. He shot a fiery glance at Aine. A wind blew down around him, jostling the bottles on the shelves and blowing the pages of manuscripts and tomes. "I asked thee about Kilfannan, and thou said you did not know," he said in a gust. "Why did thee not tell me the truth?"

"Cease, Kilcannan!" Ke-enaan's voice boomed throughout the hall.

Aine rose. The light of High Faerie shone around her. "'Twas love for thee that made me hold me tongue and keep counsel with meself," she said. "We were in peril. I could not risk that thou in thy torment might betray us to evil riding on the airwaves. Therefore I did not tell thee."

An emerald blush stained Kilcannan's cheeks. "I beg thy pardon, Mistress Aine."

"'Tis true, then, what the seal man said," Ke-enaan responded. "Fear not, Kilcannan. I asked Liam to spy on the grotto and see if he could find thy brother. When he returns, we will make a plan to rescue Kilfannan."

"I have lost my brother and my horse," Kilcannan said miserably. "Alas! All I love hast gone astray."

"Grieve not for thy horse," Doonvannan said, putting his hand supportively on Kilcannan's arm. "Finifar is in the meadow by the forge at Slieve Elva, as art all thy charges. Nala sent the horses to Doon after thou had taken to the skies on Finifar and Red Moon. Nemia found a way to escape from the stables at the Blue Buoy. With Finifar and Red Moon by her side, they travelled to me halls. I hath brought them here." Doonvannan glanced at Ke-enaan. "Where is Fercle?" he asked. "He is missing from the company."

Reaching into the pocket of his robe, Ke-enaan brought out a small translucent tetrahedron and showed it to them. "Liam found Fercle's geometric at the bottom of the sea not far from where the boat sank," he said. "The fire of Fercle's breath was extinguished by the water. I have his geometric, but we can do naught for Fercle until Braxach or Trax returns. Only the cold fire of dragons can breathe life into his geometric and return him to us."

Zarg brought wine. The company gathered round the hearth. The sylphs sat on one side of the flickering blue-flame fire; Ke-enaan and the rest of the company sat on the other.

"'Twould seem we are beset by peril on every hand," Ke-enaan said wearily, passing his hand across his brow. "If we cannot save Kilfannan, 'twill be the end for us all. The grotto of Nephelum resonates with the Cathac's hate. And at moonrise, Cthogg, Queen of the Meresna, will sacrifice Kilfannan on the bloody altar of Nephelum. 'Tis two hours to noontide. We hath time to make our plans." He sighed deeply. "I cannot go with thee on thy perilous journey to the grotto, for I have to make preparation for an attack upon my halls. Events are moving fast in the mortal world, and now our battle is at hand."

Aine frowned. "What hath happened in the world of humankind that would precipitate an attack upon Black Head?"

"Emma Cameron, the warrior of air, succeeded in her mission to retrieve the sapphire and gave it to Trevelyan for safekeeping," Ke-enaan replied. "'Twas our hope that he could take the sapphire beyond the five dimensions so the Cathac could not find it. Trevelyan made plea to the Ghrian Sidhe and Pa-za, Lord of Xonite, to take the sapphire and conceal it. They refused him, saying they had not the power to contain its glowing aura. Not knowing what else to do, Trevelyan brought the sapphire to my hall. We petitioned Uall MaCarn to secrete it in his world of eternal starlight. Uall agreed. I hid the sapphire in a secret vault beneath the forge, along with other power objects from an age long past. The light of the sapphire cannot be contained within the Faerie Worlds; its radiance is in flood upon the airwaves. The Cathac will have seen it. I fear that in the passing of the sun from one side to the other, the Cathac and his armies, led by Manannan and the demon lord Zugalfar, will lay siege to Black Head, for my hall and Slieve Elva are one in heart."

Ke-enaan's mind was full of dread and doubt as he thought about the dark sorcery that would herald the coming of the Cathac and Manannan to his halls. He and his Danaan brethren had fought the monsters in the War of Separation and defeated them. But that was an age ago. Stalwart mortals had fought alongside his people, and many clans had died in defence of the Green. But there were no human beings left to aid him. The third density had become the abode of demons, and mortal virtue had been replaced by vice, and love with hate. Ke-enaan knew his spiritual power was weakening. Demons walked upon the Burren, and the fate of Kilfannan and the HeartStar hung like a feeble thread on the sharp blade of undoing. He glanced at the sylphs. Their hearts were too innocent to enter the foul vibrations of Under-Sea. He feared for their survival. He wished he could go with them to the grotto, but he had to stay behind and make preparation for the attack that was soon to come.

Aine's voice roused him from his despair. He saw her looking at him keenly.

"When meself took to the sea to find the survivors of the wreck," she said, "I saw the Cathac free upon the waterway and my heart froze with terror. Focusing my mind on finding the company, I swam on, and saw a strange sight through the eyes of a seal. There was a great fire and smoke upon the ocean. When I reached the island, the Cathac had vanished from the sea. Doth thou know what happened?"

"'Twas Braxach that did battle with the Cathac," Ke-enaan answered. "The dragon drove the Cathac back into the Giant's Cliffs, but for how long he will remaineth there I doth not know." He paused and looked at them sadly. "I knowest naught of the dragon's fate, for he hath disappeared. I fear he is at the bottom of the sea and his flame extinguished."

The sylphs cried out in grief when they heard of Braxach's fall, and then a heavy silence descended on the room.

The stillness was suddenly broken by the sound of light footfalls on the stairs leading up from the underground river. The perfume of hyacinth stole into the room.

Aine leapt to her feet. "Nala!" she cried out in joy as her brother appeared. Starlight glimmered in his slicked-back nighted hair, and the flowers of love-lies-bleeding were blooming in his face. A sword was girthed around his waist. The fiery light of water rising gleamed from his turquoise eyes.

"Lord of Black Head," Nala said, bowing to Ke-enaan. Raising his arm, he put his clenched hand across his heart. "Meself brings news of Braxach, the dragon of Gorias."

Ke-enaan paled. "Tell on!"

"Meself was on my way to join Aine in her search for the House of Air when I saw a great fume upon the ocean. As I watched, I saw a blast of flame and then a dragon fall from the sky and crash into the rocks a league or two from where meself was watching. I hurried to him and gave him what watery fire I could to succour him, but he did only feebly revive. Fearing Braxach would be found by our enemies and destroyed, I hurried to a nearby hall of a tribe of trooping elves. Meself is known to the captain. When I told him what I had found, he ordered his troop to follow me to the dragon and return him to his hall. Braxach is safe under the mountain, but he needeth the cold fire of dragons and Pa'gnac, the healing gas, to succour his return. Neither property doth I possess, so I hath come to thee for aid."

Ke-enaan rose up. Breathing cold fire from the hearth, he summoned Pa'gnac to him. A shimmering turquoise light appeared before the wizard and coalesced into a glowing ball. Breathing out the cold fire into the turquoise gas, Ke-enaan instructed Pa'gnac to take direction from Nala's thought and go forth to heal Braxach. The turquoise ball pulsated with blue flame as it hovered for a moment over Nala's head, and then it disappeared.

Aine embraced her brother as he joined them at the fireside. After greeting the sylphs, Nala sat down beside Aine. In soft tones, Aine told him what had happened on the island and of the taking of Kilfannan to the grotto of Nephelum.

Nala's youthful face darkened, and the poisonous flowers of nightshade bloomed within his skin. "This is fell news," he said grimly. "A great evil stalks the grotto and all who enter in."

"Who amongst the company is willing to go to the grotto of Nephelum?" Ke-enaan asked.

Kilcannan, Doonvannan, and the House of An Carn got to their feet in an instant. "We pledge ourselves to the rescue of Kilfannan," they said in one voice. "For if the lord of the House of Kilfenoran perishes, so too will the Green. The HeartStar will be no more, and all living things connected to the heart will die away."

Aine and Nala rose. For a moment the glorious light of High Faerie shone from their eyes. "We are pledged to the HeartStar," they said in the rippling voice of water. "No matter how dark and dangerous the way, we will succour Kilfannan, or perish in the attempt."

Ke-enaan set his eyes upon Doonvannan. "'Tis my wish that Doonvannan of the House of Doon remaineth here with me," he said. "There is much to do to prepare for the assault. I need his help and"—he smiled—"his light-hearted company to cheer me in my doubt."

Doonvannan nodded. Raising his right arm across his heart, he said, "'Twouldst be my honour to serve thee in any way I can."

"I'd go with yees, but I can't swim," Duirmuid said despondently. "Heavy as a stone, I am."

Hearing a noise on the stairs that led down to the pool, Ke-enaan listened for a moment. Then, crossing the hall, he disappeared through the arch and down the stairs. He gasped in shock. Liam was pulling himself slowly up the steps. He was covered in blood and barking in distress.

Ke-enaan reached down, took Liam in his arms, and carried him upstairs.

"Zarg!" he called. "Bring a bowl of water and a cloth, and the jar of red unction from the herb shelf."

Ke-enaan gently laid Liam on the rushes before the dragon hearth. Kneeling down, he examined his wounds.

"Aine," he said, "sing the sound of falling water to wash away the blood while I cleanse and seal the wounds with unction."

At length the doctoring was completed. Ke-enaan brought a goblet of elixir and handed it to Liam. "Drink deep," Ke-enaan said. "The potion will knit body and soul together and give strength and clarity to thy mind. When thou art ready, pray tell us thy tidings."

Liam sipped upon the elixir. After a while, he said, "I went to the grotto of Nephelum before sunrise. The meresna normally sleep until noon, but they were awake and watching." He coughed. "It was almost like they were expecting a spy to come."

"What of Kilfannan?" Kilcannan said impatiently. He saw Ke-enaan shoot a warning look his way.

"Kilfannan is a prisoner on an island at the centre of the grotto," Liam answered. "The lagoon was wreathed in fume. I had to get close. The meresna guarding him saw me and gave alarm. As I tried to escape, they attacked me and followed me into the underwater ways. I only escaped because I'm the better swimmer and I know the twists and turns of the many flowing rivers underground."

"Let us talk of thy mission to the grotto of Nephelum," Ke-enaan said to the company. "Great evil resides there that was birthed in the War of Separation. Those that take the dark road to the grotto must be aware of the peril that is their path, for the tunnels are treacherous and there are many ways to choose from."

"So where will we find direction so as not to go astray?" Aine said worriedly.

The gashes upon Liam's body were healing fast. Raising his flipper, he said, "I will lead you to the grotto, but in this condition meself is not much of a fighter."

"Nay! Thou canst not go," Ke-enaan declared. "Thine injuries were severe and have not yet fully healed. 'Twould be wise for thee to forsake the fight. Gather thy clan to keep watch upon the Giant's Cliffs, and report to me if thou seest any movement of the Cathac and Manannan."

"Fret not, Mistress Aine," Liam said. "Meself can tell you which way to go and the rock and water marks to follow. Besides," he barked, "you have the mind of the sea. It will serve you well until the poison of the grotto puts all wholesomeness to flight."

Aine smoothed the horn upon Liam's head, murmuring endearments in the language of the water.

Zarg brought more wine. Filling up the glasses, he handed them around.

When Zarg had retired, Ke-enaan raised his goblet. "A toast," he said. "Dark may be the hour, but the green light of love will never fade if we stay strong within the HeartStar."

When they had toasted, Ke-enaan looked into their faces.

"Warriors of the Green," he said, "the Cathac and his legions believe they art invincible. Each demon is self-assured that their sorcery and blood magic will prevail against the heart. Arrogance is their weakness, and hate is their undoing. We have to look at our strengths and measure them against the weakness of our enemy." He paused, sipped upon his wine, and then continued. "Against all odds, Emma has triumphed over her mortal programme and accessed her High Faerie nature. This expansion of awareness hath strengthened the power of the House of Air in Faerie." He glanced at Cor-garran. "The power of air rising hath now increased. Thou will be able to use the updraught to fly in the dark void of Under-Earth and Under-Sea."

Cor-garran put his hand upon his heart. "Since the loss of Niamh and Caiomhin, my power to fly hath been weakened," he said. "Glad am I to know that I can take to the air again."

Ke-enaan set his eyes upon Kilcannan and Cor-cannan. "Thou will find a strengthening of the down breath, and it will succour thee in the battle that lies ahead. Your flying feet and fists will have the force of tumult air behind them."

Aine and Nala rose, and in one voice said, "Our bond is our connection to the HeartStar. The spiritual power of love will be our strength, while the enemy thinks only of itself. The High Faerie power of water rising into fire and water falling into earth will provide a spiritual force that will flow through us as one song, and we will send the music of the heart forth against the discordant noise of the Cathac and his minions." After a pause, they added, "We will not fail while the Green lives."

"Mistress Aine and Lord Nala," Liam said as they sat back down, "let me give thee directions to the grotto."

After Liam had given advice to Aine and Nala about the

water and stone marks to follow to the grotto, the company gathered in the centre of the hall.

"Thou will need to arm thyselves," Aine said to Kilcannan and Cor-cannan. She took an extra knife from her belt and handed it to Kilcannan.

"Take me blade," Duirmuid said to Cor-cannan. "'Tis sharp and light and has the power of the stone kingdoms as its virtue. Meself will have no need of it until we take the road again."

"'Tis settled then," Ke-enaan said as they stood before him. "Take heed. The meresna are from the seed of Nephelum and can reassemble their body parts once said parts have been severed. Thou must take their heads. 'Tis written in the history of the Danaans that all evil sea creatures were spawned from Nephelum and other sea clans that he conquered. The mermaid clan did not know evil until after the War of Separation. If we lose our battle against the Cathac, he will take our essence and corrupt it. We shalt become grotesque forms hungering after human flesh like the meresna and other foul creatures that are instruments of the Cathac's evil will."

Ke-enaan beckoned them towards the steps leading down to the waterfall. "'Tis time to set forth on thy mission," he said. "Let us go below to the cave of the underground river. I will put a blessing of protection upon thee."

Duirmuid, Doonvannan, and Liam followed the company down the steps and stood back while Ke-enaan gathered the company together beside the rushing water of the underground stream. Raising his arms, Ke-enaan uttered the sacred spiritual language of his Danaan lineage. The sounds bounced off the walls in flashes of outer spectrum colours. As the echo sparks multiplied, they began to flow in a spiral around the wizard as he sang. Gathering the glitter in his hands, Ke-enaan cast a protective ring of scintillating colours around the company.

"The light spell will shield you from enemies and spying eyes on thy journey to the grotto," Ke-enaan said. "Once you are there, the evil of Nephelum will overwhelm my protection, but at least you will have the element of surprise. Mark thy way to the grotto with symbols so that thou may not go astray and may return safely to my hall."

Doonvannan stepped forward with Duirmuid at his side.

"Hearts of my heart," Doonvannan said, "may the living light of the Green protect thee."

Duirmuid cupped his mouth to the wall. "I, Duirmuid, of the House of Duir," he said, sending his voice echoing through the stone, "command all rocks, boulders, crystals, and pebble stones to succour the House of Air and the House of Water on their dangerous dark road to Under-Earth and Under-Sea."

"Go now," Ke-enaan said to the company. "Long live the House of Air!"

Liam stood by the pool. "I will return to the sea and keep watch upon the cliffs. Farewell," he said, slipping into the water.

CHAPTER 11

CTHOGG

After taking leave of Ke-enaan, the company dived into the underground river. The water was cold. Kilcannan shivered and swallowed hard. The water was sapping his fiery air nature and turning his courage to despair. He was anxious about Kilfannan. The thought of what might happen to his brother if they couldn't rescue him filled him with terror. If Kilfannan were to be sacrificed, then all that was beautiful in the three worlds would die. He too would perish, and the magic music of the Green would be no more. He glanced back at Cor-cannan, who was swimming behind him, and saw the same aura of misery around his nephew. Praying to the Green to strengthen his resolve, he forced his mind into neutral and swam after Aine and Nala.

Aine took the lead with Nala behind her, followed by Kilcannan and the House of An Carn. Acting on Liam's directions, she led them along the river passage and down into sinkholes to join other rivers that were rushing to the sea. After a while they surfaced into a low, wide cavern with many waterfalls, and river passages leading off in all directions.

Climbing out of the water, they stood together in the darkness.

"There are many ways to choose from," Kilcannan declared, peering into the gloom at the myriads of water tunnels that exited the cavern. "Aine! Which way do we go?" he asked.

Aine looked about in confusion. "I hath forgotten Liam's direction from here," she said, shaking her head. She glanced at Nala. "Dost thou remember Liam's instruction?"

Nala's face paled and became a mask of perplexity. "I too, have forgotten Liam's direction," he responded with consternation. "Harpies will be watching for us from Hags Head. If we take a wrong passage, we could be washed into the ocean. They will see us and will raise the alarm."

Aine thought for a moment and then said, "Meself will contact the mind of the sea for guidance to the grotto. The rivers go for miles under the cliffs. We must take care that we do not go astray."

Stepping into the swirling water, Aine immersed herself in the mind of the sea. Focusing her attention on the grotto of Nephelum, she asked for direction. Through the eyes of a small fish, she saw one of the waterways light up for an instant. With a prayer of gratitude, she broke the surface and climbed out of the water.

"'Tis this way," she said, pointing to a river that disappeared into a sinkhole.

"I will make a mark so that we can find our passage back," Kilcannan said. Blowing the down breath into his hands, he formed a tiny ball of flame and blew it into the stone ceiling above the water passage they had just left.

The water in the sinkhole was swift, sweeping them downward and into another river. After a while, the watercourse began to narrow. They found themselves having to crawl and wriggle through fissures in the rock. Finally the passage widened and the river grew deeper.

"The water feels greasy and unclean," Aine whispered to Nala as he swam alongside her.

"Aye. It hath the stink of hell upon it."

Swimming forward, they could see a dim shimmer up ahead. An odour of decay crept into their nostrils, and unwholesome green phosphorescence became noticeable on the dripping walls. The wavering issue from the walls and ceiling grew steadily brighter. They made their way with caution. At the end of the tunnel, the group stopped. Peering out into the gloomy light, they saw a large grotto. Stalagmites covered in clinging, crawling weeds reared up in front of them. The roof was thick with glowing stalactites. The floor of the cavern was covered in human skulls. The craniums had been removed, the sirens having feasted upon the brains of their victims. Scattered amongst the piles of bones were huge stone bowls full of gold rings, coins, pocket watches, and clay pipes—trinkets that the meresna kept as souvenirs from the sailors they had seduced and eaten. Kilcannan nudged Cor-cannan and pointed to a stone bowl. Lying on top of a bunch of gold trinkets was his diamond ring and their missing enchanted bows and arrows that had been taken from them by the serpents. They would pick them up when they got an opportunity.

At the centre of the cavern was a slimy lagoon surrounded by jagged boulders and shrouded in noxious vapours that curled like snakes from the stagnant water.

Kilcannan shivered in the damp cold and looked desperately around for any sign of Kilfannan. As the clouds of poison fume engulfing the grotto cleared for a moment, he saw a pillar in the centre of the small lagoon.

Elva Thompson

Aine was staring into the fume, wondering if the meresna were trying to hide something from view. *There is an enchantment here*, she thought. *Are we walking into a trap?* She glanced at Nala and saw the same question in his eyes.

Connecting with Nala's spiritual power, Aine gazed through the shroud of vapour hanging over the centre of the lagoon, and saw a small rocky island in the middle of the lake. At the centre was a pillar. Etched into the stone was, she could see, a depiction of a horned sea serpent holding the partially eaten body of a mortal in its claw. Aine shivered. It was as the likeness of Nephelum, the father of sea serpents.

In front of the hideous statue, she saw a meresna lying on top of a huge pile of bones. The siren had purple skin, many shades darker than the bluish scaled skin of the warrior class. *That's the queen*, Aine thought to herself, noticing a tiara crowning the siren's long green hair. At the base of the statue, she saw four of the lighter-skinned warrior class guarding a body bound in thick strands of seaweed. Her intuition told her it was Kilfannan. Glancing at Kilcannan, she put her hand on her heart and then pointed to the island in the lagoon.

Aine drew her blade and, cautiously stepping out of the tunnel, looked around. Seeing a sudden movement from the corner of her eye, she ducked back into the shelter of the passage and put up her hand in a cautionary signal to the others. There were five meresna lying in the scum-filled water of a shallow rock pool. Her view was partially obscured by stalagmites. Shifting to the side to get a better look, she studied the positioning of the sirens. Two were lying on one side of the pool, and the other three were on the opposite side sitting on the rocks looking into small mirrors and combing their long green hair. Aine reasoned that if the company were careful and dodged from stalagmite to stalagmite, they could get amongst the rocks behind the pool and take the sirens by surprise. *They have to be destroyed first,* she thought. The meresna guarding Kilfannan would attack the company when they tried to claim him, and they could not afford to be assailed from in front and behind. They were already outnumbered. There was no way to know what other foul creatures may be hiding in the rocks or lurking in the dark streams that flowed into the grotto.

Gesturing to the sylphs to join her, Aine pointed to the three sirens that were grooming and then swept her finger across her throat. Kilcannan and the House of An Carn nodded in agreement.

Stealthily dodging from one stalagmite to the next, the sylphs reached the far side of the pool without detection. Hiding behind a boulder, they drew their knives and waited for Aine's signal.

Knowing the sylphs would deal with the three sirens that were grooming, Aine and Nala shape-shifted into lizards and slithered between the boulders behind the other two. Standing at their backs, they morphed into faerie form. Signalling to the sylphs to attack, they leapt forward, swinging their blades through the sirens' skinny necks, decapitating them.

At the same moment that Aine and Nala attacked the sirens, Kilcannan and the House of An Carn came out from their hiding places. Fearing no attack within their grotto, the sirens were slow to react. The sylphs quickly severed their jelly-like necks. As the heads rolled away, the company could hear a faint death croak echoing nebulously around the cavern.

Aine stiffened. The sound from the dying sirens would be immediately heard by the queen, and she would know of their presence. In an instant, Aine heard the sound of a conch horn, vibrating with the ugly tone of Under-Sea, reverberate round the cavern and along all the passages leading to the sea. The game was up.

"They are calling their sisters from the sea," Aine hissed to Nala, as Kilcannan and the House of An Carn came to her side. "We must throw away caution and fight for the life of Kilfannan, for we are few and they are many."

As the echo of the horn died away, the cavern erupted with the hissing and clicking of nameless things that were crawling and slithering amongst the rocks. Huge crablike creatures came scuttling towards them snapping their pincers, a hungry light shining from their waving stalklike eyes.

Kilcannan and Cor-cannan summoned the down breath. Dipping into fire, they advanced upon their enemies and blew a scalding wind at the snapping crabs. The fiery wind melted the crabs' bulging eyes. The line fell back in disarray and tried to retreat back into the rocks.

Seeing what was happening and determined to block the crabs from escaping and regrouping for another attack, Cor-garran called an updraught. Rising above the scuttling army, he landed at their backs and charged them from behind, while Kilcannan and Cor-cannan dashed forward, slashing off the pincers that were blindly groping for them. Fury took the House of Air. In a blasting wind, they thrust and hacked at the heaving crabs until they had hewn off every pincer, leaving only a quivering mass of blind bodies on the ground.

Amidst the seething chaos and frenzied clicking, Aine and Nala saw shadows gathering by the boulders that surrounded the lagoon. The horn had called not only the meresna but also dark wraiths and other foul creatures from Under-Sea to block the company's passage to the island. The meresna guards that were guarding Kilfannan slithered into the water and were swimming in their direction, the fell light of revenge burning in their eyes. The wraith shadows turned into coils of black smoke and began to snake through the tumult of the air towards them.

Aine and Nala transformed into their High Faerie forms and stood tall, surrounded by a blue nimbus of glittering light. The orange radiance of the water field shone from their eyes. With energetic blasts of rippling power, they threw back the shadow army as it tried to reach them. With angry hissing and bursts of foul stench, the black twisting smoke began to writhe and twist away from the pure orange light of High Faerie that had engulfed the brother and sister. Slowly, they saw the wraith light of Under-Sea dissipate and then vanish.

Aine glanced at the lagoon. The meresna guards had almost reached the circle of boulders at the edge of the water. Aine glided forward with Nala by her side. They raised their blades and charged forward to meet the guards. As the duo stepped into the water to make battle, they were arrested by an unseen and impenetrable barrier. Using their faerie power, Aine and Nala sent charges of energy at the barrier, but still it did not clear or give them access to the water. Aine realised the frequency of the lagoon was resonating on her father's will. It was his Under-Sea vibration preventing them from crossing the water and getting to the island to fight the queen. Aine knew that if they shape-shifted into reptile form they could cross the barrier, but she was deathly afraid Mannannan would feel their vibration. He would be aware of their presence in the grotto and could attack them.

They heard a cold, hissing laugh. The meresna queen was standing on her tail. Her hypnotic orange eyes sent waves of malice skimming across the lagoon towards them. Aine and Nala raised their swords and, weaving left and right, deflected the vibrations of hatred as they reached them. The queen drew out a long whip of sharpened human vertebrae and, with a mighty stroke, sent it hurtling towards them.

Aine and Nala ducked and rolled away.

"I am Cthogg, Queen of the Meresna," she hissed. A black forked tongue flickered over needle-sharp teeth as she drew back her purple lips in a sneer. "The lord of the haunted cliffs bids thee welcome."

The slits in her orange eyes expanded and contracted in such a way that Aine and Nala knew she was trying to mesmerise them into submission. They focused their eyes on the emerald in her tiara.

"Twin seed of Manannan, thou hast returned to the cavern of the serpent. Think not that thy filthy faerie blood will avail or sustain thee in our enchanted grotto. There are no sorcerous warriors here to defend thee. Thou hast been drawn into a trap." She gave a hissing laugh and flicked her whip viciously at them again. "Thou art deceived if thou think thou canst triumph over the Cathac and thy father. Victory will always be ours."

Cthogg glared hatefully at the sylphs standing by the boulders surrounding the lagoon. Drawing back her scaly arm, she sent the whip hurtling towards them.

Calling on the downdraught, Kilcannan slid under the razor-sharp bones as they cut through the air above him. Again and again, Cthogg sent the whip hurtling towards him. As he dived and ducked, he saw Cor-garran take the updraught. Hovering over the whip, Cor-garran brought his sword down with the force of falling wind upon the rippling bones. Kilcannan heard a crack and a clatter as the whip broke and vertebrae fell upon the rocks.

Swiftly, Kilcannan and Cor-cannan took the bows and

quivers from the trinket bowl amongst the weeds. Seizing the ring of resolution, Kilcannan slipped it on his finger. Then, rushing to the lakeside, they fired arrows into the sirens as they slithered onto the rocks. Using a downdraught, Kilcannan slashed the meresna with his sword as he skimmed across the water.

Cor-garran was flying above the lagoon and intuiting the queen's intention to murder Kilfannan, he flew above her as she slithered off the rocks. Then, diving down, he stabbed her from behind. If he could distract her, it would give Aine and Nala time to get to the island and rescue Kilfannan.

Cthogg struck out at Cor-garran with her scaly arm as he harried her and knocked him into the lagoon. The force of the blow winded him for a moment. But flying out of the water on the updraught, he attacked again. Cthogg whirled round, but he was too fast for her. Diving down, he stabbed her in the side and took to the air again.

The meresna guards had almost reached the boulders. Throwing caution to the wind, and knowing that in reptile form they could cross the barrier, Aine and Nala shape-shifted into giant horned lizards and slid into the water. Hacking at the guards with their claws, they tore the heads from two meresna. Seeing Cthogg glare at Kilfannan and pull out her knife, Aine knew that the queen was going to murder him. After she'd signalled to Nala, who was ripping the head from a serpent that had emerged from the pool, the two of them shape-shifted into eels and darted towards the island.

As Aine and Nala reached the island, they felt a tremor in the ground and saw the ugly vibration of Under-Sea taking shape between them and the bound body of Kilfannan. Joining their minds and thoughts as one, they watched as the hideous human shape of their father appeared before them. The sunken eyes glared out from under his broad black hat, and his cruel mouth was curled into a triumphant sneer. Clouds of blood-red light issued from Manannan's eyes. As it surrounded them, memories of lust and feasting on the world of humankind engulfed them.

Realising that in reptile form they were vulnerable to their father's sorcery and will, Aine and Nala shape-shifted into their High Faerie forms. Clothed in the shimmering blue light of the fifth dimension, they sent their spiritual power against their father. Manannan staggered back and put his arm across his eyes to shield himself from their radiance. Shape-shifting into a giant crested serpent, he sent the tainted red glow of Under-Sea billowing towards them once more. The grotto flashed red and blue and the cavern quivered with the opposing vibrations as they struggled back and forth for mastery.

Manannan raised his crested head and, opening his jaws, bared his razor teeth. Then with a thrust of his lizard neck, he struck out at Aine and Nala. Dodging his attack, the twins summoned a water vortex and sent it spinning against Manannan. The waterspout tore through the air, coiled around his body, and sent him crashing against the pillar of Nephelum. A scream of rage echoed round the cavern, the rock beneath their feet began to tremble, and with a blinding flash their father disappeared.

Cthogg had almost reached Kilfannan. Cor-garran realised that Manannan had blocked Aine and Nala's access to the island so that the queen could kill Kilfannan. What was one sylph's life, he thought, in exchange for the living light of his House of Air? He would try to kill the queen even if his own life was forfeited.

Summoning the wind, Cor-garran flew at Cthogg again

with such tornadic force that she jerked backwards. The knife fell from her hand, and her crown tumbled from her head onto the rocks. Screaming with rage, Cthogg turned on him. Ducking and weaving, he evaded her blows. Then, rotating in the air like a whirlwind, he landed on her shoulders. As she brought her arm up to grab him, he thrust his knife into her neck, cutting through the gelatinous sinew and severing her head.

Landing on the ground beside Kilfannan, Cor-garran quickly cut him loose from the seaweed bindings. "Kilfannan," he hissed, "canst thou stand?"

Kilfannan nodded. Seeing the crown set with an emerald lying on the rocks, he swiftly picked it up. The jewel was the winged emerald of the House of Air that Cthogg had stolen from his jerkin when she had stripped him naked. Clasping the emerald in his hand, he looked around. "Cor-garran," he said, "let us take to the air in the blue light of High Faerie and leave this accursed place."

The cavern was filled with vivid light as the power of High Faerie battled the sorcery of Under-Sea. Red lightning bolts struck around Kilfannan and Cor-garran as they took to the air. Weaving and ducking away from the lightning, they crossed the lagoon and joined Kilcannan and Cor-cannan, who were waiting on the shoreline.

"Come!" Aine cried out to them. "We must flee."

Rocks started to fall from the walls, passages broke open, and the sea began to rush in and flood the grotto. The roof was caving in. Stalactites were falling like swords from the ceiling, barely missing the bodies of the company as they ran across the rattling skulls and bones.

The phosphorene light was dimming; they could not see their way. Looking round in the darkness, Kilcannan saw the fire marker he had placed above their escape passage. "This way," he shouted over the grinding din and the tumult of the grotto.

The stone beneath their feet began to shake and crack as they raced towards the passageway. They heard the thunderous sound of falling rock and were suddenly covered by a cloud of dust. When it cleared, they saw a wall of solid rock before them blocking their escape.

Kilfannan heard hissing. Looking round, he saw meresna slithering towards them with their swords drawn and the fell light of revenge burning in their glowing eyes.

"Kilfannan," Nala said desperately, "let us put the power of wind and water together and create a vortex of air and a whirlpool of water that will take us through the enchantment that hath blocked our passage."

Kilfannan nodded in agreement.

Holding hands to link their spiritual energy together, the company faced the wall.

Kilfannan and Cor-garran created a whirling updraught, while Kilcannan and Cor-cannan created a spiralling downwind. At the centre of the vortex where the two winds met, Aine and Nala directed their spiritual power of water to collide with the winds and form a whirlpool. Under their focused wills, the wall began to quiver. A round shimmering space appeared in the rock.

"Go!" Aine cried out to the sylphs.

Kilfannan and Kilcannan jumped into the pulsating whirlpool, followed by Cor-garran and Cor-cannan. As Cor-cannan disappeared, the air vortex began to contract. Before Aine and Nala could get through to the other side, it had closed completely. They were trapped in the grotto, and the meresna were closing in behind them.

Kilfannan cried out in torment as the vortex closed. Aine and Nala were trapped behind the wall, and there was nothing he could think of to open it again. It took the power of both air and water to create the whirlpool vortex. There was no way that it could be recreated without Aine and Nala. A feeling of despair swept over Kilfannan. His breath caught in his throat.

He felt Kilcannan's hand upon his arm. "Brother! We must leave this place," he urged. "Come, let us return to Ke-enaan's halls and tell the wizard what hath happened to the High House of Water. We cannot tarry, for there may still be time for Ke-enaan to be of assistance to them."

The grotto suddenly grew hot and stifling. Aine and Nala found it was hard to catch their breath. In the darkness, clouds of orange flame appeared above them, surrounded by the ugly yellow tint of Lower Faerie. In the weaving light they saw the face of a man appear. His countenance had once been fair and noble but was now corrupted with sensuality and malice. From below his high forehead and arched brows, his almond eyes glowed with the lust of fire descending into water.

"I am Ngpa-tawa, Lord of Fire Descending into Water and ruler of the mortal world," he said haughtily. "Bow down and worship me, seed of Manannan."

Nala and Aine, feeling their souls shrink back in terror, joined their minds together. Ngpa-tawa's spiritual power had turned to evil. Given that his strength was fuelled by the Cathac's will and Manannan's sorcery, they knew he was formidable. They felt they did not have the spiritual strength to defeat the fire lord of the mortal world and his elemental power. Together they visualised the beauty of the Green and of flowing water to calm their minds. Then, transforming into their High Faerie forms and summoning the power of water, they turned and set their wills against Ngpa-tawa.

Doth not look at his eyes, for they are full of serpent spell, Nala thought to Aine. *Keep him in talk while I look for a way out. For he is proud and boastful, and will like to gloat before he sends his spiritual power against us.*

They heard hissing. Glancing back, they saw the meresna slithering up behind them with their knives drawn. A wall of roaring flame shot from the fire lord's eyes, blocking the sirens' attack and forcing them back.

"Daughters of Cthogg," the fire lord roared, "go back to the sea and gather thy clan. Bring me the head of the spying seal man."

Aine and Nala felt Ngpa-tawa's eyes burning through their bodies and groping for their wills. Waves of foul lusting light swirled around them, seeking a way into their minds. Nala took Aine's hand. If they were to perish, it would be together.

"Didst thou think that I did not see the fire set above the passage as a marker of return?" Ngpa-tawa sneered. "I laid a snare to catch thee. The filth from the House of Air may have escaped from my clutches, but 'twill only be a temporary respite, for Kilfannan and Kilcannan will soon be consumed, and the five dimensions will pay tribute to the Cathac and his lords."

"Thou art a murderous traitor to the HeartStar," Aine spat back defiantly. "There is naught but malice in thine soul and a nest of vipers in thine heart. When the High House of Air and Water force thee and thy dark lord to submit, thy pride will be smitten with despair. Banished ye will be to the abyss and to the dark dream that hath no ending."

"Traitor?" he mocked. "How dare thou callest me traitor. Thou art the seed of Manannan, and in thy madness thou hast destroyed Queen Cthogg, beloved of the Cathac, and slaughtered her servants. But our lord hath mercy in his heart and will give thee a chance to redeem thy traitorous, murderous ways and join thy father. Manannan desires thy return. What say thee? I counsel thee that it is useless to resist."

Knowing she had to keep the fire lord talking while Nala looked for a means of escape, Aine answered, "Thou jest! The Cathac hath no mercy. He is but a hollow reed of malice, for his heart hath fled from his iniquity."

"Jest!" the fire lord fumed, sending a blast of scalding steam into her face. "Thou art foolish to think thee and the rabble of the House of Air can beat the Cathac who is lord of all kingdoms. Thou hast been living in a dream if thou thinks the conjuror of Black Head and Trevelyan, the busybody from beyond the stars, can stop our glorious destiny." He laughed scornfully. "'Tis plain, thou art no match for me. Will thou not reconsider?"

Aine was blinded by the steam for a moment. When her sight returned, she drew herself up and said, "Meself would rather die than submit to Manannan. I Aine, daughter of Erin of High Faerie, hath spoken." Light issued from her eyes. For a moment the grotto blazed with brilliance.

While Aine was distracting Ngpa-tawa, Nala gazed desperately at the rock wall in front of him, looking for a means of escape. The stone was smooth and tight to the walls. There was no way they could get through. Bowing his head in despair, he saw a thin black streak at the bottom of the wall. Sending his mind into the rock to investigate, he saw it was a crack big enough for tiny lizards to crawl through and gain the passage to freedom. *Aine,* he said in thought. *The stone kingdom hath succoured us. Meself sees a crack at the bottom of the wall we can escape through.*

"Nala! Thine sister is a filthy turncoat," the fire lord thundered. "She prefers the delicacy of flowers over the glorious destiny of conquest that is her serpent heritage. Son of Manannan, wilt thou join thy father? What say thee?"

Before Nala could give his rebuttal, fire streamed from Ngpa-tawa's eyes and, spiralling through the air, formed a circle of flame around Nala, separating him from Aine's mind. Fear clutched at his heart. The fire lord had cut off his connection to Aine to isolate him for some evil purpose.

"Thy sister is the traitor," he heard the fire lord say. "Thou art the pure seed of Manannan, and if thou kill her, I will exalt thee to thy proper status. Thou, Lord Nala, shalt sit upon thy father's throne in his Under-Sea city for eternity. I will bring thee the most innocent and beautiful girls from the mortal world for thee to caress and feed on. With thine sister Graine, thou shalt rule the night."

Graine? Nala thought in alarm. Had his sister's will been consumed by Manannan? His mind was in turmoil. Anger flamed in his heart. "Thou art insane," he cried out. "I Nala, son of Erin, will never bow to thee, to my father, or to the demon in the Giant's Cliffs."

As the ring of fire around Nala began to pulsate, he felt the hot ecstasy of seduction course through his being. He staggered back. Putting his hands over his head, he desperately struggled to block the seething desire that crashed against his heart. He tried to take Aine's hand and find her mind, but he could not feel her presence.

"Kill her! Kill her!" the fire lord commanded. "Suck out her essence and take it unto thyself. The HeartStar is weak and knoweth not the pleasures of our lusting will."

"Yes! Yes!" Nala heard himself saying. "I will kill her. I will rule."

Aine saw Nala stagger back as the ring of fire surrounded him. Her brother was writhing back and forth, his eyes dark with terror and his arms flailing like the wings of a wounded bird. She tried to join his awareness but could find no trace of his resonance in her mind. He put his hands across his head, and she saw pain and defeat etched into his face. Then, standing erect, he turned towards her.

Aine gasped. Nala's eyes were blazing with murderous intent. The beryl and moonstones set into the silver circlet on his brow glittered with the fell light of Under-Sea. Panic seized her mind. Ngpa-tawa had possessed Nala's mind. She searched desperately for a way she could break the sorcerous spell before her brother tried to kill her.

In the stifling heat of the cavern, she suddenly felt coolness at her throat. The hare talisman Nala had given her in the exchange after the mating was vibrating. Considering it as a sign of aid, she took the talisman from her necklace and secreted it in her hand. If she could press it to Nala's heart, there might be a chance to break the fire lord's spell that had taken possession of her beloved brother.

With a scream of rage, Nala leapt towards her and pushed her to the floor. Viciously opening her mouth and putting his lips to hers, he started sucking out her essence. She felt herself ebbing away. She was weakening. In a last effort to save him and herself, she pressed the hare talisman against his heart.

With a crack, the ring of fire around Nala broke up and disappeared into the fume. She heard Nala scream as the spell that had held him was thrown back. He went limp and fell against her body.

"Nala!" she said, holding him up. "We must flee this foul place before we art undone."

The cavern quivered and erupted into flame. Then, as the fire died away, Aine and Nala heard the vengeful hissing of the meresna. The sirens had returned and were slithering towards them.

Nala, coming to his senses, grabbed Aine by the hand. They shape-shifted into tiny lizards. After darting through the hole in the wall into the passage, they morphed into faerie form. There was a rushing stream by the side of the rocky floor. Diving into the water, they felt their energy returning.

Swimming against the current, they eventually surfaced in the pool by the waterfall under Ke-enaan's hall.

CHAPTER 12

A RACE AGAINST TIME

After the company had left on their perilous mission to rescue Kilfannan, Duirmuid and Doonvannan had followed Ke-enaan back up the steps into his halls.

"Pull up chairs and let us consult the mirror," Ke-enaan said. "'Twill allow us to see the company's progress underground. I canst be ready to offer what little help I may."

While Doonvannan and Duirmuid brought their chairs, Ke-enaan sat down before the oval mirror and, imaging the company, bent his will upon the glass. The shimmering quicksilver surface rippled but did not clear. He tried again, but to no avail. A slight discolouration on the mirror's silver frame caught his attention. Peering carefully at the frame, he saw it was coated by a red sheen that looked like rust. Touching it with his finger, he immediately withdrew his hand in shock. The metal was burning hot. A tremor of fear ran through him. Another powerful spell had been laid against the looking glass.

"The mirror hath been spelled," he said in consternation to the others. "I canst not turn it to my will. I must search for a spell to break the curse."

An ominous silence stole into the room, and a shadow fell

213

upon the hall. Ke-enaan lit a candelabra and, going to a shelf, took down an old manuscript and laid it on the table. Opening the tome, he started peering at the spidery script. The hall grew hot as he turned the pages. Once he found the counter-spell, the candle flames veered wildly and then went out. The leaves of the manuscript began to smoulder, and before he could memorise the enchantment, the page suddenly tore loose and, rising into the air, burst into flame.

Ke-enaan gasped and staggered backwards. His mind was in turmoil. The spiritual protection spell he had cast around his hall when he had first taken up his abode had been breached and his security compromised. So much was happening—and so fast—that he felt overwhelmed by the magnitude of the evil forces arrayed against the House of Air and all who served the Green. It seemed to him that an irredeemable gloom had descended on his hall, and with it an intruding force that battered at his will. Doubt invaded his thoughts. It was useless to fight the Cathac in a conflict they had little chance of winning. For an instant his mind was embraced by the cold clasp of despair.

He was suddenly aware that Doonvannan was staring at him. The sylph's eyes were dark turquoise. Ke-enaan knew that Doonvannan was aware of his mental struggle and was using air rising into space to try to read his mind. He stood for a moment, slowly inhaling and exhaling. He had to pull himself together, and concentrate on staying strong and not giving into fear.

Duirmuid stirred. "Even though the mirror has been blindsided, meself might be able to track the company," he said to Ke-enaan. "Mistress Aine is water falling on leaf and rock, and we share a certain vibration within the stone kingdom.

Meself will enter the Mind of the Stone and see if I can find her on the stone waves."

Duirmuid bowed his head and, focusing on Aine, opened his awareness to the stone. Every time he located her position underground, he was immediately overcome with a choking sensation in his gullet and a sense of heat in his body that stifled his connection to her. He put his hand to his throat and coughed. "There is mischief at work," he said hoarsely. "A fey fire spell has been laid against Aine and Nala and Black Head."

Only a fire lord was capable of using flame to such advantage, Ke-enaan thought. He sensed that Ngpa-tawa the fallen fire lord had left his city of fire and travelled to the Giant's Cliffs. It was he who had cast the fire spell against his looking glass. Ke-enaan took a tense breath. Fear rose up in his throat as he realised that Kilfannan was being used as bait to capture and destroy the House of Air and the High House of Water. He had to act quickly or all would be lost. War was on his doorstep. He had to hasten to Slieve Elva and collect the power-infused objects that had lain hidden since the War of Separation. He was suddenly mindful that Doonvannan was standing before him.

"My lord," Doonvannan said, putting his clenched fist upon his heart, "what service may I do for thee?"

"And I," said Duirmuid joining Doonvannan, "are yees to command."

"I must go to Uall MaCarn's forge at the heart of Slieve Elva," Ke-enaan replied, "to collect a spell that will break the sorcery that hath been laid upon the mirror, and to gather other charms and enchantments to use against the Cathac and Manannan. I will leave my hall in thy care. If Thorn-Haw brings a message concerning Zugalfar and his airborne legion, or the number and movement of goblins and their knockers towards the Giant's Cliffs, thou must make note of the count and location. This I charge thee to do."

Noticing the wine flagon was empty, Ke-enaan called to Zarg to bring more wine.

The spriggan shuffled forward from the shadows. As Zarg put the jug upon the table, Ke-enaan thought for a fleeting moment that he could see a tiny flash of red light in Zarg's vacant eyes. When he looked again, he saw nothing but his own will staring back at him. He wondered if, in his overwrought and fearful state, he had imagined it. Shaking the thought away, he concentrated on the task at hand.

Leaving through the side door, Ke-enaan took the moss-lined passageway that led deep under the Burren to the heart of Slieve Elva. As he stepped out of the tunnel into the fragrant meadow, he thought about the events that had first brought him to the dragon-fire forge of the giant Uall MaCarn and his brother Finn McCoul.

In the last battle against the forces of the Cathac in the War of Separation, Ke-enaan's brother Creidne had taken a mortal wound. As he lay dying before the gates of Cnoc Na Dala, the great city on the Gaillimh plain, Creidne had begged him to leave the mortal world through the star-gate pyramid at Brugh and return to his own dimension. Not wanting his brother to become the food of wolves and pecking crows, he had refused to leave him and had stayed by his side until his spirit left his body. Then he had buried him and piled rocks on top of the grave. When he had finished, he drew protective runes in the earth around the mound so no wight or nightgaunt could gain access to the grave.

Numbed with grief and sadness, he had trudged through the bloody mire looking for life, but found only blood and death. A short way from the gates, he had come upon a great scene of slaughter. The dead bodies of goblins, brocshee, spriggans, and other fell creatures were littered on the ground, and in a slight clearing, he saw the hewn bodies of his lord Nuada and the latter's guard of warrior wizards. Their flag of a green star on a night sky lay trampled in the mud. He remembered with sickening clarity the mutilated bodies of Nuada and his escort. Their heads had been savagely hacked off and raised on poles; crows were picking at their eyes.

The warriors' weapons had been left where they had fallen. Ke-enaan collected four bows of black-stained yew and four quivers full of arrows. He had seen, lying in a pool of blood, Claoimh Solais, the sword of his fallen captain Nuada. The sword had been forged by the wizard Uscias in Findias, the great city of the north at the start of the War of Separation, and Nuada had carried it into battle against Manannan and the Cathac.

Beside the sword was Nuada's severed hand, and on the middle finger was a ring bearing the green star seal of his noble house. With a prayer, Ke-enaan had taken the ring from Nuada's finger and had placed it upon his own hand in memory of the fallen. Then he had stripped off the golden spider armour from the bodies of Nuada and his knights. The armour had been spun by Dinhcara, the spider queen, and was stronger and lighter than any other metal or enchanted web in Faerie.

The sword of light he had girthed around his waist. Taking the flag, he had sung the sound of falling water until the grit and mud were washed away. Then, wrapping the standard around the armour, bows, and quivers, he had turned his face southward to a freshening wind. He was alone in the world.

Not knowing where else to go, he had travelled to the giant's forge under the mountain called Slieve Elva.

The giants Uall MaCarn and Finn McCoul had fought alongside Nuada during the War of Separation. When Ke-enaan had arrived at Slieve Elva, they had given him sanctuary at the forge and bequeathed him the halls at Black Head for his dwelling.

Uall had shown him a secret vault under the faerie forge, where Ke-enaan subsequently had hidden the ring and sword of light for a future time when once again the Green would duel to the death with darkness. When the time of prophecy was at hand, the sword and ring of Nuada would unite Ke-enaan in thought with his Danaan bloodline. They were his protection, objects of connection to his Danaan heritage and the magic of the past.

The bows and quivers he had kept at Black Head, and the spider armour he had given to Uall MaCarn as a keepsake until the day it would be called forth to battle once again.

Ke-enaan wearily ran his hand over his brow and pushed back his long, silver-streaked black hair. By staying with his brother, he had been caught in the splitting of the worlds and was damned to remain within the fourth dimension. After the War of Separation, he had worked tirelessly to protect the HeartStar and the House of Air. He had guarded the western marches of the sea, and through the cunning mirror had kept watch upon the Cathac entombed in the Giant's Cliff's. He had seen goblins from the mines multiply and become emboldened; knockers walk in broad daylight; and the Cathac and Manannan break out of their spellbound prisons as the stars of prophecy aligned. The time of sorrow and battle was at hand. Ke-enaan knew with a sickening certainty that he would soon be reliving a nightmare from the past. He prayed that he would be able to remain centred and act with clarity when the darkness attacked. Nuada had been betrayed by fear and doubt—the same fear and doubt that he was now experiencing.

Striding forward through the meadow, Ke-enaan passed through a glimmering arched gate of starlight and into the smithy. He had to take possession of Claoimh Solais, the sword of light, and the green star ring of Nuada before nightfall, before the enemy attacked.

Uall MaCarn was standing by the anvil when Ke-enaan arrived, his thoughts as bitter as any brew of rue. When Ke-enaan had first told him that the lords of realities outside the six dimensions had refused to hide the sapphire, Uall knew that it was his duty to take the star-gate and that it was his destiny to fight the Cathac and Manannan. The radiance of the sapphire had exposed his hidden world to the Cathac. He wished his brother Finn McCoul were there to aid him in the battle for the Green.

Uall recalled how he and Finn had fought together alongside Nuada upon the bog of Magh Cuilen and witnessed Manannan's fall. Then they had followed the Cathac as he made his escape across the lake of Corrib. Through underground tunnels to the sea they tracked the monster, and along the coast they found cottage after cottage had been destroyed; the fisherfolk and their goats had been eaten by the monster.

While Uall and Finn were traversing the sand dunes at Fanore, the Cathac had suddenly reared up from the water and attacked them from the sea. The battle raged for a turning of the sun. The Cathac would retreat beneath the roiling waves and then attack again. Thunder roared and lightning struck around them as the Cathac's horned head and snapping jaws reared above the churning ocean. Huge lumps of turf and rocks they had thrown at him, but he dodged them, and the earth and stone had formed islands in the sea.

As night fell, Uall had heard rumbling and the beating of great wings in the sky. In plumes of fire and smoke, he had seen Braxach arrive at the Giant's Cliffs with Duir, the father of dwarves, riding on his back. They had been pursuing the legions of devils and demons that had followed the Cathac in his murderous rampage along the coast.

The dragon had settled on the beach and given them a fiery snort of greeting. Duir slid off his back. As Braxach took to the air once more, the dwarf king had told Uall and Finn of his and Braxach's plan to trap the Cathac, saying that he needed the giants' help to do it.

The sea had been calm and shadowy under a fitful moon as they waited in the darkness for the Cathac to attack. The air grew cold, and then with a churning of the waters, the Cathac had raised its horned head and, coiling its gargantuan bulk, struck at them with gaping jaws. As the Cathac attacked, Braxach had sent a blast of fire into the monster's eyes. The giants had ripped up the rock and earth in front of them, forming a great wall thousands of feet high.

Blinded, the Cathac did not see the upraised cliff and slammed into the rock face. Duir was waiting. Once the Cathac's body had made contact with the stone, Duir had called out to the burning lakes of liquid fire deep beneath the earth for aid. With his hands, the dwarf sire had woven a stone spell of molten lava and then cast the magma stream around the monster. Singing in the language of the stone, he had hardened the burning liquid into rock, trapping the Cathac within a sarcophagus of enchanted stone.

Duir had then called upon the sun and the earth to open a gateway to the abyss in the Giant Cliffs. As the words of his spell vibrated in the air, a black space appeared in the cliff beside the evil stone visage of the Cathac. On a signal from Duir, Braxach breathed out a torrent of fire and drove the legions of shrieking devils into the void. As the last demons were swept up by the pulsating darkness, Duir again cried aloud. With a roar of crashing stone, the gates to Pandemonia closed behind them.

It was so long ago, Uall thought, but to him it seemed like yesterday. He remembered Finn raising the tower on Serpent Head to keep watch on the Cathac—but it now lay deserted. He gave a great sigh. After Finn had built the Giant's Causeway and crossed the sea to Scotland, he had heard word that his brother had fallen under an evil enchantment and disappeared. All his efforts to find Finn had been in vain. He became reconciled to the idea that he would never see his brother again. The cycles of time had moved in their revolutions. Doom was at hand, and the fate of his realm and the Faerie Worlds hung like a gossamer thread before an advancing fire.

He gazed at Ke-enaan's haggard face for a moment before speaking. An age had passed. It was plain to him that the wizard was weary of his long vigil in the fourth dimension. In the War of Separation, Ke-enaan and Creidne had desperately delved into the dark magic of the enemy, trying to find a weakness in their sorcerous spells. The journey into the lower realms had left a stain upon Ke-enaan's spiritual essence, also leaving an opening for doubt and fear to enter.

"Greetings, Ke-enaan," Uall said. "All these long years we have awaited this fateful hour, and it is now upon us. We must gather what strength we can, for the onslaught of the Cathac and his legions will be swift and merciless."

There was silence for a moment, and then Uall asked, "What news of the House of Air?"

"Kilfannan hath been captured by Cthogg, Queen of the Meresna," Ke-enaan answered. "He is being held prisoner in the grotto of Nephelum. Aine and Nala, along with Kilcannan and the House of An Carn, have gone to try to rescue him." He looked at Uall with anguish in his eyes. "I fear that the enemy is one step ahead of us. They are using Kilfannan as bait to destroy the House of Air and the House of Water in one fell swoop. Ngpa-tawa hath found a way to breach the protection spell around Black Head. He hath spied upon us. When Duirmuid son of Duir tried to enter the Mind of the Stone and track his spiritual connection to Mistress Aine, his action was instantly known by the enemy, and his consciousness was attacked by a fey fire spell."

Uall's face grew dark. His bright blue eyes took on a steely, hardened look.

"Ngpa-tawa's arm is long, and his fire imps are legion," he said thoughtfully.

Ke-enaan sighed deeply. "We art few in number, and there are no Tuatha De Danaan armies or ranks of faithful men to aid us. Our hope and our strength lies in the high magic of the past. I must make haste to the vault beneath the forge and remove the sacred objects that lie in trust there."

"'Tis true that we are few in number," Uall answered. "But the spiritual strength of the Green waxes within our hearts. We are formidable and mighty in power if we can think and act as one."

A spasm of uncertainty crossed Ke-enaan's face. "I fear the House of Air and the House of Water have walked into a well-laid trap and may not return."

"Doubt hast no place in the now," Uall responded. "We

must continue without fear to blind us. Do not be distracted by thy dark thoughts, for distraction is a servant of the enemy."

Ke-enaan nodded and lowered his eyes.

Uall uttered words in the language of giants. A door appeared in the burning coals of the forge. Ke-enaan swiftly glided through the door and down a steep staircase that led to a narrow, stone-flagged passageway far underground. Passing between two pillars of tinted marble, he entered the vault. There were niches in the walls stacked with ancient grimoires and spell books. Quickly glancing at the covers, he moved from shelf to shelf until he saw the spidery runes and writing of his brother Creidne on the cover of a faded manuscript. In the War of Separation, his brother had used spells to confound and defeat the enemy, and he had left a record of enchantments to be used at the time of prophecy to come.

Putting the grimoire into his robe, Ke-enaan walked to the back of the cave and knelt down before a long dusty oblong black box with bronze hinges. Wiping away the dust of ages with his cloak, he saw on the top of the box four horizontal lines embossed in gold, with a vertical rod running down the centre. It was Eadha, the air rune of the aspen tree, which bestowed the ability to endure hardships and conquer problems.

Opening the lid of the box, Ke-enaan took out two bundles. One was wrapped in silver satin and the other in green. Inside the bundles were Delphuaan and Ennuiol, the sacred articles of the House of Air. Taking the green star ring of Nuada from the box, he placed it on his finger, and as he did so, visions of valour from the elder days ignited his will. He saw again the proud Danaan horsemen, the sun glinting on their bronze helms, and heard again the sweet sound of their silver horns.

Emboldened, Ke-enaan reached down. Bringing out Nuada's sword, he unsheathed the blade. Holding the point upward before him, he cried aloud in the sacred language of his people, calling on the Danaan wizards of old to give him clarity and strengthen his courage so that confusion and despair would not overwhelm him.

The pulsing light of the sapphire rippled upon the edges of the blade like greedy dragon fire. Sheathing the sword, Ke-enaan girthed it around his waist. Then, taking the bundles, he glided up the staircase to the forge.

While Ke-enaan was in the vault, he found that Uall had dressed himself for war. On his head was a close-fitting gold helmet. The rippling shine of spider armour covered his brawny chest, and a sword was girthed around his waist. He was waiting by the anvil when Ke-enaan returned.

"I will accompany thee to Black Head," Uall said, picking up a sling with a huge spiked metal ball attached to it. "Who will stand with us in the struggle for the sapphire that draws nigh?"

"Trevelyan, Aine and Nala of the High House of Water, Emma the High Faerie warrior in human form, and a powerful mortal," Ke-enaan answered. The two crossed the meadow and entered the passageway. "Braxach will attack the Cathac when he leaves the cliffs and takes to the sea."

"Then I will stand guard upon the beach," Uall avowed. "I will battle the Cathac if he tries to come ashore." He looked at Ke-enaan keenly. "What of the elemental lords? Why are they not coming to our aid? Was it not agreed at the council in High Faerie long ago that when peril drew nigh, the lords would join as one?"

"I have pondered long upon the question that thou hath asked, and I doth not know the answer," Ke-enaan said. "With Niamh and Caiomhin being cast into the outer darkness, the Lord of Fire Rising and the Lord of Earth are all that remains of the council. The pleas I have sent to them over the airwaves hath been met with silence."

Uall looked at him uneasily. "What can have happened to them?"

"Trevelyan is on his way to my halls with Emma and the mortal. I sense that when he travelled beyond the stars, he saw much that will be of great advantage to us. He will know the answer to our questions."

Stepping through the door into his hall, Ke-enaan heard snarling and roaring, and the stench of Lower Faerie burnt his nostrils. Zarg was standing in the middle of the room beating his scaly hands on his chest. "I am Zarg!" he bellowed, ripping off his robe. "No conjuror can tame me!"

Ke-enaan saw Doonvannan draw his sword and, leaping into the air, attack Zarg from behind, while Duirmuid began hacking with his axe at the tough sinews in the spriggan's legs.

"Zarg!" Ke-enaan thundered, drawing his sword of light.

The spriggan whipped round. Hatred blazed from his eyes as he espied the wizard. With a mighty taloned claw, Zarg grabbed Doonvannan from the air.

Holding his sword before him, Ke-enaan flung himself forward. As Zarg opened his mouth to bite off Doonvannan's head, Ke-enaan stabbed the spriggan through the heart.

Zarg gave a grunt and, stumbling forward, hurled Doonvannan against a wall. As the spriggan sunk to the ground, his scaly flesh began to smoulder and blacken. Grease began to trickle from his combusting body and form puddles on the rush floor.

"Quick!" Ke-enaan said to Uall. "I will open the door to the road. Throw the brute over the sea wall before he explodes and sets a fire in my hall. I will tend to Doonvannan."

Grabbing the spriggan's smouldering body, Uall raced through the door. Crossing the road in one stride, he flung the burning corpse over the sea wall.

Looking to the south, he saw a red fume hanging over the Giant's Cliffs. It seemed to be expanding as he watched it. Dull and poisonous fire vapours were streaking from all directions towards the evil haze, the ugly glow strengthening with every passing moment. A grey mist was rising from the sea, Uall could see the shadows of the twisted shapes of men within the gloom and smell the stench of death upon the wind.

As Uall came in, he cried, "An army is amassing at the Giant's Cliffs," and closed the door. "I hear a rumour on the wind that dead mortals are being called from the sea to fight with the Cathac's forces."

"Zombies," Ke-enaan muttered. "Hell is emptying."

Holding the broken body of Doonvannan in his arms, Ke-enaan called Pa'gnac, the turquoise gas and knitter of flesh, to him. Pa'gnac, coming from a realm of coloured space light, had been at Creidne's side on the battlefields healing the wounded Danaan warriors in the War of Separation. When the worlds separated, she had been caught up in the tumult and disconnected from her own realm of coloured bands of light. As a result of the split, she had been trapped in the fourth dimension of Faerie. After the War, she had made a new home amongst the lilies and dragonflies in the bog and fenland. Searching for Danaan resonance upon the airwaves, she had found and formed a bond with Ke-enaan at Black Head.

Pa'gnac spiralled in front of Ke-enaan, awaiting his

instruction. Directing the pulsing light into Doonvannan's body, Ke-enaan gently laid him on the rushes by the fire. The turquoise flame flowed in rivulets up and down Doonvannan's battered form. And then, in a blazing flash of turquoise light, Pa'gnac left the sylph's body and vanished into the dragon fire.

Doonvannan opened his eyes, sat up, and looked around in confusion. "What happened to meself?"

"Zarg attacked thee," Ke-enaan said, putting his hand on Doonvannan's arm. "But fear not. The spriggan hath been destroyed."

Doonvannan frowned. "Me mind is foggy. The last thing I remember is sitting with Duirmuid at the hearth." He stared at the sword girthed around Ke-enaan's waist and the green star ring upon his finger, and then gazed in wonder at Uall, who was standing alongside.

"The brute attacked us from behind," Duirmuid responded. "Wees would have been red devil food if Ke-enaan hadn't arrived and pierced his evil heart."

Ke-enaan felt guilty. He had seen the spark in the spriggan's eyes and, in his distracted state of awareness, had chosen to ignore it. It was his fault Zarg had attacked Doonvannan and Duirmuid. Because of his negligence, he had put their lives in peril. He wondered how his possession spell over Zarg's mind had been rent asunder. Spriggans were fire devils, he reasoned, and would have the same resonant patterns as the fallen fire lord. When the spell was cast on the mirror, a second spell must have freed the spriggan's mind.

Ke-enaan's thoughts rested on the company in their desperate bid to free Kilfannan. Somehow Ngpa-tawa had connected the dark spiritual powers of fire and earth and had turned them to his will. He had bound the elements with a spell so powerful that even Duirmuid, Lord of Stone, could not enter or dispel it.

Going to the mirror, Ke-enaan visualised Aine's face and bent his will upon the glass, but the surface was still and unresponsive.

"Duirmuid," he said, returning to the hearth, "the mirror is still spelled. My heart is full of worry for the company. Pray, try again and see if thou canst contact them through the Mind of the Stone."

Bowing his head, Duirmuid closed his eyes and became one with a mountain, a boulder, a crystal pebble, and a glowing gemstone. Allowing himself to flow into the stone, he tried to sense Aine's vibration. Through the Mind of the Stone, he saw Aine and Nala darting through the water towards the wizard's halls. The stifling heat and choking sensation that he had experienced when he had first tried had disappeared.

"Mistress Aine and Master Nala have triumphed over the fey fire spell," he said joyfully. "They have escaped and are returning."

Just then, they heard light footfalls on the steps leading up from the cavern. Kilfannan and Kilcannan appeared, with the House of An Carn behind them.

"Well-met!" Ke-enaan said, sending his cloak billowing around them in greeting and drawing them to him. "I thank the Green that thou art safe."

"Safe we may be," Kilfannan said, "but Aine and Nala are trapped in a tunnel by a wall of blocking stone." He then went on to tell Ke-enaan and Uall about the battle for his freedom, and the events that had followed.

"Fear not for Mistress Aine and Master Nala, for they have escaped from the blocking spell," Ke-enaan said. "Duirmuid hath seen them through the Mind of the Stone. They art returning to my halls."

The sylphs clapped their hands together in joy at the news. Ke-enaan brought a jerkin, breeches and boots for Kilfannan. "Attire for thee," he said, handing him the clothes. Kilfannan smiled appreciatively. "Many thanks."

The smile vanished from his face as he saw Doonvannan sitting on the floor by the hearth with his head in his hands.

"What ails Doonvannan?" Kilfannan asked the wizard.

"Zarg attacked him," Ke-enaan answered. "Pa'gnac has healed his wounds, but 'twill take a moment for his head to clear."

"Zarg!" Kilcannan exploded, his eyes burning with peridot fire. "I knew the brute could not be trusted. Meself should have stabbed the awful creature while I had the chance."

"Peace!" Ke-enaan thundered. "We have no energy to waste on Zarg. He is dead. The Cathac is coming for the sapphire star-gate, the entrance to nine dimensions, and he will stop at naught to get it." He turned to Kilfannan. "What are thy plans?"

Kilfannan shook his head. "I know not. My mind is in confusion and is consumed with morbid thoughts of damp and cold and death."

"Brother!" Kilcannan said, laying his hand on Kilfannan's arm and steering him towards the hearth. "Come and rest awhile by the fire. It will warm and comfort thee."

"Stay!" Uall's deep voice echoed round the chamber. "The House of Kilfenoran, come forth."

As Kilfannan and Kilcannan stood before the giant, Uall laid his huge hands upon their heads. "Lords of the House of Air, I will cleanse thee of thy fear with the mystical fire of dragon breath. May the flame in thy hearts join with the sacred dragon magic of Slieve Elva. For 'tis said in the lore of old that while the Green lives, there is a sacred mystical power in the HeartStar that could turn the tide."

A rippling blue flame appeared before their eyes; a tingling vibration ran through their being; and for a moment they saw a vision of Braxa the Red, father of all dragons, wreathed in the mystical fire of the giant's forge.

Uall's voice once more echoed round the hall. "At the start of the War of Separation," he said, "seven dragons poured their fire into the forge. Only one did not enter my domain. Nag-ta, the dragon of fire falling to water, sent word that he was fighting fire demons in the great city of the south, and apologised for his delay. Needless to say, he did not bring forth his fire to add to our dragon magic."

If only dragon fire could burn away the fear and doubts that assail me, Ke-enaan thought. He knew that his journey into dark magic in the past had left a weakness—a weakness that was now being exploited by the Cathac and his emissaries. He had to watch his thoughts and be ready to push away the doubt and fears that the enemy would send to him across the airwaves. His mind rested on Kilfannan and Kilcannan. The House of Air, having only fourth-dimensional faerie consciousness, would have no spiritual protection against the powerful forces of Under-Sea and Under-Earth that would be unleashed during the battle for the sapphire. For their own safety and that of the Green, he would have to try to persuade them to leave Black Head. He knew he had to carefully choose his words. The sylphs were headstrong and wilful, and would want to stay and face the enemy.

"Kilfannan," he said, "methinks that it would be best for the House of Air to leave my halls before the battle begins. Thou art the head of thy house and the champions of the Green.

Because of this, if Black Head falls and thou art destroyed, the Green will die. The Cathac will have vanquished all of his enemies with one foul stroke. While the House of Air lives and the sacred objects of thine house endure, there is hope for the Green, slim though it may be. My advice is that thou leave this place before nightfall."

Kilfannan rose and, addressing Ke-enaan, said, "'Twould not be prudent to send us away on the eve of battle." He glanced at Kilcannan, who nodded in agreement. "If the Cathac takes possession of the sapphire, all is lost," Kilfannan continued. "The gates to Pandemonia will open, and the Cathac and his legions will gain access not only to the Faerie Worlds but also to all nine dimensions. The power of air and the power of water combined are formidable and can breach the spells of the enemy. I would rather fight here and die amongst my relatives and friends than be caught on a lonely hillside by our enemies."

"I will not be gainsaid," Ke-enaan said, turning his piercing eyes upon Kilfannan. "We are outnumbered by the enemy in thousands, and our only defence against the Cathac and his legions is high magic. 'Tis dangerous to unleash such mighty forces within my hall and Slieve Elva. I fear that the power charges exchanged in the coming conflict may overcome thy life force and destroy thee."

A gusting wind blew up around Kilfannan and Kilcannan. Ke-enaan saw the light of battle burning in their eyes.

Giving a sigh of exasperation, Ke-enaan said, "Thy mission is to free Niamh and Caiomhin. Their revivification would be a mighty blow to the enemy. Niamh and Caiomhin are the most powerful of the elemental lords. Their liberation would strengthen our defences against the Cathac and turn the tide in our favour."

The star emerald on Kilfannan's brow blazed with the radiance of the Green as he considered the wizard's words.

"'Tis true what thou sayest," he said after a short silence. "Our mission is to find the key made of air and the coach the mortal made. Even though we desire to avenge the wrongs that have been wrought against us, the liberation of Niamh and Caiomhin hast to take priority above all else."

For a moment, Kilfannan saw the face of his mortal friend Mary, and remembered their poignant parting. She was going to the antique shop to buy the coach the thief had sold to the owner. An icy finger of fear snaked through him. He wondered what day it was in the mortal world. Faerie was timeless when compared to the realm of humankind. He thought quickly. He had left her on a Sunday. Computing the time, he realised that today was Monday in the mortal world. Mary worked from nine o' clock to five and wouldn't bring the coach to Black Head until after she had finished work. Her faerie sight would make her vulnerable to attack from Zugalfar's devil legions. He thought about the route she would take from her cottage to Black Head. She had to be warned.

"My Mary is in danger," Kilfannan said to Ke-enaan. "If she bought the coach today, 'tis possible she will bring it here and may fall victim to the battle. We must back track her route and give her warning."

"'Twill be perilous for thee upon the open road, for the dark storm will be upon us and the air alive with flying imps and devils," Ke-enaan responded.

Fey light shimmered around Kilfannan and Kilcannan. A listening hush fell upon the hall.

"If we leave an hour before the light fails, we will be miles away from here when the Cathac launches his attack. His eyes and those of his armies will be focused on Black Head and the light of the sapphire," they said as one. "We will go forth on our quest for the key with the light of the Green around us to whatever end."

The House of An Carn and the House of Doon rose. "We art servants of the Green and are bound to the House of Kilfenoran by our hearts," they said in one voice. "We art pledged to find the key and will ride with Kilfannan and Kilcannan. While the Green lives, our only focus is the will of the House of Kilfenoran."

Ke-enaan stared at them. "'Tis madness to take the open road with battle drawing nigh," he thundered. "Stay off the road, for spies will be upon it. Take the paths less trodden, and let the wood and rock flow shield thee."

"In truth!" Uall interceded. "Though it seem like madness, there is wisdom in their words. Possessing the sapphire is the focus of the Cathac. In his greed and malice, he will see naught else. The horses of the House of Air are swift, and dragon magic will help shield the company from detection and attack."

"Lord Ke-enaan," Kilfannan said, "we have failed to find the thief. His trail grows cold. 'Twould it be possible to locate him with a spell? For is it not so that the character of the key, though copy it may be, is linked by its geometry to the House of Air?"

Ke-enaan thought for a moment. Reaching into his robe, he brought out the ancient grimoire he had taken from the vault and laid it reverently on the table.

"There might be a way," he muttered, looking through the pages. He peered intently at the spidery writing. Then, going to a shelf, he took down a map and laid it next to the grimoire.

"Uall," Ke-enaan said, looking up from the page, "methinks I hath found a spell to locate the thief. Stand on one side of

the table with Kilcannan and Cor-cannan. When I give thee
the signal, fortify their downdraught with thy dragon breath.
Kilfannan and Cor-garran will stand beside me on the other
side, and together we will make a vortex on the map." He
turned to Doonvannan and Duirmuid.

"Duirmuid, place thine hands upon the map and let the
power of stone and earth guide us in our search. As for thee,
Doonvannan, take to the air. When we create the vortex, spin
it in rotation."

When all was ready, Ke-enaan raised his hand to Uall,
Duirmuid, Kilcannan, and Cor-cannan. The map began to
flatten against the table with the force of their downdraught
breath. Once Ke-enaan had signalled to Kilfannan and Cor-
garran for the updraught breath, they saw as the forces clashed
a vortex form. As the spiralling air rose, Doonvannan spun
the battling air jets and a tiny spinning whirlwind appeared
upon the map. Ke-enaan began to intone the spell of finding,
at which time the tiny twister slowly travelled inland from
Black Head.

Kilfannan watched as the tiny whirlwind travelled south,
passing by Lisdoonvarna and coming to rest in the town of
Kilfenora.

"The thief is in the Black Orchid," he said to Kilcannan.
"We must leave forthwith. With luck we may find O'Shallihan
and wrest away the key. Then we can wait for Mary at the
crossroads in Lisdoonvarna. If the thief has left by the time
we arrive, we will find Rickoreen. The clauricaun has sharp
ears and likes to listen to the mortal conversations in the bar.
He will recognise the man as the thief he saw with Grad and
will know where he may be found. There are still a couple of
hours before dark falls. Let us make ready for the road."

Booted, cloaked, and armed, the House of Air, along with Duirmuid of the House of Stone, made ready to leave.

The scent of orange blossom suddenly flooded into the hall. Aine and Nala appeared at the top of the stairs.

"Aine! Nala!" Kilfannan and Kilcannan cried out as one.

Kilfannan said, "Thank the Green thou art safe. We were worried when the vortex closed behind us and you were left to face the enemy alone."

"Dear ones," Aine said, embracing them, "the House of Air and the House of Water art as one. No enemy will come between us." She looked at them intently. "Thou art leaving?"

"Yes," Kilfannan answered. "We have a mark on the thief. He is near. We go to wrest the key made of air away from him. With luck, my Mary will have the mortal coach and before the battle starts we can free our creators. Niamh and Caiomhin art mighty in air magic and will add their power to thine."

Nala put his long, slender fingers on Duirmuid's arm. "Praise be to the House of Stone," he said with gratitude. "Rock did indeed succour us and allowed us to escape from the spell trap that had been laid."

Duirmuid smiled. "The House of Stone and the House of Water are one in heart," he said.

Ke-enaan brought out the two bundles from his cloak. "Behold the sacred power objects of the House of Air: Ennuiol, the growing tree, and Delphuaan, the silver flute." He handed the bundles to Kilfannan and Kilcannan.

"Kilfannan," Aine said, taking him aside. "I have a gift for thee that may prove useful in thy endeavour to recover the key made of air." She handed him a gold ring set with a bloodstone. "'Tis a ring of compulsion. Thou only hast to touch the thief with the stone and by using thy intent, he will follow thy command."

Taking the ring, Kilfannan put it on his finger. That way he couldn't lose or misplace it. "My lady," he said, bowing. "The House of Air is in thy debt."

Forget-me-nots flowered in Aine's face. "Debt! Nay, there is no debt for we are all one within the heart."

Uall brought goblets full of elixir on a tray and offered them around.

"Children of the HeartStar," Ke-enaan said, raising his goblet, "let us make a toast in this dark hour! Know this in thine hearts, as long as beauty endures, stone grows, rivers flow, and meadows are alive with flowers, we will sing the song of life to whatever end. That is our destiny. We will go forward into the darkness with the light of the Green around us."

With heavy hearts, the House of Air said their farewells to Aine and Nala, and then, standing before Ke-enaan and Uall, received their blessings.

"Thine horses are waiting for thee in the meadow at the forge," Ke-enaan said. "Go now, and may the HeartStar be thy guide."

A few moments after the company had left, the air in the hall shimmered and Thorn-Haw appeared before Ke-enaan. The faun's eyes were smouldering with slow anger as he spoke. "My trees have reported that goblins and their knockers are travelling south from the northern mines in Connaught to the Giant's Cliffs," he rustled. "Their number is thick like trees in a forest. Other foul broods are on the march along the east–west road. The filth art hewing down my trees to make their fires. Lord Ke-enaan," Thorn-Haw rustled, "Zugalfar and his legions have joined with the Cathac. The red stain of their being hangs like an evil thundercloud above the Giant's Cliffs. Night is drawing in. The air is full of expectant hate and malice."

Thorn-Haw looked around the hall. Bowing to Uall, Aine, and Nala, he asked, "Where is the House of Air?"

"The company is on their way to Kilfenora," Ke-enaan answered. "The thief O'Shallihan is there. Kilfannan will try to wrest the key from him."

"With thy leave," Thorn-Haw said, "I will return to me trees and keep watch upon the road to Kilfenora. My trees are in my thought. I can give warning to the House of Air if there is peril ahead or behind them."

Ke-enaan nodded. "I do not know the hour or the manner of the first wave of attack upon my hall, so I doth not know if thou will be able to return to Black Head with further tidings. I charge thee to go forth and send word to the trooping elves to stand watch upon all paths that lead to Kilfenora and kill any servants of the enemy they find."

Thorn-Haw put his knotted fingers on his heart. "Thy wish is my will," he rustled. "May the mystical power of the Green protect us all." And with a swish, he disappeared.

"My friends," Ke-enaan said to Aine and Nala, "there is much to discuss. Time is flying toward dark. Explanations are needed. Let us gather round the fire. There is much to talk and tell."

Once they were seated, Ke-enaan said, "After thou had left on thy mission to rescue Kilfannan, a fey fire spell was laid against my hall." He then went on to tell them what had happened. "Uall and I returned just in time to save Duirmuid and Doonvannan from Zarg." He looked into the dragon fire for a moment and sadly shook his head. "The mystical power that has protected Black Head from the time I took up my abode hast been infiltrated by agents of the enemy." He sighed deeply. "But for such times as these we art brought into creation." Turning his eyes on Aine and Nala, Ke-enaan said, "Tell us, what happened to thee after the House of Air made their escape from the grotto of Nephelum?"

In a hushed voice, Nala told the company how Manannan and Ngpa-tawa had conspired to trap him and his sister in the tunnel. His voice dropped and belladonna blossomed in his face when he talked of how he had succumbed to the power spell cast by Ngpa-tawa. His father, Manannan, had used the fallen fire lord to cast a possession spell upon him, causing Nala to become filled with greed and lust. Under direction from Manannan, he had tried to kill Aine and take her essence. In a last desperate bid to save him, Aine had pressed the hare charm he had given her in the exchange of talismans to his heart.

The belladonna faded from Nala's skin and love-lies-bleeding bloomed. "Once the spell had been broken by our spiritual connection," Nala said, "we saw a small crack at the bottom of the wall. Transforming into tiny lizards, we made our escape and swam back to thy pool beside the waterfall."

Uall stirred, the firelight glinting on his golden helmet. "Braxach is watching the Giant's Cliffs. I feel the heat of dragon fire upon the wind," he said. "The hour grows late. Where is Trevelyan?"

Ke-enaan sent his mind onto the airwaves to sense Trevelyan's presence. He saw him leaving a house in England with Emma and a tall man of dark complexion. "Trevelyan is leaving the third world and will be here shortly," he answered.

Putting away the map, Ke-enaan peered once more at the

pages of the ancient manuscript on the table. "This tome is full of spells and mystical enchantments used by my brother Creidne and the warrior wizards in the War of Separation," he said. "Let us see what spells we canst use to defend ourselves against the rising dark. Uall," Ke-enaan said to the giant, who was peering over his shoulder, "here is an ice spell for fire devils and a circle of containment that goblins and their knockers cannot pass. There is another spell," he said excitedly, "that will make Black Head and Slieve Elva disappear into the fifth dimension. If the battle goes ill and all else fails, in the last resort we will use it."

Before Ke-enaan could say any more, there was the sound of footsteps on the stairs leading up from the cavern. Looking up, Ke-enaan saw Trevelyan walk into his hall, accompanied by two mortals.

"Well-met!" Trevelyan said, bowing to the company.

"Let me introduce thee to Emma Cameron, the warrior of air in mortal form, and Omar St Louis, a powerful psychic and protector of the Green."

Chapter 13

THE BETRAYAL

Emma found herself in a long room with a high arched ceiling. Four figures were sitting around a great hearth that flickered and flared with a cold blue light which shined eerily upon the green rush floor. The figures rose as Trevelyan entered and turned to greet them. A tall, thin, haggard-looking man with a sombre face and steely eyes came towards them, accompanied by a stocky red-haired man.

"Well-met!" the tall man said to Emma and Omar. "I am Ke-enaan, the wizard of Black Head, and this is Uall MaCarn, the giant of Slieve Elva."

Emma stared at Uall. Dragon flame from the fire glinted on his helmet, and spidery armour rippled and glimmered on his chest. Even though he appeared to be normal in size, she could see a shimmering gargantuan silhouette around him. His energetic field was so immense in all directions that she could not comprehend the true vastness of his giant size.

Ke-enaan and Uall were followed by two beautiful faeries. "This is Aine and Nala of the High House of Water," Ke-enaan said, making the introductions.

"'Tis an honour to meet thee, faerie warrior," Aine purred to Emma. Then, smiling coquettishly at Omar, she began to visit with him. Emma was suddenly aware of Nala standing before her. "'Tis a pleasure to meet thee, my lady," he said softly, staring into her eyes.

There was something familiar about his lithe form and the sheen of stars that shone from his dark slick-backed hair that aroused her femininity. A circlet of silver set with a beryl and moonstones graced his brow. She watched in fascination as red roses budded and blossomed in his antique yet youthful face. She felt a strange pull, an intense magnetic attraction to him, and couldn't look away.

A sexual thrill ran though Nala as he gazed at Emma. She was identical in essence, bearing, and form to Aine, his beloved sister. Their heart-shaped faces held the same delicate beauty and allurement, and their eyes glittered with hidden passion.

Nala felt excited; a surge of sexual need swept through him like a hot rushing torrent, and every fibre in his body quivered with expectation. He was fused energetically to Emma the same way he was connected to Aine. Emma was his sister mate—and he wanted her.

Nala suddenly caught his thoughts. The sexual desire that had robbed his mind of all else shocked an ugly jolt into his core. What was he thinking? He closed his eyes for a moment and travelled inwards. Was the exchange of talismans not working? He felt terror slice his heart. Had his attack on Aine somehow altered things?

Examining his feelings, Nala discovered that he did not want to drain Emma but to breed her. The understanding made him think even deeper about the surreal situation he was in. It appeared that even though the compulsion to feed on earth's females for survival no longer controlled him, his sexual desire for mortals had not been quenched. He had mistakenly thought that the exchanging of talismans with Aine would also free him from his desire. He was wrong. His attraction to Emma was so strong that all he could think about in that moment was taking her to him and possessing her. Forgetting his mission and the conflict to come, he took her in his arm and, tilting up her chin, kissed her softly on the lips.

Emma gasped as Nala's fingers touched her chin. He seemed to morph into everything she found desirable in a man. Silver streaks appeared in his dark, lustrous hair, and his face took on a haughty sensuous look. She felt her self-control slipping away and desire take its place. Her pulse quickened and she began to tremble as his soft lips and questing tongue found access to her mouth. Forgotten was the battle to come. All she could think about was an overpowering urge to be part of him, and her body melting into his.

Trevelyan stared at Emma in stunned disbelief. She seemed to have forgotten the impending battle, the urgent counsel that was necessary, and the preparations to be made. Instead, she was kissing Nala. Judging from the sexual energy pulsing around them, he knew that if he did not intervene, Emma and Nala would be coupling in front of everyone in the hall.

For a moment he was in a quandary. Gathering his resolve, he tried to understand what was happening to Emma, and to Nala. Being a complete being and not split into the polarities of male or female, he had little understanding of the sexual attraction between the polarisations, and was unaware how a base nature could exert such a control over spiritual beings. He reasoned that when the Cathac had given Ngpa-tawa the mortal world, the fallen fire lord had used the polarities of the separation—male and female—to his own advantage. He had made sex a blueprint in the human psyche for the conflict of survival, just as Aine and Nala had been forced by Manannan's poisoned seed to feed upon mortals for their existence.

The more he pondered on Emma's unpredictable change, the more he realised he was in error. Bringing Emma with her incubus resonation into Nala's presence had been a terrible mistake. Their meeting had put their efforts to defend the sapphire and ultimately the Green in serious jeopardy. He had not known that Aine and Nala would be present when they arrived, so what could he have done differently? he asked himself. Trevelyan thought back into the past and tried to see the continuity of the events that had led to the present.

After the War of Separation, he had travelled into the myriads of realities in the stars, only returning to the third density when Emma was born in mortal form. He realised that while he had been on his sojourn, the enemy had plotted and schemed in furtherance of their agenda. Trevelyan felt guilt and regret that he had not paid attention to what was really occurring in the Faerie Worlds. A monstrous conspiracy had been laid and then hatched, and he and Ke-enaan had been totally unaware of the extent of the enemy's control or how far their agenda had advanced. Ngpa-tawa had murdered his own elemental kin, spied upon the council, and repeated every word that was spoken there to the Cathac. In return for his help in destroying the HeartStar and allowing access to conquer the Faerie Worlds, the Cathac had given the fallen fire lord dominion over the race of human beings. Ngpa-tawa was the god of the third dimension; a multitude worshipped him. The fire lord had turned humankind into automated bags of squirming appetites dependent on sex for the furtherance of their species. Ngpa-tawa had programmed Emma, Aine, and Nala's need through his manipulation of the fire and water field, not only in the mortal world but also in the Faerie Worlds.

The incoming black tide of hate was rushing towards them like a tidal wave—just as the enemy had planned. The poison seed that had been sown in the three worlds long ago now had bloomed. The poison flower would soon bear the fruit of misery and destruction.

Trevelyan filled himself with space to clear his mind, letting his awareness roam for a fleeting moment into the stars. He finally understood Emma's instinctual and compulsive behaviour. His heart felt sad for such a High Faerie warrior to have been snatched into dark magic from birth. All the faerie warriors had been the victims of malignant energetic powers.

Taking Emma by the arm, he pulled her away from Nala.

Emma suddenly was aware of Trevelyan's hand on her arm pulling her away. Her first instinct was to struggle.

"Let me go!" she cried out. Then, in a flash of horror and confusion, she realised what she was about to do. Nala was an incubus, one whom she had wanted to possess her there and then. The thought was like a knife strike in her mind. Her spirit recoiled at her intended actions, and her face began to burn with shame. She had acted like an alley cat in heat.

The attraction she had felt for Nala remained in her consciousness. She could still feel the sexual tension that had overcome her senses and her spiritual heritage for a moment. Embarrassed and bewildered, she stood beside Trevelyan.

"I'm sorry," she said in a small voice. "I don't know what came over me."

Trevelyan gazed at her. "Emma!" he answered, never taking his eyes off her face. "'Tis not your fault, m'dear. As a mortal, you are cursed by Ngpa-tawa's dark magic. Do not reproach yourself. Let the experience guide your heart with wisdom. Stay within the heart and put an emerald octahedron around you." His eyes softened. "May you stay strong in the power of the HeartStar."

Omar had looked in amazement at Emma standing in a steamy embrace with Nala. He couldn't believe his eyes. He had turned to Aine to ask her what was happening with her brother, when he saw to his amazement that she was no longer in her faerie bodysuit. She was wearing a short skirt, a low-cut blouse, and high-heeled shoes, and had shape-shifted into an alluring human seductress. He had found himself falling into the turquoise water of her eyes, succumbing to her sensual charm, and feeling sexual tension trying to take root in his body. There was part of him that wanted her. He had felt a jolt that jerked him from her spell and into reality. His fire and water loa had joined his being, heralding their arrival with words of warning. Putting his hand in his pocket, he had grasped the amethyst he always carried for protection, and struggled against the sexual compulsion he was feeling. Averting his eyes from Aine's magnetic gaze, he had begun praying to Jah for deliverance. He felt a hand trying to slide in between his legs. She was trying to seduce him. He had to get away. Spinning round, keeping his eyes on the floor, and keeping his hand upon the amethyst, he had quickly returned to Trevelyan's side.

"What's happenin', mon?" he said, his eyes wide with bewilderment. "Wickedness has found its way into the hall."

"An answer will be forthcoming," Trevelyan had answered. "For now, I need to think."

Trevelyan fiddled with his eyeglass. The plot against the HeartStar, which was all-encompassing, had now been exposed in all its dark dimensions. He glanced anxiously at Ke-enaan, seeing the same disbelief and confusion registering in the wizard's face. They had been blindsided, cut off from the scale of the enemy's plans. The agenda had moved stealthily forward throughout the ages of humanity, and the agenda to conquer the HeartStar was within an ace of triumph. In a plan to possess the sapphire at the time of the alignment, the Cathac and his minions had murdered all their opposition, mortal and faerie, with betrayal and dark magic. The plan that was laid before the War of Separation had come to fruition, a plot that was modified by the language of betrayal.

Trevelyan's body grew tense. They were just hours away from the battle that could decide the fate of the HeartStar, and the lords that they had relied upon to stand strong against the incoming dark tide had been murdered. Emma, Aine, and Nala had been compromised by animal desire. If the company were going to be successful in their mission, Emma had to overcome the sexual appetites Ngpa-tawa had programmed into her body. And even though Aine and Nala had overcome Manannan, it was obvious to Trevelyan that Ngpa-tawa still controlled their sexual nature through their connection to the water field.

He had to act or else their mission would fail. He thought for a moment. He would use the space field. Space was the colour blue, opposite in polarity to the yellow-orange of fire descending into the water field. If he raised a blue vibration in the hall, he could block the sexual resonance from affecting them. Then he could send them the vibrations of the HeartStar to strengthen their faerie nature.

Trevelyan breathed upon the lens of his eyeglass, creating a ball of shimmering blue light that burst into five oscillating pentagonal polyhedra. The geometrics flew around the room, clearing the air of the yellow-orange colour. Then, coming together in a ball, they separated into three spheres and entered the crowns of Emma, Aine, and Nala.

Emma's body relaxed as the light entered. Her mind became clear and free of confusion. Aine morphed back into her faerie form. Nala, embarrassed by his weakness and lack of sexual control, turned his face away and stood looking at the wall.

Searching for the physical and spiritual connection between him and Emma, Nala entered her awareness and read her past. Her father, a satanist, had used her as a vessel for his evil rituals of sodomy and rape in the temple of Cybele underneath her house. As a result, she had been parasitised by an incubus.

Nala sensed Emma's hidden shame and the insecurity she had felt as a result of the sexual trauma she had suffered. Her low self-esteem had resulted in bouts of drinking and promiscuity in her teenage years. And later, during her marriage, she had a series of sordid affairs with older men which eventually broke up the relationship with her husband and led to a divorce. Nala noticed that all her lovers bore the suave and distinguished good looks of her father.

Pushing deeper into Emma's memory, Nala noticed a faint orange glow flickering in the greens and purples that pulsed around her. In a rush of understanding, he realised there was an energetic link between Emma and the incubus that had seduced her as a child. In an ongoing effort to possess her, the incubus had sexually insinuated himself into her dreams. There she had succumbed. The sexual ecstasy of her union with the incubus tingled through Nala's body.

The understanding that Emma was still possessed by the incubus made Nala uneasy. His culpability was compounded by the fact that the incubus was from an egg he had hatched aeons ago. The ugliness and misery of Emma's life hurt his heart and made him think about his predation on the mortal world. Under the serpent spell, he had been an instrument of evil. He had preyed on multitudes of women, destroying their dreams and draining them of their life. He had felt no remorse and had not given a thought to their sensitivities or their pain. To him mortals were just animals to be ravished and then consumed in his fiery orgasm. He had never realised that they were also spiritual beings with feelings and emotions. Regret for the atrocities he had committed swept through him like a heartbreak. The emotion was so intense that he had to retreat into the flowing rivers of his water dream to wash away his torment.

When his heart had calmed, his thoughts returned to Emma. He feared for her. Even though she was coming into her High Faerie power, as a human she was still vulnerable to the subtle power of the incubus. His egg son was unredeemed. He would pursue her, and in her moments of weakness, need, and unresolved conflict, she was susceptible to his advances.

Nala also realised that he too was vulnerable to desire. Because of this, he made up his mind to watch his thoughts and try to control his own sexual appetite. He loved Emma. He felt that she was part of his own essence. Loving a mortal woman was a new experience for him. He vowed that he would protect her from his egg-born son, even if he had to kill him.

When Emma, Nala, and Aine had regained their composure, Trevelyan called the company together. Turning resolutely towards them, he cleared his throat and said, "The enemy had planned its assault on the HeartStar from the very beginning, yea, even before the War of Separation. Through the dark spell he had cast on the third dimension, Ngpa-tawa infiltrated our hall using the earth and water connection to the mortal world. This was his contingency plan to sabotage us in the final hour if Emma should escape Zugalfar's net and regain the sapphire." He glanced at Emma, Aine, and Nala. "If control had been lost while the battle raged, all of us would have been doomed," he said severely. "Take heed! You must guard your thoughts and emotions from the machinations of our enemy."

Emma felt a hot flush return to her cheeks. For an instant she wished the floor would open and swallow her up and that she would awake to find the events of the last few days all a dark dream.

Trevelyan beckoned them to the fireplace. "Come! Let us sit by the hearth, for there is much to tell and be told."

When they were seated at the hearth, Trevelyan began. "The hour grows late. I have much to tell about my journey to the stars. Space holds memory. In my dissolution, I became aware of memories and events that had happened in the Faerie Worlds at the time of Separation. Many things that had been hidden from me suddenly became clear." He sat down beside Emma and took a drink from his goblet.

"Before the Separation," Trevelyan began, "the seven lords of the elements were manifest in all three worlds and were keepers of the sapphire star-gate to the nine dimensions." He paused for a moment. Then, looking into their faces, he said, "But there was a traitor amongst them. Ngpa-tawa, Lord of Fire Falling into Water, was tempted and seduced by a lust for power. He betrayed the other lords and made a pact with the Cathac. It was agreed that he would spy on the lords of the elements and report their every move. After the loss of the third dimension of Faerie in the War of Separation, Niamh and Caiomhin called a council in Gorias to discuss how they could protect the Faerie Worlds. The loss of the world of humankind had created the curse of duality on the realms of Faerie. Niamh and Caiomhin knew that it was only a matter of time before the Cathac would find a way to break the spells laid upon him and attack the fourth and fifth dimensions. Ngpa-tawa was present at the council and told the Cathac of Becuille's vision and the future events she had seen in the oracle of Ophire.

"Ngpa-tawa revealed to the Cathac the identities of the four faerie warriors that had pledged to enter mortality when the stars aligned, and where they would be born in the mortal world. In exchange for Ngpa-tawa's betrayal of the HeartStar, the Cathac granted the fallen fire lord dominion over the mortal world. Through the elements of fire and water, Ngpa-tawa set violence, carnal lust, and endless warfare in the minds of human beings. He entered the awareness of proud lords and chieftains, men who sought power over others, and once he took control of their minds, he taught them dark magic and the blood rite of human sacrifice." Trevelyan sighed deeply and passed his hand across his brow. "Now that the stars have aligned, Ngpa-tawa has used his satanic minions to hunt down the warriors and sacrifice them. Three he has destroyed. Only Emma remains."

"Thanks to you," Emma said to Trevelyan. "Even though you warned me I was in danger, I wasn't aware of the depth of the spiritual war going on around me." She glanced at Omar, who nodded in agreement.

"Emma was frightened and confused when she sought me out, mon," Omar responded. "Praise to Jah that we got this far." Omar's face dropped. "I wish I would have had the fortitude to save my Lucy, the warrior of water, from the mamba."

Nala pricked up his ears. He was now the lord of water and had immediate interest in what had happened to the faerie warrior belonging to his house.

"The warrior of water, thou sayest?" he said to Omar. "What dost thou know of her ending?"

Omar told the company about Lucy's dreams and how he had begged her to leave Jamaica with him. His eyes welled with tears as he described the coming of the mamba and the Obeah men, and his voice lowered as he spoke of how the sorcerers had overpowered him and carried Lucy away like a trophy.

Ke-enaan brought more elixir and topped up their goblets. "Trevelyan," he said, "didst thou see in thine dissolution the fate of the warriors of earth and fire?"

Trevelyan nodded. For an instant a spasm of sorrow passed across his face.

"The warrior of fire was born in a country called Mexico," he said. "His name was Enzo. His parents left home one morning to work in the fields and never returned. Enzo was ten years old when he was orphaned. He was taken in by his uncle who was a shaman and the leader of an ancient snake cult. The necromancer was shunned by the villagers who feared his cursing powers, and those who tried to intervene on Enzo's part and take him for their own also disappeared." He put his hand across his eyes for a moment, and then said to the company, "You must excuse me. In my dissolution into the stars, I have seen much that is wicked. I have felt the agony of betrayal and of innocence destroyed ... and my heart hurts when I speak of it." He took a deep breath and then continued. "Enzo's life changed from heaven to hell. He saw the tender creatures he had loved butchered before his eyes. All he knew was toil and abuse. When he was fourteen years old, his uncle called him to a meeting of shamans and told him it was time that he was initiated into the ancient serpent cult of his ancestors. But it was a ploy. The shaman knew of Enzo's High Faerie purpose, so he gave him an ultimatum. To be worthy of the honour of being a member of the serpent cult, Enzo had to bring to the ceremony a male baby less than six months old to be sacrificed to Nephelum. Enzo refused, as the shaman knew he would. His uncle signalled to the others who were present, and Enzo was seized, bound, and kept in a squalid pit until the night of the ceremony. At the auspicious hour when the moon's full face beamed down its evil light, his uncle and other shamans in the cult came for Enzo. Unspeakable things they did to him. I cannot tell of it. Suffice to say that after they had evilly used him, the shaman bled him with scores of knife cuts. As his blood leaked into the earth, he was thrown into a pit of vipers. As the venom entered his body and he lay dying, his uncle began to chant. And as Enzo's life force began to leave his body, the shaman opened his mouth and consumed Enzo's soul."

Emma tried not to think about what Trevelyan was describing. Something similar could easily have been her fate. She felt fear trying to creep in to her mind from the negative scenarios his words were creating. Picking up her goblet, she gulped the elixir in one swallow. She felt Trevelyan's eyes upon her.

"Hold up, m'dear," he said gently. "The truth has to be told."

"As for the warrior of earth," he said, resuming, "he was born in the fjords of a country called Norway. His name was Kris. Healer of all living things, he was strong and handsome, and wise in the way of herbs and charms. When he was sixteen, he met a girl who appeared as an angel of light. She seemed to share his love of life. Not long after their first meeting, she seduced him, enslaving his flesh to hers. And, as is the way with the weakness of the flesh and the innocence of young love, he indulged her every whim. At Bealltainn, she convinced him to go with her to a fertility ceremony in the mountains to conceive a love child. Eager to please her, Kris agreed. Unbeknown to him, his lover was an old witch who had shape-shifted through blood drinking into a youth. Ngpa-tawa had alerted the witch to Kris's true identity, and she had plotted with warlocks to destroy him. When he reached the place of ceremony, the warlocks were waiting with a draugar."

Emma raised her eyebrows. "A draugar," she repeated. "What is that?"

"The undead," Trevelyan replied. "They hate the living and sustain themselves on the blood of their victims."

"It's a zombie, mon. Similar to what we have in Jamaica," Omar said. "Obeah men raise the dead from their graves and bend them to their will."

"Exactly," Trevelyan concurred. "After the warlocks had tortured and mutilated Kris, they set the draugar on him to suck out his blood and pick the flesh off his bones."

A shade fell upon the hall. The flame in the hearth retreated and burned low. It seemed that Trevelyan's recollections had brought with them menace and dark portent.

Ke-enaan got up and lit more candelabras. "Doth thou knowest the fate of the lord of earth and the lord of fire rising into air?" he asked Trevelyan. "And why, when I have connected with their resonance upon the airwaves to call for aid, I have received no answer to my summons?"

Trevelyan gazed into the fire. After a long pause, he said grimly, "The lords are dead."

"Dead!" Ke-enaan reiterated in shocked surprise.

Trevelyan nodded. "Yes. The lords were murdered long ago."

Ke-enaan looked at him with fear and incredulity in his eyes. "Tell on," he said grimly.

"The HeartStar has been betrayed from the beginning," Trevelyan began. "Ngpa-tawa invited the lords to his great city in the south as a ruse. He informed them that he had magic that could thwart the future plans of the Cathac, saying that he wished to share it with them. Such was his guile. The lords, not suspecting anything amiss, trusted him, for deceit was not present in their High Faerie nature. When they arrived at his hall, Ngpa-tawa received them with pomp and ceremony. He put on a banquet for them in his great hall of fire. Hexing their wine with a fey-fire spell, he poisoned them. Before their spirits left their bodies, Ngpa-tawa fixed their resonance on the airwaves to fool us into thinking the lords were still alive." After taking another sip of elixir, he said, "That is why even though we found their resonance on the airwaves, no word was forthcoming from the lords or aid offered, and why their warriors had no spiritual protection."

"To think we were so blind," Ke-enaan said, shaking his head.

"Do not reproach thyself," Trevelyan responded. "Ngpa-tawa plotted against us from the beginning and murdered our allies. He is well-practised in the art of deception as he has now made plain. Meself had no evidence against him, only a feeling of distrust. It was not until Braxach came to my study and told me the fire lord and his dragon had aligned themselves with Zugalfar that I knew my suspicions were well grounded."

Aine stirred. Love-lies-bleeding began to bloom in her

face as her turquoise eyes took on a darker hue. "Trevelyan," she said, "my mother, Erin, and her consort Evnass were the heads of the High House of Water and were present at the council in High Faerie long ago. After Erin was raped and abducted by Manannan, he imprisoned her in his city in Under-Sea. There she gave birth to quadruplets, meself and Nala, Graine, and Akala. After my mother gave birth to us, she killed herself." Aine paused and swallowed hard. "Dost thou know what happened to Evnass?"

Trevelyan slowly nodded. Sadness crept into his eyes as if the memory pained him. "After your mother was taken, Evnass fell into despair," he replied. "Ngpa-tawa, in league with the Cathac, saw his chance to destroy him. Unbeknown to the other lords, Ngpa-tawa had visited the great city of Murias and, using his connection to the water realm, offered Evnass his assistance to rescue Erin. Evnass was overjoyed with the fire lord's proposal, his dark despair lightening into hope. He now had a chance to rescue his beloved. A plan was made and sealed with secrecy. It was agreed they would go to Under-Sea and, with their combined power of fire and water, force Manannan to free Erin.

"On the eve of their departure, Evnass summoned the water hammer from the Mind of the Sea, the weapon he had used in the War of Separation to lay waste to Manannan's underwater city. When they arrived at the citadel, Manannan was waiting with his sea serpents to greet them. Ngpa-tawa bowed before Manannan and then turned his gloating eyes upon Evnass. In that fateful moment, Evnass realised Ngpa-tawa had betrayed him. His thoughts were in turmoil. In a desperate plea for aid, he opened his awareness to the Mind of the Sea. As Evnass's summons radiated into the water, Ngpa-tawa sent a ring of fire into the sea to cut off Evnass's vibrations. With all hope of aid dashed, Evnass drew his sword and charged at Ngpa-tawa. The fire lord became a moving flame within the water and evaded his blows. Then, with the speed of a viper, Ngpa-tawa encircled Evnass in a sheet of fell fire that the latter's water power could not quench. The ring of fire suspended Evnass in the churning water of Under-Sea. So strong was the binding spell that he did not have the power to escape it. Manannan croaked out an order in the hideous speech of Under-Sea, and his serpent lords snaked through the water and coiled like constrictors around Evnass's body. Lashing their tails, the serpents propelled him through the water to the temple of Manannan in the plaza of the weed-wracked city.

"Evnass was forced through the gaping door of the slime-ridden temple. The fire serpents suspended him over a granite slab blazing with the corrupted fire of the fallen dragon Nag-ta.

"Before Ngpa-tawa sent Evnass into the killing flame, Manannan threw open his great oilskin coat and dragged Erin out by her hair. Thrusting her forward towards the slab, he laughed and taunted Evnass, gesturing lewdly towards Erin's scratched body heavily swollen with his serpent seed. Evnass screamed and tried to struggle but found he could not move. As the serpents lowered him into the all-consuming flame, Erin was forced to witness the agonising dissolution of her lover."

The hall was quiet and the air full of sadness. Nightshade bloomed in Aine's and Nala's faces as they absorbed what had happened to Erin and Evnass. Rising from their seats, they put their hands upon their hearts in oath. "As the High House of Water," they said as one, "we will avenge Erin and Evnass, and not rest until Manannan is but dust upon the sea and Ngpa-tawa is ash upon the wind." So strong was their emotion that the candles flickered and, for a moment, their light dimmed.

"After Ngpa-tawa had destroyed the High House of Water," Trevelyan continued, "he began plotting against Niamh and Caiomhin, but the protection of the HeartStar foiled his attempts to snare them. It was not until the stars aligned that he played his final card and set his trap. Knowing that Niamh and Caiomhin would need an exact copy of their faerie coach to search for the sapphire in the world of humankind, he spied upon them from the shadows. Once Niamh and Caiomhin had found a carpenter and ordered the replica of their faerie coach, Ngpa-tawa entered the mortal's mind and laid an enchantment upon him. Then he entered the dark thoughts of the mortal O'Shallihan and, enlisting Grad the goblin, wove all three of their minds together in a spell to trap the High House of Air.

"The carpenter built the coach for Niamh and Caiomhin. So smitten was he by the couple's High Faerie beauty that he made wondrous manikins of their likeness. When Niamh and Caiomhin returned and saw the dolls, Caiomhin, telling the carpenter it was forbidden to make their High Faerie images visible in the mortal world, ordered him to destroy them." Trevelyan sighed deeply. "But Ngpa-tawa entered the carpenter's mind in a dark dream and appealed to his vanity. He told him the dolls were beautiful and that it was unreasonable and petty of the High House of Air to ask him to destroy his wonderful creations. Under the fire lord's spell, the carpenter became vain and resentful, so he disobeyed Caiomhin's order. As a consequence, the High House of Air became trapped within the dolls.

"For many years, Ke-enaan and I suspected a traitor in

our midst, but neither of us bargained that Ngpa-tawa's reach had grown so long. It seems that his fingers were in many evil plots against the Green."

Trevelyan's explanation made everything clear to Emma. The fallen fire lord had been the mover and shaker behind the scenes. He had cursed the four warriors with a moon spell of forgetfulness cast out of his own watery nature. He had destroyed their High Faerie protection by murdering the lords, and had left the warriors defenceless. Then he and Zugalfar had conspired with satanists to track the warriors down and destroy them. Three were dead. She was the only one left, and that was because of Trevelyan's vigilance and protection. She wondered why he had not been able to defend the other three warriors. When she glanced at him, he must have read her mind, because he looked at her and said, "M'dear, your resonance is air rising into space. You have a genetic connection to Niamh and Caiomhin. Therefore, as Lord of Space, I pledged to protect thee in the mortal world."

Emma looked at him in astonishment. "You are the Lord of Space?"

"Yes, m'dear. I am the all and nothingness that surrounds the nine dimensions."

Emma pondered over Trevelyan's words. Having been born into a devil-worshipping family and had been satanically abused as a child, she wondered why he had not been there to protect her from the incubus. She decided to ask him when time allowed.

Trevelyan's eyes took on a steely cast as he continued. "The lords of fire, water, and earth were given the responsibility of protecting their warriors as the stars aligned and prophecy was fulfilled. Meself and Ke-enaan assumed that the lords would protect their warriors. We did not realise that Ngpa-tawa had destroyed them and left their warriors with no defence." He took a drink from his goblet and then turned his eyes upon the company. "The battle for the sapphire cannot be won by force," he said. "For we are few and would be overrun in the first swell of attack. 'Twill be the force field of our being that we will set against them. Their hate vibration is low and slow, but our connection to the Green is high and fast. We have the power of space, wind, and water to defend ourselves, energies that the enemy does not possess. But take heed! Our only weakness in this battle is the doubt or fear we harbour. Fear will make a tear in our frequency that the enemy will exploit in order to break through our defences and destroy us. Fear and doubt are the only things that can betray us. If we can stay as one mind, we can use our intent to create a separate reality from which to launch our magic against theirs."

Fear, Emma thought. For them to succeed in repelling the attack, she had to be fearless. She suddenly felt tense and realised she was sweating. She'd been in fear all her life, and she prayed that when the attack came, she could hold herself together and wouldn't be the weak link in the chain.

"Fear has always been the weapon of wickedness, mon," Omar piped up. "Fear is Ngpa-tawa's curse upon our world. He is a devil. That's why we have to stay in Jah love and positive vibrations."

Emma nodded to herself. She needed to stay positive, keep in the now, and not let fear into her mind. To bolster her courage, she began to sing a Bob Marley song about positive vibrations over and over in her head. She would use the song as a mantra, a set of words to calm her. She remembered the mantra she had used as a child in the terror of her half-conscious nightmares: *This is only a dream. This is only a dream.*

Ke-enaan brought more elixir. Glancing anxiously out of

his window at the sky, he said, "'Twill be a while before the darkness falls. We must discuss the nature of our defence."

"Before we start to weave our defences," Trevelyan responded, "I will cast the energy of the stars around us. It will create a force field that will repel any emissary of the Cathac that may try to spy upon us while we make ready."

Trevelyan opened his mouth. In the darkness of his throat, galaxies appeared. A rain of small silver specks issued forth from the whirling nebulae, filling the hall with scintillating particles of light. Then, turning his back to the fire, he joined Ke-enaan at the table.

Calling the rest of the company to him, Ke-enaan laid his hands upon the grimoire. Uttering the words of replication, he made two more manuscripts appear, each pertaining to the special spells they would use against their selected targets. He handed one copy to Emma and Omar and the other to Aine and Nala.

"My brother Creidne wrote down the instructions for the binding and blinding spells of fire, earth, and ice; curses and enchantments; and the nature of their casting," Ke-enaan said. "He has left a written record of geometric properties, incantations, herbs, and crystals for each spell that, when used together in a sequence, creates fields of force, vibrating shields of power that can withstand and repel the energetic attacks of our enemy. As the shadows fall," he said solemnly, drawing himself up to his full height, "the armies of the Cathac led by the arch-demon Zugalfar will be waiting for the signal to attack Black Head while Manannan and Ngpa-tawa will make their charge against the magic of Slieve Elva.

"The enemy will attack as one force against us," Ke-enaan continued. "His whole focus will be to gain possession of the sapphire, and destroy us in the process." He gazed at Emma and Omar for a moment and then turned his eyes on Aine and Nala.

"Each of us has our own spiritual gifts and strengths within the energies of earth, water, fire, air, and space," he said. "Therefore, I think it best that we do not attack our assailants as one force, as they will do with us, but pick our adversaries and pit our will and unique spiritual strengths against them."

Nala put his hand upon his heart. "Meself and Aine will use the power of the High House of Water against Manannan," he declared with fire in his eyes. "Manannan is no longer our sire. When we exchanged talismans and destroyed his lie that we would perish if we did so, the spell he had cast over us was broken asunder and we were liberated from his serpent seed. We triumphed over him when he came against us in the sea, and we escaped from Ngpa-tawa in the grotto of Nephelum. He fears us as our High Faerie power waxes. 'Twas Manannan who sent the dark fire lord to set the spell against us in the grotto, for he desired that I kill Aine, take her talisman, and then return with Ngpa-tawa to my father's city in Under-Sea." He took Aine's hand and kissed it. "But sister love delivered me from his snare and we escaped. Therefore he will be in double doubt. We have to find a way to increase his fear. In his uncertainty lies his weakness."

Ke-enaan nodded in agreement. "As doubt assails us, so doubt assails our enemies—and we can use their uncertainty against them. Manannan fears thee. And what thou say is true: in his insecurity he will act rashly, and his recklessness may well lead to his undoing." He thought for a moment, and then said, "I hath an idea that will give us advantage over him."

Aine and Nala joined their minds together and gazed at Ke-enaan intently.

Ke-enaan looked into their memory, and through his resonance with the sea, he saw the events that had led up to Aine's triumph over Manannan. He saw her rise from the sea clothed in the brilliant light of High Faerie. Violet lightning burst forth from the clouds as a host of High Faerie knights rose from the depths to join her.

Holding the vision in his mind, Ke-enaan withdrew from Aine's memory and entered his own thought. Swiftly he began to make an energetic copy of the scene. He would create a thought form of the confrontation, a spell of projection to challenge Manannan at the start of the conflict and undermine his will.

When the image was complete, he said to Aine and Nala, "Thou hast triumphed over thine father. His defeat on the sea will be fresh in his mind. If we can project an image through the water field of thy rising from the sea clad in the radiance of High Faerie surrounded by the knights that accompanied thee, it will cause Manannan to rage but also to doubt. Methinks it will knock him from his arrogant perch for a moment." He paused. Looking into their eyes, he said, "Thou must exploit his instant of doubt with an immediate blasting wave of spiritual power. It may be that thy radiant energy can force him back to Under-Sea, and as a result, he and his serpents and other fell creatures will be powerless to help the Cathac take possession of the sapphire."

If Aine and Nala were pitted against Manannan, Emma thought, and Braxach against the Cathac, only two adversaries remained, Zugalfar and Ngpa-tawa. The thought of Zugalfar made her cringe. She felt a stab of fear rake her being. Even though she had triumphed over the arch-demon on several occasions, taken his ruby daggers, and wrested the sapphire from him, she had acted on instinct and only escaped him by the skin of her teeth. The understanding that she was still not totally connected to her faerie power, and could not summon it at will, made her afraid. She worried that her ability to merge with her mystical nature might desert her in the battle.

Picking up her goblet, Emma gulped the elixir. She felt herself expressing the very doubt that Trevelyan had warned about. Nervously rubbing her hand across the back of her neck, she glanced at Omar.

Omar put his hand supportively on her shoulder. "Fear is the tool of wickedness. We have to try to overcome it, mon," he said, "Just like we did at the sabbat and the ceremony at Sue's. It's better to fight the devil we know than one we don't. If we can stay in neutral, loa can help us. Let's pit our will against Zugalfar and send the wicked son of Babylon back to the abyss."

"Yes. I agree." Emma nodded nervously. She was trying to appear confident, but her doubt about her abilities remained. How she wished she'd brought the tobacco with her. She could use a smoke to calm her nerves. Glancing at Trevelyan, she saw he was absorbed in the manuscript. Suddenly as if disturbed from his reading by her attention he looked up at her. "M'dear," he said gently. "I know of your misgivings. I have a gift that will empower you." Waving his fingers rhythmically in the air, Emma saw Naka, the whirlwind blade of Gorias, appear in his hand. "This is yours, m'dear," he said, giving her the dagger.

The moment Emma took the dagger, she was inundated with memory. The blade gave her a sudden rush of strength. Power flowed from the deep memories the blade shared with her. She saw herself as a High Faerie warrior wielding the whirlwind blade of Gorias in the War of Separation, and recalled how Naka had saved her from the incubus in the temple of Cybele underneath her house.

"You found Naka!" she cried out joyfully. "I thought it was lost in my struggle against the incubus."

"The dagger returned to Gorias, and Braxach brought it to me," Trevelyan said. "You will need it to cast a protection spell against Zugalfar."

Having Naka, Trevelyan, and the company with her strengthened Emma's resolve, boosted her failing sense of confidence. Pushing away her anxieties, she said, "What's the plan?"

"Zugalfar will be hot with revenge," Trevelyan replied. "But just as Manannan was, he too will be in doubt. We will compound his doubt. I will create a thought form of the ruby daggers to confound him. I will show them to him on the airwaves as he launches his attack. The power of his daggers, not yet having been recreated by the satanists, has blocked his entry into the third dimension. Zugalfar will think they are still in our possession. That will inflame his desire for them. In his eagerness we will have a chance to trap him and send him back to hell."

Trevelyan looked into their faces. "'Tis settled then. We must each be responsible for our adversaries and coordinate our attack from different angles all at once. Meself and Ke-enaan will cast our power against Ngpa-tawa. The fallen fire lord has fey fire. We will need our combined spiritual power to overcome his dark sorcery and defeat him."

Ke-enaan opened his grimoire and peered at the spidery writing of his brother Creidne. A few moments into the text, he looked up in consternation. "Trevelyan!" he said in alarm. "To cast a spell that will create a separate world in which to imprison Ngpa-tawa requires a fire elemental to act as a focus."

"What news of Fercle?" Trevelyan asked. "Did he leave with the House of Air?"

Ke-enaan shook his head. Reaching into his robe, he brought forth a small yellow tetrahedron. "Liam found Fercle's geometric on the bottom of the seabed not far from where the boat had sunk and brought it to my halls," he said. "I have not been able to resurrect Fercle, for Braxach hath not returned and there is no other dragon to breathe life into his form." Turning to Uall, who was peering at the geometric, Ke-enaan said, "Doth thou think that the dragon fire of thy forge could revive Fercle and his dragon familiar Trax?"

"To that I know not the answer," Uall replied. "But we can try."

Trevelyan was uneasy. Ke-enaan's halls had been breached. It was possible that evil had also entered Slieve Elva. The sapphire was visible on the airwaves, so Ngpa-tawa would be aware of its position and would try to get it. Trevelyan was worried that a snare may have been laid against the dragon forge and that those who entered Slieve Elva could be at risk.

"Black Head and Uall's realm are one heart," Trevelyan said. "So we must assume that Slieve Elva has also been infiltrated."

"'Tis my thought as well," Ke-enaan replied grimly, girthing the sword of light around his waist. "Uall and I must make haste to the forge at Slieve Elva. Guard my halls while we are gone. Thou will find all the requirements for the spelling in the bottles on the shelves."

CHAPTER 14

NGPA-TAWA

Ke-enaan's mind was restive as he left Black Head and followed Uall along the passage to Slieve Elva. The spectacle of Emma's and Nala's sexual compulsion, and Aine's advances towards Omar, had stunned him to the core. A foul spell of lust had penetrated the protection around his halls and had tried to sabotage their efforts to defend themselves. It seemed that their defences were falling apart before the battle had even started.

As he thought about Aine and Nala's wanton behaviour, he became aware that there had to be an energetic connection between them and Ngpa-tawa. Nala had told him that when they were trapped in the grotto of Nephelum, the fallen fire lord had ordered him to kill Aine. The fire lord's hold on Nala's mind had been so strong that Nala had acted upon the former's murderous command. Even though Aine and Nala had escaped from the grotto, he reasoned, the stain of Ngpa-tawa's spell was still upon Nala's soul. A spell had been cast to sabotage their defence of the sapphire by stealth, and Nala had unwittingly been the conduit for a lustful destructive energy to gain access to his halls.

Ke-enaan did not fault Nala. The incubus was struggling

to overcome his sexual connection to the mortal world and transcend into his High Faerie nature. Emma was the first mortal woman he had encountered since the exchanging of the talismans. When he saw her, he had not been able to resist his old nature.

Emma too was blameless. The stain of an incubus was already in her aura, and she had succumbed to her instinctual sexual desire, the automatic programme of the mortal world that could not be denied.

Tension mounted in Ke-enaan's body. He swallowed hard. Ngpa-tawa was the evil force behind the animalistic scenes he had witnessed, and the fire lord's machinations from the time of the Separation to the present awed and frightened him.

It seemed to him that the Cathac, Ngpa-tawa, and his ally Zugalfar had not only set their schemes and plots but also had covered all the angles of win or lose. They had made contingency plans for every possibility and eventuality, having all bases covered. Ke-enaan rubbed his fingers thoughtfully across his mouth. He was beginning to see the true picture and dimension of the plot to destroy the HeartStar, and how the Cathac's strategies had unfolded through the ages.

The murder of the lords and three faerie warriors had almost guaranteed the enemy's success to gain the sapphire; open the gates to Pandemonia; destroy the HeartStar of the Faerie Worlds; and then go on to conquer the nine dimensions.

The Cathac and his dark company had been thwarted in their attempts to get the sapphire in the mortal world. Emma had defeated them. She had taken the sapphire from Zugalfar and given it to Trevelyan. But Ngpa-tawa had planned for all eventualities.

After Zugalfar's failure to deliver the sapphire, Ngpa-tawa would have been well aware that Trevelyan's only chance to find refuge for the sapphire would be in worlds outside the nine dimensions. He also knew that Trevelyan would have little choice of where to take it. Only Alfaan of the Ghrian Sidhe and Paza, Lord of Xonite, had conquered time and space and created realities of their own beyond the nine dimensions.

Ke-enaan also suspected that Ngpa-tawa, to cover any eventuality, had visited Alfaan and Paza. He would have bragged to them about his murder of the elemental lords, and cautioned them with veiled threats, giving them forewarning of what might happen if they took the sapphire. Once Alfaan and Paza had learnt that Ngpa-tawa had destroyed the elemental lords of the fifth dimension, it would have put fear in their hearts. If the Cathac conquered the fifth dimension, it would not be long before his sorcerers would find a way to subjugate the other four. Once in control of the nine dimensions, the Cathac would launch an attack upon their worlds.

Ke-enaan sighed deeply and passed his hand wearily across his brow. No doubt, Ngpa-tawa would have offered Alfaan and Paza the Cathac's protection for their goodwill and come away with an agreement.

In light of his machinations, Ngpa-tawa was confident that Alfaan and Paza would refuse to take the sapphire. Black Head would then be its only place of refuge. The fire lord had set it up that way. He was dictating the play like a chess master moves pieces on the game board.

The depth and magnitude of the deception was now apparent to Ke-enaan. The shockwave of this revelation was so overwhelming that he stumbled to a stop and leant against the side of the passageway to collect his scrambled mind. The enemy's plans had slowly advanced through the ages from the Separation to the time of prophecy. What confounded him was the fact that he had been unaware of the scale of the secret monstrous plot executed against them with martial skill. It seemed he had been stuck in time and unable to see clearly what was going on around him. Somehow the enemy had found a way to block the true magnitude of their evil onslaught on the Faerie Worlds from his awareness. He had believed that when the stars aligned and the sapphire became visible on the airwaves, he would stand with the lords of the elements and, with the strength of High Faerie, defeat the Cathac. But he had been ignorant of the true reality facing him. He had also been deceived.

Fear's cold finger poked at his heart. Black Head and Slieve Elva were one in heart and mind. The spell of protection he had cast around the Burren was waning. Fell creatures stalked the roads looking for human prey, and knockers and their maggs walked upon his sacred land. He shivered as the icy finger poked his heart again. If his protection around Black Head was failing, the mystical protection around Uall's dragon forge would also be failing. Doubt tried to claw at his mind. Ngpa-tawa had been one step ahead again. Ke-enaan feared that they might be too late to take possession of the sapphire.

He was suddenly aware that he had stopped and Uall was at his side.

"Friend in heart! What ails thee?" Uall said urgently, putting his hand on Ke-enaan's shoulder.

Ke-enaan took a tense breath before replying. "Every fibre in my body is tingling with warning," he responded. "Our domains art as one. Methinks that Ngpa-tawa is already attacking Slieve Elva. He wants the sapphire and will do everything he can to acquire it." His eyes burned feverishly. "We must beat him to the jewel if we can."

"How far Ngpa-tawa's will and sorcery has encroached upon the forge, we shalt soon see," Uall answered grimly. "Let us hasten to the dragon forge and pray we are in time."

As they approached the arched entrance to Slieve Elva, the air grew rank with the stink of corruption and decay. Uall coughed and put his hand over his face.

"'Tis as I feared," Ke-enaan hissed. "Evil is here to greet us."

"We have no choice but to go on to whatever end," Uall answered, forging ahead to the entrance of his land. "To defeat Ngpa-tawa, we have to revive Fercle. He is our only hope."

They stepped out of the passageway into the meadow. Uall gasped with shock and staggered backwards. His star-spangled velvet sky had disappeared. The flowers in the meadow were dying, their sweet perfume sullied by a stench of rot and acrid smoke. From the heaving darkness of the shadow-litten sky, a blazing red sun was glaring balefully down upon the forge.

A quiver of anger ran through Uall's frame. His face grew hot and he could hear his blood pounding in his temples. The red light was an insult to all he held dear, an eye in the clouds waiting and watching for their arrival.

Expanding in size to giant form, Uall swiftly crossed the meadow in a stride and stood by the forge. Then, gathering his power of super speed and impact, he let fly first one fist and then the other into the glaring red eye. Blow after blow he rained upon the blasphemy that had usurped and desecrated his realm.

The red light was instantly extinguished. There was a scream of pain fused with rage. Sparks burst forth from the seething clouds, and jagged forks of fey fire lightning struck around his feet.

"Quick!" Uall said to Ke-enaan who had summoned the downdraught wind and was close behind him. Uall ushered the wizard through the door to the forge and bolted it behind them. "Even though the watcher's red eye has been blinded," Uall said breathlessly, "the necromancer will find another spyhole. He will use it as a focus of intent and will, by foul spell, force an entry into my realm. I will raise the dragon flame and will try to bring fire back into Fercle's being whilst you go below to the vault and get the sapphire."

Turning towards the fire, he stiffened with shock. His mind numbed into a mixture of denial, anger, and then loss. The great dragon fire sired by Braxa, father of all dragons, had withered to a flicker. Not since its beginning had it died in flame. He realised in despair that Ngpa-tawa had found a way to drain the everlasting fire.

Grabbing the bellows, he tried frantically to revive the flame. The great veins on his neck stood out like cords as renewed anger coursed through his blood and being. Beads of sweat appeared upon his face and arms as he furiously pumped the bellows. He cried out to Braxa the Red across the airwaves in long booming sounds, asking for aid.

The flame rose in a tremble, and tried to recombine, but it petered out and sank once more to a flicker.

Ke-enaan's mind was in turmoil. Without the dragon fire, the door to the vault beneath the forge would not open and the stairway to the ancient chamber would be blocked. Uall's realm was dying. And when the breach in Slieve Elva was wide enough for Ngpa-tawa and his imps to enter, it was only a matter of time before the fire lord would seize control of the forge—and seize the sapphire.

He suddenly felt trapped and defeated. Fear slithered into his awareness like a snake. He tried to stay centred in his intent, but doubt consumed him. Sinking to his knees, he covered his face with his hands. "'Tis too late," he hissed. "We have tarried too long in blindness. The enemy's arm hath lengthened. We art undone."

Uall looked at him in dismay. "Rise, Ke-enaan, brother of Creidne!" he boomed. "Thou art the wielder of the sword of light and the green star ring of Nuada. Where is thy mettle?"

Hearing the rebuke, Ke-enaan's cheeks grew hot with shame. The ring of Nuada on his finger was shimmering with the light of his green star, and in his mind he heard again the words of his captain on the eve of the final conflict. *While the green star of eve and morn glows, and its fire burns in my heart, I will fight the enemy of life until my spirit leaves and my body crumbles into dust.*

"'Tis not only the enemy without we fight, but also the enemy within," Uall said, desperately pumping the bellows. "Let our intent to succeed in our mission be our only guide."

Ke-enaan gazed into the ring of Nuada. Taking a deep shuddering breath, he tried to pull his courage together. Getting to his feet, he straightened his back and stood tall beside Uall.

"Here is Fercle's geometric," Ke-enaan said, reaching into his robe and bringing out the small yellow tetrahedron. Holding it over the flickering flame, he began to utter the language of his lineage. Phonetics that had been lost to him since the Separation suddenly surged into his awareness, and memories appeared as visions. He saw again the Danaan warriors with their tall plumes astride their grey horses going into battle, and for a moment his ears rang with the sweet sound of their silver horns.

The ring of Nuada on his finger began to glow, energising his will. Raising his hand into the air, Ke-enaan stood in front of the flickering flame. Mighty were his words and the power that flowed through them. In ringing tones, he chanted an incantation from elder days commanding the elements of air and fire to obey him. Then, placing the geometric in the embers, he made passes with his hands over the fire and uttered words of summoning to the elemental forces.

Courage rose in his heart as the sacred words echoed around the smithy. The fire began to crackle and roar and the air in the forge grew warm. Symmetry appeared within the struggling flames. Fercle's tetrahedral geometric lit up with a burst of blue light crackling with fire. The glow began to oscillate and expand in all directions. In the midst of the spinning light, Fercle's yellow eyes appeared, followed by the round contours of his face and the rest of his portly form.

Ke-enaan breathed a sigh of relief. With the resurrection of Fercle, they now stood a chance to forge a separate fire reality and create a spellbound prison in which to confine Ngpa-tawa.

Fercle stepped out of the dragon fire onto the brick floor and looked around the forge in confusion. "Where am I?" he said to Ke-enaan.

"Thou art in the faerie forge of Uall MaCarn at Slieve Elva," Ke-enaan answered, not taking his eyes from the fire. The blue flame was roaring. He was waiting anxiously for the door to the underground vault to appear.

Before the door could form within the blaze, there was a quiver in the ground and the floor began to quake and roll. Tongs, pokers, swords, and maces fell from the shaking walls, and small rocks and stones began to tumble from the ceiling.

Ke-enaan looked up as rubble fell around him. He ducked

as a bronze quenching pot sailed over head and crashed into the anvil.

"By the stars! What is going on?" Fercle asked, dodging the falling debris.

"Suffice to say, we art under siege. If we live, I will tell thee later," Ke-enaan responded curtly, staring back into the flames.

The shaking ceased and all became quiet. As the outline of the door began to form in the dragon fire, the entrance to the forge was buffeted by a mighty wind. Then it burst open, crashing against its hinges.

A stench of decay gusted around the fire, quelling the newborn flame to a flicker. The doorway to the vault disappeared. The walls of the forge shook again and more rock fell from the ceiling.

Rushing to the entrance of the forge, Ke-enaan desperately cast a shutting spell upon the door, wresting control away from the force that was trying to keep it open.

Returning to Fercle's side, he said anxiously, "Drawn by the radiance of the sapphire, Ngpa-tawa hath sent a fey-fire spell against the forge. The magic of this land is dying. We must get the sapphire from the Vault of Ages that lies beneath the dragon flame. The furnace hast to burn with vigour before the entrance will appear. But as thou canst see, the fire is dying and the door is hidden. Now that thou art whole within the flame, callest Trax, for 'tis only dragon fire that can succour the blue flame forge, reveal the door, and give us what little hope there may be left."

Fercle's face darkened into sombre red, his cheeks glowed yellow, and his eyes became orbs of blue flame. Going inwards to his fire core, he called upon his dragon Trax. He felt a stirring heat spiralling upward from the depth of his being and quivered as dragon fire coursed through him. Drawing in his breath, Fercle opened his mouth and exhaled a mighty jet of coiling fire. The flame coalesced into form. Trax appeared before him.

"Fire Lord of Gort," Trax flared. "Thou callest!"

"We are in need of haste," Fercle answered. "Ngpa-tawa has breached Slieve Elva. He is destroying the dragon forge. Send thy breath into the dying flame to succour and renew it."

Fire issued from Trax's nostrils. Slowly his golden scales began to pulse and ripple. As his form expanded, small flames ran up and down the pointed armour on his back. With a mighty roar, he lifted his proud head and sent a blast of sparking flame into the dimming fire.

Blast after blast Trax sent into the fire, while Uall pumped the bellows. Higher and higher leapt the flames. In the midst of the blaze, Ke-enaan saw the outline of the door appear. Hastening forward, he stepped through the sheet of fire. Opening the door, he hastened down the steep stairway to the vault.

Moving swiftly to a corner of the room to the ancient box where he had hidden the sapphire, Ke-enaan opened the lid and looked in. The jewel glittered darkly. As he touched the star-gate, he was caught up in the pulsing blue spectrum of nine dimensions. Picking up the sapphire, he put it in his robe, and then with all the speed he could muster, he raced back up the stairs before the fire waned and the door closed against him.

As Ke-enaan joined Uall and Fercle in the forge, they heard a roaring sound. The smithy was buffeted by a mighty gale. The walls began to shiver and shake. The floor heaved; they could hardly keep their footing. The door to the smithy crackled with wisps of fey fire and suddenly flew open. Gusts of acrid smoke billowed into the forge. The air grew thick and hot, burning their eyes and nostrils until they could hardly breathe or see.

"We must flee before the forge collapses," Uall shouted, picking up a spiked mace that had fallen on the ground.

Surrounded by the brilliance of the sapphire, they rushed to the door, but before they could reach it, their exit was slammed shut against them.

"The enemy is trying to stop our escape," Uall roared. With a mighty kick, he knocked the door off the hinges and sent it flying into the darkness. The ground rumbled as they raced outside into the choking shadow. They heard the crash of falling brick behind them.

Trax had contracted in size to a small dragoneen. Flying above the company as they raced through the door, he landed on the ground in front of them.

"Trax act as shield; company escape with sapphire." The dragoneen flared, expanding into fearsome size.

Bidding the company get behind him, Trax breathed a jet of flame into the gloom. In answer, bolts of jagged lightning lit up the churning clouds and struck the turf around them. Above the blackened meadow, a ring of noxious yellow-orange light became visible within the dark and heaving clouds. The glow became brighter. In the centre of the ring a more evil hue appeared. In the shifting vapours, a pair of red almond-shaped eyes formed, followed by the contours of a long face.

The air became alive with malice and sorcery. Looking down upon them from the lurid light was the sneering face of Ngpa-tawa. Bound about his brow was a circlet of gold bearing a single glittering ruby. Lust and excess had etched themselves into deep creases on his once noble face, and his long hair that in elder days had rivalled the sun in its golden glory now hung in greasy drab locks about his shoulders.

Streaks of fire dropped like darts around the company. Overhead, shadowy fliers were hovering on silent wings, waiting for Ngpa-tawa's signal to attack.

Erupting in a blaze of flame, Trax stood before the company.

"Betrayer of sacred fire," he hissed at Ngpa-tawa, "leave!" His eyes glowed yellow as fire rippled along his spine. "Trax, son of Braxa, burn thee into ash."

"The power of thy fire, Trax, is weak compared to mine," the fire lord said, gloating. Tiny sparks shot outwards from his curved, voluptuous lips. "Not even Braxach the Green hath power to match me. I am the lord of all the fire worlds, wielder of the fey flame, so 'tis useless to resist. Give me the sapphire and I will let thee live so thee can skulk away."

Trax lifted his head and glared at Ngpa-tawa, and then with a snort sent a scalding jet of flame into the fire lord's face. The image of Ngpa-tawa blurred for a moment, and then a stream of rushing fey fire issued from his eyes. Surrounded by the firestorm, Trax writhed in pain. Flapping his wings, he staggered back.

"See!" Ngpa-tawa thundered, streaming the fey fire back into himself. "Thy weak flame is no match for my fey fire. Thou art outmatched." Sniggering, he raised his hand and extended it towards them. "Canst thou not see thy cause is lost?"

The claw-like armour covering Ngpa-tawa's fingers was dripping with green sylph blood. Ke-enaan's heart went cold, and for a moment his will failed. The House of Air had left Black Head before the light failed and the attack upon his halls began. Was it possible they had been attacked and destroyed upon the road?

Fercle tugged on Ke-enaan's robe and motioned his head towards Trax.

"Green blood; illusion," the dragon hissed at Ngpa-tawa. "Trax sense fire-lie."

"How astute of thee to divine my little falsehood," Ngpa-tawa sniggered. "Trax, son of Braxa," he said in a soft, cajoling tone, "my dragon Nag-ta is dead, but thou art alive." There was pause, and then he said, "For the present." Bolts of fiery darts shot from his eyes, but before they could reach the company, Trax consumed them with his breath.

"I say again," Ngpa-tawa thundered to Trax, "thy cause is doomed. Why not join me in the fey-fire world, where dragons are free to feed upon the flesh of men? I will exalt thee, and all will tremble before thy fiery breath. Thou wilt conquer Braxa the Red and take the dragon world of Axar as thy own. What say thee?"

Fercle stepped up beside Trax. Planting his feet firmly on the ground, he laughed in the fire lord's face. "My, oh my." Fercle chuckled. "Is one as great as you trying to recruit me and my dragon familiar? Why bother with, as you say, one so weak of flame?"

"Thou hast the audacity to question me?" Ngpa-tawa boomed. Fireballs exploded around the company. The air was fraught with arrogance and hate.

"You have betrayed the sacred fire," Fercle shouted defiantly. "All your deception will come to naught." He felt a sudden rush of dragon fire to his heart as Trax joined his mind.

Prepare run, the dragon thought to him. *Be fast in escape. Trax will buy thee time.*

Fercle felt a chill strike his heart. Trax was no match for the fey fire of Ngpa-tawa. He was going to sacrifice himself so the company could get away.

Taking to the air in a gush of roaring flame, Trax blasted the hateful image in the sky. Whirling away from the fire lord's eyes, he circled the glowing cloud and kept up his attack.

Uall took on giant form. Singing the war song of giants, he swung his mace into Ngpa-tawa's leering face. Then, picking up Ke-enaan and Fercle, he crossed the dead meadow in a stride.

The sky was wracked with jets of flame and bolts of fey fire, the crackle of lightning sounded, and a bitter rain began to fall.

Once they gained the entrance to the passageway, Fercle looked back towards the forge. The image of Ngpa-tawa had vanished and the hideous red eye had reappeared. Trax was wheeling round, making ready to join them at the passageway, when lurid bolts of fey fire shot out from the glaring eye. From the streaks of fire, a fire serpent appeared. Whipping its tail around Trax's neck, it swiftly coiled around his body. Trax squirmed and twisted desperately, trying to escape from the binding spell. Roaring his distress in torrents of flame, Trax was sucked into the smouldering red sun.

Fercle screamed in anguish as the red sun plucked Trax from the sky. Overcome with horror, he stood still before the entrance to the passage with his head bowed. With the loss of his dragon, part of his fire energy had been seized. He felt drained and giddy. As his legs gave way, he felt himself falling.

Seeing Fercle sinking to the ground, Ke-enaan grabbed his arm and propelled him into the passage while Uall stood on guard at the entrance. Fercle's firepower had been partially drained by the loss of Trax. Taking Fercle to his breast,

Ke-enaan called out the phonetics of the faerie fire world. Feeling the sacred flame stream through him, he sent a charge of energy into Fercle's heart.

Fire streamed from Fercle's eyes as Ke-enaan's power coursed through him. The weakness seemed to leave Fercle, but the anger and the sadness over Trax's loss remained.

"I need thee to go to Black Head and give warning of what has happened," Ke-enaan said to him. "Give this message to Trevelyan. If Uall and meself doth not return within five mortal minutes, he is to block the door to Slieve Elva with the most powerful spell he has. Our absence means that Slieve Elva has fallen to Ngpa-tawa and that we are dead." He paused for a moment, his eyelids narrowing. He felt a vague terror tingle through his awareness as if a deeply buried fear had suddenly been reignited.

"Yes, Lord Ke-enaan," Fercle answered. "I will deliver your message verbatim." He turned away along the passage, when he heard Ke-enaan call after him. "Tell Trevelyan to look in my brother's manuscript of spells and influences. He will find a dark spell to call the Hex, a being with the strongest of magic." He caught Fercle's eye. "Tell him the time of restraint is over. Even if it is perilous to set the Hex free in the world, I pray thee release it, for we are in dire straits."

Ke-enaan stood with Uall at the entrance to the passage. The sky was dark. From the fuming clouds, fire imps came swooping down upon them. Their hideous bodies were a sticky crimson, raw with flesh like skinned children. Hate burned in their eyes, and in their claws were jagged fey-fire knives that spelled death by contact.

The imps were now a swarm. Ke-enaan could hear the droning of their bat-like wings swelling to a roar. Knowing that even a pinprick of fey fire would kill them, Ke-enaan called upon the elemental power of water. Commands in the language of the sea flowed from his lips. Curling his hands into a ball, he felt power pulsing in his palms. With the water field ready to his command, he summoned the earth power of Black Head. Slowing down the vibration of the water, he transformed it into ice. Hailstones formed within his hands. With a mighty cry he let loose a driving wall of spiked ice crystals into the hordes of imps, trying to gain access to the tunnel. Some of the imps evaded the hailstorm and came rushing towards the company, but Uall was ready for them. Swinging his mace, he cut their quivering flesh into pieces.

The front line of Ngpa-tawa's ranks fell back under Ke-enaan's onslaught and then closed in again with renewed fury.

"Ngpa-tawa and his demons have to be blocked from entering the passageway," Uall hissed to Ke-enaan. "Only a sealing of the passage will contain them. Stand back!"

Reaching down, Uall pulled up the rock-strewn ground before the entrance into a wall of stone. Then, morphing into a smaller version of himself, he urged Ke-enaan forward along the passage. "We must make haste to thy halls. I have shaken the foundation of Slieve Elva. The vibrations through the stone will cause a landslide that will sever the connection between Slieve Elva and Black Head forever."

Uall felt numbed as the door to Slieve Elva was sealed, along with its fate. The unthinkable had happened. His beloved starlit land, dragon-fire forge, and perfumed meadows had been consumed by a destroying darkness. His awareness twisted in torment and loss, and for a moment he felt the cold clasp of despair. Slieve Elva had been unassailable in the War of Separation, but like Ke-enaan, Uall too had been lulled by a hidden deception into a sense of false security. He thought back to the timeless days before the Separation when his brother Finn had been with him in the forge. The smithy walls were always full of silver offerings, and their meadow was filled with horses to be faerie shod. He sighed deeply, breathing out his pain. His realm was gone and his future now uncertain.

The tunnel began to shake and judder. Rocks started falling from the ceiling as Ke-enaan and Uall fled to Black Head. Behind them they heard the roar and slither of sliding soil and rock.

CHAPTER 15

STAIN OF EVIL

After Uall and Ke-enaan left for Slieve Elva, Emma and Omar, under Trevelyan's supervision, cleared away the rushes from the flagstone floor and constructed a pentacle surrounded by a double circle in accordance with the instructions in the ancient book of spells. Trevelyan told them that their battle against Zugalfar and Ngpa-tawa would be rooted in the lower astral plane of the third and fourth dimensions. Therefore it was necessary to construct a pentacle that would serve as a potent defence in the mortal world, and as a protection in Faerie as well.

When the geometric was completed, apart from a narrow space for them to enter, Trevelyan went to Ke-enaan's shelves and sorted through the bottles. He returned with five tall jars and five spear-shaped blue obsidian crystals. Putting down the jars by the side of the outer ring, he walked round the circle and placed one crystal at each point of the star.

"After the War of Separation, the Danaan wizards were attacked by the Cathac's sorcerous druids," Trevelyan said when he had completed his task. "The obsidian crystals enabled the wizards to anchor their souls to their bodies and become one with their spells."

Emma raised her eyebrows and looked at him quizzically. "What do you mean, become one with their spells?"

"The frequency of the crystals binds the physical elements of earth, water, fire, air, and space together with their spiritual or energetic counterparts, m'dear." Noticing Emma's blank look, he said, "Let me explain further. Because you and Omar are mortal, your bodies belong to the third dimension, but your faerie essence belongs to the fourth dimension of the heart. The crystals allow the two to become one within your third-dimensional awareness. This connection allows for conscious expansion and full spectrum interaction, along with the power of High Faerie to command any spells that you may cast." He waved his eyeglass at them. "Do you both understand?"

"Full spectrum dominance, mon," Omar said excitedly, pushing back his dreads and flashing a smile at Emma. "The obsidian crystals allow us to connect to all aspects of ourselves, physical and spiritual. We can then become conscious three-world walkers instead of only walkin' in two worlds, mon. We'll be able to drive out wickedness from every dark nook and cranny."

Hearing Omar's explanation, Emma nodded in agreement. When she had given Trevelyan the sapphire, he had told her she was a three-world walker, but she hadn't understood what he had meant. Now she understood. Humans walk in one world, and for most that is all there is. Those with the gift of faerie sight walk in two worlds, and because she accessed her High Faerie nature, she could walk in three.

"Exactly so, Omar!" Trevelyan responded, pouring three goblets of elixir and handing them around. "When we can connect our physical vibrations with our spiritual energy, we become one within the spell. The enchantment affects quantum reality, which will then determine physical reality."

"Tell us more about the obsidian crystals, mon," Omar said. "My loa tells me they are fire stones."

"Yes, they are fire stones born in the magma heart of a volcano and thrown into the air," Trevelyan answered, dramatically raising his arm upward. "Symbolically the crystals represent fire rising into air and give you the ability to transcend the third dimension and reconnect with the HeartStar of the fourth and fifth dimension, the Faerie realities that the Cathac stole from you at the time of Separation." He paused to give them time to assimilate the information. After a while, he carried on. "'Tis the energetic link beyond time and space that will power you in both worlds. That is their gift." He looked at them searchingly and then said, "Do not try to understand with intellect. Envision the connection with your heart and become three-world walkers."

Emma sipped on her drink. Trevelyan's explanation and the hope that it offered was what she needed to hear. The thought that she might not be able to shift at will into her faerie nature was nagging at her mind, and she wished she had a cigarette .... a brandy ... any fucking thing to break the gulf of alienation that she felt between her and sanity and the normalcy of mundane reality. She wondered about Jim. He had cracked up. She couldn't blame him. She was cracking up herself. It seemed that her fears and self-assurance fought each other over and over again, and her mind kept swinging from confidence to insecurity. She felt like her head was going to split in two—and part of her welcomed oblivion.

Trying to steady her mind and get centred, Emma gazed at the crystals in the tips of the star. She could see the obsidian points were all connected in a throbbing pentagon of primary earth-based hues and outer spectrum colours that waxed and waned like the pulse of a beating heart. She was suddenly conscious of the beating of her own heart. In a rush of understanding she realised that all she had to do to connect with her quantum spiritual power was to synchronise her heartbeat with the crystals.

Omar was thinking about full spectrum spiritual interaction with loa and what it would mean to be a three-world walker. He sniffed. He couldn't even cope with walking through the spiritual darkness in his own world, let alone another two.

Suddenly aware of Emma's thoughts and of the beating of his heart, he closed his eyes, focusing his inner sight on the pulsing crystal grid.

Trevelyan was eavesdropping on their minds. He was relieved that they had seen the grid and divined their course of action. Because Ke-enaan and Uall had not yet returned from Slieve Elva, he thought he would take advantage of the time and provide further explanation.

"While you are in the pentacle, the obsidian crystals will help you regain that which you lost at the fall," he began.

"The fall of man, mon?" Omar asked, interrupting.

Trevelyan nodded. "'Tis called the fall of man for good reason." He drained his goblet and refilled it from the decanter on the table. "Before the Separation, the race of man had multidimensional awareness and was part of the Faerie Worlds. After the war, man became mortal and, due to Ngpa-tawa's sorcery, lost the ability to see into the higher realms of Faerie and High Faerie. With the loss of immortality, the connection to the heart and spiritual reality was severed, and a once spiritual race became sense-bound and life became a narrow, physical sensory experience of three dimensions with five senses. The awareness of spiritual reality was lost."

"Lord Trevelyan!" Nala called in alarm from the hearth. "The dragon fire is dying. Its flame is almost spent."

Jerking his head round, Trevelyan stared at the dying flames in dismay. The fire in Ke-enaan's hall burned with dragon fire from Uall's forge, so the dying flames could only mean one thing: Slieve Elva had been breached and seized by Ngpa-tawa.

Peering into the space field to see what information he could garner about Slieve Elva, Trevelyan was suddenly aware of a subtle change in the energy of the hall. He sensed a contraction around Black Head, a shrinking of free space, a containment of energy like a net had been cast and was being slowly pulled in. Slieve Elva had fallen. He wondered if Ngpa-tawa was trying to contain the frequency of Black Head and drag it down to a lower vibration. He glanced again at the fire. The flames had diminished to a flicker. The assault on Black Head was beginning. Suddenly realising that the protective circle for Emma and Omar was not complete, he chided himself for having delayed. They were running out of time. He should not have tarried.

"Uncork the jars," he said urgently to Emma and Omar. "The sacred herbs each carry a different energetic frequency. They will guard each point of the star. We must make haste, for I fear Uall's dragon forge has fallen and been taken by the enemy."

The understanding that Slieve Elva had fallen frightened Emma. She could feel her chest tighten. It was hard for her to breathe. In desperation, she surrounded herself in an emerald octahedron and tried to calm herself. She glanced at Nala and saw he was looking at her. *Be strong, my love,* his voice whispered in her mind. *Shut out everything but the now and set thy intent to master thy adversary.*

"Follow me!" Trevelyan's voice jerked her into action. Taking a handful of yellow flowers from one of the jars, Trevelyan put the broom flowers at the apex of the pentacle. "Broom creates sacred space," he said. "We will use the plant ally to guard the space inside the pentacle."

Emma and Omar followed him around the outer circle as he placed the other herbs in the other four valleys of the star. Agrimony he used to ground the energy of air; angelica to ground the energy of fire; boneset to focus the power of water; and dandelion the garblus, to protect the sacred fire of High Faerie.

"The five plants will protect the energetic integrity of the pentacle," he informed them. "They will power the sacred space within the geometric. Keep it at a high vibration so that fear and doubt cannot enter." He fiddled with his eyeglass. "Come! Let us consult the manuscript and make sure we have not forgotten anything."

Aine and Nala had constructed an icosahedron on the flagstone floor from alder twigs, the sacred tree of Pan. To ground the energy of water, they used tiny orange crystals and moonstones they had found on Ke-enaan's shelves. When they had finished placing the glittering stones around the edges of the geometric, they joined Trevelyan, Emma, and Omar at the table.

"We have found a water hammer spell that can break the foundations of Manannan's underwater city," Nala reported. "Dost Ke-enaan have antimony in his store of herbs and metals? We need it to create a magnetic bond with the hammer so we can wield it."

Trevelyan nodded. Going to one of the shelves, he returned with a piece of flaky metal.

"Antimony," he said, handing the silver shard to Nala, "the ancient metal of protection."

"And energy connection," Nala added. "If we can use the hammer to attack Manannan's city, he will feel the drain in his power and be forced to return. Then we can assail him with the Mind of the Sea."

Before they could talk further, there was a noise. Fercle burst through the side door into the hall.

"Trevelyan! Meself brings word from Ke-enaan," he said breathlessly. "He told me to repeat to you this message. 'If Uall and meself doth not return within five mortal minutes, Trevelyan is to block the door to Slieve Elva with the most powerful spell at his disposal. Our absence means that Slieve Elva has fallen to Ngpa-tawa and that we are dead. Tell Trevelyan to look in my brother's manuscript of spells and influences. He will find a dark spell to call the Hex, a powerful being with the strongest of magic. The time of restraint is over. Even if it is perilous to set the Hex free in the world, I pray thee release it, for we are in dire straits.'"

For a moment there was a stunned silence. The fire went out, and shadows seemed to lengthen in the hall.

Trevelyan closed his eyes and let his mind dissolve into the space field. He needed clarity. Ke-enaan and Uall either would return or would not. He must stay focused and not be distracted by negative scenarios lest he bring his ideations to pass. He had to wait five minutes before he would have an answer.

Glancing at Emma and Omar, Trevelyan asked, "Are either of you wearing a watch?"

Emma shook her head.

"I am, mon," Omar said.

"Tell me when five mortal minutes have gone by,"

Trevelyan said abruptly. Putting on his eyeglass, he returned to the manuscript on the table.

Trevelyan was shocked to the core by the latter part of Ke-enaan's message. What the wizard had asked him to do was inconceivable. The Hex was an old and virulent evil that preyed on the mortal world, a singularity of all negative emotion that had come into being at the time of the Separation. The Hex was a hungry hateful spirit from the realm of Under-Ice that not even the Cathac could contain.

Why, he wondered, *would Ke-enaan even suggest such a thing ... unless,* he mused, *Ke-enaan had used the Hex before.*

He put his hand across his face and thoughtfully rubbed his cheek. Ke-enaan had told him that he had delved into dark magic at the time of the Separation. In a desperate situation, he and Creidne must have called the Hex, Trevelyan reasoned. Even though they had found a counter-spell and banished the demon once it had finished its task, its dark energy still resonated in Ke-enaan's consciousness. They were still linked by the evil of the past. Slieve Elva had fallen. It was likely that the Hex had used Ke-enaan's fear and despair to overtake the latter's will, and the stain upon his soul to access his awareness.

Before Trevelyan could follow his train of thought further, Ke-enaan and Uall came through the side door. The hall was suddenly flooded in sapphire light.

"Well-met!" Trevelyan said to Uall and Ke-enaan. Crossing the room, Trevelyan clasped Ke-enaan's hands to his breast. "Friend of Ages," he said, "'tis good to see your safe return. And yours, Uall MaCarn, my friend in heart."

Ke-enaan's fingers closed around Trevelyan's wrists like a vice. His eyes were blazing with the fell light of madness. The sweat of fever was on his brow.

"The enemy is at hand," he cried shrilly, pulling Trevelyan within inches of his face. "We must make ready for battle!"

In Ke-enaan's grip, Trevelyan could feel the power of the former's Danaan lineage coursing through the wizard's body, but he also sensed a malignant shadow of hateful intent sneaking alongside.

It was as he feared. Ke-enaan had been compromised by evil. The Hex had hungrily waited for payment and, using its dark connection to Ke-enaan's energy, had found a chance to exploit and influence the wizard's thoughts and will to further its agenda. Trevelyan would have to keep a close eye on Ke-enaan in case the Hex took total control of the latter's mind and tried to destroy them all. He also realised that he must be ready to deal with Ke-enaan as an enemy and, if necessary, destroy him.

Pulling away from Ke-enaan's grasp, Trevelyan cast a fleeting glance at Fercle. The fire elemental was sitting in a chair, gazing into the dead embers of the fire. Trevelyan swallowed hard. He feared that with the loss of Trax, Fercle would not have the strength to focus their spell against Ngpa-tawa. If that were the case, then they would have to find another way to counter the fire lord's attack, and that could present a problem. Without Fercle to focus their spell, Ke-enaan would be uncertain what to do. He couldn't use the sapphire to create a prison world for Ngpa-tawa, because his intent would be visible on the airwaves and the fire lord would divine their plan and make a move to stop them. It would be in Ke-enaan's confusion that the Hex would make its move, putting its long-awaited desire for revenge against the wizard into action. It would offer Ke-enaan its services to defeat Ngpa-tawa. Trevelyan was worried that Ke-enaan, in his fear, would succumb to its will. What was of greater concern was that the wizard was in possession of the sapphire and could summon the Hex at any time.

Uall stood before Trevelyan and Ke-enaan. "My lords," he said. "As stone blocked the passageway from Slieve Elva to Black Head, I had a vision of my brother Finn McCoul. Finn is dead and cast in stone. The dragon forge lies cold and lifeless. All that I love has withered." A tear came to his eye. "I am the last of the Faerie giants, and I will now go forth to the Giant's Cliffs and join Braxach in the battle against the Cathac and his legions." Uall bowed to the company. "May the living light of the Green protect thee." Picking up his mace, Uall crossed the hall and disappeared through the door.

"Trevelyan! Fercle!" Ke-enaan said agitatedly. "There is no time to lose. We need to build a specific fire geometric from which to cast our spell and create a prison world for Ngpa-tawa."

The three of them formed a triangular shape before the dead fire. Trevelyan and Ke-enaan stood side by side, with Fercle at the apex.

"Trevelyan and I will create a star tetrahedron around us," Ke-enaan said to Fercle. "Speak thy fire words of summoning."

Fire phonetics resonated around the hall and tiny yellow sparks appeared within the sapphire light. Ke-enaan made passes with his hands and, uttering words of power, wove the sparks into the golden outline of a star tetrahedron. Once the star was complete, Trevelyan began to create the space for a fire world to form. Opening his mouth, he breathed galaxies and whirling nebulae into the geometric.

Sending forth jets of flame from his fingers, Fercle formed an arc of fire that blazed like a sun above the star tetrahedron. As a ring of fire started to form, he suddenly clutched at his heart, staggering backwards.

Ke-enaan caught him as he fell. Seeing with dismay that the blazing arc had been extinguished, Ke-enaan hissed, "What ails thee?"

"Without Trax, my fire heart wanes and is too weak to hold the fire gate open," Fercle said miserably, recovering his balance. "Forgive me, my lord. Meself has failed you."

Ke-enaan's mind was in conflict, see-sawing between clarity and confusion. His plan to use Fercle to ground the containment spell around the fire lord had failed. He had gambled and lost. Going to the table, he picked up the manuscript, and rifling through the pages, desperately searched for an enchantment that could defeat or at least defend against Ngpa-tawa's assault upon Black Head.

Ke-enaan suddenly felt uneasy. Exploring the cause of his fear, he sensed an evil presence in his awareness, an alien will that seemed to be patiently and stealthily biding its time before attacking him. A chill ran down his spine. A voice was whispering, trying to force its will upon him and urging him to use the Hex to defeat Ngpa-tawa.

No! He pushed the thought away. He had been weak with fear and sorrow when he had asked Trevelyan to use the Hex. Ke-enaan now recognised himself to have been the target of a hungry hostile force for even having considered such a monstrous thought. He was a Danaan. With Trevelyan, the lord of space, by his side, he would use high magic to repel the fire lord's attack—or perish in the doing.

The ring of Nuada glowed eerily on his finger; the pulsing green star seal was turning the sapphire light around him to turquoise. Ke-enaan swallowed hard. He had to find a spell to stop Ngpa-tawa from capturing the sapphire.

Returning his attention to the manuscript, he peered at the spidery writing of his brother Creidne, and was transported back into the past to the evil that had led to the stain upon his soul.

In the final hours of the War of Separation, the Cathac's druids had tracked Nuada and his company as they fled north to the pyramid at Brugh. Weak with exhaustion, the company had camped in a glen. As they rested, the Cathac's druids had sent sorcery against them. In a black sheet of squirming bodies, giant vampire bats had silently swooped down upon the sleeping knights. Before the warriors could awake, the bats had fastened their fangs into the veins of the sleeping company. By the time Ke-enaan and Creidne had realised what had happened, half the company lay drained of blood and in a death swoon.

Their spells of protection had failed to safeguard the warriors. In a desperate gamble, they had summoned the dark magic of the Hex. A bargain had been struck. In return for the Hex's aid, the demon had demanded twelve of the finest warriors who were left alive. Creidne had sent a thought into Ke-enaan's mind telling him that the bargain would not be fulfilled and that after the Hex had destroyed the bat spell, they would use Under-Earth sorcery to banish him back to his world of Under-Ice. It was perilous to summon the Hex, and an even greater risk to banish him. But it was a desperate chance that had to be taken, or all of them would have perished.

Ke-enaan shivered as he recalled the summoning of the thin black shade and the endless icy malevolence that surrounded it. Sticky grey webbing had issued from its half-formed fingers, and the air in the glen had grown inky and opaque. He had heard the panicked shrieking and strangulated squeaking of the bats as the Hex consumed them, and simultaneously had smelled the choking stench of blood upon the air.

When the Hex returned to collect payment, they had

put their plan into action. Using forbidden magic, they had contained the demon in a ring of Under-Earth vibration. Then, with blasphemous incantations, they had created confining geometry. Imprisoning the Hex in a cube squared into a circle, they had forced the demon back to its ice world.

The Hex would remember the double-cross and would exact a price that Ke-enaan was not prepared to pay. But the thought kept sneaking into Ke-enaan's mind that summoning the Hex was the only way to defeat Ngpa-tawa.

Feeling another will trying to take root in his awareness, Ke-enaan put his hands to his head and desperately tried to shut out the intruder. The Hex was whispering, urging him to use the calling spell. Ke-enaan found himself once again weighing the pros and cons.

"Thy plan hath failed," the Hex whispered. "Thou canst use thy own Danaan strengths and the power contained within the ring of Nuada to an uncertain end, or thou canst ally with me, the Hex. Together we are formidable and can rout the lord of fire."

Searching his memory for the blocking spells he had used in the War of Separation to combat possession of his will, Ke-enaan felt what seemed to be a crushing weight settling on his thinking. He could only recall vague outlines of the spells. Instructions flashed through his mind, but before he could focus on them, they diminished and faded away. Desperately trying to collect his scattered wits, he suddenly became aware of the star seal ring on his finger. The green jewel was now blazing with shimmering pulses. He felt a stirring in the recesses of his mind. A kaleidoscope of visions flashed before his eyes, and he sensed an awareness that was neither the being that called itself Ke-enaan nor the whispering voice of the Hex.

Tall men with clear grey eyes and flowing silver hair were

sending a voice across time and space to aid him. His ancestors were speaking, but try as he may, he could only understand a little of what they were trying to impart. The Hex was interfering with his mind, jamming the connection with his ancestors. To support his courage and gain clarity, Ke-enaan put his hand upon the sword of light girthed around his waist. Power flowed through him as his fingers touched the sword hilt. Instruction seemed to become etched into his memory, even though in that instant he could not comprehend it.

Without warning, his concentration began to waver, his mind began to wander to trivial things, and his efforts to focus on the present became harder and harder. The connection to his ancestors began to diminish. He knew with a sinking heart that the Hex was using the dark spell of connection from long ago to take over his thinking. In the recesses of his mind, he could hear the voice of his ancestors. The instructions they were giving him beat in his brain, but the Hex beat them back again and again.

"Ngpa-tawa is coming for the sapphire," the Hex whispered. "I lust for the fire lord's energy. If I consume his fire, I will have release from the world of Under-Ice. Help me to conquer him, and I will forgive thee and thy brother's transgression of old. Use me!" the Hex commanded.

Ke-enaan's will began to waver, and with it came a change of mind. Yes, he thought, he would summon the Hex and allow it to enter his hall through the sapphire. Once the Hex had defeated Ngpa-tawa, he would use the sapphire to banish the demon back to Under-Ice.

Moving towards the manuscript to read the spell of calling, Ke-enaan saw Trevelyan pick up the grimoire and hold it to his breast. Ke-enaan paused and, scowling darkly, said, "Clear the way."

"Stay your plan," Trevelyan thundered, raising his eyeglass. "We will combine our power and find another way to defeat our enemy." Emerald light issued from the lens, bathing the hall in a show of strength. "For the sake of the three worlds, I beg you, do not summon the Hex."

In that instant a shockwave rippled through the hall as if a mighty psychic hammer had struck it. The walls shivered and the emerald light disappeared. Jars and bottles fell from the shelving, and with a crash the cunning mirror shattered, sending a rain of pointed shards flying towards the company.

Trevelyan spun on his heel. Using his eyeglass, he held the shards in suspended animation. Then with a downward motion of his hand, he sent the projectiles harmlessly to the floor.

Turning back towards the company, Trevelyan saw Ke-enaan making gestures with his arms. Up to the sky the wizard's palms turned, and were suddenly brought to ground. Then, in shrill tones, he uttered a thunderous incantation that slowly rolled through his hall like a rising sea.

Trevelyan took a quick intake of breath. "The power of Ke-enaan's spell is dominating the hall and trying to master the wills of all that oppose it," he said desperately to Emma and Omar. "Go into the pentacle of protection and close the circle behind you."

As Emma and Omar entered the circle, Trevelyan glanced at Ke-enaan. The wizard's eyes were blazing with the pale fell light of Under-Ice, and a shadow was forming around him, shaping itself into a long, thin outline. Sensing a ruthless will, Trevelyan looked deep into the ether. Pale malignant eyes were gleaming out from the deepening shadow around the wizard's head. The temperature in the hall was dropping.

Fear stabbed throughout Trevelyan's being. He felt sick at heart. It was as he had feared. Ke-enaan's mind was now the accursed focus of the ice demon's will. For a moment, he was at a loss. Then, in an instant of action, he stepped out in front of Ke-enaan. Putting his hand on the wizard's arm, he cried out, "In the name of the HeartStar, I command you to stop! Friend of Ages, it is not too late. Cease thy spell!"

The incantation stopped, and the hall fell into brooding silence.

Ke-enaan's brow furrowed and his mouth turned into a frown as he gazed at Trevelyan's restraining hand upon his arm. In a moment of lucidity, he wondered why his friend was trying to stop him. He felt a sudden loss of concentration, an inability to focus on his thoughts. His mind was confused. And even though he wanted to believe that he was rational, his heart was telling him this wasn't the truth.

"Stay thy hand! I, not thou, am master of this hall," Ke-enaan hissed, shaking off Trevelyan's grasp.

An icy force hit Trevelyan in the heart. Dropping the manuscript on the table, he was forced backwards to the edge of the pentacle. The table began to turn and then spin, and the pages of the manuscript were ripped from their bindings and came to lay scattered on the floor.

Trevelyan felt as if he had been whipped up into a different set of frequencies and was shooting dizzily downward into breathtaking chaos and confusion. Ke-enaan's spell had ripped a hole in the Faerie Worlds. Trevelyan had to get to the safety of the pentacle before he got sucked into Under-Earth. The obsidian crystals at the points of the star would offer him, Emma, and Omar some protection against the Hex. Using his eyeglass, he created a space in the protective rings. Stepping inside the pentacle, he closed it up behind him.

"The fate of the sapphire and the HeartStar will soon be decided," he said, gazing at Emma and Omar with grave, deliberate eyes. Then, taking their hands, he created a linked circle at the centre of the pentacle. "Our fate floats like gossamer in a gale," he said. "Ke-enaan is undone by the stain of the past and is about to bring ruin upon the worlds. We have to shut out our fear and to focus, become one, with the intent of reaching my house in England. Come! Let us ..."

Before he could finish his sentence, the sapphire light within the hall began to redden. Through the gaping void of the mirror, a shadow lengthened across the floor, slithering like a red snake upon the blackening rushes.

Wreathed in fire, the figure of Ngpa-tawa appeared before them. A Danaan sword was girthed about his waist, a trophy taken from some great captain in the War of Separation. The ruby on his brow shone with the sullied red light of Under-Fire, and his flame-flecked eyes blazed forth in mocking triumph. Licking flame began to creep up the walls and crawl across the ceiling. Hordes of fire imps came swarming through the broken mirror and gathered silently behind Ngpa-tawa.

"The lord of fire is in thy hall," the Hex whispered in Ke-enaan's ear. "Finish thy spell of summoning, and then seal it with thy blood. Cut thy ring finger, and let thy life force drip upon the sapphire. Then I will manifest to aid thee."

The will of the Hex receded. As Ngpa-tawa rose before him, Ke-enaan was consumed with panicked fear. The unthinkable had happened: his hall had been breached and doom was upon him. His courage deserted him. He felt an immense and overwhelming drain upon his power. It seemed to him that his form had become translucent and that his awareness was just a reflection in a glass.

"We meet at last," Ngpa-tawa said mockingly, stretching out his arm towards the wizard.

Ke-enaan flinched. The cruel claw-like extensions on the fire lord's fingers were inches from his face.

"For an age thou hast evaded me," Ngpa-tawa said gloatingly, gouging Ke-enaan's cheek with his claws. "Thou hast been hiding in thy hovel of a hall, hatching plots, sorceries, and illusions against my master, the Cathac, and his lords. But all thy scheming is in vain. The Cathac will possess the sapphire and conquer the nine dimensions, and"— he leered—"my master will savour the conquest of thy green star. Know that I, Ngpa-tawa, the Cathac's mighty champion, will ravish and enslave thy kin. Mortal thou shalt be. Kneel before me and pay homage," he snarled.

"Beaten though I may be," Ke-enaan responded, defiantly shaking his head, "I will not bend my knee before thee. I am the master of Black Head."

Suddenly he felt the Hex surge into his awareness, blotting out his will. "Summon me," the ice demon demanded. "Make haste! Finish the spell before it is too late."

"Meddler, thy hall will soon lie in ruin. Thou art finished!" Ngpa-tawa spat contemptuously. "'Tis now the time of reckoning for thee and thy filthy rabble." He glared around the hall at the company. Turning back to Ke-enaan, he said, "I will gouge out thine eyes and feed them to my imps and then suck out thine essence into myself. All the knowledge of thy spell lore and the enchantments thou hast gathered throughout the ages will be mine."

Ice that burned like fire seemed to settle in Ke-enaan's heart. His mind trembled. The very foundations of his strength and courage were shaken. He could hear the urgent whisperings of the Hex commanding him to use the calling spell. As Ngpa-tawa's gold claws reached for his eyes, Ke-enaan shouted the final words of summoning for the Hex.

Grabbing the quill from the inkpot, he jabbed the end into his finger. As blood spurted out, he thrust his injured hand into his robe and brought out the sapphire. Then, uttering a mighty cry that seemed to echo beyond the Faerie Worlds, he placed the blood-soaked star-gate in his mouth and swallowed it.

Trevelyan gasped in shock, his mind reeling in terror. By swallowing the sapphire, Ke-enaan had allowed the deadly stream of power emanating from Ngpa-tawa and the Hex to pour into him unopposed. With a sinking heart, Trevelyan realised that the Cathac could now access Ke-enaan's knowledge and that of his ancestors, and all the defences and enchantments the Danaan wizards had used against him in the War of Separation to the present would be laid bare. The Cathac had no one to oppose him. The Green of the Faerie Worlds would turn to dust, and the higher dimensions would become a fiefdom of the demon lords. Even Trevelyan's own realm of space would be assailed. His anguish was so encompassing that for a moment all thought left him and fled away into the safety of the stars.

As Trevelyan's fourth-dimensional awareness returned, the floor began to rock and the air grew icy with the chilled embrace of death. The walls of the hall writhed and thrashed into distorted shapes and prismatic colours. A great roaring sound swept overhead, filling all free space with rushing darkness, and then a spinning twilight abyss appeared, with still vaster shadowed realms beyond it.

Emma began to shiver. A cold sweat broke out across her forehead as she clung to Trevelyan's and Omar's hands. Waves of fear hammered at her mind. She clutched their fingers even tighter.

The torment in the hall suddenly subsided. All became deathly quiet in the choking, freezing darkness.

Trevelyan felt disorientated as the roaring died away. He had no clear impressions or understandings of the giddy space that surrounded their astral fortress. Probing the cloying darkness with his awareness, he could hear nothing but the sound of water dripping and rivers rushing deep beneath the ground.

Sending his intent into the crystals to produce more light, Trevelyan looked around and stiffened. He, Omar, and Emma were alone in a long, dank, empty cave. The walls were dripping and covered in black slime. It seemed that Ke-enaan's hall had been swallowed up in an unfathomable gulf of shadow, until nothing familiar remained. An evil vortex had sucked up Ke-enaan's essence and dissolved any trace of his faerie presence from Black Head. There was no sign of Aine or Nala, and their icosahedral geometric had disappeared. Fercle was also missing. Trevelyan could only trust that Ke-enaan had made a strategy for such eventuality while still in his right mind. Was it possible that if all turned ill, the wizard had planned to swallow the sapphire and sacrifice himself for the Green? Trevelyan also wondered if by ceasing to resist the evil forces arrayed against him, Ke-enaan had been able to absorb his enemy's power and use it to increase his own.

He felt a hand upon his arm and heard Emma's voice crying out in panic: "What's happening to the crystals?"

The sound of Emma's voice and the pressure of her fingers jerked him back to the ultimate horror of their situation. Looking at the tips of the five-pointed star, he realised that the energy he had put into the crystals was fading and darkness was once more closing in around them.

"Where are Aine, Nala, and Fercle? Everybody has disappeared but us!" Emma's voice was shrill. Trevelyan stared at her for a moment in an intense and helpless silence.

"When Ke-enaan swallowed the sapphire, he destroyed the connection between the Faerie Worlds and the third dimension," Trevelyan answered slowly. "The act negated the quantum power provided by the obsidian crystals, which are now being drained by the hungry sucking energy that exists between the realms." Sighing deeply, he unlinked their hands, breaking the circle. "Where our friends are, I do not know. All I can tell you is that the faerie realms have vanished and we are trapped in the space between the third and fourth dimensions."

Emma looked at Trevelyan in stunned shock as the implications of his words took root in her mind. "Caught between the worlds?" she repeated anxiously.

"It means we are stuck in limbo, mon," Omar muttered nervously, chewing on his lip.

Trevelyan passed his hand over his eyes for a moment and let his breath escape softly through his teeth. "And there is more that you should know. We are trapped in goblin space. And once we leave this cave, if we cannot escape from this abyss, we will be hunted by denizens of the pit and ultimately destroyed."

"So what are we going to do?" Emma cried out in alarm.

"First, m'dear, we have to stay calm and find a way out of this cave. Otherwise it will become our prison and our tomb." He glanced at Omar. "Can you summon your fire elemental to give us light?"

Omar nodded. Focusing his awareness in inner space, he called his loa. Again and again he called for them, but each time he was met with empty silence. He ran his hand over his dreads in despair. "My loa are gone, mon. I and I cannot reach them."

Switching to faerie sight, Emma peered into the shadow but could see nothing but swirling darkness. "My faerie sight is blocked. I cannot sense the airwaves," she said grimly.

"Our faerie sight is blocked by the slow vibration in this fell place," Trevelyan answered. "And the calling of the Hex has left behind a legacy of evil. We must leave before all is lost and the portal gate is closed against us. I cannot cast spells to help us escape, for even though you are with me underground, I am energetically compromised in this vibration. We must make haste! There is not much time."

Hearing furtive sounds outside that trembled on the brink of audibility, Trevelyan inclined his head and listened. He could hear faint scratching at the walls and above the ceiling punctuated with panting hideous grunts. Demons were hunting for them.

Gesturing at Emma and Omar with his eyeglass, he pressed his finger to his lips as a signal for them to stay quiet. *We are being hunted,* he said in their minds. *Do not move. If we stay motionless within our astral fortress, we must trust they will not find us.*

Emma could not see anything in the darkness, but she sensed shapes moving through the cave, some crawling across the ground and others flying around like bats. Every now and then she heard a squeal and the sound of ripping flesh as one of the demons devoured another, weaker member of its troop. The stench of rotten flesh was almost suffocating, and the terror of the experience was deepening with every passing second. Emma was screaming inside. She prayed she could hold herself together.

The three of them stood huddled at the centre of the pentacle until the ebb and flow of evil that crept, slithered, and flew had withdrawn from the cave. Trevelyan listened as the sounds of their enemies died away.

We must find a way out, he said in their minds. *There may still be time to reach the portal.*

Emma, suddenly feeling a draught blowing on the back of her neck, turned round to face it, trying to pinpoint where the waft was coming from. After a couple of moments, she detected a cold current of air flowing through the west wall that faced the sea.

I feel a draught, she said in their mental conversation. *Follow me!*

The darkness in the cave was absolute. Linking hands, Omar and Trevelyan followed Emma along the side of the cave. The draught grew stronger. Emma stopped.

"There is a narrow crevice here that leads outside," she said, feeling the wall with her hands. "It is big enough for us to crawl through."

They squirmed blindly through the crevice to a narrow opening in the rock.

Wait here while I check the road, Trevelyan said in their minds.

Stepping out of the crevice into a leaden light, he cautiously looked around. The sea was flat and still; the narrow road and grey stone wall seemed two-dimensional. Black Head towered above him like a cardboard cut-out silhouetted against the steely sky. He could no longer see the likeness of Ke-enaan's face within the rock. Seeing no sign of enemies, he whispered, "'Tis all clear. Follow me!"

The grey cliffs of the Burren loomed up in front of them, but before they could reach the spriggan's stair, the ground began to groan and shake. Looking south towards the Giant's Cliffs, Trevelyan saw a flash of vivid sapphire light blaze into the red fume and then fade away. The lurid glare of Zugalfar and his legions had also disappeared. For a moment, Trevelyan's feet faltered as his mind tried to fathom what was happening.

He was suddenly aware of shadows on the road ahead creeping towards them with a swift directiveness that made him shudder.

"Climb!" Trevelyan cried out. "Enemies are on our trail. Let us pray the portal to England is still open."

Printed in the United States
By Bookmasters